Vikas Swarup is a member of the Indian Foreign Service and *Q&A* is his first novel. A prize-winning international sensation, it has been translated into over forty languages, and was recently made into the multiple Oscar-winning film SLUMDOG MILLIONAIRE. His new novel *Six Suspects* is also available as a Black Swan paperback. To find out more about Vikas Swarup, visit his website: www.vikasswarup.net

Acclaim for *Q&A*

'Not simply the story of a quiz, but rather a reminder of the various, often apparently random, ways in which knowledge can be acquired by the adventurous, the curious and the observant . . . Swarup is an accomplished storyteller, and *Q&A* has all the immediacy and impact of an oral account' *Daily Mail*

'An inspired idea . . . Through Ram's life story, Swarup is able to give us snapshots of Indian society . . . at its most lurid and extreme. If the prose style suggests social realism, the spirit of the novel is cinematic, even cartoon-like . . . A broad and sympathetic humanity underpins the whole book. Perhaps that is why, when it was finally time for Ram's good luck to hold, I was moved as well as relieved' *Sunday Telegraph*

'India is equally chaotic, enchanting and corrupt in this spirited novel' *Sunday Times*

'The premise of Vikas Swarup's picaresque début is enticing . . . His vivid characterisation covers the full social spectrum (prostitutes, glue-sniffers, film stars, diplomats, slum-dwellers), and paints a colourful, generous and admirably unvarnished portrait of contemporary India, where not all the poor are angels, not all the wealthy are villains' *Literary Review*

'Gloriously fantastical . . . the flashbacks he relates build into a picture of his life and of his remorselessly tough world: a mafia underworld that cripples children and trains them as beggars, arrogant whites oppressing their servants, families who prostitute a daughter, the dreary meanness of the rich, the desperate criminal measures to which poverty drives ordinary people' *The Times*

'I can see it all on the big screen now' Mariella Frostrup 'Open Book' Radio Four

'This page-turning novel reels from farce to melodrama to fairytale' *You Magazine*

D1395673

'An enthusiastic début worth devouring. Vikas Swarup weaves a delightful yarn ... the story stays with the reader for its remarkable and magical story of a young boy who believes that "a waking dream is always more fleeting than a sleeping one". So go ahead and read this enchanting tale of the good over the baneful' *Sunday Tribune*

'A bloody good book. No two ways about it ... The characters we encounter in the novel, be it the guileless Salim, the dutiful Lajwanti, or Nita, the whore pining for redemption, are all stereotypical and yet entirely believable. It is easy to feel for them. It is also easy to wish for a ride into the sunset with them ... a roller coaster ride – part quiz show, part morality tale' *Deccan Herald*

'Riveting drama ... Ram's life must pass through multiple filters, it must be told and retold in different ways. From the questions posed to him – and the record provided on the DVD – to his backgrounders for Smita, to the final tying up of all the loose ends, Ram is perhaps being put to a higher test. At the age of 18, his crowded life must be straightened out to disclose a compact honesty. For Swarup the quiz show is also a template to tell the story of modern India. It is a depiction with a moral edge' *Indian Express*

'Rescued from a dustbin where he is dumped after his birth, Ram's life follows a singular path. One of survival in the face of great odds. From the moment he is picked up by Father Timothy to the time he meets a crazy Australian mole, Ram's life is one of existing by instinct, which never fails him. Predictably as he tells his story against the backdrop of each question put to him on the show, there unfolds a saga of human greed, abuse, homosexuality, friendship and compassion. *Q&A* touches a chord somewhere even as it lets you believe in magic' *The Hindu*

'Swarup's début novel is impressive. At one level, there is nothing in his protagonist's history that can be called truly fantastic. Each event – from winning the game show to getting employed by an Australian diplomat who fancies himself as a spymaster – could have happened to someone. What is interesting is the way these plausible incidents are stitched together to create a fantastic tale' *Business World*

'A polished début ... bang on the publisher's pulse. The linguistic style is simple, peppy and very *Life of Pi*. It is not often that we get such fast paced action, which, like a breathless express train, stops only at special stations, punch lines or when the quizmaster says, "You just won a 100 million rupees!"' *The Week*

'Just the book for a long journey. If you aren't going away somewhere, don't start if you intend to get any sleep at night' *Sydney Morning Herald*

Q & A

Vikas Swarup

BLACK SWAN

Q & A
A BLACK SWAN BOOK : 9780552776165

Originally published in Great Britain by Doubleday,
a division of Transworld Publishers

PRINTING HISTORY
Doubleday edition published 2005
Black Swan edition published 2006
Black Swan edition reissued 2009

2 4 6 8 10 9 7 5 3 1

Set in 11/13pt Melior by
Falcon Oast Graphic Art Ltd.

Black Swan Books are published by Transworld Publishers,
61–63 Uxbridge Road, London W5 5SA,
a division of The Random House Group Ltd

Addresses for Random House Group Ltd companies outside the UK
can be found at: www.randomhouse.co.uk/offices.htm

Printed and bound in Great Britain by
Cox & Wyman Ltd, Reading, Berkshire.

The Random House Group Limited supports The Forest Stewardship
Council (FSC), the leading international forest certification organisation
All our titles that are printed on Greenpeace approved FSC certified paper
carry the FSC logo. Our paper procurement policy can be found at:
www.rbooks.co.uk/environment

For
my parents,
Vinod and Indra Swarup

and my late grandfather,
Shri Jagadish Swarup

CONTENTS

Prologue   11

1,000   The Death of a Hero   31

2,000   The Burden of a Priest   48

5,000   A Brother's Promise   68

10,000   A Thought for the Crippled   90

50,000   How to Speak Australian   123

100,000   Hold On To Your Buttons   153

200,000   Murder on the Western Express   173

500,000   A Soldier's Tale   194

1,000,000   Licence to Kill   223

10,000,000   Tragedy Queen   244

100,000,000   X Gkrz Opknu
(or, A Love Story)   273

1,000,000,000   The Thirteenth Question   343

Epilogue   358

Acknowledgements   363

Reading Group Guide   365

PROLOGUE

I have been arrested. For winning a quiz show.

They came for me late last night, when even the stray dogs had gone off to sleep. They broke open my door, handcuffed me and marched me off to the waiting jeep with a flashing red light.

There was no hue and cry. Not one resident stirred from his hut. Only the old owl on the tamarind tree hooted at my arrest.

Arrests in Dharavi are as common as pickpockets on the local train. Not a day goes by without some hapless resident being taken away to the police station. There are some who have to be physically dragged off by the constables, screaming and kicking all the while. And there are those who go quietly. Who expect, perhaps even wait for, the police. For them, the arrival of the jeep with the flashing red light is actually a relief.

In retrospect, perhaps I should have kicked and screamed. Protested my innocence, raised a stink, galvanized the neighbours. Not that it would have helped. Even if I had succeeded in waking some of the residents, they would not have raised a finger to defend me. With bleary eyes they would have watched the spectacle, made some trite remark like 'There goes another one,' yawned, and promptly gone back to sleep. My departure from Asia's biggest slum would make no difference to their lives. There would be the same queue for water in the morning, the same daily struggle to make it to the seven-thirty local in time.

They wouldn't even bother to find out the reason for my arrest. Come to think of it, when the two constables barged into my hut, even I didn't. When your whole existence is 'illegal', when you live on the brink of penury in an urban wasteland where you jostle for every inch of space and have to queue even for a shit, arrest has a certain inevitability about it. You are conditioned to believe that one day there will be a warrant with your name on it, that eventually a jeep with a flashing red light will come for you.

There are those who will say that I brought this upon myself. By dabbling in that quiz show. They will wag a finger at me and remind me of what the elders in Dharavi say about never crossing the dividing line that separates the rich from the poor. After all, what business did a penniless waiter have to be participating in a brain quiz? The brain is not an organ we are authorized to use. We are supposed to use only our hands and legs.

If only they could see me answer those questions. After my performance they would have looked upon me with new respect. It's a pity the show has yet to be telecast. But word seeped out that I had won something. Like a lottery. When the other waiters heard the news, they decided to have a big party for me in the restaurant. We sang and danced and drank late into the night. For the first time we did not eat Ramzi's stale food for dinner. We ordered chicken biryani and seekh kebabs from the five-star hotel in Marine Drive. The doddery bartender offered me his daughter in marriage. Even the grouchy manager smiled indulgently at me and finally gave me my back wages. He didn't call me a worthless bastard that night. Or a rabid dog.

Now Godbole calls me that, and worse. I sit crosslegged in a ten-by-six-foot cell with a rusty metal door and a small square window with a grille, through which a shaft of dusty sunlight streams into the room. The lock-up is hot and humid. Flies buzz around the mushy remains of an over-ripe mango lying squished on the stone floor. A sad-looking cockroach lumbers up to my leg. I am beginning to feel hungry. My stomach growls.

I am told that I will be taken to the interrogation room shortly, to be questioned for the second time since my arrest. After an interminable wait, someone comes to escort me. It is Inspector Godbole himself.

Godbole is not very old, perhaps in his mid forties. He has a balding head and a round face dominated by a handlebar moustache. He walks with heavy steps and his overfed stomach droops over his khaki

13

trousers. 'Bloody flies,' he swears and tries to swat one
circling in front of his face. He misses.

Inspector Godbole is not in a good mood today. He
is bothered by these flies. He is bothered by the heat.
Rivulets of sweat run down his forehead. He smears
them off with his shirt sleeve. Most of all, he is
bothered by my name. 'Ram Mohammad Thomas –
what kind of a nonsense name is that, mixing up all
the religions? Couldn't your mother decide who your
father was?' he says, not for the first time.

I let the insult pass. It is something I have become
inured to.

Outside the interrogation room two constables stand
stiffly to attention, a sign that someone important is
inside. In the morning they had been chewing *paan*
and exchanging dirty jokes. Godbole literally pushes
me into the room, where two men are standing in front
of a wall chart listing the total number of kidnappings
and murders in the year. I recognize one of them. He is
the same man, with long hair like a woman – or a rock
star – who had been present during the recording of
the quiz show, relaying instructions through a headset
to the presenter. I don't know the other man, who is
white and completely bald. He wears a mauve-
coloured suit and a bright-orange tie. Only a white
man would wear a suit and tie in this stifling heat. It
reminds me of Colonel Taylor.

The ceiling fan is running at full speed, yet the room
feels airless in the absence of a window. Heat rises
from the bleached white walls and is trapped by
the low wooden ceiling. A long, thin beam bisects the
room into two equal parts. The room is bare except for

a rusty table in the centre with three chairs around it. A metal lampshade hangs directly over the table from the wooden beam.

Godbole presents me to the white man like a ring-master introducing his pet lion. 'This is Ram Mohammad Thomas, Sir.'

The white man dabs his forehead with a hand-kerchief and looks at me as though I am a new species of monkey. 'So this is our famous winner! I must say he looks older than I thought.' I try to place his accent. He speaks with the same nasal twang as the prosperous tourists I'd seen thronging Agra from far-off places like Baltimore and Boston.

The American eases himself into a chair. He has deep-blue eyes and a pink nose. The green veins on his forehead look like little branches. 'Hello,' he addresses me. 'My name is Neil Johnson. I represent NewAge Telemedia, the company that licenses the quiz. This is Billy Nanda, the producer.'

I remain quiet. Monkeys do not speak. Especially not in English.

He turns to Nanda. 'He understands English, doesn't he?'

'Are you out of your mind, Neil?' Nanda admonishes him. 'How can you expect him to speak English? He's just a dumb waiter in some godforsaken restaurant, for Chrissake!'

The sound of an approaching siren pierces the air. A constable comes running into the room and whispers something to Godbole. The Inspector rushes out and returns with a short, corpulent man dressed in the uniform of a top-level police officer. Godbole beams at

Johnson, displaying his yellow teeth. 'Mr Johnson, Commissioner Sahib has arrived.'

Johnson rises to his feet. 'Thank you for coming, Mr Commissioner. I think you already know Billy here.'

The Commissioner nods. 'I came as soon as I got the message from the Home Minister.'

'Ah yes . . . He is an old friend of Mr Mikhailov's.'

'Well, what can I do for you?'

'Commissioner, I need your help on *W3B*.'

'*W3B?*'

'Short for *Who Will Win A Billion?*'

'And what's that?'

'It's a quiz show that has just been launched – in thirty-five countries – by our company. You may have seen our advertisements all over Mumbai.'

'I must have missed them. But why a billion?'

'Why not? Did you watch *Who Wants To Be A Millionaire?*'

'*Kaun Banega Crorepati?* That show was a national obsession. It was mandatory viewing in my family.'

'Why did you watch it?'

'Well . . . because it was so interesting.'

'Would it have been half as interesting if the top prize had been ten thousand instead of a million?'

'Well . . . I suppose not.'

'Exactly. You see, the biggest tease in the world is not sex. It's money. And the greater the sum of money, the bigger the tease.'

'I see. So who's the quiz master on your show?'

'We have Prem Kumar fronting it.'

'Prem Kumar? That B-grade actor? But he's not half

as famous as Amitabh Bachchan, who presented
Crorepati.'

'Don't worry, he will be. Of course, we were partly
obliged to choose him because he has a 29 per cent
stake in the Indian subsidiary of NewAge Telemedia.'

'OK. I get the picture. Now how does this guy, what's
his name, Ram Mohammad Thomas, fit into all this?

'He was a participant in our fifteenth episode last
week.'

'And?'

'And answered all twelve questions correctly to win
a billion rupees.'

'What? You must be joking!'

'No, it's no joke. We were as amazed as you are. This
boy is the winner of the biggest jackpot in history. The
episode has not been aired yet, so not many people
know about it.'

'OK. If you say he won a billion, he won a billion. So
what's the problem?'

Johnson pauses. 'Can Billy and I talk to you in
private?'

The Commissioner motions Godbole to leave. The
Inspector glowers at me and exits. I remain in
the room, but no one takes any notice. I am just a
waiter. And waiters don't understand English.

'OK. Now tell me,' says the Commissioner.

'You see, Commissioner, Mr Mikhailov is not in a
position to pay a billion rupees right now,' says
Johnson.

'Then why did he offer it in the first place?'

'Well . . . it was a commercial gimmick.'

'Look, I still don't understand. Even if it was a

gimmick, won't your show do even better now that someone has won the top prize? I remember that whenever a contestant won a million on *Who Wants To Be A Millionaire?*, viewing figures doubled.'

'It's the timing, Commissioner, the timing. Shows like *W3B* cannot be dictated by chance, by a roll of the dice. They have to follow a script. And according to our script, a winner was not due for at least eight months, by which time we would have recouped most of our investment through ad revenues. But now this fellow Thomas has wrecked all our plans.'

The Commissioner nods. 'OK, so what do you want me to do?'

'I want your help to prove that Thomas cheated on the show. That he couldn't have known the answers to all twelve questions without an accomplice. Just think. He's never been to school. He's never even read a newspaper. There's no way he could have won the top prize.'

'Well ... I'm not so sure.' The Commissioner scratches his head. 'There have been cases of boys from poor backgrounds turning out to be geniuses in later life. Wasn't Einstein himself a high-school drop-out?'

'Look, Mr Commissioner, we can prove right now that this guy is no Einstein,' says Johnson. He gestures to Nanda.

Nanda approaches me, running his fingers through his luxuriant hair. He addresses me in Hindi. 'Mr Ram Mohammad Thomas, if you were indeed brilliant enough to win on our show, we would like you to prove it by taking part in another quiz for us, now.

These will be very simple questions. Almost anyone of average intelligence will know the answers.' He sits me down on a chair. 'Are you ready? Here comes question number one. What is the currency of France? The choices are a) Dollar, b) Pound, c) Euro, or d) Franc.'

I keep silent. Suddenly, the Commissioner's open palm swoops down and hits me tightly across my cheek. 'Bastard, are you deaf? Answer or I'll break your jaw,' he threatens.

Nanda starts hopping around like a madman – or a rock star. 'Pleeeeze, can we do this the civilized way?' he asks the Commissioner. Then he looks at me. 'Yes? What's your answer?'

'Franc,' I reply sullenly.

'Wrong. The correct answer is Euro. OK, question number two. Who was the first man to set foot on the moon? Was it a) Edwin Aldrin, b) Neil Armstrong, c) Yuri Gagarin, or d) Jimmy Carter?'

'I don't know.'

'It was Neil Armstrong. Question number three. The Pyramids are situated in a) New York, b) Rome, c) Cairo, or d) Paris?'

'I don't know.'

'In Cairo. Question number four. Who is the President of America? Is it a) Bill Clinton, b) Colin Powell, c) John Kerry, or d) George Bush?'

'I don't know.'

'It's George Bush. I am sorry to say, Mr Thomas, that you didn't get a single answer right.'

Nanda turns to the Commissioner, and reverts to English. 'See, I told you this guy's a moron. The only way he could have answered those questions last week was by cheating.'

'Any idea how he could have cheated?' asks the Commissioner.

'That's what beats me. I have got you two copies of the DVD footage. Our experts have gone over it with a microscope, but so far we have got zilch. Something will turn up eventually.'

The hunger in my belly has now risen to my throat, making me dizzy. I double up, coughing.

Johnson, the baldy American, looks at me sharply. 'Do you remember, Mr Commissioner, that case of the Army Major who won a million pounds on *Who Wants To Be A Millionaire?* It occurred in England, a few years ago. The company refused to pay. The police launched an investigation and succeeded in convicting the Major. It turned out he had a professor as an accomplice in the audience who signalled the correct answers through coded coughs. It's a cert something similar has happened here.'

'So do we need to look out for a cougher in the audience?'

'No. There's no evidence of coughing. He must have used some other signal.'

'What about being buzzed by a pager or mobile?'

'No. We are pretty sure he had no gadgets on him. And neither pager nor cellphone would have worked in the studio.'

The Commissioner is struck by an idea. 'Do you think he might have a memory chip implanted in the brain?'

Johnson sighs. 'Mr Commissioner, I think you have

been watching too many science-fiction films. Look, whatever it is, you have to help us find it. We don't know who the accomplice was. We don't know what signalling system was used. But I am one hundred per cent sure this boy is a con. You have to help us prove it.'

'Have you considered buying him off?' the Commissioner suggests hopefully. 'I mean he probably doesn't even know the number of zeros in a billion. I imagine he would be quite happy if you threw him just a couple of thousand rupees.'

I feel like punching the Commissioner's lights out. Admittedly, before the quiz show I didn't know the value of a billion. But that's history. Now I know. And I am determined to get my prize. With all nine zeros.

Johnson's answer reassures me. 'We can't do that,' he says. 'It would make us vulnerable to a law suit. You see, he is either a bona fide winner or a crook. Therefore either he gets a billion or he goes to jail. There's no halfway house here. You have to help me ensure he goes to jail. Mr Mikhailov would have a coronary if he had to shell out a billion now.'

The Commissioner looks Johnson directly in the eye. 'I understand your point,' he drawls. 'But what's in it for me?'

As if on cue, Johnson takes him by the arm into a corner. They speak in hushed tones. I catch just three words: 'ten per cent'. The Commissioner is clearly excited by what he is told. 'OK, OK, Mr Johnson, consider your job done. Now let me call in Godbole.'

The Inspector is summoned. 'Godbole, what have you got out of him so far?' the Commissioner asks.

Godbole gazes at me balefully. 'Nothing, Commissioner Sahib. The bastard keeps on repeating the same story that he just "knew" the answers. Says he got lucky.'

'Lucky, eh?' sneers Johnson.

'Yes, Sir. I have so far not used third degree, otherwise he would be singing like a canary by now. Once you permit me, Sir, I can get the names of all his accomplices out in no time.'

The Commissioner looks quizzically at Johnson and Nanda. 'Are you comfortable with that?'

Nanda shakes his head vigorously, sending his long hair flying. 'No way. No torture. The papers have already got wind of the arrest. If they find out he has been mistreated, we will be finished. I've enough problems on my plate already without having to worry about being sued by a bloody civil rights NGO.'

The Commissioner pats him on the back. 'Billy, you have become just like the Americans. Don't worry. Godbole is a professional. There won't be a single mark on the boy's body.'

Bile rises in my stomach like a balloon. I feel like retching.

The Commissioner prepares to depart. 'Godbole, by tomorrow morning I want the name of the collaborator and full details of the MO. Use any means necessary to extract the information. But be careful. Remember, your promotion depends on this.'

'Thank you, Sir. Thank you.' Godbole puts on a plastic smile. 'And don't worry, Sir. By the time I am through with this boy, he will be ready to confess the murder of Mahatma Gandhi.'

I try to recall who murdered Mahatma Gandhi, who is known to have said 'Hey Ram!' just before dying. I remember this because I had exclaimed, 'That's my name!' And Father Timothy had gently explained that it was the name of Lord Ram, the Hindu god who had been banished into the jungle for fourteen years.

Godbole, meanwhile, has returned after seeing off the Commissioner and the two men. He wheezes into the interrogation room and slams the door shut. Then he snaps his fingers at me. 'OK, motherfucker, strip!'

Sharp, throbbing pain oozes from every pore of my body. My hands are tied to the wooden beam with coarse rope. The beam is nine feet above the ground, so my legs dangle in the air and my hands and feet feel like they are being pulled apart. I am completely naked. The ribs on my chest jut out like those on starving African babies.

Godbole has been punishing me for more than an hour but he has still not finished. Every half-hour or so he comes up with a new instrument of torture. First he inserted a wooden rod into my anus. With chilli powder smeared on it. It felt as if a molten, searing spike was being driven through my backside. I choked and gagged with pain. Then he thrust my head into a bucket of water and held it there till my lungs were about to explode. I spluttered and gasped and quite nearly drowned.

Now he is holding a live wire in his hand like a sparkler on Diwali. He dances around me like a drunken boxer and suddenly lunges at me. He jabs at the sole of my left foot with the naked wire. The electric current shoots up my body like hot poison. I recoil and convulse violently.

Godbole shouts at me. 'Bastard, you still won't tell me what trick you used on the show? Who told you the answers? Tell me, and this torture will end. You will get a nice hot meal. You can even go home.'

But home seems like a far-off place right now. And a hot meal would make me vomit. If you don't eat for a long time, the hunger just shrivels and dies, leaving only a dull ache in the pit of your stomach.

The first wave of nausea is beginning to assail me now. I am blacking out. Through a thick mist, I see a tall woman, with flowing black hair. The wind is howling behind her, making her jet-black hair fly across her face, obscuring it. She is wearing a white sari of thin fabric that flutters and vibrates like a kite. She opens her arms and cries, 'My son . . . my son . . . what are they doing to you?'

'Mother!' I scream and reach out for her across the chasm of mist and fog, but Godbole grabs me roughly by the neck. I feel as if I am running without moving forward. He slaps me hard and the blackness lifts.

Godbole is holding out the pen once again. It is black with a shiny golden nib. Blue ink glistens at its tip. 'Sign the confession statement,' he orders.

The confession statement is quite simple. 'I, Ram Mohammad Thomas, do hereby state that on 10 July I was a participant in the quiz show *Who Will Win A Billion?* I confess that I cheated. I did not know the answers to all the questions. I hereby withdraw my claim to the top prize or any other prize. I beg forgiveness. I am making this statement in full control of my senses and without any undue pressure from anyone. Signed: Ram Mohammad Thomas.'

I know it is only a question of time before I sign this statement. I will not be able to hold out much longer. We were always told never to pick a quarrel with the police. Street boys like me come at the bottom of the food chain. Above us are the petty criminals, like pickpockets. Above them come the extortionists and loan sharks. Above them come the dons. Above them come the big business houses. But above all of them are the police. They have the instruments of naked power. And there is nobody to check them. Who can police the police? So I will sign the statement. After ten, maybe fifteen, more slaps. After five, perhaps six, more shocks.

All of a sudden, I hear a commotion at the door. Constables are shouting. Voices are raised. The door shudders and slams open. A young woman bursts into the room. She is of average height and slim build. She has nice teeth and lovely arched eyebrows. In the middle of her forehead she wears a large round blue *bindi*. Her dress consists of a white salwar kameez, a blue *dupatta* and leather sandals. Her long black hair is loose. A brown bag hangs from her left shoulder. There is a certain presence about her.

Godbole is so flustered he touches the live wire to his own hand, and yelps in pain. He is about to grab the intruder by the collar, then realizes she is a woman. 'Who the hell are you, bursting in like this? Can't you see I am busy?'

'My name is Smita Shah,' the woman announces

calmly to Godbole. 'I am Mr Ram Mohammad Thomas's lawyer.' Then she looks at me, at my condition, and hastily averts her eyes.

Godbole is stunned. He is so stunned that he does not notice that I am equally stunned. I have never seen this woman before. I don't have money to hire a taxi. I can hardly hire a lawyer.

'Come again?' Godbole croaks. 'You are his lawyer?'

'Yes. And what you are doing to my client is completely illegal and unacceptable. I want an immediate end to this treatment. He reserves the right to prosecute you under sections 330 and 331 of the Indian Penal Code. I demand to be shown the papers regarding his arrest. I see no evidence of any FIR having been recorded. No grounds for arrest have been communicated as required under Article 22 of the Constitution and you are in breach of Section 50 of the CrPC. Now unless you can produce his arrest warrant, I am removing my client from the police station to consult with him in private.'

'Er . . . mmm . . . I . . . I will have to speak to . . . to the Commissioner. Please wait,' is all Godbole can say. He looks at the woman with a helpless expression, shakes his head, and slinks out of the room.

I am impressed. I didn't know lawyers wielded such power over the police. The food chain will have to be revised.

I don't know at what point Godbole returns to the room, what he says to the lawyer, or what the lawyer says to him, because I have passed out. From pain and hunger and happiness.

* * *

I am sitting on a leather couch with a cup of hot, steaming tea in my hands. A rectangular desk is strewn with papers. On top is a glass paperweight and a red table lamp. The walls of the room are painted rose pink. The shelves are lined with thick black books with gold letters on the spines. There are framed certificates and diplomas on the walls. A potted money plant grows sideways in one corner of the room.

Smita returns with a plate and a glass in her hands. I smell food. 'I know you must be hungry, so I've brought you some chapattis, some mixed vegetables and a Coke. It was all I had in my fridge.'

I grasp her hand. It feels warm and moist. 'Thank you,' I say. I still don't know how she got to the police station, or why. All she has told me is that she read about my arrest in the papers, and came as soon as she could. Now I am at her house in Bandra. I will not ask her when she brought me here, or why. One doesn't question a miracle.

I begin eating. I eat all the chapattis. I polish off all the vegetables. I drink all the Coke. I eat till my eyes bulge out.

It is late evening now. I have eaten and slept. Smita is still with me, but now I am in her bedroom, sitting on a large bed with a blue bedspread. Her bedroom is different from that of my former employer, the film star Neelima Kumari. Instead of the huge mirrors and trophies and acting awards lining the shelves, there are books and a large brown teddy bear with glass eyes. But, like Neelima, she has a Sony TV and even a DVD player.

Smita is sitting with me on the edge of the bed holding a disc case in her fingers. 'Look, I've managed to get a copy of your show's DVD footage. Now we can go over it with a toothcomb. I want you to explain to me exactly how you came to answer all those questions. And I want you to tell me the truth.'

'The truth?'

'Even if you did cheat, I am here to protect you. What you tell me cannot be used against you in a court of law.'

The first doubts start creeping into my mind. Is this woman too good to be true? Has she been planted by that baldy Johnson to ferret out incriminating truths from me? Can I trust her?

Time to take a decision. I take out my trusted one-rupee coin. Heads I cooperate with her. Tails I tell her ta-ta. I flip the coin. It is heads.

'Do you know Albert Fernandes?' I ask her.

'No. Who is he?'

'He has an illegal factory in Dharavi which makes watch-strap buckles.'

'And?'

'He plays matka.'

'Matka?'

'Illegal gambling with cards.'

'I see.'

'So Albert Fernandes plays matka and last Tuesday he had an amazing game.'

'What happened?'

'He came up with fifteen winning hands in a row. Can you believe it? Fifteen hands in a row. He cleaned out fifty thousand rupees that evening.'

'So? I still don't see the connection.'

'Don't you see? He got lucky in cards. I got lucky on the show.'

'You mean you just guessed the answers and by pure luck got twelve out of twelve correct?'

'No. I didn't guess those answers. I knew them.'

'You *knew* the answers?'

'Yes. To all the questions.'

'Then where does luck come into the picture?'

'Well, wasn't I lucky that they only asked those questions to which I knew the answers?'

The look of utter disbelief on Smita's face says it all. I can take it no longer. I erupt in sadness and anger. 'I know what you are thinking. Like Godbole, you wonder what I was doing on that quiz show. Like Godbole, you believe I am only good for serving chicken fry and whisky in a restaurant. That I am meant to live life like a dog, and die like an insect. Don't you?'

'No, Ram.' She grasps my hand. 'I will never believe that. But you must understand. If I am to help you, I have to know how you won that billion. And I confess, I find it difficult to comprehend. Heavens, even I couldn't answer half those questions.'

'Well, Madam, we poor can also ask questions and demand answers. And I bet you, if the poor conducted a quiz, the rich wouldn't be able to answer a single question. I don't know the currency of France, but I can tell you how much money Shalini Tai owes our neighbourhood moneylender. I don't know who was the first man on the moon, but I can tell you who was the first man to produce illegal DVDs in Dharavi. Could you answer these questions in my quiz?'

'Look, Ram, don't get agitated. I meant no offence. I really want to help you. But if you didn't cheat, I must know how you knew.'

'I cannot explain.'

'Why?'

'Do you notice when you breathe? No. You simply know that you are breathing. I did not go to school. I did not read books. But, I tell you, I knew those answers.'

'So do I need to know about your entire life to understand the genesis of your answers?'

'Perhaps.'

Smita nods her head. 'I think that is the key. After all, a quiz is not so much a test of knowledge as a test of memory.' She adjusts her blue *dupatta* and looks me in the eye. 'I want to listen to your memories. Can you begin at the beginning?'

'You mean the year I was born? Year number one?'

'No. From question number one. But before we start, promise me, Ram Mohammad Thomas, that you will tell me the truth.'

'You mean like they say in the movies, "The truth, the whole truth and nothing but the truth"?'

'Exactly.'

I take a deep breath. 'Yes, I promise. But where is your Book of Oaths? The Gita, the Koran or the Bible, any one will do.'

'I don't need a book. I am your witness. Just as you are mine.'

Smita takes the shiny disc from its cover and slips it into the DVD player.

1,000

THE DEATH OF A HERO

The third bell has sounded. The purple velvet curtain is about to be raised. The lights are progressively dimming, till only the red signs showing EXIT remain, glowing like embers in the darkened hall. Popcorn sellers and cold-drink vendors begin to leave. Salim and I settle down in our seats.

The first thing you must know about Salim is that he is my best friend. The second is that he is crazy about Hindi films. But not all Hindi films. Just the ones featuring Armaan Ali.

They say that first there was Amitabh Bachchan. Then there was Shahrukh Khan. Now there is Armaan Ali. The ultimate action hero. The Indian Greek God. The heart-throb of millions.

Salim loves Armaan. Or, more accurately, he worships Armaan. His tiny room in the chawl is a shrine. It is lined with posters of all kinds depicting the hero in various poses. Armaan in a leather jacket. Armaan on a motorbike. Armaan with his shirt off, baring his hairy chest. Armaan with a gun. Armaan on a horse. Armaan in a pool surrounded by a bevy of beauties.

We are occupying seats A21 and A22 in the very first row of the Dress Circle in Regal Talkies in Bandra. We shouldn't really be sitting here. The tickets in my front pocket do not say DRESS CIRCLE Rs.150. They say FRONT STALLS Rs.25. The usher was in a good mood today and did us a favour. He told us to go and enjoy the balcony, because the stalls were practically deserted. Even the balcony is almost empty. Apart from Salim and me, there are no more than two dozen people in the rows ahead of us.

When Salim and I go to the movies, we usually sit in the front stalls. It enables us to make catcalls and whistle. Salim believes the nearer you sit to the screen, the closer you are to the action. He says he can lean forward and almost touch Armaan. He can count the veins on Armaan's biceps, he can see the whites of Armaan's hazel-green eyes, the fine stubble on Armaan's cleft chin, the little black mole on Armaan's chiselled nose.

I am not particularly fond of Armaan Ali. I think he acts the same way in every movie. But I, too, like to sit in the front rows, as close to the giant screen as possible. The heroine's breasts appear more voluptuous from there.

The curtain has now lifted and the screen flickers to life. First we have the advertisements. Four sponsored by private companies and one by the government. We are told how to come first at school and become a champion in cricket by eating Corn Flakes for breakfast. How to drive fast cars and win gorgeous girls by using Spice Cologne. ('That's the perfume used by Armaan,' exclaims Salim.) How to get a promotion and have shiny white clothes by using Roma soap. How to live life like a king by drinking Red & White Whisky. And how to die of lung cancer by smoking cigarettes.

After the adverts, there is a little pause while the reels are changed. We cough and clear our throats. And then the censor certificate appears on the cinema-scope screen. It tells us that the film has been certified U/A, has seventeen reels and a length of 4,639.15 metres. The certificate is signed by one Mrs M. Kane, Chairman of the Censor Board. She is the one who signs all censor certificates. Salim has often asked me about this lady. He really envies her job. She gets to see Armaan's pictures before anyone else.

The opening credits begin to roll. Salim knows everyone in this film. He knows who is the wardrobe man, who is the hair stylist, who is the make-up man. He knows the names of the production manager, the finance controller, the sound recordist and all the assistants. He doesn't speak English very well, but he can read names, even the ones in really small print. He has watched this film eight times already and every time he memorizes a new name. But if you were to see the concentration on his face right now, you would think he was watching the First Day First Show with black-market tickets.

Within two minutes, Armaan Ali makes his grand

entrance by jumping down from a blue and white helicopter. Salim's eyes light up. I see the same innocent excitement on his face as when he first saw Armaan, a year ago. In person.

Salim comes running through the door and collapses face-down on the bed.

I am alarmed. 'Salim! . . . Salim!' I shout. 'What's happened to you? How come you are back so early?' I turn him on his back. He is laughing.

'The most amazing thing has happened today. This is the happiest day of my life,' he declares.

'What is it? Have you won a lottery?'

'No. Something even better than winning a lottery. I have seen Armaan Ali.'

Bit by breathless bit, the whole story comes out. How Salim caught a glimpse of Armaan Ali while doing his daily round in Ghatkopar. The star was alighting from his Mercedes Benz to enter a five-star hotel. Salim was travelling on a bus to deliver his last tiffin box to a customer. The moment he spotted Armaan, he jumped down from the speeding vehicle, narrowly missing being run down by a Maruti car, and ran towards the actor, who was passing through the hotel's revolving door. He was stopped by the tall, strapping uniformed guard at the entrance and prevented from entering the hotel. 'Armaan!' Salim called, trying desperately to catch the star's attention. Armaan heard the cry, stopped in his tracks and turned around. His eyes made contact with Salim's. He gave a faint smile, an imperceptible nod of acknowledgement and continued walking into the lobby. Salim forgot all about the tiffin and came racing home to give me the news of his dream having come true. A customer of Gawli Tiffin Carriers went hungry that afternoon.

'Does Armaan look different from the way he appears on screen?' I ask.

'No. He is even better in real life,' says Salim. 'He is taller and more handsome. My ambition in life is to shake his hand, at least once. I probably won't wash it for a month after that.'

I reflect on how good it is to have simple, un-complicated ambitions, like shaking a film star's hand.

Meanwhile, on screen, that hand is holding a gun and pointing it at a group of three policemen. Armaan plays a gangster in this movie. A gangster with a heart. He loots the rich and distributes money to the poor. In between he falls in love with the heroine, Priya Kapoor, an up-and-coming actress, sings six songs and fulfils his beloved mother's wish by taking her on a pilgrimage to the shrine of Vaishno Devi. At least, that's the story till the interval.

Priya Kapoor's entry in the film is greeted with cat-calls from the stalls. She is a tall, good-looking actress who won the Miss World title a few years ago. Her body is sculpted like that of a classical beauty, with heavy breasts and a slim waist. She is my favourite actress these days. She pouts a lot in the film, and keeps on saying 'Shut up' to the comedian. We laugh.

'Your ambition is to shake Armaan's hand,' I say to Salim. 'But what do you think is Armaan's ambition in life? He seems to have it all – face, fame and fortune.'

'You are wrong,' Salim replies solemnly. 'He does not have Urvashi.'

The papers are full of the Armaan–Urvashi break-up, after a whirlwind romance lasting nine months. There is speculation that Armaan is completely heartbroken. That he has stopped eating and drinking. That he might be suicidal. Urvashi Randhawa has returned to her modelling career.

I see Salim crying. His eyes are red and wet with tears. He has not eaten all day. The heart-shaped glass frame containing a picture of Armaan and Urvashi, on which he had spent almost half his meagre salary, lies on the ground, shattered into a hundred pieces.

'Look, Salim, you are being childish. There is nothing you can do about it,' I tell him.

'If only I could meet Armaan. I want to comfort him. To hold his hand and let him cry on my shoulder. They say crying makes the heart lighter.'

'And what good will that do? Urvashi will not come back to Armaan.'

Suddenly Salim looks up. 'Do you think I could speak to her? Maybe I could persuade her to come back to Armaan. Tell her that it was all a mistake. Tell her how sad and contrite he is.'

I shake my head. I don't want Salim tramping all over Mumbai looking for Urvashi Randhawa. 'It's not a good idea to poke your nose into other people's affairs, or make other people's troubles your own, Salim. Armaan Ali is a mature man. He will deal with his troubles in his own way.'

'At least I will send him a gift,' says Salim.

He goes and buys a large bottle of Fevicol glue and sets about sticking the shattered pieces of the heart-shaped frame back together again. It takes him a week, but finally the heart is whole, a grid of criss-crossing black streaks the only reminder of the fault lines on which it broke.

'I will now send it to Armaan,' he says. 'It is a symbol that even a broken heart can be put together again.'

'With Fevicol?' I ask.

'No. With love and care.'

Salim wraps it up in cloth and sends it to Armaan Ali's home address. I don't know whether it reached Armaan or not. Whether it was broken by the postal department, smashed by the security guards or trashed by Armaan's secretary. The important thing is that Salim believes it reached his hero and helped to heal his wound. It made Armaan whole again, and enabled him to resume giving blockbusters, such as this one. Which I am seeing for the first time and Salim for the ninth.

A devotional song is playing on the screen. Armaan and his mother are climbing towards the shrine of Vaishno Devi.

'They say if you ask Mata Vaishno Devi sincerely for anything, she grants your wish. Tell me, what would you ask?' I say to Salim.

'What would you ask?' he counters.

'I guess I would ask for money,' I say.

'I would ask for Armaan to be reunited with Urvashi,' he says without thinking even for a second.

The screen says INTERVAL in bold red letters.

* * *

Salim and I stand up and stretch our arms and legs. We buy two soggy samosas from the food vendor. The boy selling soft drinks looks at the empty seats mournfully. He will not make a good profit today. We decide to go to the toilet. It has nice white tiles, banks of urinals and clean washbasins. We both have our designated stalls. Salim always goes to the one on the extreme right, and I always take the sole urinal on the left side wall. I empty my bladder and read the graffiti on the wall. FUCK ME . . . TINU PISSED HERE . . . SHEENA IS A WHORE . . . I LOVE PRIYANKA.

Priyanka? I rail against the graffiti artist who has defaced the last inscription. I spit into my hand and try to remove the extra letters, but they have been written with permanent black marker and refuse to budge. Eventually I use my nails to scratch them off the wall and succeed in restoring the graffiti to its original state, just as I had inscribed it four months ago: I LOVE PRIYA.

The second bell sounds. The interval is over. The film is about to resume. Salim has already briefed me on the remaining plot. Armaan and Priya will now sing a song in Switzerland, before Priya is murdered by a rival gang. Then Armaan will kill hundreds of bad guys in revenge, expose corrupt politicians and police officers, and finally die a hero's death.

We return to A21 and A22. The hall goes dark again. Suddenly, a tall man enters through the balcony door and takes the seat next to Salim. A20. He has two hundred seats to choose from, but he selects A20. It is impossible to see his face, but I can make out that he is an old man with a long, flowing beard. He is wearing what appears to be a pathan suit.

I am curious about this man. Why is he joining the film halfway through? Did he pay half price for his ticket? Salim is not bothered. He is craning forward in anticipation of the love scene between Armaan and Priya which is about to begin.

Armaan has come to Switzerland, ostensibly to locate a contact, but actually to romance Priya and sing a song, in which he is joined by twenty white female dancers wearing traditional costumes that are rather skimpy for a cold mountainous country. The song and dance over, he is now sitting in his hotel room, where a crackling fire burns in the fireplace.

Priya is taking a bath. We hear the sound of running water and Priya humming a tune, and then we see her in the bath. She applies soap to her legs and back. She raises a leg covered in bubbles and uses the shower-head to wash it clean. We hope she will also use it on her ample chest and make all the bubbles disappear, but she disappoints us.

Finally, she emerges from the bath with just a pink towel around her body. Her jet-black hair hangs loose behind her shoulders, glistening with moisture. Her long legs are smooth and hairless. Armaan takes her in his arms and smothers her face with kisses. His lips move down to the hollow of her neck. Soft romantic music begins to play. Priya undoes the buttons on his shirt and Armaan slips out of it languidly, exposing his manly chest. The glow of the fire envelops the two lovers in a golden tint. Priya makes soft moaning noises. She arches her back and allows Armaan to caress her throat. His hand snakes to her back and tugs at her towel. The pink fabric loosens and falls at her feet. There is a tantalizing glimpse of thigh and back, but no shot of breasts. Salim believes this is where the censors inserted a cut. And why he envies Mrs Kane.

Armaan has now locked Priya in his embrace. We are shown the swell of her breasts, her heavy breathing, the perspiration forming on her forehead. There are catcalls and whistles from the stalls. The old man sitting next to Salim shifts uncomfortably in his seat, crossing his legs. I am not sure, but I think his hand is massaging his crotch.

'The oldie next to you is getting frisky,' I whisper to Salim. But he is oblivious to the old man and me. He is gaping at the intertwined bodies thrusting in synchronized rhythm to the music in the background. The camera pans over Armaan's heaving back and zooms in on the fireplace, where golden-yellow flames are licking the logs with increasing abandon. Fade to black.

There is a fire of similar proportions in our kitchen when I enter the chawl, but instead of logs, Salim is using paper. 'Bastards! . . . Dogs!' he mutters while tearing a thick sheaf of glossy paper into pieces.

'What are you doing, Salim?' I ask in alarm.

'I am taking revenge on the bastards who have maligned Armaan,' he says as he tosses more sheets of paper on to the pyre.

I notice that Salim is tearing pages from a magazine.

'Which magazine is this? It looks new.'

'It is the latest issue of *Starburst*. I will destroy as many copies as I can lay my hands on. I could only buy ten from the news-stand.'

I grab a copy that has not yet been mangled. It has Armaan Ali on the cover, with a screaming headline: 'THE NAKED TRUTH ABOUT THIS MAN'.

'But it has your idol on the cover. Why are you destroying it?' I cry.

'Because of what they say inside about Armaan.'

'But you can't read.'

'I read enough and I can hear. I overheard Mrs Barve and Mrs Shirke discussing the scurrilous accusations made against Armaan in this issue.'

'Like what?'

'That Urvashi left him because he could not satisfy her. That he is gay.'

'So?'

'You think they can abuse my hero in this fashion and get away with it? I know this report is a load of nonsense. Armaan's rivals in the industry are jealous of his success. They have hatched this plot to destroy his reputation. I will not allow them to succeed. I will go to the *Starburst* office and set fire to it.'

Salim's anger is white hot. And I know why. He hates gays. To tarnish his idol with the brush of homosexuality is the ultimate insult in his book.

I, too, know of perverts and what they do to un-suspecting boys. In dark halls. In public toilets. In municipal gardens. In juvenile homes.

Luckily, *Starburst* retract their allegation in the next issue. And save a *dabbawallah* from becoming an arsonist.

*   *   *

Meanwhile, things are hotting up off screen, in seat A20. The old man slides closer to Salim. His leg casually brushes against Salim's. The first time, Salim thinks it is his own fault. The second time, he thinks it is an accident. The third time, he is convinced it is deliberate.

'Mohammad,' he whispers to me, 'I am going to give a tight kick to the bastard sitting next to me if he doesn't stop his wandering leg.'

'Look how old he is, Salim. It's probably just tremors in his leg,' I counsel.

The fight sequence has started and Salim is busy watching the action. Armaan has entered the villain's den and all hell is breaking loose. The hero uses all manner of feints and tackles – boxing, karate, kung fu – to give his opponents a licking.

The old man's hands are also getting into action. He presses his elbow against the common armrest and lets his arm slide next to Salim's, touching it ever so lightly. Salim hardly notices this. He is engrossed in the film, which is reaching its climax.

The most famous scene of the movie is about to happen. The one in which Armaan Ali dies after killing all the bad guys. His vest is soaked in blood. There are bullet wounds all over his body. His trousers are coated with dust and grime. He drags himself along the ground towards his mother, who has just arrived on the scene.

Salim is in tears. He leans forward and says poignantly, 'Mother, I hope I have been a good son. Don't cry for me. Remember, dying an honourable death is better than living a coward's life.'

Armaan's head is in his mother's lap. He is mimicking Salim: 'Mother, I hope I have been a good son. Don't cry for me. Remember, dying an honourable death is better than living a coward's life.' The mother is crying too as she cradles his bleeding head in her lap. Tears fall from her eyes on Armaan Ali's face. He grips her hand. His chest convulses.

Tears fall into my lap. I see another mother who kisses her baby many times on his forehead before placing him in a clothes bin, rearranging the clothes around him. In the background the wind howls. Sirens sound. The police have arrived, as usual, too late. After the hero has done all the work for them. They cannot do anything for him now.

I see that the bearded man's left hand has moved on. It is now placed in Salim's lap and rests there gently. Salim is so engrossed in the death scene he does not register it. The old man is emboldened. He rubs his palm against Salim's jeans. As Armaan takes his last few breaths, the man increases his pressure on Salim's crotch, till he is almost gripping it.

Salim erupts. 'You bloody motherfucker! You filthy pervert! I am going to kill you!' he screams and slaps the man's face. Hard.

The man hastily removes his hand from Salim's lap and tries to get up from his seat. But before he can lift himself completely, Salim makes a grab for him. He fails to catch the man's collar, but gets hold of his beard. As Salim tugs, it comes off in his hand. The man leaps out of his seat with a strangled cry and dashes towards the exit, which is hardly twenty feet away.

At that very instant the electrical power in the theatre fails and the generator kicks in. The screen goes blank and the dark hall is dazzled as the emergency lights flick on. The man is caught unawares, like a deer in a car's headlamps. He whirls around, unsure of himself.

Just as suddenly, the power comes back. It was only a momentary interruption. The film resumes on the screen, the emergency lights are extinguished. The man rushes past the black curtains to the red EXIT sign, slams open the door and disappears.

But in that split second Salim and I have seen a flash of hazel-green eyes. A chiselled nose. A cleft chin.

As the credits begin to roll over the screen, Salim is left holding in his hand a mass of tangled grey hair smelling vaguely of cologne and spirit gum. This time he does not see the name of the publicity designer and the PRO, the light men and the spot boys, the fight director and the cameraman. He is weeping.

Armaan Ali, his hero, has died.

Smita is staring at me with sceptical eyes. 'When exactly did this incident happen?'

'About six years ago. When Salim and I lived in a chawl in Ghatkopar.'

'And do you realize the significance of what you have just recounted to me?'

'What?'

'That if this incident was made public, it could destroy Armaan Ali, end his film career. Of course, that will happen only if what you just told me is true.'

'So you still don't believe me?'

'I didn't say that.'

'I can see the doubt in your eyes. If you still don't believe me, you do so at your own peril. But you cannot disregard the evidence on this DVD. Should we see the first question?'

Smita nods her head and presses 'Play' on the remote.

The studio lights have been dimmed. I can hardly see the audience sitting around me in a circle. The hall is illuminated by one spotlight in the centre, where I sit in a leather revolving chair opposite Prem Kumar. We are separated by a semicircular table. There is a large screen in front of me on which the questions will be projected. The studio sign is lit up. It says 'Silence'.

'Cameras rolling, three, two, one, you're on.'

The signature tune comes on and Prem Kumar's booming voice fills the hall. 'Here we are once again, ready to find out who will make history today by winning the biggest prize ever offered on earth. Yes, ladies and gentlemen, we are ready to find out Who Will Win A Billion!'

The studio sign changes to 'Applause'. The audience begins clapping. There are some cheers and whistles, too.

The signature tune fades out. Prem Kumar says, 'We have three lucky contestants with us tonight, who have been selected at random by our computer. Contestant number three is Kapil Chowdhary from Malda in West Bengal. Contestant number two is Professor Hari Parikh from Ahmedabad, but our first contestant tonight is eighteen-year-old Ram

Mohammad Thomas from our very own Mumbai. Ladies and gentlemen, please give him a big round of applause.'

Everyone claps. After the applause dies down, Prem Kumar turns to me. 'Ram Mohammad Thomas, now that's a very interesting name. It expresses the richness and diversity of India. What do you do, Mr Thomas?'

'I am a waiter in Jimmy's Bar and Restaurant in Colaba.'

'A waiter! Now isn't that interesting! Tell me, how much do you make every month?'

'Around nine hundred rupees.'

'That's all? And what will you do if you win today?'

'I don't know.'

'You don't know?'

'No.'

Prem Kumar scowls at me. I am not following the script. I am supposed to 'vibe' and be 'entertaining' during the 'small talk'. I should have said I will buy a restaurant, or a plane, or a country. I could have said I will host a big party. Marry Miss India. Travel to Timbuktu.

'OK. Let me explain the rules to you. You will be asked twelve questions, and if you answer each one correctly, you stand to win the biggest jackpot on earth: one billion rupees! You are free to quit at any point up until question number nine and take whatever you have earned up to then, but you cannot quit beyond question number nine. After that, it is either Play or Pay. But let's talk about that when we come to that stage. If you don't know the answer to a question, don't panic, because you have two Lifeboats available to you – A Friendly Tip and Half and Half. So I think we are all set for the first question for one thousand rupees. Are you ready?'

'Yes, I am ready,' I reply.

'OK, here comes question number one. A nice easy one on popular cinema, I am sure everyone in the audience can answer. Now we all know that Armaan Ali and Priya Kapoor have formed one of the most successful screen pairings of recent times. But can you name the blockbusting film in which Armaan Ali starred with Priya Kapoor for the very first time. Was it a) *Fire*, b) *Hero*, c) *Hunger*, or d) *Betrayal*?'

The music in the background changes to a suspense tune, with the sound of a ticking time bomb super-imposed over it.

'D. *Betrayal*,' I reply.

'Do you go to the movies?'

'Yes.'

'And did you see *Betrayal*?'

'Yes.'

'Are you absolutely, one hundred per cent sure of your answer?'

'Yes.'

There is a crescendo of drums. The correct answer flashes on the screen.

'Absolutely, one hundred per cent correct! You've just won one thousand rupees! We will now take a quick commercial break,' declares Prem Kumar.

The studio sign changes to 'Applause'. The audience claps. Prem Kumar smiles. I don't.

2,000

THE BURDEN OF A PRIEST

If you have been to Delhi by train, you must have visited Paharganj. In all probability you would have arrived at the noisy and dusty Paharganj railway station. You would have exited the station and almost certainly headed left towards Connaught Place, bypassing the crowded market with the cut-price guest houses and cheap prostitutes for tourists. But if you had gone right, past the Mother Dairy and J. J. Women's Hospital, you would have seen a red building, with a large white cross. That is the Church of St Mary. That is where I was born eighteen years ago on Christmas Day. Or, to be more precise, that is where I was left on the cold winter night of 25 December. Dumped in the large bin the sisters had put out for old clothes. Who left me there and why, I do not know to this day. The finger of suspicion has always pointed towards the maternity ward of J. J. Hospital. Perhaps I was born there and my mother, for reasons known only to her, was forced to abandon me.

In my mind's eye I have often visualized that scene. A tall and graceful young woman, wearing a white sari, leaves the hospital after midnight with a baby in her arms. The wind is howling. Her long black hair blows across her face, obscuring her features. Leaves rustle near her feet. Dust scatters. Lightning flashes. She walks with heavy footsteps towards the church, clutching the baby to her bosom. She reaches the door of the church and uses the metal ring knocker. But the wind is so strong, it drowns out the sound of the knock. Her time is limited. With tears streaming from her eyes, she smothers the baby's face with kisses. Then she places him in the bin, arranging the old clothes to make him comfortable. She takes one final look at the baby, averts her eyes and then, running away from the camera, disappears into the night . . .

The sisters of St Mary ran an orphanage and an adoption agency, and I was put up for adoption, together with a clutch of other orphan babies. All the other babies were collected, but no one came for me. A prospective mother and father would see me and exchange glances with each other. There would be an imperceptible shake of the head, and then they would move on to the next cradle. I do not know why. Perhaps I was too dark. Too ugly. Too colicky. Perhaps I didn't have a cherubic smile, or I gurgled too much. So I remained at the orphanage for two years. Oddly enough, the sisters never got round to giving me a name. I was just called Baby – the baby that no one wanted.

I was finally adopted by Mrs Philomena Thomas and her husband Dominic Thomas. Originally from Nagercoil in Tamil Nadu, they now lived in Delhi. Mrs Thomas worked as a cleaner in St Joseph's Church and her husband as the gardener. Because they were in their forties without any children of their own, Father Timothy Francis, the parish priest, had been urging them to consider adopting to fill the void in their life. He even directed them to St Mary's Orphanage. Mr Thomas must have taken one look at me and immediately passed on to the next baby, but Mrs Philomena Thomas selected me the moment she saw me. I was a perfect match for her dark skin!

The Thomases spent two months completing the paperwork for my adoption, but within three days of taking me home and even before I could be christened, Mr Thomas discovered that the void in his wife's life had already been filled. Not by me, but by a Muslim gentleman by the name of Mastan Sheikh, who was the local ladies' tailor, specializing in short skirts. Mrs Philomena Thomas ditched her old husband and newly adopted baby and ran off with the tailor, reportedly to Bhopal. Her whereabouts are not known to this day.

On discovering this, Mr Thomas went into a rage. He dragged me in my cradle to the priest's house and dumped me there. 'Father, this baby is the root cause of all the trouble in my life. You forced me to adopt him, so now you decide what to do with him.' And before Father Timothy could even say 'Amen', Dominic Thomas walked out of the church. He was last seen buying a train ticket for Bhopal with a shotgun in his hands. So willy-nilly I became Father Timothy's responsibility. He gave me food, he gave me shelter and he gave me a name: Joseph Michael Thomas. There was no baptism ceremony. No priest dipped my head into a font. No holy water was sprinkled. No white shawl was draped over me. No candle was lit. But I became Joseph Michael Thomas. For six days.

On the seventh day, two men came to meet Father Timothy. A fat man wearing white *kurta* pyjamas, and a thin, bearded man wearing a *sherwani.*

'We are from the All Faith Committee,' the fat man said. 'I am Mr Jagdish Sharma. This is Mr Inayat Hidayatullah. Our third board member, Mr Harvinder Singh, representing the Sikh faith, was also to come, but he is unfortunately held up at the Gurudwara. We will come straight to the point. We are told, Father, that you have given shelter to a little orphan boy.'

'Yes, the poor boy's adoptive parents have dis-appeared, leaving him in my care,' said Father Timothy, still unable to figure out the reason for this unexpected visit.

'What name have you given this boy?'

'Joseph Michael Thomas.'

'Isn't that a Christian name?'

'Yes, but—'

'How do you know that he was born to Christian parents?'

'Well, I don't.'

'Then why have you given him a Christian name?'

51

'Well, I had to call him something. What's wrong with Joseph Michael Thomas?'

'Everything. Don't you know, Father, how strong the movement is against conversion in these parts? Several churches have been set fire to by irate mobs, who were led to believe that mass conversions to Christianity were taking place there.'

'But this is no conversion.'

'Look, Father, we know you did not have any ulterior motive. But word has got around that you have converted a Hindu boy.'

'But how do you know he is Hindu?'

'It won't matter to the lumpen elements who are planning to ransack your church tomorrow. That is why we have come to help you. To cool things down.'

'What do you suggest I do?'

'I suggest you change the boy's name.'

'To what?'

'Well . . . giving him a Hindu name might do the trick. Why not name him Ram, after one of our favourite gods?' said Mr Sharma.

Mr Hidayatullah coughed gently. 'Excuse me, Mr Sharma, but aren't we replacing one evil with another? I mean, what is the proof that the boy was a Hindu at birth? He might have been Muslim, you know. Why can't he be called Mohammad?'

Mr Sharma and Mr Hidayatullah debated the respective merits of Ram and Mohammad for the next thirty minutes. Finally, Father Timothy gave up. 'Look, if it takes a name change to get the mob off my back, I will do it. How about if I accept both your suggestions and change the boy's name to Ram

Mohammad Thomas? That should satisfy everyone.'
Luckily for me that Mr Singh did not come that day.

Father Timothy was tall, white and comfortably middle aged. He had a huge house in the church compound with a sprawling garden full of fruit trees. For the next six years, he became my father, mother, master, teacher and priest, all rolled into one. If there has been anything approximating happiness in my life, it was in the time I spent with him.

Father Timothy was from the north of England, a place called York, but had been settled in India for very many years. It was thanks to him that I learnt to read and speak the Queen's English. He taught me Mother Goose Tales and nursery rhymes. I would sing 'Twinkle Twinkle Little Star' and 'Baa Baa Black Sheep' in my horribly off-key voice, providing, I suppose, an amusing diversion for Father Timothy from his priestly duties.

Living in the church compound, I felt part of a much larger family. Apart from Father Timothy, his faithful manservant Joseph stayed in the house and Mrs Gonzalves, the maid, also lived close by. And then there was a whole bunch of street kids belonging to the plumbers, cobblers, sweepers and washermen, who lived practically next door and did not hesitate to use the church grounds for their cricket and football games. Father Timothy taught me about the life of Jesus, and Adam and Eve, and this extended family instructed me on the rudiments of other religions. I came to know about the Mahabharata and the Holy Koran. I learnt about the Prophet's flight from Mecca to

Medina and of the burning down of Lanka. Bethlehem and Ayodhya, St Peter and the Hajj all became part of my growing-up.

This is not to suggest, though, that I was a particularly religious child. I was like any other child, with three main preoccupations: eating, sleeping and playing. I spent many an afternoon with the neighbourhood kids of my age, catching butterflies and frightening birds in Father Timothy's garden. While Joseph, the old retainer, dusted curios in the drawing room, I would sneak out and try to pluck ripe mangoes, under the watchful eye of the gardener. If caught, I would give him generous abuse in Hindi. I would dance with abandon in the monsoon rain, try to catch little fish in the small muddy pools of rain water and end up coughing and sneezing, much to the consternation of Father Timothy. I would play football with the street kids, come back battered and bruised, and then cry the entire night.

Father Timothy lived an active life. He would go for a walk every morning, play golf, volleyball and tennis, read voraciously and take vacations three times a year to meet his aged mother in England. He was also an expert violinist. Most evenings he would sit out in the moonlit garden and play the most soulful melodies you can imagine. And when it rained at night during the monsoon season, I would think of the sky as weeping from hearing his sad tunes.

I enjoyed going into the church. It was an old building built in 1878, with stained-glass windows and a spectacular roof made of timber. The altar was beautifully carved. Above it was a large crucifix of Christ and the letters INRI. There were sculptures of the Virgin and Child enthroned and of many saints. The pews were made of teak wood, but they were full only on Sundays. Father Timothy would give a long sermon from the pulpit, during which I would doze off, to wake only when he gave everyone the wafer and wine. I also enjoyed hearing the organ and the choir. I fell in love with Easter eggs and Christmas trees, which unfortunately came only once a year, and church weddings, which were held in all seasons. I would wait for Father Timothy to say, 'And you may now kiss the bride.' I would always be the first to throw the confetti.

My relationship with Father Timothy was never precisely defined. It was never made clear to me whether I was servant or son, parasite or pet. So for the first few years of my life, I lived under the happy illusion that Father Timothy was my real father. But gradually I began to realize something was amiss. For one, all those who came to Mass on Sunday mornings would call him Father, and it intrigued me that he was the father of so many people, and that I had so many brothers and sisters, all much bigger than me. I was also perplexed by the fact that he was white and I was not. So one day I asked him, and he shattered the fantasy world in which I had lived till then. In the gentlest possible way, he explained to me that I was an orphan child left behind by my mother in the clothes bin of St Mary's Orphanage, and that was why he was white and I was not. It was then, for the first time, that I understood the distinction between father and Father. And that night, for the first time, my tears had nothing to do with physical pain.

Once the realization sank in that I did not have a biological connection with Father Timothy and was living in the church only due to his generosity, I became determined to repay, at least in part, the debt I owed him. I began doing little chores for him, like taking the clothes from the laundry basket to the washing machine. Sitting in front of the machine, watching the drum spin round and round and wondering how the clothes came out so magically clean. Once putting some dusty books inside the washing machine as well. Doing the dishes in the kitchen sink. Breaking fine china. Slicing vegetables. On occasion almost chopping off my finger.

Father Timothy introduced me to many of his parishioners. I met old Mrs Benedict, who came religiously to Mass every day, come hail or rain, till she slipped on the pavement one day and died of pneumonia. I attended the wedding of Jessica, who cried so much her father had a heart attack. I was taken once to high tea at the house of Colonel Waugh, who was the Australian Defence Attaché in Delhi and who seemed to speak to Father Timothy in a completely foreign language. I went on a fishing trip with Mr Lawrence, who caught nothing, then purchased a large trout from the fish market to deceive his wife.

All the people I met had nothing but praise for Father Timothy. They said he was the best priest this diocese had ever had. I saw him comfort the bereaved, attend to the sick, lend money to the needy and share a meal even with lepers. He had a smile on his face for every member of the parish, a cure for every problem and a quotation from the Bible for every occasion – birth, Baptism, Confirmation, First Communion, marriage or death.

It is Sunday and the church is full of people gathered for the Mass. But today Father Timothy is not standing alone behind the altar. He has another man with him, also wearing a cassock and a white band at his neck. He looks more like a boxer than a priest. Father Timothy is introducing him. '. . . And it is a great pleasure for us to welcome Father John Little, who has joined the Church of St Joseph as Associate Priest. Father John, as you can see, is much younger than me, and even though he was ordained only three years ago, is vastly experienced. I am sure he will be able to relate much more effectively to our younger worshippers, who, I am well aware, have been referring to me behind my back as "that old fogy".' The congregation titters.

That evening, Father Timothy invites Father John for dinner. Joseph is supposed to serve them, but in my enthusiasm to impress Father Timothy, I pick up the heavy bowl of soup from the kitchen and walk with unsteady steps towards the dining table. As is to be expected from an ill-trained seven-year-old, instead of depositing the soup bowl on the table, I spill it all on Father John. He gets up in a hurry, and the first words that appear on his lips are 'Bloody Hell!' Father Timothy raises an eyebrow, but doesn't say anything.

Three days later, Father Timothy goes away to England on holiday, leaving the church, and me, in the hands of Father John. I meet him two days later coming down the steps of the church.

'Good evening, Father,' I say politely.

Father John looks at me with disdain. 'You're that idiot orphan boy who spilled soup on me the other day! You'd better behave yourself in Father Timothy's absence. I'll be watching you very carefully.'

Joseph has sent me with a glass of milk to Father John's room. He is watching a movie on the TV. He invites me in. 'Come in, Thomas. Do you want to watch this film with me?' I look at the TV. It is an English film – about priests, I think, because I see a priest in a black cassock talking to another priest in a white cassock. I am relieved Father John is fond of watching good, religious films. But the very next scene sends a chill down my spine, because it shows a young girl, about my age, sitting on a bed. She does not appear to be a normal girl, because she has a funny expression on her face and her eyes are going all over the place. The priest in the black cassock enters her room with a cross in his hand. He points it at her, and she starts speaking the most filthy language I have ever heard, and that too in the hoarse voice of a grown-up man. I put my fingers in my ears, because Father Timothy has instructed me not to listen to such dirty words. Suddenly she stops speaking. She starts laughing, like a mad girl. Then she opens her mouth and horrible, gooey green stuff spews out of it like a jet of water from a garden pipe and lands on the priest. I feel like vomiting. I cannot watch any longer and run down to my room. I hear Father John squealing with laughter. 'Come back, you idiot orphan boy, it's just a film,' he calls out.

I get bad dreams that night.

Three days later I am out shopping with Joseph. We purchase meat and eggs and vegetables and flour. As we are returning to the church late in the evening, I hear the sound of a motorcycle behind me. Before I can look back, the motorcycle rider is upon us. He slaps me on the head and screams away, raising a plume of dust. I catch sight only of his back. He seems like a heavy-set man wearing a leather jacket and tight black trousers, with another similarly dressed man riding pillion. I wonder who the rider is and why he rapped me on the head. It doesn't occur to me that it could be Father John. After all, I am only an idiot orphan boy.

A week later, I have to deliver some mail to Father John, but he is taking a bath. 'Leave the post on the table,' he shouts from the bathroom. I am about to leave the room when I catch sight of something peeping out from underneath his mattress. I look closely. It is a magazine. I pull it out. And then I find a whole bunch of them under the mattress. They are not very thick but they have nice glossy covers. They have strange titles like *Gay Parade* and *Out* and *Gay Power*. But the men on their covers do not seem very happy and gay. They are all hairy and naked. I hastily put the magazines back under the mattress. I am about to go out when Father John emerges from the bathroom. He has a towel around his waist. But his chest is covered in strange patterns made in black ink and there are snakes painted on his arms. 'What are you doing here?' he admonishes me. 'Bugger off!'

Why Father John has all these strange designs on his body and keeps those strange magazines under his bed, I don't know. I am just an idiot orphan boy.

I often see strange-looking young men entering the church at night and going to Father John's room. Visitors used to come to meet Father Timothy as well, sometimes at odd hours of the night, but they never came by motorcycle wearing leather jackets and thick metal chains around their necks. I decide to follow one of these visitors to Father John's room. He knocks and enters and Father John closes the door. I peer through the little keyhole. I know I am doing a very bad thing, but my curiosity is killing me. Through the keyhole I see Father John and the young leather-clad man sitting on the bed. Father John opens his drawer and takes out a plastic packet, which has some white powder in it. He spreads the powder in a thin line on the back of his left hand. Then he does the same to the left hand of his friend. They both bend their faces to the powder and inhale deeply. The white powder seems to disappear into their noses. Brother John laughs, like that mad girl in the film. His friend says, 'This is good stuff, man! Way too good for a priest. How did you get into this Church shit in the first place?'

Father John laughs again. 'I liked the dress,' he says, and gets up from the bed. 'Come,' he tells his friend and puts out his hand. I hastily retreat.

Why Father John puts talcum powder into his nose

I don't know. But then I am just an idiot orphan boy.

Father Timothy finally returns from his holiday in England and I am delighted to see him again. I am pretty sure he has heard lots of complaints about Father John, because within just two days of his return there is a big argument between them in the study. Father John rushes out of the room in a huff.

Easter is over. All my Easter eggs have been eaten. And Mrs Gonzalves, the house maid, is sniggering.

'What's the matter, Mrs Gonzalves?' I ask her.

'Don't you know?' she whispers confidentially. 'Joseph caught Father John in the church with another man. But don't tell anyone, and don't whisper a word to Father Timothy, otherwise there'll be hell to pay.'

I don't understand. What's wrong if Father John was with another man in the church? Father Timothy is with other men all the time in the church. Like when he listens to confessions.

Today, for the first time, I am in the confession box.

'Yes, my son, what have you come to tell me?' asks Father Timothy.

'It is me, Father.'

Father Timothy almost jumps out of his chair. 'What are you doing here, Thomas? Haven't I told you this is not a joking matter?'

'I have come to confess, Father. I have sinned.'

'Really?' Father Timothy softens. 'What wrong have you done?'

'I peeped inside Father John's room through the keyhole. And I looked at some of his things without his permission.'

'That's quite all right, my son. I don't think I want to hear about that.'

'No, you must, Father,' I say, and proceed to tell him about the magazines under the mattress, the designs on the body, the leather-clad visitors at night, and the snorting of the talcum powder.

That evening there is the mother of all showdowns in the study between the two priests. I listen at the door. There is a lot of shouting. Father Timothy ends the discussion by threatening to report Father John to the Bishop. 'I am a priest,' he says. 'And to be a priest, you have to carry a heavy burden. If you can't do this, then return to the seminary.'

An English backpacker passing through Delhi came to church this morning and Father Timothy found out that he is also from York. So he brought him home and is allowing him to stay for a few days. He introduces him to me. 'Ian, meet Thomas, who lives with us here. Thomas, this is Ian. Do you know he is also from York? You are always asking me about my mother's city; now you can ask him.'

I like Ian. He is fifteen or sixteen years old. He has fair skin, blue eyes and golden hair. He shows me pictures of York. I see a large cathedral. 'It's called York Minster,' he says. He shows me pictures of lovely gardens and museums and parks.

'Have you met Father Timothy's mother? She also lives in York,' I ask him.

'No, but I will meet her after I return, now that I have her address.'

'What about your own mother? Does she also live in York?'

'She used to. But she died ten years ago. A motorcycle rider crashed into her.' He takes out a picture of his mother from his wallet and shows it to me. She had fair skin, blue eyes and golden hair.

'So why have you come to India?' I ask him.

'To meet my dad.'

'What does your father do?'

Ian hesitates. 'He teaches at a Catholic school in Dehradun.'

'Why don't you also live in Dehradun?'

'Because I am studying in York.'

'Then why doesn't your dad live with you in York?'

'There are reasons. But he comes to visit me three times a year. This time I decided to meet him in India.'

'Do you love your dad?'

'Yes, very much.'

'Do you wish your dad could stay with you for ever?'

'Yes. What about your dad? What does he do?'

'I don't have a dad. I am an idiot orphan boy.'

Three evenings later, Father Timothy invites Father John to dinner with Ian. They eat and talk late into the night and Father Timothy even plays his violin. Father John leaves some time after midnight, but Father Timothy and Ian continue chatting. I lie in bed listening to the sound of laughter drifting from the open window. I have trouble sleeping.

It is a moonlit night and a strong wind is blowing. The eucalyptus trees in the compound are swaying, their leaves making a rustling noise. I feel like going to the lavatory and get up. As I am walking towards the bathroom, I see a light inside Father John's room. I also hear sounds. I tiptoe to the door. It is closed, so I peer through the keyhole. What I see inside is frightening. Ian is stooped over the table and Father John is bending over him. His pyjamas have fallen down to his feet. I am totally confused. I may be an idiot orphan boy, but I know something is wrong. I rush to Father Timothy, who is fast asleep. 'Wake up, Father! Father John is doing something bad to Ian!' I shout.

'To whom? To Ian?' Father Timothy is immediately alert. Both of us rush to Father John's room and Father Timothy bursts inside. He sees what I have just seen. His face goes so pale, I think he is about to faint. He grips the door to keep himself from collapsing. Then his face becomes red with anger. He almost starts frothing at the mouth. I am scared. I have never seen him this angry before. 'Ian, go to your room,' he thunders. 'And you too, Thomas.'

I do as I am told, even more confused than before.

I am woken early next morning by the sound of two bangs, coming from the direction of the church. I sense immediately that something is wrong. I rush to the church and witness a scene which shakes me to my core. Father Timothy is lying in a pool of blood near the altar, just below the statue of Jesus Christ on the cross. He is wearing his cassock and looks to be kneeling in prayer. Ten steps away from him lies the body of Father John, splattered with blood. His head appears to have been shattered and little pieces of his brain stick to the pews. He is dressed in leather. There are images of dark serpents on his arms. A shotgun lies clenched in his right hand.

I see this scene, and I feel the breath being choked out of my lungs. I scream. It is a piercing cry, which shatters the stillness of the morning like a bullet. It frightens away the crows sitting on the eucalyptus trees. It causes Joseph, dusting ornaments in the drawing room, to pause and listen. It impels Mrs Gonzalves to finish her shower quickly. And it wakes up Ian, who comes running into the church.

I am bent over Father Timothy, wailing like an eight-year-old wails when he has lost everything in his life. Ian comes and sits beside me. He looks at the lifeless body of Father Timothy and begins crying too. We hold hands and cry together for almost three hours, even after the police jeep with the flashing red light comes, even after the doctor in a white coat arrives with an ambulance, even after they cover the bodies with white cloth, even after they cart away the corpses in the ambulance, even after Joseph and Mrs Gonzalves take us away to the house and try their best to comfort us.

Later, much later, Ian asks me, 'Why did you cry so much, Thomas?'

'Because today I have really become an orphan,' I reply. 'He was my father. Just as he was Father to all those who came to this church. But why were you crying? Is it because of what you did with Father John?'

'No, I was crying because I have lost everything too. I have become an orphan like you.'

'But your father is alive. He is in Dehradun,' I cry.

'No, that was a lie.' He begins sobbing again. 'Now I can tell you the truth. Timothy Francis may have been your Father, but he was my dad.'

Smita has a sad expression on her face. 'What a tragic story,' she says. 'I now understand what Father Timothy must have meant when he spoke of the burden of a priest. It is amazing how he lived a double life all those years, as a priest who was also secretly a married man and a father. So what happened to Ian, finally?'

'I don't know. He went back to England. To some uncle, I think.'

'And you?'

'I got sent to a Juvenile Home.'

'I see. Now tell me about the second question,' says Smita and presses 'Play' on the remote.

We are still in the commercial break.

Prem Kumar leans forward and whispers to me, 'Let me tell you what the next question is going to be. I will ask you what FBI stands for. You have heard of this organization, haven't you?'

'No.' I shake my head.

He grimaces. 'I knew it. Look, we would like you to win at least a little more money. I can change the question for something else. Tell me quickly, are there any abbreviations you are familiar with?'

I think for a while before replying. 'I don't know about FBI, but I know INRI.'

'What's that?'

'It's what's written on top of a cross.'

'Oh! OK, let me check my data bank.'

The commercial break ends. The signature tune comes on.

Prem Kumar turns to me. 'I am curious, Mr Ram Mohammad Thomas, as to your religion. You seem to have all the religions in your name. Tell me, where do you go to pray?'

'Does one have to go to a temple or a church or a mosque to pray? I believe in what Kabir says. Hari is in the East, Allah is in the West. Look within your heart, and there you will find both Ram and Karim.'

'Very well said, Mr Thomas. It looks like you are an expert on all religions. And if that is the case, the next question should be fairly easy for you. OK, here it comes, question number two for two thousand rupees. What is the sequence of letters normally inscribed on a cross? Is it a) IRNI, b) INRI, c) RINI or d) NIRI? Is the question clear, Mr Thomas?'

'Yes,' I reply.

'OK. Then let's hear your reply.'

'The answer is B. INRI.'

'Are you absolutely, one hundred per cent sure?'

'Yes.'

There is a crescendo of drums. The correct answer flashes.

'Absolutely, one hundred per cent correct! You have just won two thousand rupees.'

'Amen,' I say.

5,000

A Brother's Promise

You should take a good look at all sides of an issue before making a decision. Put something away in case of an emergency. New neighbours will bring good cheer. A small problem may occur at home base, but you will solve it quickly and correctly. Don't offer smart advice unless you are really asked to comment.

This is what the daily horoscope in the *Maharashtra Times* has predicted today for those who are Capricorns like me, born in the last week of December.

I don't read the *Maharashtra Times*. In fact, I don't read any newspaper. But I occasionally pilfer a copy from Mr Barve's rubbish bin. It is useful for stoking the fire in the kitchen, and sometimes, when I have nothing else to do, I flip through its pages as a time pass before they are reduced to ash.

I also don't believe in horoscopes. If I did, I should be dead by now, as per the prediction made by Pandit Ramashankar Shastri. But today's daily horoscope does appear to contain a kernel of truth. New neighbours are moving into the room next door and there is indeed a small problem at home base.

We have just returned from the matinée at Regal Talkies and Salim is in a blind rage. He is tearing down all the posters of Armaan Ali which have adorned the walls of our small room for nearly three years. The poster of Armaan in a leather jacket has been torn to shreds. Armaan on a motorbike has been dismembered with a knife. Armaan with his shirt off, baring his hairy chest, is now in the bin. Armaan with a gun has been diced into tiny pieces and Armaan and his horse have both been roasted over the fire. With all the posters gone, our room, with just two beds, is suddenly looking even more bare than before, and the mildew patches on the whitewashed walls are no longer hidden.

Despite the warning in the daily horoscope, I cannot resist offering some smart advice to Salim. 'Do you now realize the truth of what I told you ten months ago, when you were busy trying to fix Armaan's relationship with Urvashi? I told you not to poke your nose into other people's affairs, or make other people's troubles your own. Remember this as a lesson for the future.'

Salim hears me sullenly as he stomps on the poster of Armaan in a pool surrounded by a bevy of beauties.

I hear footsteps and voices outside the room. It looks as if the new tenants are finally moving into the room next to ours. I am excited. It is always good to meet new people. I hope the new tenants have boys of my age. Putul and Dhyanesh are good company, but they rarely get permission from their parents to come and play with me on Sundays, which is the only day I don't have to go to work. Ajay, the show-off, is also getting on my nerves. He made fun of me in front of the whole chawl when I told him I had joined a foundry. I know working in a foundry is not half as exciting as working for a film star, but at least it is better than sitting in the street.

After the time I spent with the actress Neelima Kumari, living in her flat, I had almost forgotten life in a chawl. A bundle of one-room tenements occupied by the lower-middle classes, chawls are the smelly armpit of Mumbai. Those who live here are only marginally better off than those who live in slums like Dharavi. As Mr Barve told me once, the rich people, those who live in their marble and granite four-bedroom flats, they enjoy. The slum people, who live in squalid, tattered huts, they suffer. And we, who reside in the over-crowded chawls, we simply live.

Living in a chawl does have certain advantages. What happened to Neelima Kumari would never happen here, because in a chawl everyone knows everything that is going on. All the residents have a common roof over their heads and a common place where they shit and bathe. The residents of the chawl may not meet each other for social occasions, but they have to meet while standing in a queue outside the common lavatories. In fact, it is rumoured that Mr Gokhale met Mrs Gokhale while waiting outside the latrine and fell in love. They got married within a month.

There is no chance of my falling in love with any girl in the chawl. They are all fat and ugly, not even remotely like my favourite actress, Priya Kapoor. Besides, they all like stupid things like dolls and cannot play any decent games like boxing and *kabaddi*. Not that I get much time to play these games. The whole day I work at the foundry, returning only at six in the evening. And smelting metal is a tough job. The molten iron smothers you with its heat and your eyes are often blinded by the bright-orange flames.

'Thomas!' I hear a voice. It is Mr Ramakrishna, the administrator of the chawl, calling me. He is a very important man. We go to Mr Ramakrishna whenever the bulb goes out or the water pressure becomes low. We beg Mr Ramakrishna when we don't have enough money to pay the monthly rent. We have been after Mr Ramakrishna to repair a section of the first-floor wooden railing which has become weak and wobbly and poses a safety hazard.

I come out of the room and see Mr Ramakrishna standing with a short, middle-aged man who frowns and looks as though he has not gone to the toilet for a long time. 'Thomas, meet Mr Shantaram. He is our new tenant, who will be staying in the flat next to yours. I have told Mr Shantaram that you are a very responsible boy, so please help him and his wife and

71

daughter settle down. OK, Mr Shantaram, I will now take my leave.'

'Oh no,' I think to myself. 'No boys.' I try to see his wife and daughter, but only catch a fleeting glimpse of a woman with grey hair, and a girl, older than me, with long black hair tied back, sitting on the bed. Shantaram sees me peering into his flat and hastily closes the front door.

'What do you do?' I ask Shantaram.

'I am a scientist, an astronomer. You won't understand. But these days I am taking a break. I am working as the sales manager in the Vimal showroom. This room here is a very temporary arrangement. We will be shifting to a de luxe apartment in Nariman Point very soon.'

I know Mr Shantaram is lying. Those who can afford to live in Nariman Point never stay in chawls, not even temporarily.

The walls of the rooms inside the chawl are very thin. If you put your ear against the common wall and concentrate hard or, even better, if you put an inverted glass against the wall and put your ear against it, you can listen to almost everything going on in the next room. Salim and I do this often with our neighbours on the left, whose room adjoins our kitchen wall. Mr and Mrs Bapat are not a young couple any more. It is rumoured that Mr Bapat even beats Mrs Bapat, but they obviously make up at night because Salim and I often hear their heavy breathing and panting, their 'oohs' and 'aahs', and we snicker.

I adjust a stainless-steel cup against the wall

adjoining Mr Shantaram's room and bury my ear in it.
I can hear Shantaram speaking.

'This place is nothing less than a black hole. It is
totally beneath my dignity to be staying here, but just
for the sake of you two, I will endure this humiliation
till I get a proper job. Listen, I don't want any of the
street boys to enter the house. God knows what hell
holes they have come from. There are two right next to
us. Rascals of the highest order, I think. And Gudiya,
if I catch you talking to any boy in the chawl, you will
receive a hiding with my leather belt, understood?' he
thunders. I drop the cup in panic.

Over the next couple of weeks, I hardly see Shantaram
and I never see his wife or daughter. She probably goes
to college every day, but by the time I return home
from the foundry, she is inside her house and the door
is always firmly shut.

Salim doesn't even notice that we have new neighbours. He hardly gets any spare time from his work as
a tiffin delivery boy. He wakes up at seven in the
morning and gets dressed. He wears a loose white
shirt, cotton pyjamas and puts a white Nehru cap on
his head. The cap is the badge of identification of all
dabbawallahs in Mumbai, and there are nearly five
thousand of them. Over the next two hours he collects
home-cooked meals in lunch boxes from approximately twenty-five flats. Then he takes them to the
Ghatkopar local train station. Here the tiffins are
sorted according to their destination, each with
colour-coded dots, dashes and crosses on the lids, and
then loaded on to special trains to be delivered

promptly at lunch time to middle-class executives and blue-collar workers all over Mumbai. Salim himself receives tiffins by another train, which he delivers in the Ghatkopar area after deciphering the dots and dashes which constitute the address. He has to be very careful, because one mistake could cost him his job. He dare not hand over a container with beef to a Hindu, or one with pork to a Muslim or one with garlic and onions to a Jain vegetarian.

It is nine at night. Salim is flipping through the pages of a film magazine. I am kneeling on my bed with my left ear inside a stainless-steel cup held to the wall. I hear Shantaram speaking to his daughter. 'Here, Gudiya, see through the eyepiece. I have adjusted the telescope now. Can you see the bright-red object in the middle? That is Mars.'

I whisper to Salim, 'Quick, get a cup. You must hear this.'

Salim also glues his ear to the wall. Over the next thirty minutes, we listen to a running commentary on the state of the sky. We hear about stellar con-stellations and galaxies and comets. We hear about the Great Bear and the Little Bear. We hear of something called the Milky Way and the Pole Star. We learn about the rings of Saturn and the moons of Jupiter.

Listening to Shantaram, I am filled with a strange longing. I wish I too had a father who would teach me about stars and planets. The night sky, which till now was just a big black mass to me, suddenly becomes a place of meaning and wonder. As soon as Shantaram's tutorial ends, Salim and I crane our necks out of our

first-floor window and try to find the celestial landmarks pointed out by him. Without the aid of a
telescope we see only little white dots in the dark sky,
but we squeal with delight when we recognize the
seven stars of the Great Bear, and even the knowledge
that the dark patches on the moon are not blemishes
but craters and seas fills us with a sense of satisfaction,
as though we have unlocked the mysteries of the
universe.

That night I don't dream about a woman in a fluttering white sari. I dream about rings around Saturn and
moons around Jupiter.

A week later, I am alerted by a totally new sound coming from Shantaram's room. 'Meow!' I scramble to the
wall with my stainless-steel listening device in hand.

I hear Gudiya speaking. 'Papa, look, I've got a cat.
Isn't he lovely? My friend Rohini gave him to me from
her cat's new litter. Can I keep him?'

'I am not in favour of any pets,' Mrs Shantaram
grumbles. 'There's hardly space in this room for
humans – where will we keep an animal?'

'Please, Mummy, he is such a tiny thing. Papa,
please agree,' she pleads.

'OK, Gudiya,' says Shantaram. 'You can keep him.
But what will you call him?'

'Oh, thank you, Papa. I was thinking of calling him
Tommy.'

'No, that is such a commonplace name. This cat is
going to live in an astronomer's family, so it should be
named after one of the planets.'

'Which one? Should we call him Jupiter?'

'No. He is the smallest in the family, so he can only be called Pluto.'

'Great, I love the name, Papa. Here, Pluto! Pluto, come and have some milk.'

'Meow!' says Pluto.

These little snippets force me to reconsider my opinion of Shantaram. Perhaps he is not so bad after all. But, once again, I learn that appearances can be deceptive and the dividing line between good and bad is very thin indeed.

I see Shantaram come home one evening, completely drunk. His breath stinks of whisky. He walks with unsteady steps and needs help to climb up the flight of stairs. This happens the next day, and the day after that. Pretty soon it is common knowledge in the chawl that Mr Shantaram is a drunkard.

Drunkards in Hindi films are invariably funny characters. Think of Keshto Mukherjee with a bottle and you cannot help bursting out laughing. But drunkards in real life are not funny, they are frightening. Whenever Shantaram comes home in a stupor, we don't need listening devices. He hurls abuses at the top of his voice and Salim and I quiver with fear in our room as if we are the ones being shouted at. His swearing becomes such a ritual that we actually wait for the sound of his snoring before falling asleep ourselves. We come to dread the interval between Shantaram's return from work and his crashing out in bed. This interval is, for us, the zone of fear.

We think this is a passing phase and that Shantaram will eventually recover. But it actually gets worse.

Shantaram begins drinking even more and then he starts throwing things. He begins with plastic cups and books, which he throws at the wall in disgust. Then he starts breaking pots and pans. The ruckus he creates makes living next door very difficult. But we know complaining to Mr Ramakrishna is out of the question. The voices of a thirteen-year-old and an eleven-year-old habitual rent offender do not carry much weight. So we simply duck in bed whenever an object thuds on to our common wall and cringe in fear whenever we hear the sound of a plate crashing or china breaking.

Even this phase does not last long. Pretty soon, Shantaram starts throwing objects at people. Mainly his family members. He reserves maximum ire for his wife. 'You bloody bitch! You are the one who has brought me down in life. I could be writing research papers on black holes, and instead I am showing blouse pieces and saris to wretched housewives. I hate you! Why don't you die?' he would holler, and throw a peppershaker, a glass, a plate. At his wife, his daughter, her cat.

One night he exceeds all limits and throws a piping-hot cup of tea at his wife. Gudiya tries to shield her mother and the burning liquid falls on her instead, scalding her face. She shrieks in agony. Shantaram is so drunk he doesn't even realize what he has done. I rush out to get a taxi for Mrs Shantaram to take her daughter to hospital. Two days later, she comes to me and asks whether I will go with her to visit Gudiya. 'She gets very lonely. Perhaps you can talk to her.'

So I accompany Mrs Shantaram on my first-ever visit to a hospital.

The first thing that assails your senses when you enter a hospital is the smell. I feel nauseated by the cloying, antiseptic smell of disinfectant, which permeates every corner of the dirty wards. The second thing that strikes you is that you don't see any happy people. The patients lying on their green beds are moaning and groaning and even the nurses and doctors seem grim. But the worst thing is the indifference. No one is really bothered about you. I had imagined there would be doctors and nurses swarming all over Gudiya, but I find her lying all alone on a bed inside the Burns Unit with not a single nurse on duty. Her face is completely bandaged; only her black eyes can be seen.

'Gudiya, look who has come to see you,' Mrs Shantaram says, beaming at me.

I feel diffident approaching the girl. She is obviously much older than me. I am just a voyeur who has heard some snippets from her life; I hardly know her. I don't see her lips, but I can see from her eyes that she is smiling at me and that breaks the ice between us.

I sit with her for three hours, talking about this and that. Gudiya asks me, 'How did you get such an unusual name – Ram Mohammad Thomas?'

'It is a very long story. I will tell you when you are well.'

She tells me about herself. I learn that she is about to finish her Intermediate and start University. Her ambition is to become a doctor. She asks me about myself. I don't tell her anything about Father Timothy or what happened to me later, but I recount my experiences in the chawl. I tell her about life as a foundry worker. She listens to me with rapt attention and makes me feel very important and wanted.

A doctor comes and tells Mrs Shantaram that her daughter is lucky. She has received only first-degree burns and will not have any permanent scars. She will be discharged within a week.

The three hours that I spend with Gudiya enable me to learn a lot about her father. Mrs Shantaram tells me, 'My husband is a famous space scientist. Rather, he was a scientist. He used to work in the Aryabhatta Space Research Institute, where he investigated stars with the help of huge telescopes. We used to live in a big bungalow on the Institute's campus. Three years ago he discovered a new star. It was a very important scientific discovery but one of his fellow astronomers took credit for it. This shattered my husband completely. He started drinking. He started having fights with his colleagues and one day he got so angry with the director of the Institute he almost beat him to death. He was thrown out of the Institute immediately and I had to beg the director not to have him arrested by the police. After leaving the Institute, my husband got a job as a physics teacher in a good school, but he could not keep his drinking and his violent temper in check. He would thrash boys for minor lapses and was kicked out in just six months. Since then he has been doing odd jobs, working as a canteen manager in an office, as an accountant in a factory, and now as a sales assistant in a clothes showroom. And because we have exhausted all our savings, we are forced to live in a chawl.'

'Can't Mr Shantaram stop drinking?' I ask her.

'My husband swore to me he would not touch alcohol again and I had begun to hope that the worst was over. But he couldn't stick to his promise, and look what has happened.'

'Do me a favour, Ram Mohammad Thomas,' Gudiya says. 'Please look after Pluto till I return home.'

'Definitely,' I promise.

Suddenly she stretches out her arm and takes my hand in hers. 'You are the brother I never had. Isn't he, Mummy?' she says. Mrs Shantaram nods her head.

I do not know what to say. This is a new relationship for me. In the past, I have imagined myself as someone's son, but never as someone's brother. So I just hold Gudiya's hand and sense an unspoken bond pass between us.

That night I dream of a woman in a white sari holding a baby in her arms. The wind howls behind her, making her hair fly across her face, obscuring it. She places the baby in a laundry bin and leaves. Just then, another woman arrives. She is also tall and graceful, but her face is swathed in bandages. She plucks the baby from the bin and smothers him with kisses. 'My little brother,' she says. 'S-i-s-t-e-r,' the baby gurgles back. 'Meeeow!' A strangled cry from a cat suddenly pierces the night. I wake up and try to figure whether the cry I heard came from the dream or the adjacent room.

I discover Pluto's limp and mangled body the next morning, lying in the same dustbin in which Mr Barve disposes of his copy of the *Maharashtra Times*. The cat's neck has been broken and I can smell whisky on his furry body. Shantaram tells his wife that Pluto has run away. I know the truth, but it is pointless mentioning it. Pluto has indeed run away. To another, better world, I think.

'I like Gudiya very much,' I tell Salim. 'I have to ensure that Shantaram does not repeat what he did to her.'

'But what can you do? It is his family.'

'It is our business as well. After all, we are neighbours.'

'Don't you remember what you told me once? That it's not a good idea to poke your nose into other people's affairs, or make other people's troubles your own, Mohammad?'

I have no response to this.

Gudiya comes home, but I don't get to see her because Shantaram will not permit a boy to enter his house. Mrs Shantaram tells me that her husband has realized what he has done and will now reform, even though in her heart of hearts she knows that Shantaram is beyond redemption. But even she did not know the depths to which her husband could descend.

Barely a week after Gudiya returns from the hospital, he does something to her again. He tries to touch her. But not like a father. At first, I don't understand. All I hear is some references to Gudiya being his moon and then Mrs Shantaram crying, and Gudiya screaming, 'Papa, don't touch me! Papa, please don't touch me!'

Something snaps in my brain when I hear Gudiya's plaintive cry. I want to rush into Shantaram's room and kill him with my bare hands. But even before I can gather my courage, I hear Shantaram's loud snores. He has crashed out. Gudiya is still weeping. I don't need a glass to hear her sobbing.

Her crying affects me in a strange way. I don't know how a brother should react on listening to his sister's sorrow, because I have no experience of being a brother. But I know that somehow I have to comfort her. Unfortunately, it is not very easy to comfort someone when there is a wall, howsoever thin, between you. I notice then that right at the bottom of the wall, where the water pipes go into the other flat, there is a small circular opening, large enough to thrust an arm through. I jump down from the bed and, lying spread-eagled on the ground, push my hand through the opening. 'Sister, don't weep. Here, hold my hand,' I cry. And someone does grasp my hand. I feel fingers caress my arm, my elbow, my wrist, like a blind man feeling someone's face. Then fingers interlock with mine and I feel a magical transference of power, energy, love, call it what you will; the fact is that in that instant I become one with Gudiya and I feel her pain as if it is my own.

Salim, meanwhile, is still sitting on his bed, watching the scene in amazement. 'Are you mad, Mohammad? Do you realize what you are doing?' he admonishes me. 'This hole through which you have pushed your hand is the same hole through which rats and cockroaches come into our room.'

But I am oblivious to Salim and to everything else. I don't know how long I hold Gudiya's hand, but when I wake up the next morning I find myself lying on the ground with my hand still thrust through the hole and a family of cockroaches sleeping peacefully inside my shirt pocket.

The next night, Shantaram again comes home in a drunken stupor and tries to molest Gudiya. 'You are more beautiful than all the stars and planets. You are my moon. You are my Gudiya, my doll. Yesterday you evaded me, but today I will not let you leave me,' he says.

'Stop behaving like this!' Mrs Shantaram cries, but her husband takes no notice.

'Don't worry, Gudiya, there is nothing wrong in my love for you. Even Shahjahan, the great emperor, fell in love with his own daughter, Jahan Ara. And who can deny a man the privilege of gathering fruit from a tree he himself has planted.'

'You are a demon,' Mrs Shantaram yells, and Shantaram hits her. I hear a bottle break.

'No!' I hear Gudiya scream.

I feel as though an oxyacetylene torch has pierced my brain and molten metal has been poured over my heart. I can tolerate it no more. I run to Mr Ramakrishna's room and tell him that Shantaram is doing something terrible to his own wife and daughter. But Ramakrishna behaves as if I am talking about the weather.

'Look,' he tells me. 'Whatever happens inside the four walls of a home is a private matter for that family and we cannot interfere. You are a young orphan boy. You have not seen life. But I know the daily stories of wife-beating and abuse and incest and rape, which take place in chawls all over Mumbai. Yet no one does anything. We Indians have this sublime ability to see the pain and misery around us, and yet remain unaffected by it. So, like a proper Mumbaikar, close your eyes, close your ears, close your mouth and you will be happy like me. Now go, it is time for my sleep.'

I rush back to my room. I hear Shantaram snoring and Gudiya screaming that she is dirty. 'Don't touch me! Nobody touch me! I will infect whoever comes near me.'

I think she is losing her mind. And I am losing mine.

'Infect me,' I say, and thrust my hand through the hole in the wall.

Gudiya catches it. 'I will not live much longer, Ram Mohammad Thomas,' she sobs. 'I will commit suicide rather than submit to my father.' Her pain floats through the hole and envelops me in its embrace.

I begin crying. 'I will never allow this to happen,' I tell her. 'This is a brother's promise.'

Salim gives me a dirty look, as if I have committed a criminal act by making this promise. But I am beyond right and wrong. I feel Gudiya's bony fingers, the flesh on her hands, and know that we are both hunted animals, partners in crime. My crime was that I, an orphan boy, had dared to make other people's troubles my own. But what was Gudiya's crime? Simply that she was born a girl and Shantaram was her father.

I carry out my promise the next evening, when Shantaram returns from work and climbs the rickety stairs to the first floor. He walks with slow, bumbling steps. Even his clothes reek of whisky. As he is about to pass that section of the railing which has not yet been fixed by Mr Ramakrishna, I charge at him from behind. I slam into his back and he slams into the wooden railing. The railing is already weak and wobbly. It cannot take his weight. It cracks and splinters. Shantaram loses his balance and topples to the ground below.

In films, they show a villain falling from the roof of a skyscraper and it seems as if he is floating in the air; he twists his legs and flaps his arms and screams, 'Aaaaaaaaaaaah!' In real life, it doesn't happen like that at all. Shantaram drops down like a rock. There is no flapping of hands or legs. He hits the ground face-down and lies spread-eagled, hands and legs outstretched.

Only when I see Shantaram's limp body on the ground do I realize what I have done. And then I visualize the consequences of my act.

The crime-scene officers arrive in a jeep with a flashing red light and make a nice neat outline in chalk. They take photos and say, 'This is where the body fell.' Then they look up and see me on the first floor. The inspector points at me. 'That is the boy who pushed him down. Arrest him!' I am taken to jail, where I am stripped and beaten. Then I am presented in court, where a stern-faced judge sits in a black robe with a ceiling fan above him. A faded and dusty golden sign with the words *Satyameva Jayate* – Truth Always Prevails – is fixed on the wall behind him. The judge takes one look at me and pronounces his verdict. 'Ram Mohammad Thomas, I find you guilty of the pre-meditated murder of Mr Shantaram. Under Section

302 of the Indian Penal Code, I hereby sentence you to death by hanging.'

'No!' I cry and try to run, but my legs are shackled and my wrists are handcuffed. I am blindfolded and led to the execution cell. A noose is placed around my neck, a lever is pulled. I shriek in pain as my legs suddenly dangle in the air and the breath is choked from my lungs. I open my eyes and find that I am in heaven. But heaven seems just like the chawl and I look down and see the body of Shantaram lying spread-eagled on the ground. People are gathering around it now. Someone shouts, 'Call the police!'

I don't wait another moment. I scramble down the stairs and start running. I run past the gate and the milk booth and the multi-storey building. I run to the local station and take the Express to Victoria Terminus. I search every platform for a particular train. I find it at last and jump inside just as it is pulling away.

I left Mumbai, I left Gudiya, I left Salim, and ran away to the only other city I knew. Delhi.

Throughout this story, Smita remains perfectly silent. I can see now that she has been deeply affected. I detect a hint of a teardrop in the corner of her eye. Perhaps, being a woman, she can relate to Gudiya's torment.

I pick up the remote. 'Let us see question number three,' I say, and press 'Play'.

Prem Kumar swivels on his chair and addresses me. 'Mr Thomas, you have answered two questions correctly to win two thousand rupees. Now let us see whether you can answer the third question for five thousand rupees. Are you ready?'

'Ready,' I reply.

'OK. Question number three. This is from the field of—'

Just then the central spotlight goes off, plunging Prem Kumar and me into darkness.

'Oops! Houston, we have a problem,' says Prem Kumar. The audience laughs. I don't get the joke.

'What did you just say?' I ask Prem Kumar.

'Oh, that is a famous line from the film *Apollo Thirteen*. I am sure you don't see English films. You use this line when you suddenly have a major problem, and we do have a major problem here. The show cannot proceed till we fix the spotlight.'

As the technicians start checking out the wiring of the spotlight, Prem Kumar listens to a voice on his headset. Then he leans forward and whispers in my ear, 'OK, buster, your golden run has lasted all of two questions and is now about to end. The next question is really tough, especially for a waiter. I would love to help you win more, but the producer has just informed me he wants to move on to the next contestant, a maths professor. Sorry, tough luck!' He takes a sip of lemonade and smacks his lips.

The spotlight is now fixed. The studio sign changes to 'Applause'.

As the clapping dies down, Prem Kumar looks at me. 'Mr Thomas, you have answered two questions correctly to win two thousand rupees. Now let us see whether you can answer the third question for five thousand rupees. Are you ready?'

'Ready,' I reply.

'OK. Our next question is from the world of astronomy. Tell me, Mr Thomas, do you know how many planets there are in our solar system?'

'What are my choices?'

'That is not the question, Mr Thomas. I am just asking whether you know the number of planets in the solar system.'

'No.'

'No? I hope you know the name of the planet we are living on.'

The audience laughs.

'Earth,' I reply sullenly.

'Good. So you do know the name of a planet. OK, are you ready for question number three?'

'Ready,' I reply.

'OK. Here is question number three. Which is the smallest planet in our solar system? Is it a) Pluto, b) Mars, c) Neptune or d) Mercury?'

A sound escapes my lips even before the music can commence, and it is 'Meow!'

'Excuse me?' says Prem Kumar in astonishment. 'What did you say? For a moment I thought I heard a meow.'

'What I said was "A".'

'A?'

'Yes. The answer is A. Pluto.'

'Are you absolutely, one hundred per cent sure that it is A?'

'Yes.'

There is a crescendo of drums. The correct answer flashes.

'Absolutely, one hundred per cent correct! Pluto is indeed the smallest planet in our solar system. Mr Thomas, you have just won five thousand rupees!'

The audience are impressed with my general knowledge. Some people stand up and clap.

But Smita is still silent.

10,000

A THOUGHT FOR THE CRIPPLED

The sun seems weaker, the birds less chirpy, the air more polluted, the sky a shade darker.

When you have been plucked from a beautiful big bungalow, with a lovely sunlit garden, and dumped in a crumbling house where you are forced to live in a crowded dormitory with dozens of other kids, I suppose you do acquire a somewhat jaundiced view of life.

And it doesn't help if you actually have jaundice. Jaundice is a pretty uncomfortable disease, but it has one very good outcome. You are removed from the stuffy dormitory and put in a room all by yourself. It is a huge room with a metal bed and green curtains. It is called the isolation ward.

I have been confined to bed for the last two weeks. But it seems as if I have been sick ever since they

90

picked me up from the church after Father Timothy's death. They didn't come for me in a jeep with a flashing red light. They came in a blue van with wire-meshed windows. Like the type they use to round up stray dogs. Except this one was for rounding up stray boys. If I had been younger they would probably have sent me to an adoption home and promptly put me up for sale. But since I was eight years old, I was sent to the Delhi Juvenile Home for Boys, in Turkman Gate.

The Juvenile Home has a capacity of seventy-five, and a juvenile population of one hundred and fifty. It is cramped, noisy and dirty. It has just two toilets with leaky washbasins and filthy latrines. Rats scurry through its hallways and kitchen. It has a classroom with ramshackle desks and a cracked blackboard. And teachers who haven't taught in years. It has a sports ground where grass grows as tall as wickets and where, if you are not careful, you can graze yourself against stones the size of footballs. There is a sports instructor in crisp white cotton bush shirt and knife-edge pressed trousers. He keeps cricket and badminton equipment in a nice glass case, but never allows us to touch it. The mess hall is a large room with cheap flooring and long wooden tables. But the surly head cook sells the meat and chicken that is meant for us to restaurants, and feeds us a daily diet of vegetable stew and thick, blackened chapattis. He picks his nose constantly and scolds anyone who asks for more. The warden, Mr Agnihotri, is a kind, elderly man who wears starched *kurta* pyjamas made of *khadi* cotton cloth, but we all know that the real power is wielded by his deputy, Mr Gupta, nicknamed the Terror of Turkman Gate. He is the worst of the lot, a short, hairy man who smells of leather and chews *paan* all day. He wears two thick gold chains around his neck which jangle when he walks, and carries a short bamboo cane with which he whacks us whenever he feels like it. There are dark rumours that he calls boys to his room late at night, but nobody will discuss it. We want to talk about the good things. Like being allowed to watch television in the common room for two hours every evening. We huddle around the twenty-one-inch Dyanora TV and watch Hindi film songs on Channel V and middle-class soaps on Doordarshan. We especially like watching the films on Sunday.

These films are about a fantasy world. A world in which kids have mothers and fathers, and birthdays. A world in which they live in huge houses, drive in huge cars and get huge presents. We saw this fantasy world, but we never got carried away by it. We knew we could never have a life like Amitabh Bachchan's or Shahrukh Khan's. The most we could aspire to was to become one of those who held power over us. So whenever the teacher asked us, 'What do you want to become when you grow up?' no one said pilot or prime minister or banker or actor. We said cook or cleaner or sports teacher or, at the very best, warden. The Juvenile Home diminished us in our own eyes.

I came to know many boys in the Home very intimately. Some younger, mostly older. I met Munna and Kallu and Pyare and Pawan and Jashim and Irfan. Being sent to the Juvenile Home from Father Timothy's house was like a transfer from heaven to hell for me. But only when I met the other boys did I realize that for many of them this was their heaven. They came from the slums of Delhi and Bihar, from the shanty-towns of UP and even from as far away as Nepal. I heard their stories of drug-addicted fathers and prostitute mothers. I saw their scars from beatings at the hands of greedy uncles and tyrannical aunts. I learnt of the existence of bonded labour and family abuse. And I came to fear the police. They were the ones responsible for sending most of the boys to the Juvenile Home. Boys caught stealing bread from a roadside stall or hawking black-market tickets at a theatre, and unable to bribe the constable. Or, most often, framed simply because the inspector didn't like their faces.

Many of these boys were 'repeaters', which meant that they had been returned to the Juvenile Home even after someone had taken custody of them from the Juvenile Welfare Board. Munna returned after being ill-treated by his stepmother. Jashim was hounded out by his cruel brother. Pawan returned because the relative he was restored to put him to work in a seedy motel and the police caught him. Despite such experiences, many boys still pined to be 'restored', ready to exchange a known hell for an unknown one.

Without even trying, I became their leader. Not because I was bigger, not because I was more aggressive, but because I spoke English. I was the orphan boy who could speak and read the magic language, and its effect on the officials was electric. The head warden would ask how I was doing from time to time. The sports teacher allowed me to set up a makeshift cricket pitch in the front courtyard, where we got in four or five decent games before Munna broke the warden's window and all sports were banned. The stern cook occasionally obliged me with a second helping. Gupta never called me to his room at night. And the doctor instantly put me in the isolation ward without the usual delay, thereby preventing me from infecting the whole dormitory.

I had been enjoying my exclusive stay in the isolation ward for over two weeks when another bed was moved into the room. A new boy had arrived, I was told, in a very bad condition. He was brought in on a stretcher in the afternoon, wearing a torn orange vest, stained and scuffed shorts, and a yellow *tabeez* around his neck. And that was my first meeting with Salim Ilyasi.

Salim is everything that I am not. He has a wheatish complexion and a cherubic face. He has curly black hair and when he smiles his cheeks dimple. Though he is only seven years old, he has a keen, questioning mind. He tells me his story in short, halting sentences.

He comes from a very poor family, which used to live in a village in Bihar. The village was mostly made up of poor peasants, but there were also a few rich landowners. It was predominantly Hindu, but there were a couple of Muslim families too, like Salim's. His father was a labourer, his mother a housewife, his elder brother worked in a tea stall. Salim himself attended the village school. They lived in a small thatched hut at the edge of the *zamindar*'s compound.

Last week, in the cold and frosty month of January, an incident took place in the village's Hanuman temple. Someone broke into the sanctum sanctorum at night and desecrated the idol of the monkey god. The temple's priest claimed he saw some Muslim youths lurking near the grounds. *Bas*, that was it! The moment the Hindus heard this they went on a rampage. Armed with machetes and pickaxes, sticks and torches, they raided the homes of all the Muslim families. Salim was playing outside the hut and his father, mother and brother were having tea inside when the mob attacked. Before his very eyes, they set fire to the hut. He heard his mother's shrieks, his father's cries, his brother's wails, but the mob would not allow anyone to escape. His whole family was burnt to death in the inferno. Salim ran to the railway station and jumped on to the first train he saw. It took him to Delhi with no food, no clothes and not one familiar face. He lay on the platform for two days, cold and hungry, delirious with fever and grief, before a constable discovered him and sent him to the Juvenile Home.

Salim says he has bad dreams at night. He hears the sounds of the mob. His mother's shrieks echo in his ears. He shudders when he visualizes his brother writhing in the flames. He says he has begun to hate and fear all Hindus. He asks my name.

'Mohammad,' I tell him.

Over time, Salim and I become very good friends. We have many things in common. We are both orphans, with no hope of being 'restored'. We both love playing marbles. And we both love watching films. I use my influence to get him a bed next to mine when we move back to the dormitory.

Late one night, Salim is summoned to Gupta's room. Gupta is a widower and lives alone on the compound. Salim is worried. 'Why is he calling me?' he asks me.

'I don't know,' I reply. 'I've never been to his room. But we can find out today.'

So Salim walks down to Gupta's room and I tiptoe behind him.

Gupta is sitting in his room wearing crumpled *kurta* pyjamas when Salim knocks on the door. 'Come . . . come, Salim,' he says in a slurred voice. He has a glassful of golden liquid in his hand. He gulps it down and wipes his mouth. His eyes look like big buttons. I watch from the little space between the two curtains in the doorway. He strokes Salim's face, tracing his fingers over his bony nose and thin lips. Then abruptly he orders, 'Take off your shorts.'

Salim is confused by this request.

'Just do as I say, bastard, or I will give you a tight slap,' Gupta snarls.

Salim complies. He pushes down his shorts hesitatingly. I avert my eyes.

Gupta approaches Salim from behind, his gold chains jangling. 'Good,' he mutters. I see him unfasten the cord of his pyjamas and lower them. I can see his hairy backside. Salim has still not understood what is happening, but a fog is lifting from my brain. With startling clarity I suddenly comprehend what had happened in Father John's room that night. And what had followed the next day.

I let out a piercing scream that shatters the silence of the night like a bullet. It wakes up the boys sleeping peacefully in the dormitories; it wakes up the cook, snoring in the kitchen; it wakes up the warden in his bedroom; it even wakes up the stray dogs, which begin to bark madly.

Gupta doesn't know what has hit him. He hastily pulls up his pyjamas and tries to shoo Salim away. But the cook, the warden and the guards are already on their way to Gupta's room. They discover his dirty secret that night (though they do nothing about it). But Gupta also discovers me lurking behind the curtains. From then on he becomes my mortal enemy. Salim is shaken, but unhurt. He had given up his animus against Hindus a long time ago. But a fear of abuse is embedded in him for the rest of his life.

It is a beautiful spring day. And it appears even more beautiful because we are outside the confines of the Juvenile Home. We have all been taken on a day trip by an international NGO. We travel by air-conditioned bus all over Delhi. We have lunch in the zoo and see the animals. For the first time we see a hippopotamus and kangaroos and giraffes and the giant sloth. We see pelicans and flamingos and the duck-billed platypus. Then we are taken to the Qutub Minar, the highest tower in India. Laughing and jostling, we climb the stairs and peer out from the first-floor balcony. The men and women on the ground seem like ants. We shout 'Hooooo' and listen for the sound to peter out before it reaches the ground. Finally, we are taken to India Gate to see a big carnival. We are each given ten rupees to spend on any attraction we choose. I want to ride on the giant wheel, but Salim tugs at my sleeve and pulls me to another booth. 'Pandit Ramashankar

Shastri,' it says. 'World-famous Palmist. Only Rs.10 per reading.' An old man is sitting inside the booth, wearing a *dhoti kurta*. He has a white moustache, a vermilion *tilak* on his forehead, and thick lenses. A black *choti* juts out from the back of his head.

'I want to show my hand,' Salim says. 'It is only ten rupees.'

'Don't be foolish,' I tell him. 'These chaps are conmen. They cannot know your future. And, in any case, there's not much in our future worth knowing.'

'I want to show my hand just the same.' Salim is adamant.

'Fine.' I give in. 'You go ahead, but I'm not spending my ten rupees on this crap.'

Salim pays the money and eagerly extends his left hand. The pandit shakes his head. 'No, not the left hand. That is for girls. Boys have to show their right hand.'

Salim quickly extends his right palm. The palmist peers at it with a magnifying glass, and analyses the scrabbly lines as if they were a map of buried treasure. Finally he puts down the magnifying glass and lets out a satisfied sigh. 'You have a remarkable hand, my boy. I have never seen a better fate line. I see a very bright future for you.'

'Really?' Salim is delighted. 'What will I become?'

Mr Shastri has obviously not thought about that. He closes his eyes for ten seconds, then opens them. 'You have a beautiful face. You will be a very famous actor,' he declares.

'Like Armaan Ali?' squeals Salim.

'Even more famous,' says the pandit. He turns to me.

'Do you also want to show your hand? It is only ten rupees.'

'No, thank you,' I say and begin to move away, but Salim bars my way.

'No, Mohammad, you have to show your hand. For my sake, please.'

With a resigned look, I fork out my ten rupees and extend my right hand.

The pandit scowls at me as he adjusts his thick glasses and examines my palm. He pores over it for more than five minutes. He makes some notes, does some calculations.

'What's the matter?' Salim asks, alarmed.

The palmist frowns slightly and shakes his head. 'The line of head is strong, but the line of heart is weak. And, most importantly, the line of life is short. The stars do not seem to be right. The alignment of the planets is inauspicious. The Mount of Jupiter is good, but the Mount of Saturn cancels it out. There are obstacles and pitfalls. I can do something to ease your way, but it will cost you.'

'How much?'

'Around two hundred rupees. Why don't you ask your father? Isn't he the one who owns the big bus?'

I laugh. 'Ha! Panditji, before spinning this yarn about my future, you should have checked out who we really are. We are not rich kids. We are orphans from the Delhi Juvenile Home in Turkman Gate and this bus doesn't even belong to us. Still, you conned us into parting with twenty rupees.' I pull Salim. 'Come, let's go. We have wasted enough time here.'

As we are walking away, the palmist calls me. 'Listen! I want to give you something.'

I return to the booth. The pandit gives me an old one-rupee coin.

'What's this, Panditji?'

'It's a lucky coin. Keep it. You will need it.'

I hold it in my fist.

Salim wants an ice cream, but we have just one rupee and that won't buy us anything. We watch the other kids enjoying their rides. I flip the coin aimlessly and it slips out of my fingers and rolls underneath a bench. I bend down to pick it up. It has come up heads. Next to it lies a ten-rupee note, dropped by someone. Like Magic. Salim and I buy ice creams. I slip the coin carefully into my pocket. It is indeed my lucky charm.

Salim is sad that my future has not turned out to be as bright as his, but he is also excited about becoming a film star. In front of us is a huge billboard of a new film. In lurid colours, it shows the hero with a gun in his hands, blood on his chest and a black bandanna around his head; a villain wearing a twisted grin; a heroine with big breasts. Salim stares at it, transfixed.

'What are you looking at, Salim?' I ask.

'I am trying to see if the black headband will suit me,' he replies.

We are sitting in class, but Mr Joshi, our portly teacher who specializes in burping and picking his nose, is not teaching. He is reading a novel, which is carefully hidden inside the textbook he holds in his hands. We pass the time making paper aeroplanes, etching patterns on the wooden desks and dozing. Suddenly Munna, who has been instructed to monitor the corridor, comes running in. 'Masterji, Masterji,' he says breathlessly, 'Warden Sahib is coming.'

Mr Joshi lets out a loud burp and quickly jettisons his novel. He snaps his fingers and stands up. 'OK boys, so what were we discussing? Yes. You were all telling me what you want to become when you grow up. Who wants to go next?'

Salim puts up his hand. The first time he has ever done this.

'Yes, Salim, what do you want to become?'

'I will become a famous actor, Masterji. An astrologer has told me,' he says triumphantly.

The class squeals with laughter.

There are two versions of who the big man is. Some say that he is a very rich diamond merchant with no offspring of his own. So from time to time he comes to the Juvenile Home to adopt children, who are then taken to his palatial home in Mumbai. Others say that he actually owns a school in Mumbai, where he takes children he finds promising for proper training. Either way, one thing is clear. If you are selected by Sethji, your life is made.

Salim doesn't care whether Sethji is a diamond merchant or a school owner. He is mainly concerned with the fact that the big man is from Mumbai – the centre of the film industry. He is convinced that Sethji has come to pluck him from here and take him to the glittering world of Bollywood. It is his destiny. The palmist's prediction is going to come true.

We are all lined up in the mess hall for an inspection by Sethji. Salim has taken a bath. Actually, he has taken three baths, scrubbing himself again and again to remove every trace of dirt. He has put on his best clothes. His hair is nicely combed. He is the most presentable boy in the Home. But I fret at his desperation. If he is not selected, he will be shattered.

Sethji finally arrives, accompanied by two other men. He doesn't look like a diamond merchant. He looks more like a gangster. But then, we've never seen a diamond merchant. Perhaps they look like gangsters. He is very swarthy and has a thick black moustache, like the dacoit Veerappan's. He wears a white *bandgala* suit. A long, thick gold chain dangles down from his neck to his second button. His fingers are loaded with rings with different coloured gems. Some red, some green, some blue. The two henchmen with him look exactly like henchmen. I learn later that they are called Mustafa and Punnoose. Gupta is also with them, leading the way. His two gold chains look modest in comparison with Sethji's.

'Sethji, you seem to have forgotten us, coming after such a long time. Many new boys have arrived since your last visit. I am sure you will find many to your liking,' Gupta tells him.

The inspection begins. All of us put on our best smiles. Sethji goes over each boy, appraising him from head to toe. I don't know what he is looking for, because he does not ask us any questions, just looks at our faces. He completes one round of inspection. He does not even glance at me twice. Then he goes over the line once again. When he comes to Salim, he stops.

'What is your name?' he asks in a heavy South Indian accent.

'S . . . Salim Ilyasi,' Salim stammers in his excitement.

'When did he arrive?' he asks Gupta.

'About eleven months ago, from Chhapra in Bihar.'

'How old is he?'

'Eight.'

'Does he have anyone?'

'No, Sethji. His whole family died in a communal disturbance.'

'How sad,' says Sethji. 'But he is just the kind of boy I need. Can you sort out the paperwork?'

'You just have to tell me, Sethji. Whoever you want will be restored to you in no time. For this boy, we'll show Mustafa as the uncle. The Welfare Board will not create any problems. In fact, they want to get rid of as many kids as possible.'

'Fine. For this visit, let's settle on just this one kid.'

Gupta looks at Salim, and then he looks at me, standing next to Salim. 'What about him?' He points at me.

Sethji looks me in the eye, and shakes his head. 'He is too old.'

'No, Sethji, he is only ten. Name is Thomas, speaks perfect English.'

'Makes no difference to me. I don't need him. I want the other one.'

'They are thick as thieves, these two. If you take Salim, you have to take Thomas as well.'

Sethji gets annoyed. 'I've told you, Gupta, that I don't want any Thomas Womas. I am only taking one boy and that is Salim.'

'I am sorry, Sethji, but I insist. If you take Salim, you will have to take Thomas. It is a package deal.'

'Package deal?'

'Yes. Buy one, get one free. I won't charge you for Thomas.' Gupta grins, displaying his *paan*-stained teeth.

Sethji goes into a huddle with his henchmen.

'OK,' he tells Gupta. 'Prepare the papers for these two. I'll collect them on Monday.'

Salim rushes into my arms. He is on top of the world. That night, he doesn't sleep from sheer excitement. He has celluloid dreams of life in Mumbai. Of golden sunsets on Marine Drive with Amitabh and rose-coloured dawns on Chowpatty with Shahrukh. I don't sleep that night either. I toss and turn in my bed. But I don't dream of stardom and paradise. I dream that I am a hawker on the pavement, selling fruits. A dark swarthy man bends down to buy some mangoes from me. I see his gold chain dangling. He tosses me some change. I put a nice juicy mango in his bag, and then quietly slip in a rotten banana. For free.

The train journey to Mumbai is uneventful. Salim and I travel in the second-class sleeper compartment with the henchmen Mustafa and Punnoose. Sethji, we are told, has gone ahead by plane. Mustafa and Punnoose wear *lungis*, smoke *beedis* and sleep most of the time. They tell us very little about Sethji. They say his real name is Babu Pillai, but everybody calls him Maman, meaning 'Uncle' in the Malayalam language. He is originally from Kollam in Kerala, but has been settled in Mumbai for a long time. He is a very kind man, who runs a school for disabled kids, helping them rebuild their lives. Maman believes that disabled children are closer to God. He rescues children from juvenile homes, which he believes are nothing but jails under another name. If Maman had not saved us, we would have ended up cleaning car windscreens at traffic lights or sweeping floors in private houses. Now we would be taught useful skills and groomed for success. Mustafa and Punnoose are excellent salesmen. By the end of the trip, even I am convinced that being picked by Maman is the best thing that has ever happened to me and that my life will now be transformed.

From time to time, the train passes through slum colonies, lining the edges of the railway tracks like a ribbon of dirt. We see half-naked children with distended bellies waving at us, while their mothers wash utensils in sewer water. We wave back.

The sights and sounds of Mumbai overwhelm us. Churchgate station looks exactly as it did in *Love in Bombay*. Salim half expects to bump into Govinda singing a song near the church. Mustafa points out the beach at Marine Drive. I am fascinated by my first sight of the ocean, where giant waves crash and roll against the rocks. Salim doesn't see the majestic ocean. He looks at the stalls selling soft drinks and snacks. 'That is where Govinda and Raveena had *bhel puri*,' he points out excitedly. We pass through Haji Ali's *dargah*. Salim raises his hands to Allah when he sees the shrine, exactly like he saw Amitabh Bachchan do in the film *Coolie*. We pass through the districts of Worli, Dadar and Mahim, Mustafa and Punnoose pointing out major landmarks to us. At Mahim Fort, Salim gestures the taxi driver to stop.

'What's the matter?' Mustafa asks.

'Nothing. I just wanted to see the place where the smugglers offload their consignment in the film *Mafia*!'

As we approach Bandra, Juhu and Andheri, dotted with the sparkling residences of film stars, with their high boundary walls and platoons of uniformed guards, Salim becomes maudlin. Through the taxi's tinted windows, we gape at the sprawling bungalows and high-rise apartment blocks like villagers on a first trip to the city. It is as if we are seeing Mumbai through a chromatic lens. The sun seems brighter, the air feels cooler, the people appear more prosperous, the city throbs with the happiness of sharing space with the megastars of Bollywood.

We reach our destination in Goregaon. Maman's house is not the palatial bungalow we had come to expect. It is a large decrepit building set in a courtyard with a small garden and two palm trees. It is ringed by a high boundary wall topped with barbed wire. Two dark, well-built men sit in the porch smoking *beedis* and wearing thin, coloured *lungis*. They are holding thick bamboo sticks in their hands. They cross their legs and we catch a glimpse of their striped underwear. A strong smell of arrack radiates from them. Punnoose speaks to them in quick-fire Malayalam. The only word I can catch is 'Maman'. They are obviously guards employed by Mr Babu Pillai.

As we enter the house, Mustafa points out a set of

corrugated-iron structures beyond the courtyard, like huge sheds. 'That is the school Maman runs for crippled children. The children live there as well.'

'How come I don't see any children?' I ask.

'They have all gone out for vocational training. Don't worry, you will meet them in the evening. Come, let me show you to your room.'

Our room is small and compact, with two bunk beds and a long mirror built into the wall. Salim takes the top bed. There is a bathroom in the basement which we can use. It has a tub and a shower curtain. It is not as luxurious as the houses of film stars, but it will do. It looks as though we are the only children living in the house.

Maman comes to meet us in the evening. Salim tells him how excited he is to be in Mumbai and how he wants to become a famous film star. Maman smiles when he hears this. 'The first and foremost requirement for becoming a film star is the ability to sing and dance. Can you sing?' he asks Salim.

'No,' says Salim.

'Well, don't worry. I will arrange for a top music teacher to give you lessons. In no time at all you will be like Kishore Kumar.'

Salim looks as if he might hug Maman, but restrains himself.

At night we go to the school for dinner. It has a mess hall similar to the one in our Juvenile Home, with cheap linoleum flooring, long wooden tables, and a head cook who is a carbon copy of ours back at the Home. Salim and I are told to sit at a small round table with Mustafa. We are served before the other kids come in. The food is hot and tasty, a definite improvement on the insipid fare we got in Delhi.

One by one the children start trickling in, and instantly challenge our definition of hell. I see boys with no eyes, feeling their way forward with the help of sticks; boys with bent and misshapen limbs, dragging themselves to the table; boys with two gnarled stumps for legs, walking on crutches; boys with grotesque mouths and twisted fingers, eating bread held between their elbows. Some of them are like clowns. Except they make us cry instead of laugh. It is good Salim and I have almost finished our meal.

We see three boys standing in one corner, watching the others eat, but not being served themselves. One of them licks his lips. 'Who are these boys?' I ask Mustafa. 'And why aren't they eating?'

'They are being punished,' Mustafa says. 'For not doing enough work. Don't worry, they'll eat later.'

The music teacher comes the next day. He is a youngish man, with an oval, clean-shaven face, large ears and thin, bony fingers. He carries a harmonium with him. 'Call me Masterji,' he instructs us. 'Now listen to what I sing.' We sit on the floor in rapt attention as he sings, '*Sa re ga ma pa dha ni sa.*' Then he explains, 'These are the seven basic notes which are present in each and every composition. Now open your mouth and sing these notes loudly. Let the sound come not from your lips, not from your nose, but from the base of your throat.'

Salim clears his throat and begins. '*Sa re ga ma pa dha ni sa.*' He sings full-throated, with abandon. The room resonates with the sound of his clear notes. His voice floats over the room, the notes ringing pure and unsullied.

'Very good.' The teacher claps. 'You have a natural, God-given voice. I have no doubt that with constant practice, you will very soon be able to negotiate the entire range of three and a half octaves.' Then he looks at me. 'OK. Now why don't you sing the same notes.'

'*Sa re ga ma pa dha . . .*' I try to sing, but my voice cracks and the notes shatter and fragment like a fistful of marbles dropped on the floor.

The teacher inserts a finger in his ear. '*Hare Ram . . . Hare Ram . . .* You sing like a buffalo. I will have to work really hard on you.'

Salim comes to my rescue. 'No, Masterji, Mohammad has a good voice too. He screams really well.'

Over the next two weeks, Masterji teaches us several devotional songs by famous saints and how to play the harmonium. We learn the *dohas* of Kabir and the *bhajans* of Tulsidas and Mirabai. Masterji is a good teacher. Not only does he teach us the songs, he also explains the complex spiritual truths portrayed through these songs in the simple language of common people. I particularly like Kabir, who says in one of his verses:

> *Maala pherat jug bhaya,*
> *mita na man ka pher,*
> *kar ka manka chhod de,*
> *man ka manka pher.*

> You have been counting rosary beads for an era,
> But the wandering of your mind does not halt,
> Forsake the beads in your hand,
> And start moving the beads of your heart.

The fact that Salim is Muslim is of little consequence to Masterji as he teaches him Hindu *bhajans*. Salim himself is hardly bothered. If Amitabh Bachchan can play the role of a Muslim coolie and if Salman Khan can act as a Hindu emperor, Salim Ilyasi can sing *Thumaki Chalat Ram Chandra Baajat Painjaniya* with as much gusto as a temple priest.

During this period, Salim and I come to know some of the other boys in the cripple school, despite subtle attempts by Mustafa and Punnoose to prevent us from mixing too much with those they mispronounce as 'handclapped' kids. We learn the sad histories of these boys and discover that when it comes to cruel relatives and policemen, Mumbai is no different from Delhi. But as we learn more and more about these kids, the truth about Maman also starts to unravel.

We befriend Ashok, a thirteen-year-old with a deformed arm, and receive our first shock.

'We are not schoolchildren,' he tells us. 'We are beggars. We beg in local trains. Some of us are pickpockets as well.'

'And what happens to the money you earn?'

'We are required to give it to Maman's men, in return for food and shelter.'

'You mean Maman is a gangster?'

'What did you think? He is no angel, but at least he gives us two square meals a day.'

My belief in Maman is shattered, but Salim continues to lay faith in the innate goodness of man.

We have an encounter with Raju, a blind ten-year-old.

'How come you were punished today?'

'I didn't earn enough.'

'How much are you required to give each day?'

'All that we earn. But if you give less than one hundred rupees, you are punished.'

'And what happens then?'

'You don't get food. You sleep hungry. Rats eat your belly.'

'Here, take this chapatti. We saved it for you.'

We speak to Radhey, an eleven-year-old with a leg missing.

'How come you never get punished? You always make enough money.'

'Shhh . . . It's a secret.'

'Don't worry. It's safe with us.'

'OK. But don't let any of the other boys know. You see, there is this actress living in Juhu Vile Parle. Whenever I am a little short, I go to her. She not only gives me food, she also gives me money to cover the shortfall.'

'What is her name?'

'Neelima Kumari. They say she was quite famous at one time.'

'What does she look like?'

'She must have been very beautiful in her youth, but

111

Q & A

now she is getting old. She told me she is in need of domestic help. If I didn't have a leg missing, I would have run away from here and taken up a servant's job in her house.'

I dream that night of going to a house in Juhu Vile Parle. I ring the bell and wait. A tall woman opens the door. She wears a white sari. A strong wind begins howling, making her long black hair fly across her face, obscuring it. I open my mouth to say something, and then discover that she is looking down at me. I look down and discover with a shock that I have no legs.

I wake up, drenched in sweat.

We get introduced to Moolay, a thirteen-year-old with an amputated arm.

'I hate my life,' he says.

'Why don't you run away?'

'Where to? This is Mumbai, not my village. There is no space to hide your head in this vast city. You need to have connections even to sleep in a sewage pipe. And you need protection from the other gangs.'

'Other gangs?'

'Yes. Two boys ran away last month. They came back within three days. They couldn't find any work. Bhiku's gang wouldn't allow them to operate in their area. Here, at least we get food and shelter, and when we are working for Maman none of the other gangs bother us.'

'We don't want to get involved with any gangs,' I tell him and recite a *doha*. '*Kabira Khara Bazaar Mein, Mange Sabki Khair, Na Kahu Se Dosti, Na Kahu Se*

112

Bair. Kabir is in the market place, wishing the welfare of all; He wants neither friendship nor enmity with anyone at all.'

We meet Sikandar, the import from Pakistan.

A ripple of excitement goes round the mess hall. A new kid has arrived. Mustafa brings in the new inmate and we all crowd around him. Mustafa is the most excited. 'We got him this morning from Shakeel Rana's consignment,' he says and slaps his thighs in delight.

The boy is no more than twelve years old. We touch him as though he is a caged animal. But he doesn't look like an animal. He looks more like the alien we saw in a Britannia biscuits commercial on TV, with an oval, tapering head, Chinese eyes, a thick nose and thin lips. Mustafa tells Punnoose, 'He is from the Shrine of Shah Dola in Pakistani Punjab. These boys are called "Rat Children".'

'How do they get a head like that?'

'I have heard that they put iron rings on the baby's head to stop it growing. That is how you get this unique head design.'

'I think he has a lot of potential. Maman will be pleased,' says Punnoose.

'Yes,' Mustafa concurs. 'A real high-value item.'

For some reason, the rat boy reminds me of a bear I saw once with Father Timothy in Connaught Place. He had a tight collar round his neck and a black mask covering his mouth. His owner would poke him hard with a pointed stick and he would stand on both his hind legs, saluting the people gathered round him. They would throw coins at him. The owner would pick up the money and pull him away for another performance. I was struck by the eyes of the bear, which seemed so sad that I had asked Father Timothy, 'Do bears cry?'

I discover Jitu, hiding in a closet.

He holds a plastic bag in his hand with a yellowish-white substance inside. He opens the end over his nose and mouth and inhales deeply, pressing the bottom of the bag towards his face. His clothes smell of paint and solvent. There is a rash around his nose. His mouth is sweaty and sticky. After he inhales, his half-closed eyes turn glassy and his hand begins to tremble.

'Jitu! . . . Jitu!' I shake him. 'What are you doing?'

'Don't disturb me,' he says in a drowsy voice. 'I am floating on air. I am sleeping on the clouds.'

I slap him. He coughs up black phlegm.

'I am addicted to glue,' he tells me later. 'I buy it from the cobbler. Glue takes the hunger away, and the pain. I see bright colours, and occasionally my mother.'

I ask him for some glue and try it. After I inhale, I start to feel a little dizzy, the floor beneath me appears to shift and I begin to see images. I see a tall woman, clad in a white sari, holding a baby in her arms. The wind howls, making her hair fly across her face, obscuring it. But the baby reaches out his tiny hand, and with gentle fingers smooths away her tresses, prises open her face. He sees two haggard, cavernous eyes, a crooked nose, sharp pointy teeth glistening with fresh blood, and maggots crawling out of the folds of her lined and wrinkled skin which sags over her jaw. He shrieks in terror and tumbles from her lap.

I never try glue again.

Meanwhile, our musical training is coming to an end. Masterji is extremely pleased with Salim's progress. 'You have now mastered the art of singing. Only one lesson is left.'

'And what is that?'

'The *bhajans* of Surdas.'

'Who is Surdas?'

'He is the most famous of all *bhakti* singers, who composed thousands of songs in praise of Lord Krishna. One day he fell into an abandoned well. He could not get out. He remained there for six days. He went on praying and on the seventh day he heard a child's voice asking him to hold his hands so that he could pull him out. With the boy's aid, Surdas got out of the well, but the boy disappeared. The boy was none other than Lord Krishna. After that Surdas devoted his life to composing songs in praise of Krishna. With the single-stringed *ektara* in his hand, he began singing songs depicting Krishna's childhood.' Masterji begins singing, '*Akhiyan hari darshan Ki Pyasi* – My eyes are hungry for your presence, Lord Krishna.'

'Why are his eyes hungry?' I ask.

'Didn't I tell you? Surdas was completely blind.'

On the last day of our musical training, Masterji showers accolades on Salim for singing one of Surdas's *bhajans* perfectly. I am testy and distracted.

My encounters with Maman's boys have left me distraught. Though in a sense we are all children of a lesser god, Maman's boys seem to me to be a particularly disadvantaged lot.

Punnoose comes into the room to talk to Masterji. They speak in low voices, then Punnoose takes out his purse and begins counting out some money. He hands over a sheaf of notes to the music teacher, who tucks it gratefully in the front pocket of his *kurta*. They leave the room together, leaving me alone with Salim and a harmonium.

'I should never have left Delhi,' I tell Salim. 'You have at least become a good singer, but I have gained nothing from this trip.'

It is then that I notice a hundred-rupee note lying on the floor. Punnoose must have dropped it while counting the money. My first impulse is to pocket it, but Salim snatches it from my hand and insists that we must return it. So we go down the corridor to the room Maman uses as his office, where Punnoose and Mustafa hang out.

As we approach the door, we hear voices coming from inside. Maman is talking to Punnoose.

'So what did the Master say after finishing his lessons? He is getting more and more expensive.'

'He said that the older one is useless, but the young kid has a lot of potential. He says he's never trained a more talented boy before.'

'So you think he can bring in at least three hundred?'

'What is three hundred? When he sings it is magic. And his face? Who can resist his face? I would say easily a potential of four to five hundred. We have hit the jackpot, Maman.'

'And the other boy? The tall one?'

'Who cares? The bastard will have to fend for himself. Either he gets us a hundred each night or he remains hungry.'

'OK. Send them out on the trains from next week. We will do them tonight. After dinner.'

A chill runs down my spine as I hear these words. I catch Salim's hand and rush back to our room. Salim is confused about the conversation we heard, and the reference to numbers. But the jigsaw is piecing itself together in my brain.

'Salim, we have to escape from this place. Now.'

'But why?'

'Because something very bad is going to happen to us tonight, after dinner.'

'I don't understand.'

'I understand everything. Do you know why we were taught the *bhajans* of Surdas?'

'Because he was a great poet?'

'No. Because he was blind. And that is what we are going to become tonight, so that we can be made to beg on local trains. I am convinced now that all the cripple boys we have met here have been deliberately maimed by Maman and his gang.'

But such cruelty is beyond Salim's comprehension. He wants to stay.

'Why don't you run away alone?' he asks me.

'I can't go without you.'

'Why?'

'Because I am your guardian angel, and you are part of my package deal.'

Salim hugs me. I take out the one-rupee coin from my pocket. 'Look, Salim,' I tell him. 'You believe in destiny, don't you? So let this coin decide our future. Heads we leave, tails we stay, OK?'

Salim nods. I flip the coin. It is heads.

Salim is finally reconciled to escaping from Maman's den, but his mind is full of doubt. 'Where will we go? What will we do? We don't know anyone in this city.'

'I know where we will go. Remember that actress Neelima Kumari that Radhey told us about? She needs a servant. I have her address and I also know which local train goes there.'

'How about going to the police?'

'Are you out of your mind? Haven't you learnt anything since Delhi? Whatever you do, wherever you go, never go to the police. Ever.'

We are inside the bathroom in the basement, listening to the steady beat of water dripping from a leaky tap. Salim is on my shoulder with a knife in his hand, trying to work the bolts holding the wire-mesh window in place.

'Hurry,' I whisper through clenched teeth.

Upstairs, Maman's guards trample through our room, opening closets and cupboards. We hear shouts and abuses. A bottle crashes, jangling our frayed nerves even more. Salim is terrified. He is breathing quickly in short gasps. The beating of my heart intensifies till I can almost hear its pounding. Footsteps come closer.

'Only one is left,' says Salim. 'But it is jammed. I don't think I can open it.'

'Please . . . please try again!' I urge him. 'Our lives depend on it.'

Salim tackles the bolt with renewed urgency, twisting the knife into it with all his strength. Finally, it gives way. He takes out the four bolts and lifts the wire mesh. We can see the palm trees outside swaying gently in the breeze. There is just enough space for us to crawl out. Maman's men are about to come down the stairs to the basement when Salim manoeuvres himself through the window. Then he grasps my hand and helps me slither out. We clamber on to a mound of gravel and rubble, gasping and panting. The moon is full, the night is calm. We take in deep gulps of fresh air. It smells of coconuts.

We are sitting in a local train going away from Goregaon towards the centre of this vast metropolis. The train is not crowded at this time of night and there are only a few passengers in our compartment. They read newspapers, play cards, criticize the government, fart. A soft-drinks vendor enters the compartment carrying a plastic cool-box filled with multi-coloured bottles. 'Coke, Fanta, Thums Up, Limca, 7 Up,' he shouts in a high-pitched voice. The bottles are chilled, we can see tiny droplets of moisture beading their surface. Salim looks at the soft drinks and passes his tongue over his parched lips. He feels his front pocket and pats it reassuringly. The vendor looks at him hopefully. Salim shakes his head and the man moves on.

Soon another pedlar enters the compartment, a bearded old man wearing round glasses. There is a large tray hanging from his neck, filled with a plethora of rusty tins, cloudy glass bottles and small plastic packets containing an assortment of gnarled roots, dry leaves, powders and seeds. 'Yusuf Fahim, Travelling Hakim,' he announces. 'I have a treatment for every ailment. From cancer to constipation, just name your condition.' Unfortunately for him, there are no sick persons in the compartment, and he departs shortly, leaving behind a pungent smell of turmeric and ginger.

We watch the flickering lights of the city as the train rushes past housing colonies and sports stadiums. We catch fleeting glimpses of people sitting in their drawing rooms, watching TV, eating dinner, making beds. When our destination is only two stops away, we hear shuffling footsteps from the far side of the compartment.

A small, undernourished boy of about seven or eight appears. He is wearing a blue top and dusty shorts. He walks with the help of a stick and holds an *ektara* in his hands. We do not recognize him: he is not one of Maman's boys.

He stops no more than fifteen feet from us and breaks into a full-throated rendition of '*Sunire Maine Nirbal Ke Balaram* – I have heard that Krishna comes to the aid of the weak', one of Surdas's most famous poems.

We cringe as the singer's melodious voice cascades over the compartment. Images of Maman's boys come flooding back to us. Raju and Radhey and Ashok and

Moolay. Salim squeezes up to me and I shift deeper into the corner of my seat. But like a radar the singer's head tracks us. He seems to look at us accusingly through unseeing eyes. For five tortuous minutes we listen to him complete his song. Then he takes out a begging bowl and asks for alms. Only a handful of passengers are left in the compartment and nobody even bothers to hunt for change.

As the empty-handed singer is about to pass our side, Salim takes something from his front pocket. He holds it in a clenched fist and looks guiltily at me. I nod silently. With a pained expression, Salim opens his fist over the singer's outstretched hand. A crumpled, hundred-rupee note drifts into the beggar's bowl.

Smita shivers involuntarily. 'I cannot imagine there are still people in this day and age who can inflict such cruelty on innocent children.'

'It is sad, but true. If Salim and I had not escaped that night, perhaps we would still be singing songs on local trains, like that blind singer,' I reply.

'So did you finally land that job with Neelima Kumari?'

'Yes, I did.'

'And what happened to Salim?'

'Neelima Kumari arranged a room for him in a chawl in Ghatkopar.'

'But in the last story, weren't you working in a foundry and living in the chawl?'

'That was after I had left Neelima Kumari – or rather, after she had left me.'

'Meaning?'

'You will soon find out.'

Smita shakes her head, and presses 'Play' on the DVD remote.

Prem Kumar faces the camera. 'We now move on to question number four for ten thousand rupees. This one is also straightforward, but only if you know your devotional singers. Mr Thomas has told us he believes in all the religions. Let's hope he knows his *bhajans*.' He turns to me. 'Are you ready?'

'Ready,' I reply.

'OK. Question number four. Surdas, the blind poet, was a devotee of which god: a) Ram, b) Krishna, c) Shiva or d) Brahma?'

The music commences.

'B. Krishna.'

'Are you absolutely, one hundred per cent sure?'

'Yes.'

There is a crescendo of drums. The correct answer flashes.

'Absolutely, one hundred per cent correct! You have just won ten thousand rupees!' declares Prem Kumar. The audience claps. Prem Kumar grins. I don't.

50,000

HOW TO SPEAK
AUSTRALIAN

'Name, sex and age, please, Sir,' says the timid-looking census man standing in the porch wearing thick, black-rimmed glasses. He carries a sheaf of forms with him and fiddles with a blue felt pen.

Colonel Taylor has an irritated expression on his face as he begins the introductions. He is dressed in a cream-coloured linen suit. He wears suits all the time, in summer and in winter. They suit his tall frame. He has an oval face with a thick pepper-coloured moustache, thin lips and ruddy cheeks. His sandy hair is swept back. The entire Taylor family and all the servants are gathered on the front porch as if for a group photograph. 'I am Colonel Charles Taylor, male, forty-six. This is my wife Rebecca Taylor, female, forty-four.' He points out Mrs Taylor, thin, blonde and dressed in a long skirt. 'This is our son Roy, male, fifteen.' Roy is fidgeting with his mobile phone. He is tall and lanky and wears his trademark faded jeans, T-shirt and sneakers. 'This is our daughter Maggie, female, seventeen.' Maggie is not so tall, but quite good looking with a round face, blue eyes and golden hair. She wears a really short skirt.

Colonel Taylor draws himself to his full height and puts more force into his voice. 'I am the Australian Defence Attaché. We are diplomats, so I don't think you need to enumerate us in your census. The only people from this house who should go into your report are our servants. That is Bhagwati, standing near the gate. He is our driver-cum-gardener, male, fifty-two. We have a maid, Shanti, female, eighteen I think, who is not in the house at the moment. That is Ramu, our cook, male, twenty-five, and this is Thomas, male, fourteen. Will that be all?'

'No, Sir, I will need to ask your servants some questions, Sir. For the latest census they have introduced a long questionnaire. All kinds of weird things, such as which TV programmes you watch, which foods you eat, which cities you have visited, and even,' he sniggers, 'how often you have sex.'

Mrs Taylor whispers to her husband, 'Oh Charles, we don't want Ramu and Thomas wasting their time on this silly exercise. Can't you get rid of this drongo?'

Colonel Taylor pulls out a packet of cigarettes from his pocket. 'Look, Mister whatever your name is, my servants really don't have the time to go through your full questionnaire. So why don't you accept this packet of Marlboros and move on to the next house? I am sure you can afford to exclude four people from your survey.'

The census man eyes the packet, then licks his lips. 'Well . . . Sir, you are very kind. But you see, I don't smoke, Sir. However, if you have some Black Label . . . or even Red Label whisky, I would be happy to oblige, Sir. After all, what difference does it make if we take out four drops from an ocean? No one will miss four people out of a billion!' He laughs nervously.

Colonel Taylor gives the census man a dirty look. Then he stomps off into the drawing room and returns with a bottle of Johnny Walker Red Label. 'Here, take this and rack off. Don't ever bother us again.'

The census man salutes Colonel Taylor. 'Don't worry, Sir. I won't bother you for the next ten years.' He walks off happily.

Mrs Taylor is also happy. 'These bloody Indians,' she smiles. 'Give them a bottle of whisky and they'll do anything.'

Bhagwati grins from the gate. He has no clue what is happening. But he smiles whenever Sahib and Memsahib smile. Ramu is also grinning. He smiles whenever he gets to see Maggie in her short skirts.

I am the only one not smiling. Granted, we servants are invisible people, not to be heard during parties and family occasions, but to be left out even from our country's head count is a bit too galling. And I do wish the Taylors would stop their snobbish references to 'bloody Indians'. This must be the fiftieth time I have heard them use this expression since I have been with them. Every time I hear it, my blood boils. OK, so the postman and the electrician and the telephone repair man and the constable, and now even the census man, have a weakness for whisky. But it doesn't mean that all Indians are drunkards. I wish I could explain this to Mrs Taylor some day. But I know I won't. When you live in a posh locality of Delhi in a nice house, get three hot meals a day and a salary of one thousand five hundred, yes, one thousand five hundred rupees a month, you learn to swallow your pride. And smile whenever Sahib and Memsahib smile.

To be fair to the Taylors, though, they have been very kind to me. Not many people would employ you if you turned up on their doorstep suddenly one day from Mumbai. Moreover, I gave all the wrong references. Colonel Waugh was Colonel Taylor's predecessor, twice removed. And the Taylors, being Anglicans, had nothing to do with Father Timothy's Roman Catholic Church. It was pure luck that they needed a servant urgently, having just kicked out the previous domestic help.

In the fifteen months I have been with the family, five more servants have been dismissed. All because of Colonel Taylor. He is The Man Who Knows. Just as there is an omniscient God above, there is Colonel Taylor below. Jagdish, the gardener, stole fertilizer from the shed and Colonel Taylor knew. Result: dismissed the next day. Sheela, the maid, picked up a bracelet from Mrs Taylor's room and Colonel Taylor knew. Result: dismissed the next day. Raju, the cook, opened the liquor cabinet and drank some whisky at night. Result: beaten up and dismissed the next day. Ajay, the new cook, hatched a plan to steal some money and mentioned this to a friend on the phone.

Result: dismissed the next day and both he and his friend arrested by the police. Basanti, the new maid, tried on one of Maggie's dresses. Result: yes, dismissed the next day. How Colonel Taylor gets to know these things that take place behind closed doors, in the dead of night, or on the telephone, with no one around, is a real mystery.

I am the only one who has survived. I admit, occasionally I am also tempted to pocket the loose change lying around on Mrs Taylor's dressing table or grab one of the delicious Swiss chocolates from the fridge, but I keep such urges in check. Because I know that Colonel Taylor is The Man Who Knows. And the family trusts me. The fact that I have a Christian name and speak English helps, too. Apart from Shanti, who was employed just two months ago, I am the only one to have exclusive access to the family's private quarters. I can enter all the bedrooms and I am the only one allowed to watch TV and occasionally to play Nintendo with Roy in the living room. But even I am not allowed to enter Colonel Taylor's office, known as the Den. It is the small room adjacent to the master bedroom. It has a sturdy brown wooden door, protected by a thick iron grille. The iron grille has three locks: two small ones and one huge golden padlock that says, 'Yale. Armoured. Boron Shackle.' On the wall next to the padlock is a small white electronic panel with a picture of a skull and two bones and numbers 0–9 like on a telephone keypad. You can open the padlock only after punching in a code. If you try to open it forcibly you get a 440-volt current and you die. A little light on the panel burns red when the room is closed. Whenever Colonel Taylor enters the room, the light changes to green. No member of the household is allowed to enter this room. Not even Mrs Taylor, Maggie or Roy.

The time I have spent with the Taylors has helped me forget the traumatic events in Mumbai. Shantaram and Neelima Kumari have become painful but distant memories. For the first few months I lived in constant dread, cringing whenever a police jeep with a flashing red light passed the compound. Over time, the feeling of being hunted began to dissipate. I often thought about Gudiya, too, and wondered what had happened to her, but it is difficult to sustain a memory if you don't have a face to associate with the name. Gradually, she disappeared into the dustbin of my past. But Salim I couldn't forget. I was often racked with guilt for having left him behind. I wondered how he was coping, whether he was still working as a *dabbawallah*, but I refrained from contacting him, worried that this might reveal my whereabouts to the police.

Living with the Taylors, I have learnt to do barbies and make fondue. I have become an expert at mixing drinks and measuring whisky by the peg. I have tasted kangaroo steaks and crocodile dumplings imported directly from Canberra. I have become a fan of rugby, tennis, and something called Aussie Rules, which I watch with Roy. But even after all this time, I still struggle with the Australian accent. Every evening I sit in my room and practise speaking like an Australian.

'G'day Maite, see you at aight at India Gaite,' I say, and burst out laughing.

I especially enjoy going shopping with Mrs Taylor. She gets most of her provisions from Australia. But from time to time she buys imported products from Super Bazaar and Khan Market. We purchase Spanish chorizo and Roquefort cheese and gherkins in brine and red chillies in olive oil. The best days are when she takes Maggie and Roy with her to Kids Mart, the biggest kids' store in the whole world. It has clothes and toys and bikes and cassettes. Maggie and Roy buy sweatshirts and jeans and I get to go on the free merry-go-round.

Roy and Maggie get a magazine every month. It is called *Australian Geographic*. I think it is the best magazine on earth. It is crammed with page upon page of photos of the most gorgeous places in the world, all of which are in Australia. There are beaches with miles of golden sand. Islands fringed with lovely palm trees. Oceans full of whales and sharks. Cities teeming with skyscrapers. Volcanoes spewing out deadly lava. Snow-covered mountains nestling against tranquil green valleys. At the age of fourteen, my only ambition is to see these beautiful places. To visit Queensland and Tasmania and the Great Barrier Reef before I die.

My life with the Taylors is comfortable, too, because I do not have much work to do. Unlike in the actress's house, where I was the only servant, there are three others here sharing the work. Ramu is the cook and the kitchen is completely under him. Shanti makes the beds and does the washing. I have only to do the vacuuming and the cleaning. From time to time, I also polish the silver cutlery, stack up books in Colonel Taylor's library and help Bhagwati trim the hedges. All of us live in the servants' quarters attached to the main house. We have one large and two small rooms to ourselves. Bhagwati lives in the large one with his wife and son. Shanti lives alone in the second. And I share the third with Ramu. The room has bunk beds. I sleep in the one on top.

Ramu is a nice bloke. He joined the Taylors four months ago and is an excellent cook. His main claim to fame is that he knows French cooking, having previously worked for a French family. He can make *gâteau de saumon* and *crêpes suzette* and *cervettes au gratin*, which is my favourite dish. Ramu is well built and his face, if you ignore the pockmarks, is quite good looking. He loves to see Hindi movies. His favourite films are those in which the rich heroine runs off with the poor hero. I have a suspicion that Shanti fancies Ramu. The way she looks at him, winking occasionally, makes me think she is trying to give Ramu a signal. But Ramu does not care for Shanti. He is in love with someone else. He has made me swear not to mention this to anyone, so I cannot reveal the name. But I suppose I can mention that she is a beautiful girl with blue eyes and golden hair.

Although I live in the servants' quarters, the Taylors treat me almost as part of the family. Whenever they go for an outing to McDonald's, they remember to buy me a kids' meal. When Roy and Maggie play *Scrabble*, they always include me. When Roy watches cricket in the TV room, he always invites me to join him (though he gets nasty whenever Australia is losing). Every time the Taylors travel to Australia on holiday, they make a point of getting me a small gift – a keyring saying I LOVE SYDNEY or a T-shirt with a funny message. Sometimes all this kindness makes me cry. When I am eating a slice of Edam cheese or drinking a can of root beer, I find it difficult to believe that I am the same orphan boy who was eating thick blackened chapattis and indigestible stew in a filthy juvenile home not far from here just five years ago. At times I actually start imagining myself as part of this Australian family. Ram Mohammad Taylor. But when one of the servants is scolded or dismissed or when Colonel Taylor wags a finger and says 'You bloody Indians,' my dream world comes crashing down and I begin to think of myself as a mongrel peeping through a barred window into an exotic world which does not belong to me.

But there is one thing that does belong to me, and that is the money piling up from my salary, though I have yet either to see or touch it. After bad experiences with a string of servants, Colonel Taylor decided not to give me a monthly salary on the grounds that I am a minor. He gives me only fifty rupees per month as pocket money. I am supposed to receive the rest of my salary as accumulated savings only on termination of employment. And only then if I have behaved well. Otherwise, like Raju and Ajay, it is bye bye without pay. Unlike me, Ramu gets his salary every month. A full two thousand rupees. He has already accumulated a kitty of eight thousand rupees which he keeps safely hidden inside a hollow space in the mattress of his bed. I have only a hundred rupees in my pocket, but I have a little red diary in which I keep adding up my salary every month. As of today, the Taylors owe me 22,500 rupees. Just the thought of owning all this money makes me giddy. Every night I dream of visiting the places I see in *Australian Geographic*. Ramu has bigger ambitions. He dreams of marrying a beautiful white girl and honeymooning in Sydney, and starting a chain of French restaurants where he will serve venison and *crème brûlée*.

The neighbourhood junk-dealer, or *kabariwalla*, is here. Mrs Taylor is selling him all the newspapers and magazines we have hoarded over the past six months. They must have cost at least ten thousand rupees to purchase. But we are selling them at fifteen rupees per kilo. Ramu and I bring out heavy bundles of the *Times of India*, *Indian Express*, the *Pioneer* and the *Hindu*. We pull out the stacked copies of *India Today*, *Femina*, *Cosmopolitan* and *The Australian*. The *kabariwalla* weighs them on his dusty scales. Suddenly Roy appears on the scene. 'What's happening?' he asks his mother.

'Nothing. We are just getting rid of all the junk newsprint in the house,' she replies.

'Oh, is that right?' he says and disappears into the house. He comes out after five minutes armed with thirty copies of *Australian Geographic*. My jaw drops in shock. How can Roy even think of selling off these magazines?

But before I can say anything, the *kabariwalla* has weighed the glossy magazines. 'These come to six kilos. I will give you ninety rupees for them,' he tells

Roy. The boy nods. The transaction is completed. I race back to my room.

As soon as the *kabariwalla* leaves the house, I accost him on the road. 'I am sorry, but Memsahib wants those magazines back,' I tell him.

'Too bad,' he shrugs. 'I have bought them now. They have excellent quality paper which will fetch a good price.' Eventually I have to give him my hundred rupees, but I get back the issues of *Australian Geographic*. They are now mine. That evening, I spread all of them out in my tiny room and watch the images of mountains and beaches, jellyfish and lobsters, kookaburras and kangaroos float up before my eyes. Somehow, these exotic places seem a little more accessible today. Perhaps the fact that I now own the magazines means that I also own a tiny part of their contents in my heart.

Another notable thing that happens this month is the debut of *Spycatcher* on Star TV. This serial has taken Australia by storm. Set in the 1980s, it is about the life of an Australian police officer called Steve Nolan who catches spies. Colonel Taylor becomes completely addicted to it. Almost every evening he disappears into his Den to come out only for dinner. But come Wednesday night, he sits in the TV room with his stubby of Foster's beer and watches Steve Nolan catch dirty foreigners (called Commies) selling secrets to some Russian organization called the KGB. I like the serial because of the car chases, death-defying stunts and cool gadgets, such as a pen which doubles up as a miniature camera, and a tape recorder which becomes a gun. And I am fascinated by Steve Nolan's car – a bright red Ferrari which hurtles through the streets like a rocket.

The Taylors' garden party is a regular fixture during the summer season, but today's party is something special. It is in honour of a visiting general from Australia and even the HC – High Commissioner – will be attending. Ramu and I and, for once, even Bhagwati are 'laired up' – clad in spotless white uniforms with round golden buttons. We wear white gloves and black shoes. Big white turbans with little tails sit uncomfortably on our small heads. They are of the type worn by grooms at weddings. Except we don't look like grooms on horseback. We look like fancy waiters at a fancy garden party.

The guests have begun to arrive. Colonel Taylor welcomes them on the well-manicured rear lawn. He is dressed in a light-blue suit. Ramu is busy grilling skewers of chicken, pork, fish and mutton over the barbecue pit. Bhagwati is serving cocktails to the guests on a silver tray. I am manning the bar. Only I can understand the guests when they ask for a Campari with Soda or a Bloody Mary. Shanti is busy helping out in the kitchen. Even she is wearing a smart skirt instead of her usual sari.

The guests are mostly white and from other embassies. There is a sprinkling of Indians as well – a couple of journalists and officials from the Defence Ministry. The whites drink Kingfisher beer and cocktails. The Indians, as usual, ask only for Black Label whisky.

The conversation at the garden party falls into two

categories. The Indians talk about politics and cricket. The diplomats and expatriates exchange gossip about their servants and colleagues and crib about the heat. 'It's so bloody hot, I wish they'd declare a holiday.' 'My maid ran away the other day with the gardener, and after I had given both of them a raise.' 'It's so difficult to get good help these days. Most of these bloody servants are thieves.'

The arrival of the HC with a smartly attired man, who, I am told, is the general, creates a buzz. Mrs Taylor almost falls over herself in her rush to greet the HC. There is a lot of kissing and pressing of hands. Colonel Taylor looks pleased. The party is going well.

By eleven o'clock, all the guests have gone. Only the two Indian journalists and one official from the Defence Ministry called Jeevan Kumar are still sitting, nursing their tenth peg of Johnny Walker. Mrs Taylor looks at them with disdain. 'Charles,' she tells her husband, 'why do you have to invite these bloody journos? They are always the last to leave.'

Colonel Taylor makes sympathetic noises. The Ministry of Defence official, a dark, heavy-set man, lurches into the house. 'Can I have a word with you, Mr Taylor?' he calls out. Colonel Taylor hurries after him.

It is past midnight and Ramu is still not asleep. I hear him tossing and turning in his bunk bed. 'What's the matter, Ramu? Can't you get to sleep tonight?' I ask him.

'How can I sleep, Thomas? My darling is tormenting me.'

'You are stupid. How often have I told you not to entertain this fanciful idea? If Colonel Taylor finds out he will have you slaughtered.'

'Lovers have to be prepared to sacrifice themselves for their love. But at least now I have a piece of my love with me.'

'What? What have you got?' I climb down from my bed.

'Shhh . . . I can only show it to you if you swear not to reveal it to anyone.'

'OK, OK, I swear. Now show me what you have got.'

Ramu pushes his hand underneath his pillow and brings out a piece of red fabric. He holds it close to his nostrils and inhales deeply. Even I can smell a faint perfume.

'What is it? You have to show it.'

Ramu unfurls it like a flag. It is a red bra. I jump up in shock and hit my head against the wooden rail.

'Oh, my God! Where the hell did you get this from? Don't tell me it is hers.'

'Here, see for yourself.' Ramu hands the bra to me.

I turn the bra up and down. It seems like a very expensive piece, full of lace embroidery. It has a small white label near the hooks which says 'Victoria's Secret'.

'Who is Victoria?' I ask him.

'Victoria? I don't know any Victoria.'

'This bra belongs to Victoria. It even has her name. Where did you get it from?'

Ramu is confused. 'But . . . but I stole it from Maggie's room.'

'Oh my God, Ramu! You know you are not allowed

to go to the children's bedrooms. Now you will get into real trouble.'

'Look, Thomas, you promised not to tell anyone. Please, I beg you, don't reveal this secret.'

I cross my heart as I climb back into my bed. Soon Ramu begins snoring. I know he is dreaming about a girl with blue eyes and golden hair. But I am dreaming about a jeep with a flashing red light. I am convinced that Ramu is heading for trouble. Because Colonel Taylor is The Man Who Knows.

Sure enough, two days later a jeep with a flashing red light comes screeching to the house. A Police Inspector wearing goggles swaggers into the drawing room. He is the same Inspector Tyagi who took away Ajay. He asks for Ramu, and the constables drag the cook out of the kitchen and take him to his room. I scamper behind them. It is my room too. They rummage through Ramu's bed. They find the money he keeps inside his mattress. They also discover a diamond necklace nestling under his pillow. How it got there I have no idea, but I know Ramu is no thief. Then the constables start rummaging through my things. They find my *Australian Geographic* magazines, neatly stacked in one corner. They find my keyrings and my T-shirts. And then they find a crumpled red bra underneath my mattress. How it got there I have no idea, but I know it is the same bra Ramu stole from Maggie's room.

I am brought before the Taylors like a notorious convict. 'Taylor Sahib, you were only talking about one crook in the house, and we did find the diamond necklace and a lot of stolen cash in his bed. But look at what we found in this little bastard's bed. We found these magazines, which he must have stolen from the children –' he drops the stack of *Australian Geographic* on the floor, 'and we found this.' The Inspector unfurls the red bra like a flag.

Maggie begins crying. Ramu looks as if he is about to faint. Colonel Taylor has a murderous glint in his eyes.

'Strewth! You too, Thomas?' says Mrs Taylor, in complete shock. Then she goes into a rage and slaps me four or five times. 'You bloody Indians,' she rants. 'All of you are just the same. Nothing but ungrateful bludgers. We feed you and clothe you and this is what you give us in return, trying to flog our stuff?'

Colonel Taylor comes to my rescue. 'No, Rebecca,' he tells his wife. 'Fair crack of the whip. Thomas is a good bloke. That bastard Ramu hid this in his bed. Trust me, I know.'

Colonel Taylor proves yet again that he is The Man Who Knows. His omniscience saves me that day, and I get back my collection of *Australian Geographic*. But the beaches of Queensland and the wildlife of Tasmania do not entice me any longer. Ramu weeps and confesses to pocketing the bra, but continues to maintain that he did not steal the necklace. He points an accusing finger at Shanti. But it is all to no avail. The Inspector takes him away in his jeep. He also takes away a bottle of Black Label whisky from Colonel Taylor, smiling toothily. 'Thank you very much, Taylor Sahib. Any time you need my services, just give me a ring. It will be a pleasure to serve you. Here's my card.'

Colonel Taylor takes the card abstractedly and leaves it on the side table in the drawing room.

There is a lot of excitement in the house. The Taylors have got a pet dog for Maggie. The Colonel brings him in on a leash. He is small and furry, with a tiny wet nose and a long tail. He looks like a doll and yelps rather than barks. Maggie says he is an Apso. She decides to call him Rover.

There is excitement in the house again. A new cook has arrived. His name is Jai. He does not know half the things that Ramu knew. Never mind cooking French cuisine, he cannot even pronounce *au gratin*. But he gets the job because he is a mature, married man, with a wife and two girls who live in some nearby village. I am not very happy to share my room again. I was enjoying sleeping alone in the bunk beds. On some nights I would sleep in the top bed and on others in the bottom.

I take an instant dislike to Jai. He has shifty eyes. He smokes secretly in the room (smoking in the Taylors' residence is prohibited). And he treats me like a servant. 'What is your ambition in life?' he asks me like the teacher in the Juvenile Home.

'To own a red Ferrari,' I lie. 'What is yours?'

He lights up another cigarette and sends smoke rings spinning out of his mouth. 'I want to open a garage, but it will cost money. I have a very rich friend, Amar, who has promised that if I can arrange a hundred and fifty thousand, he will put together the rest. How much money do you think these *firangs* have in the house?'

I keep my mouth shut. So from the very first week, Mr Jai has begun plotting a robbery. Good that he doesn't know about The Man Who Knows. He will find out soon enough.

Colonel Taylor starts going on early-morning walks with Rover to Lodhi Garden, which is close to the house. Till the Delhi Government brings out a new law under which people with pet dogs have to scoop up the dog litter or face hefty fines. From then on I am instructed to accompany master and dog and act as sweeper to Rover. I hate this chore. Imagine having to get up from bed at five-thirty and go running with scoop and pan after a dirty, stupid dog which shits every two minutes. Lodhi Garden, though, is a nice place for a morning walk. It has a lot of greenery and a crumbling ancient monument called Bara Gumbad in the centre. In the morning the park is full of joggers. I see fat old ladies doing yoga and thin anorexic girls doing aerobics. I also begin to notice that sometimes Colonel Taylor disappears from my view for long periods when I am busy scooping Rover's poop. This intrigues me, so one morning I leave Rover to his own devices and decide to follow Colonel Taylor. I see him go past the Bara Gumbad and move towards a little thicket. I peer from behind a dense bush and see him greet the same Indian from the Ministry of Defence who had come to the garden party.

'Do you know, Mr Kumar, that I followed you last night from your house in South Ex all the way to the sweet shop, and you didn't have a clue?' says Colonel Taylor.

Jeevan Kumar is sweating profusely and is clearly fidgety. He seems very contrite. 'Oh, I am really sorry, Colonel Sahib. I will be more careful in the future. I know people should not see us together.'

'Of course, Mr Kumar, that goes without saying. But if you continue to be lax about your security I am afraid we will have to terminate these face-to-face meetings. Just remember a simple rule: CYTLYT.'

'CYTLYT?'

'Yes. Confuse Your Trail, Lose Your Tail. It's actually quite simple. What it means is that you must never take a direct route to your destination. Change roads, change cars, duck into one shop, come out of another, anything to confuse your trail. Once you do that, you make it extremely difficult to be followed. Whoever is tailing you will give up.'

'OK, Colonel Sahib, I will remember that. But let me tell you the good news. I think I will be able to give you what you have been wanting from me all this while. Meet me on Friday the fourteenth in the car park behind Balsons in South Ex. It is generally quite deserted. At eight pm. OK?'

'OK.'

The meeting ends. I hurry back to Rover before Colonel Taylor returns.

My eyes are wide open on Friday the fourteenth and my ears extra sensitive. Colonel Taylor discloses his plans early in the morning to his wife. 'McGill, the new Commercial Attaché, wants me to show him a couple of places in the city after work. So I'll be a bit late, Rebecca. Don't wait for me at dinner.'

141

'That's fine. The HC's wife has asked me to a bridge party, so I'll be out too,' says Mrs Taylor.

I can put two and two together. Why did Colonel Taylor lie to his wife about his meeting? He falls in my estimation that day. I feel a terrible sadness for Mrs Taylor.

After Ramu, it is Roy's turn. Colonel Taylor has caught him kissing Shanti in his bedroom. Shanti swears on her dead mother that there is nothing going on between her and Roy *baba* and that this is the very first time Roy kissed her – and that, too, by mistake. But all her pleading is to no avail. The result is all too predictable: immediate dismissal. But at least she gets her wages. Roy will probably get a thrashing for getting too close to the 'bloody Indians', and all his shopping in Kids Mart will be stopped. I decide not to do any cleaning in Maggie's bedroom for the next ten days as a precautionary measure.

If I had, I could probably have saved her. Because barely two weeks after Roy, his sister is in the dock. The Man Who Knows has obtained irrefutable proof that she has been smoking in her room, despite strict instructions. Maggie tries to deny the charge, but Colonel Taylor produces the carton of cigarettes she has hidden inside her *almirah* and even the stubs she has forgotten to dispose of. That is the end of Maggie's shopping trips to Kids Mart as well.

Believe it or not, two months later Colonel Taylor catches someone else cheating. His own wife. Mrs Rebecca Taylor. Turns out she was having an affair with someone in the Embassy. 'You bloody bitch!' he screams at her in their bedroom. 'I am going to fix you and that half-arsed lover of yours.' I hear the sound of a slap and of something being broken, like a vase. Mrs Taylor doesn't come down for dinner that evening. Maggie and Roy also maintain a respectful distance from their father. I cannot help commiserating with Mrs Taylor. Her husband has discovered her little affair but she doesn't have an inkling of his own dirty secret. I want to spill the beans on Colonel Taylor. How he meets up with old Jeevan Kumar in deserted car parks. But those who live in glass houses cannot throw stones and the constant fear nagging me is that The Man Who Knows might find out how I pushed Shantaram through the railing. And that he might know things about me that even I don't know.

While all these crazy things are happening in the Taylor family, Jai is getting on my nerves. His cooking has gone from bad to worse. His clear soups are clear of all taste, his curries make me worry, and even Rover will not eat his steaks. He bores me to death by talking about his stupid garage and getting the hundred and fifty thousand. I have almost made up my mind to complain about him to Colonel Taylor when tragedy strikes the family. Colonel Taylor's mother dies in Adelaide. Everyone is very sad. For the first time we see the softer side of the military officer. 'We are all going to be away for a week,' he tells Jai in a subdued tone. 'The house will be locked. You and Thomas can eat outside.' Maggie and Roy are weeping. Mrs Taylor's eyes are red. Naturally, Bhagwati is also crying. Even my eyes are misting with tears. There is only one person smiling slyly behind the kitchen wall. It is Jai.

That night, Jai breaks into the Taylors' house. He doesn't go to the children's rooms or the master bedroom. He goes straight to the Den. First he switches off the electricity at the mains. Then he short-circuits the electronic panel, cuts the padlock with a chainsaw, pushes aside the iron grille and kicks open the wooden door.

I am woken by the sound of violent screaming coming from the Taylor residence. At three am I rush into the house and discover Jai's handiwork. He is inside the Den, beating his head against the wall. 'These bastards. They live like kings and don't have a penny in the house,' he seethes.

Alarm bells are ringing in my mind. I am convinced that The Man Who Knows will find out about Jai's treachery even while he is attending a funeral ten thousand miles away. And that I will also be implicated by association.

'Jai, you fool, what have you done?' I yell at him.

'Nothing more than what I came here to do. I am a professional thief, Thomas. Spent eight years in Tihar Jail. I thought that with all this security, that bastard Taylor was keeping the family jewels in this room. But there's not a penny here. Six months of effort has gone completely to waste. OK, I am restoring the electricity and then I'm off. I am taking the VCD player and the three-in-one in the TV room. They are crumbs, but I have to respect my profession. You can clean up after me. And if you try and call the police I will break every bone in your body.'

After Jai has gone, I look around the room. It is full

of strange-looking gadgets: microphones like tiny sun-flowers and miniature cameras like disembodied eyes. There are pads saying 'Cipher' with nonsense combinations of numbers and letters. There are some books: *The Art of Espionage, Essentials of a Good Counter Agent, Spying for Dummies.* There are papers bearing labels like 'Top Secret' and 'For Your Eyes Only', drawings of various kinds, one saying 'Advanced Technology Vessel nuclear reactor design' and another 'submarine schemata'. And there is a drawer full of miniature VHS tapes. I look at the labels on the tapes, arranged alphabetically: Ajay, Bhagwati, HC, Jeevan, Jones, Maggie, McGill, Raj, Ramesh, Rebecca, Roy, Shanti, Stuart. And Thomas. Hidden inside the second drawer is a portable video player. With trembling hands I pull out my tape and insert it into the player. The screen comes alive with images from my room. I see myself reclining on my bed; writing in my red diary; talking to Ramu; sleeping. I fast-forward to see whether there are any pictures of Shantaram on the tape. I then insert the tape with Mrs Taylor's name. She is sitting on her bed. A man enters surreptitiously and takes her in his arms. I can only see his back. He kisses her long and hard. Suddenly there is a knock and the man whirls around and looks me straight in the eye. I almost die of fright. It is the High Commissioner. I hastily take out the tape and switch off the video player. For a couple of minutes I stand absolutely still, worried that a secret camera might be in action even in this room. Then I breathe deeply. Now I know how Colonel Taylor became The Man Who Knows. He has bugged the whole house and probably the whole High Commission. He is a spy. But I'm not Steve Nolan from *Spycatcher*. I get 1,500 rupees a month, which I have totted up to 43,500 rupees in my red diary. And I don't want all this money to remain only in a diary. I want to touch the bundles of currency, feel the smooth surface of the crisp new notes. So I will keep my mouth shut. And smile whenever Sahib and Memsahib smile.

I call up Colonel Taylor on his cellphone number. 'I am sorry to disturb you, Sir, but there has been a robbery in the house. Jai has taken away the VCD player and the three-in-one. And he also broke into the Den.'

'What???'

'Yes, Sir. I am sorry, Sir.'

'Look, Thomas, this is what I want you to do. I want you to secure the Den immediately. Take out the broken padlock. You don't have to enter the room. Just put any lock on the door and do not allow anyone to enter it. It is very important that you don't call the police. If the alarm sounds, just punch in the following code on the keypad on the door: 0007. You got it? 0007 and it will stop. I am taking a flight back immediately and should be in Delhi by tomorrow afternoon, but till I arrive I want you to make sure that no one enters the Den. Have you understood?'

'Yes, Sir.'

Colonel Taylor returns to Delhi without even attending his mother's funeral. He rushes into the Den as soon as the taxi pulls up outside the house. He comes out looking relieved. 'Thank God, nothing has been taken from the room. Well done, Thomas. I knew I could rely on you.'

* * *

Over the next six months, my life slips back into the
same groove as before. A new cook is hired who has
not been within a thousand miles of Tihar Jail.
Bhagwati is dismissed for taking the car without permission for a wedding in his family. Maggie's new
boyfriend James is discovered and banned from entering the house. Roy is caught taking drugs and given a
thrashing. Mrs Taylor and her husband continue to
speak to each other with icy formality. Colonel Taylor,
I presume, continues to meet Jeevan Kumar in lonely
alleys and deserted car parks.

Maggie and Roy are playing *Scrabble* in the living
room. They ask me to join them. I have learnt many
new words playing this game with them, such as
'bingle' and 'brekkie' and 'chalkie' and 'dosh' and
'skite' and 'spunk'. Maggie always wins these games.
Her vocabulary is really good. She is the only one who
knows eight-letter words and once she even made a
nine-letter word. I am the worst. I make words like 'go'
and 'eat' and 'sing' and 'last'. Once in a blue moon, I
do get six- or seven-letter words, but I still end up with
the least points. Sometimes I think Roy invites me as a
third player just so that he doesn't come last. Today,
my letters have not been good. Lots of Xs and Js and Ks
and Ls. The game is about to end. Maggie has 203
points, Roy has 175 and I have 104. My last seven letters
are G, P, E, E, S, A and I. I am thinking of making 'page'
or 'see'. Then Roy uses an O from one of Maggie's words
to make 'on' and I latch on to it in a flash. I put E, S, P
and I before O and A, G and E after N. 'Espionage'. That's

147

a total of seventeen points, and triple that for putting it on a red square and add fifty points for using all seven tiles. 101 points. Take that, Maggie!

I have been hovering around the phone all day. Maggie is expecting a call from James and she has instructed me to pick up the phone before her father does from the Den. The phone finally rings at seven-fifteen pm. I lift the receiver in a flash. But Colonel Taylor has already beaten me to it. 'Hello,' he says.

There is heavy breathing at the other end. Then Jeevan Kumar's voice floats over the static. 'Meet me tomorrow, Thursday, at eight pm at the Kwality Ice Cream Shop near India Gate. I have dynamite stuff.'

'Good,' says Colonel Taylor and disconnects the line.

Colonel Taylor sits with his stubby of Foster's in the living room, watching the latest episode of *Spycatcher*. This time Steve Nolan is in a real dilemma. He has discovered that his best friend, the one he went to college with, the one who was best man at his wedding, is a Commie spy. He is very sad. He doesn't know what to do. He sits in a bar in a dishevelled condition and drinks loads of whisky. Then the bartender tells him, 'It's a dirty world out there, but if no one agrees to do the washing, the whole country goes down the shit house.' Steve Nolan hears this and gets all charged up. He rushes to the Commie spy's house in his red Ferrari. 'You are a good man, doing a bad job,' he tells his friend, before taking out his gun. 'Friendship is important. But the country comes first. I am sorry,' he says and shoots him dead.

*   *   *

The next night a police jeep and an Ambassador car with flashing red lights come screeching to the house at ten pm. The same Inspector who arrested Ramu gets out, together with the Commissioner of Police. Colonel Taylor is with them, looking like Steve Nolan in the bar. Within ten minutes, the High Commissioner also arrives, looking very grim. 'What's all this?' he asks the Police Chief. 'Why has Colonel Taylor been declared *persona non grata* and asked to leave within forty-eight hours by the Foreign Office?'

'Well, Your Excellency, we have evidence of your officer indulging in activities incompatible with his diplomatic status. I am afraid he will have to leave the country,' the Police Chief replies.

'But what's the charge against him?'

'We caught him red-handed taking sensitive and top-secret documents from a man by the name of Jeevan Kumar, who is a clerk in the Ministry of Defence.'

Colonel Taylor looks ashen. He doesn't say these Indians are bloody fibbers. He just stands in the middle of the drawing room with his head bowed.

The High Commissioner lets out a sigh. 'I must say this is the first time in my long career that any of my officers has been PNG'd. And believe me, Charles is no spy. But if he has to go, he has to go.' Then he takes the Police Chief aside. 'Mr Chopra, I have sent you many cases of Black Label over the years. Can you do me a favour and answer one question?'

'Sure.'

'Just for my information, can you tell me how did

you come to know about Charles's meeting today? Did this fellow Kumar lead you to him?'

'Funny you should ask. It was not Jeevan Kumar. Quite the contrary, it was one of your own guys. Called up Inspector Tyagi this morning and told him to go to India Gate at eight pm to catch Colonel Taylor receiving some secret documents.'

'I don't believe it. How can you be so sure it was an Australian?'

Inspector Tyagi steps in. 'Well, Mr Ambassador, the accent was a dead give-away. The man said something like, "G'day maite, go to India Gaite, tonight at aite." I mean, only an Australian would speak like that, wouldn't he?'

The next day, Colonel Taylor leaves Delhi alone on a Qantas flight. Mrs Taylor and the kids will follow later. I am leaving the Taylors, too. With three keyrings, six T-shirts, thirty *Australian Geographic* magazines which I will sell to a *kabariwalla*. And 52,000 rupees. In crisp new notes.

I say my hooroos to the Taylor family. Roy behaves like a whacker. Since he started taking drugs he has kangaroos loose in the top paddock. Maggie's pashing James. And I am not worried about Mrs Taylor. With the HC around, I know she'll be apples. As for me, I'm off to meet Salim in Mumbai. It'll be a bonzer!

Smita looks at her watch. It shows the time as one-thirty am. 'Are you sure you want to carry on?' I ask.

'Do we have a choice?' she replies. 'They will file

formal charges against you by tomorrow.' She presses the 'Play' button again.

We are in yet another commercial break. Prem Kumar taps his desk. 'You know what, Mr Thomas, your luck has finally run out. I am ready to bet you that you cannot answer the next question. So prepare to use one of your Lifeboats.'

The signature tune begins.

Prem Kumar turns to me. 'We now move on to question number five for fifty thousand rupees. This one pertains to the world of diplomacy. When a government declares a foreign diplomat *persona non grata*, what does it mean? Is it a) that the diplomat is to be honoured, b) that the diplomat's tenure should be extended, c) that the diplomat is grateful or d) that the diplomat is not acceptable? Have you understood the question, Mr Thomas?'

'Yes,' I reply.

'OK. Then let's have your reply. Remember, both Lifeboats are still available to you. You can get A Friendly Tip, or you can ask me for Half and Half and I will remove two wrong answers, leaving you with just two choices. What do you say?'

'I say D.'

'Excuse me?'

'I said D. The diplomat is not acceptable.'

'Is that a guess? Remember, you stand to lose the ten thousand rupees you've already won if you give the wrong answer. So if you want, you can quit right now.'

'I know the answer. It is D.'

There are gasps from the audience.

'Are you absolutely, one hundred per cent sure?'

'Yes.'

There is a crescendo of drums. The correct answer flashes.

'Absolutely, one hundred per cent correct! You have just won fifty thousand rupees!' declares Prem Kumar. The audience stands up and cheers. Prem Kumar wipes the sweat from his brow. 'I must say, this is remarkable,' he says out aloud. 'Tonight Mr Thomas really seems to be The Man Who Knows!'

100,000

HOLD ON TO YOUR BUTTONS

'*Khallas*. Finished,' I say, speaking in monosyllables. 'No more whisky. Bar closed now. Go home.'

'Noooo. Plizz don't say that. Ged me one m-more peeeg. Lasht one,' the customer pleads and holds out his empty glass. I look at my watch. It is twelve forty-five am. Technically, the bar does not close till one. With a grimace I pick up the bottle of Black Dog rum. 'Hundred rupees, please,' I demand. The man takes a crumpled note from his shirt pocket and I pour a care-fully measured peg into his glass.

'Thang you, b-b-b-artender,' he says, takes a swig of the rum and crashes down on the table, shattering his glass on the floor, spilling the bottle of soda and over-turning the bowl of mint chutney. Within seconds he will be fast asleep. Now I not only have to clear up the big mess he has created, but also call a taxi, help him to his feet and somehow send him home. And though I was

153

smart enough to charge him for the drinks in advance, I can forget about getting any tip from this customer.

Perhaps I myself am to blame for getting into this situation. The customer was displaying all the tell-tale signs of crashing out any minute. But I thought he could stomach one last peg. As usual, I was wrong.

Even after two months at Jimmy's Bar and Restaurant, I am unable to assess accurately a drinker's capacity. I have, though, evolved a rough classification system for drunkards. Top of my list are the horses. These can hold as many as eight pegs without slurring their speech. Then come the asses, who start braying and babbling after just two or three, or become maudlin and sentimental and begin crying. Then come the dogs. The more they drink, the more they want to get into an argument or a fight. Some of them also get frisky with Rosie. Below them are the bears, who drink and then drift off to sleep. And at the bottom are the pigs. They are the ones who vomit after their last peg. This classification is not watertight. I have seen customers who start like horses but end up like pigs. And dogs who turn into bears. Mercifully, this customer has ended up a bear rather than a pig.

I get rid of the last drunkard and look at the clock on the wall. It is one-ten am. Ever since Rosie and her dad pushed off to Goa for a holiday, I have been returning to my cubby-hole of a house in Dharavi after midnight almost every night. This is partly my fault. If I had not told the manager that I knew how to mix drinks and measure whisky by the peg, that I could tell the difference between a Campari with Soda and a Bloody

Mary, I wouldn't have been asked to officiate as the bartender in Alfred's absence.

Jimmy's Bar and Restaurant in Colaba has fading prints on the walls, mirrors behind the bar, sturdy wooden furniture, and the best menu in South Mumbai. Because the food is so good and the prices so cheap, it attracts customers from all walks of life. On any given day you can find a top-level executive nursing his drink at the bar next to a lowly factory worker. The manager insists that we strike up conversations with customers at the bar, because people drink more when they have company. Rosie's dad, the doddery bartender Alfred D'Souza, is adept at chatting up patrons. He knows most of the regulars by name and sits with them for hours, listening to their tales of woe and adding steadily to their liquor bill. Rosie herself is becoming quite an expert bar girl. She sits at the bar wearing a low-cut blouse and a tight skirt, occasionally bends down to display some cleavage and entices the customers into ordering expensive imported whisky instead of the cheap Indian brands. Sometimes, though, her antics land her in trouble with boorish customers who fancy her as a cheap lay. I then have to act as informal bouncer.

Mr Alfred D'Souza thinks there is something brewing between Rosie and me and watches me like a hawk whenever she is around. He is completely mistaken. Rosie is a sweet girl. She is short and bosomy. The way she tilts her head at me and occasionally winks, I feel she might be trying to give me a signal. But my brain is now incapable of receiving it. It is overloaded with memories of just one person: Nita. The doctors in Agra have said it will take at least four months for Nita to recover from her injuries. And I know Shyam will never allow me to meet her. That is why I have returned to Mumbai: to exorcise the ghosts of Agra, both of the living and of the dead. But I cannot escape my own history in this city. Memories of the past way-lay me at every intersection. Shantaram, the failed astronomer, mocks me in the streets. Neelima Kumari, the actress, calls out to me on the local train. And Salim, my friend, looks down at me from every bill-board. But I have taken a conscious decision not to meet Salim. I do not want him to get sucked up in the vortex of my crazy life and my crazy plans.

I live in a corner of Mumbai called Dharavi, in a cramped hundred-square-foot shack which has no natural light or ventilation, with a corrugated metal sheet serving as the roof over my head. It vibrates violently whenever a train passes overhead. There is no running water and no sanitation. This is all I can afford. But I am not alone in Dharavi. There are a million people like me, packed in a two-hundred-hectare triangle of swampy urban wasteland, where we live like animals and die like insects. Destitute migrants from all over the country jostle with each other for their own handful of sky in Asia's biggest slum. There are daily squabbles – over inches of space, over a bucket of water – which at times turn deadly. Dharavi's residents come from the dusty backwaters of Bihar and UP and Tamil Nadu and Gujarat. They came to Mumbai, the city of gold, with dreams in their hearts of striking it rich and living upper-middle-class lives. But that gold turned to lead a long time ago, leaving behind rusted hearts and gangrenous minds. Like my own.

Dharavi is not a place for the squeamish. Delhi's Juvenile Home diminished us, but Dharavi's grim landscape of urban squalor deadens and debases us. Its open drains teem with mosquitoes. Its stinking, excrement-lined communal latrines are full of rats, which make you think less about the smell and more about protecting your backside. Mounds of filthy garbage lie on every corner, from which rag-pickers still manage to find something useful. And at times you have to suck in your breath to squeeze through its narrow, claustrophobic alleys. But for the starving residents of Dharavi, this is home.

Amidst the modern skyscrapers and neon-lit shopping complexes of Mumbai, Dharavi sits like a cancerous lump in the heart of the city. And the city refuses to recognize it. So it has outlawed it. All the houses in Dharavi are 'illegal constructions', liable to be demolished at any time. But when the residents are struggling simply to survive, they don't care. So they live in illegal houses and use illegal electricity, drink illegal water and watch illegal cable TV. They work in Dharavi's numerous illegal factories and illegal shops, and even travel illegally – without ticket – on the local trains which pass directly through the colony.

The city may have chosen to ignore the ugly growth of Dharavi, but a cancer cannot be stopped simply by being declared illegal. It still kills with its slow poison.

I commute daily from Dharavi to Jimmy's Bar and

Restaurant. The only good thing about working in Jimmy's establishment is that I don't have to come to work till at least midday. But this is more than offset by the late nights spent serving drunken louts from all over the city and listening to their pathetic tales. The one conclusion I have reached is that whisky is a great leveller. You might be a hot-shot advertising executive or a lowly foundry worker, but if you cannot hold your drink, you are just a drunkard.

After my traumatic experience with Shantaram, I thought I would never be able to tolerate a drunk. But Jimmy's was the only establishment that offered me a job. I console myself with the thought that the smell of whisky is less pungent than the stench from the communal latrine near my shack, and that listening to a drunkard is less painful than listening to the heart-rending stories of rape, molestation, illness and death that emanate daily from the huts of Dharavi. So I have now learnt to fake an interest and say 'Ummmm' and 'Yes' and 'Really?' and 'Wow!' to the tales of cheating wives and miserly bosses that are aired every night at Jimmy's Bar and Restaurant, while simultaneously encouraging customers to order another plate of Chicken Fry and another bowl of salted cashew nuts to go with their drinks. And every day I wait for a letter to arrive from the *W3B* people, to tell me if I have been selected to participate in the show. But the postman delivers nothing.

A sense of defeat has begun to cloud my mind. I feel that the specific purpose for which I came to Mumbai is beyond me. That I am swimming against the tide. That powerful currents are at work which I cannot overcome. But then I hear my beloved Nita's cries and Neelima Kumari's sobs and my willpower returns. I have to get on to that show. And till that happens, I will continue to listen to the stories of the drunkards in this city. Some good. Some bad. Some funny. Some sad. And one downright bizarre.

It is past midnight, but the lone customer at the bar refuses to budge. He has come by chauffeur-driven Mercedes, which is parked outside. He has been drinking steadily since ten pm and is now on his fifth peg. His uniformed driver is snoring in the car. Perhaps he knows that his employer will not come out in a hurry. The man is in his early thirties and is dressed in a smart dark suit with a silk tie and shiny leather shoes.

'My dear brother, my dear brother,' he keeps repeating every two minutes, in between sips of Black Label whisky and bites from the plate of shammi kebabs.

The manager snaps his fingers at me. 'Thomas, go and sit with him and ask him about his brother. Can't you see the poor fellow is distraught?'

'But . . . Manager Sahib, it is past midnight. We should tell him to leave or I'll miss the twelve-thirty local.'

'Don't you dare argue with me or I'll break your jaw,' he snarls at me. 'Now go, engage the customer in conversation. Get him to order the Scottish single malt which came in yesterday. He has come in a Mercedes.'

I glare at the manager like a schoolboy at a bully. Reluctantly, I return to the bar and slide closer to the customer.

'Oh, my dear brother, I hope you will forgive me,' he

moans, and nibbles at the shammi kebab. He is behaving like an ass, but at least he is in the lucid phase, with a couple of pegs in his system and words bubbling out of his mouth.

'What happened to your brother, Sir?' I ask.

The man raises his head to peer at me with half-closed eyes. 'Why do you ask? You will only increase the pain,' he says.

'Tell me about your brother, Sir. Perhaps it will lessen your pain.'

'No. Nothing can lessen the pain. Not even your whisky.'

'Fine, Sir. If you do not want to talk about your brother, I will not ask. But what about you?'

'Don't you know who I am?'

'No, Sir.'

'I am Prakash Rao. Managing Director of Surya Industries. The biggest manufacturer of buttons in India.'

'Buttons?'

'Yes. You know, buttons on shirts, pants, coats, skirts, blouses. We make them. We make all kinds of buttons from all kinds of materials. We use mostly polyester resins, but we have also made buttons of cloth, plastic, leather and even camel bone, horn-shell and wood. Haven't you seen our ad in the newspapers? "For the widest range of buttons – from fastening garments to pulling drawers – come to Surya. Buttons R Us." I am quite sure that the shirt you are wearing has buttons manufactured by my company.'

'And your brother, what is his name?'

'My brother? Arvind Rao. Oh, my poor brother. Oh, Arvind,' he starts moaning again.

'What happened to Arvind? What did he do?'

'He used to be the owner of Surya Industries. Till I replaced him.'

'Why did you replace him? Here, let me pour you a peg from this single malt which we got direct from Scotland.'

'Thank you. It smells good. I remember going to Mauritius for my honeymoon, to Port Louis, and there I had my first taste of single malt whisky.'

'You were mentioning replacing your brother.'

'Ah yes. My brother was a very good man. But he had to be replaced as MD of Surya Industries because he went mad.'

'Mad? How? Here's a fresh bowl of cashew nuts.'

'It is a long story.'

I use one of Rosie's lines. 'The night is young. The bottle is full. So why don't you begin?'

'Are you my friend?' he says, looking at me with glassy eyes.

'Of course I am your friend,' I reply with a toothy grin.

'Then I will tell you my story, friend. I am drunk, you know. And a drunken man always speaks the truth. Right, friend?'

'Right.'

'So, friend, my brother, my dear, dear brother Arvind, was a great businessman. He built Surya Industries from scratch. We used to sell beads in the Laadbazaar market of old Hyderabad. You know, the one near Charminar. It was he who painstakingly built up the business empire which I have inherited.'

'But you must have helped your brother in his business.'

'Hardly. I was a failure. Couldn't even complete my matriculation. It was my brother's greatness that he took me under his wing and employed me in the sales division of his company. I did my best and, as time went by, my brother's confidence in my abilities increased. Eventually he made me Head of International Sales and sent me to New York, where our international office is located.'

'New York? Wow! That must have been great!'

'Yes, New York is a great place. But I had a tough job, going out every day, meeting the dealers and distributors, processing the orders, ensuring timely delivery. I was busy from morning till night.'

'OK. So what happened next? Just hold on for a minute while I bring you another plate of shammi kebabs.'

'Thank you, friend. It was in New York that I met Julie.'

'Julie? Who is she?'

'Her real name was Erzulie De Ronceray, but everyone called her Julie. She was dark and sultry with thick curly hair and pouting lips and a slim waist. She worked as a cleaner in the apartment block where I rented my office. She was an illegal immigrant from Haiti. Have you heard of Haiti?'

'No. Where is it?'

'It is a tiny country in the Caribbean, near Mexico.'

'OK. So you met Julie.'

'Well, I would occasionally exchange a greeting with

her. One day, the INS caught her working without a green card. She begged me to show her as my employee so that her stay in the US could be regularized. In a fit of generosity I agreed to sponsor her. In return, she gave me love, respect, and the most mindblowing sex I had ever had. Believe me. I am drunk. And a drunken man always speaks the truth. Right?'

'Right. Why don't you take another peg? This single malt from Scotland is really good, isn't it?'

'Thank you, friend. You are very kind. Much kinder than Julie. She really manipulated me, you know. Preyed on my weaknesses. I was a lonely man in a large city. One thing led to another and I ended up marrying her.'

'And then you went for your honeymoon to Port Louis, correct?'

'Correct. But when I returned from the honeymoon I discovered there was a different, darker side to Julie. I visited her flat for the first time after we got married and found it to be full of strange stuff – rum bottles decorated with sequins and beads, a whole bunch of weird-looking dolls, stones of various shapes, crosses, rattles and even parchment made of snake skin. She also had a black cat called Bossu, which was very mean and nasty.

'The first time I discovered that there was more to Julie than met the eye was when I was attacked in the Bronx by a mugger with a knife. I was lucky to escape alive, but received a deep gash in my arm. Julie wouldn't allow me to go to the hospital. Instead, she applied some herbs to my arm and recited some chants, and within just two days the wound was completely gone, not even a scar remaining. And then she told me that she was a voodoo priestess.'

'Voodoo? What's that?'

'You don't want to know, my friend. Voodoo is a religion in Haiti. Its practitioners worship spirits called *loas* and believe that the universe is all inter-connected. Everything affects something else. Nothing is an accident, and everything is possible. That is why people who know voodoo can do all kinds of amazing things. Like bringing a dead man to life.'

'You must be joking.'

'No, not at all. These dead people are called zombies. I told you I am drunk. And a drunken man always tells the truth, right?'

'Right.' By now I am drawn completely into his story. I forget to ply him with more whisky and cashew nuts.

'Julie turned my life upside-down. She had been a poor cleaning woman, but now she wanted to be a part of high society. She forgot that she was married to the brother of a rich industrialist, not the industrialist himself. She wanted money all the time. Money which I couldn't give her because it didn't belong to me. It belonged to my brother, to the company.

'She forced me into stealing. It started with trifling things – a few dollars pocketed from a false taxi claim. Then it moved on to bigger things. Money received from a client and not shown on the ledger. A contract signed, the advance received and not sent to head office. Over time, the embezzled amount became half a million dollars. And then my brother, who lived here in Mumbai, discovered it.'

'Oh, my God! What happened then?'

'Well what do you think? My brother was furious. If he had wanted to, he could have got me arrested by the police. But blood is thicker than water. I begged for mercy and he forgave me. Of course, he transferred me from America, put me in a small office in Hyderabad and insisted that I repay at least half of the embezzled amount over a twenty-year period out of my salary.

'I was quite happy to accept these terms. Anything to avoid going to jail. But Julie was furious. "How can your brother behave with you like this?" she egged me on. "You have an equal stake in the company, you must fight for your rights."

'Over time, her constant nagging began to have an impact. I started thinking of Arvind as a devious and cunning man who had given me a raw deal. Then one day Arvind came to Hyderabad to visit my small office. He found evidence again of some petty thievery and lost his temper. In front of all the staff he abused me, called me names, said I was good for nothing and threatened to terminate my association with the company.

'I was devastated. For the first time I felt like hitting back at my brother. I recounted the incident to Julie and she became incandescent with rage. "The time has come to teach your brother a lesson," she told me. "Are you ready now to take your revenge?" "Yes," I replied, because my brain had been numbed by his insults. "Good, then get me a button from one of your brother's unwashed shirts and a little snippet of his hair." "Where will I get a snippet of his hair from?" I asked. "That's your lookout," said Julie. Hey, why don't you give me another peg?'

I hastily refill his glass. 'So how did you get your brother's hair and a button from his shirt?'

'Simple. I visited him for a day in Mumbai, stayed at his house and pulled a button from a shirt he had just put in the laundry basket. Then I found the barber he used and bribed him to give me a lock of his hair the next time he had a haircut. I told him I needed it for an offering to Lord Venkateshwara in Tirupathi.

'So within a month I got Julie both the button and the hair. What Julie did next was amazing. She took a male doll made of cloth with all kinds of funny black lines on it. She stitched the button over the doll's chest and stuck the hair on the doll's head. Next she killed a rooster and drained all its blood in a pan. She dipped the doll's head in the rooster's blood. She then took it into her room, uttered various incantations and applied strange-looking herbs and roots to the doll. Then she took out a black pin and said, "The voodoo doll is ready. I have infused it with your brother's spirit. Now, whatever you do to the doll with this black pin will happen to your brother in Mumbai. For instance, if I press this pin on the doll's head, your brother will have a splitting headache. And if I stick it deeply into the button, your brother will have severe chest pain. Here, try it." I thought she was joking, but just to humour her I pressed the black pin into the white button on the doll's chest. Within two hours I received a call from Mumbai to say that Arvind had had a minor heart attack and had been admitted to Breach Candy Hospital.'

'My God! That's amazing,' I cry.

'Yes. You can imagine my shock. Not because

Arvind had had a heart attack, but because now I knew that Julie had indeed created a black-magic voodoo doll.

'Over the next two months, the doll became a little secret toy for me. I poured all my frustration, all my latent resentment against my brother into it. I took a perverse pleasure in causing him pain and suffering. It became a source of demented amusement for me. I would take the doll to Mumbai and watch Arvind squirm on his lawn while I gently teased the button on the doll with the black pin. Gradually I started employing the doll on occasions when others were also present. I took it with me to a five-star hotel where Arvind was entertaining some Japanese clients. I sat unobtrusively at a corner table. I heard my brother speaking. ". . . Yes, Mr Harada, we do have plans to open a subsidiary in Japan, but the response from Nippon Button Company has not been very positive. We are also—" Suddenly I inserted the black pin into the doll's head. "Owwwwwwww!" my brother screamed and caught his head with both hands. His foreign clients left without having dinner.

'I took the doll to a family wedding in Bangalore to which I had been invited with my brother. Just when Arvind was about to bless the bride and groom, I used the black pin. "May God bless both of owwwwwwwwwwwwww!" he screamed, and head-butted the groom to the chagrin of all the guests. Many people commiserated with me that evening, saying how sorry they were that Arvind was slowly going mad.

'I took the doll to a function where my brother was

to receive an award for best entrepreneur. Arvind was giving his acceptance speech with the gleaming crystal trophy in his hands. "Friends, I feel really very honoured to be holding this beautiful trophy. All my life I have believed in the motto that hard work and owwwwwwwwwwwwwwwww!" The glass trophy slipped from his hands and broke into a million pieces.

'Arvind went to a doctor, who did an MRI scan and found nothing physically wrong with his head. The doctor advised him to consult a psychiatrist.

'Finally, I took the doll to the annual shareholders' meeting, and sat in the very last row. Arvind was giving the MD's report. "And my dear shareholders, I am happy to report that our company's performance in the last quarter represented a significant increase in our gross owwwwwwwwwwwwwwwwwwwwwww!" There was utter pandemonium thereafter, with the agitated shareholders demanding an immediate resignation from the mad MD. He was forced to resign within a week. I became the new MD and my brother was locked up in a mental institution.

'My brother remained in the mental asylum for two years. During this time I became wealthy beyond my imagination. Julie finally had everything she had ever wanted. She summoned her mother and brother from Port-au-Prince to come and live with us in Mumbai. But as I acquired all the trappings of a rich man, I also started contemplating my life, the means I had adopted to gain all this wealth. And then I met Jyotsna.'

'Who's she?'

'Officially she's just my new secretary, but actually she is much more than that. She is my soul-mate. I have so much in common with her that I will never have in common with a foreigner like Julie. She's the exact antithesis of Julie. It is Jyotsna who made me realize the terrible injustice I had done to my elder brother. I resolved to get Arvind out of the mental asylum.'

'So were you able to get him out?'

'No. It was too late. They tortured my brother in the asylum, gave him electric shocks. Two weeks ago, he died.'

'What?'

'Yes. My poor brother is dead,' he wails. 'My dear brother is dead.' He holds his head in his hands. 'And I killed him.'

I snap out of my stupor. Mr Rao is rapidly degenerating from an ass into a dog.

'That bitch Julie, I will now expose her. I will throw her fat mother out of the house and get rid of her good-for-nothing brother. I will kill her mean cat and I will kick Julie out of Mumbai. Let her rot in hell in Haiti. Ha!'

'But how do you plan to do this?'

There is a sly glint in his eye. 'You are my friend, and I am drunk. A drunken man always tells the truth. So I should tell you that I have already met a lawyer and drawn up the divorce papers. If Julie accepts it, well and good, otherwise I have something else as well. See.' He takes out an object from his trouser pocket. It is a small, snub-nosed revolver, very compact, no bigger than my fist. The metal is smooth and shiny with no markings at all. 'Look at this beauty. I am going to use this to blow her head off. Then I will marry Jyotsna. You are my friend. I am drunk. And a drunken man always speaks the owwwwwwwwwwwwwwwwwwwwwwwwwwwww!!!' He suddenly screams in agony, clutches at his heart and crashes face-down on the table, upturning the bottle of single malt and scattering cashew nuts all over the floor.

Looks like I have missed out on my tip once again.

The police jeep with the flashing red light arrives after half an hour. An ambulance comes with a doctor in a white coat, who pronounces Prakash Rao dead owing to a massive heart attack. They go through his pockets. They discover a wallet full of banknotes, a picture of a beautiful Indian girl, a sheaf of papers saying 'Divorce'. They do not find any gun. In any case, dead men don't need guns.

Smita is looking at me with an amused expression on her face. 'You don't expect me to believe this mumbo-jumbo nonsense, do you?'

'I make no judgement. I merely related to you what was told me by Prakash Rao. What I heard, what I saw.'

'Surely there can be no truth in such things?'

'Well, all I can say is that at times truth is stranger than fiction.'

'I cannot believe that Rao was killed by someone pricking a voodoo doll. I think you made up this story.'

'Fine, don't believe in the story, but then how do you explain my answer to the next question?'

Smita presses 'Play'.

Prem Kumar taps his desk. 'Ladies and gentlemen, we now move on to our next question, question number six for one lakh rupees. This is the perennial favourite in all quiz shows. Yes. I am talking about countries and capitals. Mr Thomas, how familiar are you with capital cities? For example, do you know the capital of India?'

The audience titters. They are prepared to believe that a waiter might not even know the capital of his country.

'New Delhi.'

'Very good. And what is the capital of the United States of America?'

'New York.'

Prem Kumar laughs. 'No. That is not correct. OK, what is the capital of France?'

'I don't know.'

'And the capital of Japan?'

'I don't know.'

'How about the capital of Italy. Do you know that?'

'No.'

'Well, then I don't see how you can answer the next question without making use of one of your Lifeboats. So here comes question number six for a hundred thousand rupees. What is the capital of Papua New Guinea? Is it a) Port Louis, b) Port-au-Prince, c) Port Moresby or d) Port Adelaide?'

The suspenseful music commences.

'Do you have any clue at all, Mr Thomas, about this question?'

'Yes, I know which are the incorrect answers.'

'You do?' Prem Kumar says incredulously. The members of the audience begin whispering amongst themselves.

'Yes. I know it is not Port-au-Prince, which is the capital of Haiti, or Port Louis, which is in Mauritius. And it is also not Port Adelaide, because Adelaide is in Australia. So it has to be C. Port Moresby.'

'This is amazing. Are you absolutely, one hundred per cent sure?'

'Yes, I am.'

There is a crescendo of drums. The correct answer flashes.

'Absolutely, one hundred per cent correct! It is Port Moresby. You have just won a hundred thousand rupees, you are now a *lakhpati*!' declares Prem Kumar. The audience stand up and cheer. Prem Kumar wipes more sweat from his brow. 'I swear the way you are giving these answers, it's almost like magic.'

Smita laughs. 'It's not magic, you idiot,' she tells Prem Kumar on the screen. 'It's voodoo!' Suddenly her eyes dart down to something lying on the bedroom carpet. She bends to pick it up. It is a small button with four slits. The type used on shirts. She looks at my shirt. The third button is indeed missing. She hands it to me. 'Here. Better hold on to your buttons.'

200,000

MURDER ON THE WESTERN EXPRESS

New Delhi's Paharganj railway station is humming with sound and crawling with people. The grey platforms are bathed in white light. Train engines belch smoke and whistle like impatient bulls.

If you were to search for me in this crowded maze, where would you look? You would probably try to find me among the dozens of street children stretched out on the smooth concrete floor in various stages of rest and slumber. You might even imagine me as an adolescent hawker, peddling plastic bottles containing tap water from the station's toilet as pure Himalayan aqua minerale. You could visualize me as one of the sweepers in dirty shirt and torn pants shuffling across the platform, with a long swishing broom transferring dirt from the pavement on to the track. Or you could look for me among the regiments of red-uniformed

173

porters bustling about with heavy loads on their heads.

Well, think again, because I am neither hawker, nor porter, nor sweeper. Today I am a bona fide passenger, travelling to Mumbai, in the sleeper class, no less, and with a proper reservation. I am wearing a starched white bush shirt made of one hundred per cent cotton and Levi jeans – yes, Levi jeans, bought from the Tibetan Market. I am walking purposefully towards platform number five to board the Paschim Express for Mumbai. There is a porter trudging along by my side carrying a light-brown suitcase on his head. The porter has been hired by me and the suitcase on his head belongs to me. It contains a few clothes, some old toys, a bunch of *Australian Geographic* magazines and an electronic game for Salim. The suitcase does not contain any money. I have heard too many stories about robbers on trains who drug you at night and make off with your belongings to take the chance of keeping the most precious cargo of my life in the suitcase – my salary from the Taylors. The manila envelope full of crisp thousand-rupee notes – fifty of them – is therefore with me, hidden in a place where no one can see it. Inside my underwear. I have used the remaining two thousand to finance the trip. From it I have paid for my clothes, my ticket and the game for Salim, and now I will pay the porter and buy some food and drink. I take a quick look at the loose notes in my front pocket. I reckon I will have just enough to take an auto-rickshaw from Bandra Terminus to Salim's chawl in Ghatkopar. Won't Salim be surprised to see me arrive in a three-wheeler instead of the local train?

And when he sees the game, I hope he doesn't faint from happiness.

Platform number five is more crowded than Super Bazaar. Hawkers are out in as much force as touts outside a government office. Passengers hunt for their names on the reservation chart with the same fervour as students scanning examination results. I find that the railway department has completely mangled my name, making it T. M. Ram. I am happy, nevertheless, to see that I have been allotted lower berth three in coach S7.

The coach is almost at the end of the long train, and the porter is tired and sweating by the time we enter it. I settle down on my designated berth, which is right next to the door, and arrange the suitcase neatly in the space underneath. I pay the porter twenty rupees. He argues for more, points out the long distance from the station's entrance to the coach, and I tip him a further two rupees. Having disposed of the porter, I survey the scene around me.

My cabin has a total of six berths. One above me, two in front of me and two on the side. Sitting on the lower berth opposite me is a family of four, a father, mother and two children – a boy, around my age, and a girl, slightly older. The father is a middle-aged Marwari businessman dressed in the trademark black waistcoat and black cap. He has bushy eyebrows, a pencil moustache, and a stern expression on his face. His wife is of a similar age and is equally grim looking. She wears a green sari and a yellow blouse and looks at me with suspicious eyes. The boy is tall and gangly and looks friendly, but it is the girl sitting next to the window who draws my attention like a magnet. She is thin and fair, wearing a blue salwar kameez with the *chunni* pulled down over her chest. Her expressive eyes are lined with kohl. She has a flawless complexion and lovely lips. She is the most beautiful girl I have seen in a long time. One who demands a second look. And a third. I think I can lose myself in those bewitching eyes of hers. But before I can reflect on her beauty any further, my attention is distracted by a baby who starts crying loudly. It is a baby boy, just a few months old, sitting on the side berth in his mother's lap. The mother is a young, morose-looking woman wearing a crumpled red sari. It looks as if she is travelling alone. She tries to calm the baby with a rubber pacifier, but the baby continues to wail. Finally she pushes up her blouse and offers a breast to the baby's lips. He suckles contentedly and she rocks him to sleep. From my seat I glimpse the underside of her plump brown breast and it makes my mouth dry, till I catch the Marwari businessman looking directly at me and I shift my eyes to the window behind her.

A tea vendor enters the compartment. I am the only one who asks for a cup. He dishes out tepid tea in an earthen receptacle, which tastes vaguely of mud. He is followed by a newspaper boy. The businessman purchases a copy of the *Times of India*. His son buys an *Archie* comic. I buy the latest issue of *Starburst* from my fast-dwindling change.

The train gives a final whistle and begins to move off, an hour and a half behind schedule. I glance at my watch, even though I can clearly see 18:30 displayed on the platform's digital clock. I shake and twist my wrist, hoping that the others, particularly the girl, will notice that I am wearing a brand new Kasio digital watch, made in Japan, with day and date, which cost me a whopping two hundred rupees in Palika Bazaar.

The father immerses himself in the newspaper, the son in his comic. The mother starts making arrangements for the family's dinner. The other young mother has gone off to sleep, the baby still glued to her breast. I pretend to read the film magazine. It is open at the centrefold, which displays the latest sex symbol, Poonam Singh, in a bikini, but I have no interest in her vital assets. I keep casting furtive glances at the girl, who is looking abstractedly at the urban scenery rushing past the window. She doesn't look at me even once.

At eight pm a black-waistcoated ticket examiner enters the compartment. He asks for all our tickets. I whip mine out with a flourish, but he doesn't even read it. He simply punches it and returns it to me. As soon as he has gone, the mother opens up rectangular cardboard boxes containing food. Lots of it. I see shrivelled *puris*, yellow potatoes, red pickles and dessert. The mouth-watering aroma of home-made *gulab jamuns* and *barfees* fills the compartment. I am beginning to feel hungry too, but the pantry boy has still not come to take orders for dinner. Perhaps I should have picked up something from the station.

The Marwari family eats heartily. The father gobbles *puri* after *puri*. The mother polishes off the golden-yellow potatoes, taking a juicy chilli pickle after each bite. The boy makes a beeline for the soft *gulab jamuns* and even slurps up the sugary syrup. Only the girl eats lightly. I lick my lips in silence. Strangely enough, the boy offers me a couple of *puris*, but I decline politely. I have heard many stories of robbers disguised as passengers who offer drug-laced food to their fellow travellers and then make off with their money. And there is no reason why boys who read *Archie* comics cannot be robbers. Though if the girl had offered me food I might – no, I would – have accepted.

After finishing dinner, the boy and girl start playing a board game called *Monopoly*. The father and mother sit side by side and chat. They discuss the latest soaps on TV, something about buying property and travelling to Goa for a holiday.

I pat my abdomen gently where fifty thousand rupees in crisp new notes nestle inside the waistband of my underwear, and feel the power of all that money seep insidiously into my stomach, my intestines, my liver, lungs, heart and brain. The hunger gnawing at my stomach disappears miraculously.

Looking at the typical middle-class family scene in front of me, I don't feel like an interloper any more. I am no longer an outsider peeping into their exotic world, but an insider who can relate to them as an equal, talk to them in their own language. Like them, I too can now watch middle-class soaps, play Nintendo and visit Kids Mart at weekends.

Train journeys are about possibilities. They denote a change in state. When you arrive, you are no longer the same person who departed. You can make new friends en route, or find old enemies; you may get diarrhoea from eating stale samosas or cholera from drinking contaminated water. And, dare I say it, you might even discover love. Sitting in berth number three of coach S7 of train 2926A, with fifty thousand rupees tucked inside my underwear, the tantalizing possibility which tickled my senses and thrilled my heart was that I might, just might, be about to fall in love with a beautiful traveller in a blue salwar kameez. And when I say love, I don't mean the unrequited, unequal love that we profess for movie stars and celebrities. I mean real, practical, possible love. Love which does not end in tears on the pillow, but which can fructify into marriage. And kids. And family holidays in Goa.

I had only fifty thousand rupees, but every rupee had a technicolour dream written on it and they stretched out on a cinemascope screen in my brain to become fifty million. I held my breath and wished for that moment to last as long as it possibly could, because a waking dream is always more fleeting than a sleeping one.

After a while, the brother and sister tire of their board game. The boy comes and sits next to me. We begin talking. I learn that his name is Akshay and his sister is Meenakshi. They live in Delhi and are going to Mumbai to attend an uncle's wedding. Akshay is excited about his Playstation 2 and his computer games. He asks me about MTV and surfing the Internet and mentions some porn sites. I tell him that I speak English, read *Australian Geographic*, play *Scrabble* and have seven girlfriends, three of them foreign. I tell him that I have a Playstation 3 console and a Pentium 5 computer and I surf the Internet day and night. I tell him that I am going to Mumbai to meet my best friend,

Salim, and I will be taking a taxi from Bandra Terminus to Ghatkopar.

I should have known that it is more difficult to fool a sixteen-year-old than a sixty-year-old. Akshay sees through my deception. 'Ha! You don't know anything about computers. Playstation 3 hasn't even been released. You are just a big liar,' he mocks me.

I cannot resist it. 'Oh, so you think it is all a big lie, eh? Well, Mr Akshay, let me tell you that right here, right now, I have fifty thousand rupees in my pocket. Have you ever seen so much money in your life?'

Akshay refuses to believe me. He challenges me to show the money, and the prospect of impressing him is too tempting for me. I turn around, push my hand into my pants and bring out the manila envelope, slightly damp and smelling of urine. I surreptitiously take out the sheaf of crisp thousand-rupee notes and flutter them before him triumphantly. Then I quickly put them back and deposit the envelope in its former resting place.

You should have seen Akshay's eyes. They literally popped out of their sockets. It was a victory to be savoured for eternity. For the first time in my life, I had something more tangible than a dream to back up a claim. And for the first time in my life, I saw something new reflected in the eyes that saw me. Respect. It taught me a very valuable lesson. That dreams have power only over your own mind. But with money you can have power over the minds of others. And once again it made the fifty thousand inside my underwear feel like fifty million.

* * *

It is ten pm now and everybody is about to turn in for the night. Akshay's mother pulls out bed linen from a green holdall and begins preparing the four berths her family will use. The young mother with the baby is sleeping on the side berth, without worrying about pillows and bed sheets. I don't have bedding and I am not that sleepy, so I sit next to the window and feel the cold wind caress my face, watching the train tunnel through the darkness. The lower berth directly opposite me is taken by Akshay's mother, the upper by Meenakshi. The father climbs up on the berth above me and Akshay takes the upper berth on the side, above the mother and child.

The father goes to sleep straight away – I can hear him snoring. The mother turns on her side and pulls up her sheet. I crane my neck to catch a glimpse of Meenakshi, but I can only see her right hand, with a gold bangle on her wrist. Suddenly she sits up in bed and bends down in my direction to drop her shoes. Her *chunni* has slipped and I can clearly see the top of her breasts through the V neck of her blue kameez. The sight sends an involuntary shiver of pleasure down my back. I think she catches me watching her, because she quickly adjusts her *chunni* over her chest and gives me a disapproving look.

After a while I, too, drift off to sleep, dreaming middle-class dreams of buying a million different things, including a red Ferrari and a beautiful bride in a blue salwar kameez. All with fifty thousand rupees.

I am woken up by something prodding my stomach. I open my eyes and find a swarthy man with a thick black moustache jabbing at me with a thin wooden stick. It is not the stick which bothers me. It is the gun in his right hand, which is pointed at no one in particular. 'This is a dacoity,' he declares calmly, in the same tone as someone saying, 'Today is Wednesday.' He wears a white shirt and black trousers and has long hair. He is young and looks like a street Romeo or a college student. But then I have never seen a dacoit outside a movie hall. Perhaps they look like college students. He speaks again. 'I want all of you to climb down from your berths, slowly. If no one tries to act like a hero, no one will get hurt. Don't try to run, because my partner has the other door covered. If all of you cooperate, this will be over in just ten minutes.'

Akshay, Meenakshi and their father are prodded similarly and made to climb down from their berths. They are groggy and disoriented. When you are woken up suddenly in the middle of the night, the brain takes some time to respond.

We are all sitting on the lower berths now. Akshay and his father sit next to me, and Meenakshi, her mother and the woman with the baby sit opposite us. The baby is getting cranky again and begins to cry. The mother tries to soothe it but the baby begins crying even more loudly. 'Give her your milk,' the dacoit tells her gruffly. The mother is flustered. She pushes up her blouse, and instead of one, exposes both breasts. The dacoit grins at her and makes a show of grabbing one of her breasts. She screams and hastily covers it. The dacoit laughs. I don't get titillated this time. A loaded gun pointed at your head is more riveting than an exposed breast.

Now that the dacoit has everyone's undivided attention, he gets down to business. He holds aloft a brown gunny sack in his left hand, with the gun in his right. 'OK, now I want you to hand over all your valuables. Put them in this sack. I want the men to hand me their wallets and watches and any cash in their pockets, the ladies to hand me their purses, bangles and gold chains. If there is anyone who does not comply with my instructions, I will shoot him dead instantly.' Meenakshi's mother and the young mother scream simultaneously when they hear this. We hear cries coming from the far side of the compartment. The dacoit's partner is, presumably, issuing similar instructions to passengers on his side.

The dacoit takes round the open sack to all of us one by one. He starts with the mother and child. With a terrified expression she takes her brown leather purse, opens it quickly to remove a pacifier and a bottle of milk, then drops the bag into the sack. Her baby, whose breastfeeding has been interrupted momentarily, begins wailing again. Meenakshi looks stunned. She takes off her gold bangle, but as she is about to put it in the sack, the dacoit drops the sack and grabs her wrist. 'You are much more beautiful than a bangle, my darling,' he says as Meenakshi desperately tries to escape the man's vice-like grip. The dacoit lets go of her wrist and makes a grab for her kameez. He catches her shirt by the collar, she pulls back, and in the process the shirt almost tears in half, exposing her bra. We all watch, horrified. Meenakshi's father can take it no longer. 'You bastard!' he cries and tries to punch the dacoit, but the man has panther-like reflexes. He releases Meenakshi's shirt and hits her father with the butt of his pistol. A deep gash opens up instantly on the businessman's forehead, from which blood starts oozing out. Meenakshi's mother starts screaming again.

'Shut up,' the dacoit growls, 'or I will kill all of you.'

These words have a sobering impact and we all become absolutely still. A lump of fear forms in my throat and my hands become cold. I listen to everyone's laboured breathing. Meenakshi sobs quietly. Her mother drops her bangles and her purse into the sack, her father puts in his watch and his wallet with shaky fingers, Akshay asks whether he should put in the *Archie* comic. This infuriates the dacoit. 'You think this is a joke?' he hisses and slaps the boy. Akshay yelps in pain and begins nursing his cheek. For some reason I find the exchange rather funny, like a comic interlude in a horror film. The dacoit berates me. 'What are you grinning at? And what have you got?' he snaps. I take out the remaining notes and change from my front pocket and drop them in the sack, leaving only my lucky one-rupee coin. I begin to unfasten my wristwatch, but the dacoit looks at it and says, 'That is a fake. I don't want it.' He appears to be satisfied with the haul from our cabin and is about to move on when Akshay calls out, 'Wait, you have forgotten something.'

I watch the scene unfold as if in slow motion. The dacoit whirls around. Akshay points at me and says, 'This boy has got fifty thousand rupees!' He says it softly, but it seems to me the entire train has heard it.

The dacoit looks menacingly at Akshay. 'Is this another joke?'

'N-no,' says Akshay. 'I swear.'

The dacoit looks underneath my berth. 'Is it in this brown suitcase?'

'No, he has hidden it in his underwear, in a packet,' Akshay replies, smirking.

'Ah ha!' the dacoit exhales.

I am trembling – I don't know whether from fear or anger. The dacoit approaches me. 'Will you give me the money quietly or should I make you strip in front of all these people?' he asks.

'No! This is my money!' I cry, and instinctively protect my crotch like a footballer blocking a free kick. 'I have earned it. I will not give it to you. I don't even know your name.'

The dacoit gives a raucous laugh. 'Don't you know what dacoits do? We take money which doesn't belong to us, from people who don't even know our name. Now are you giving me the packet or should I pull down your pants and take it out myself?' He waves the pistol in my face.

Like a defeated warrior, I surrender before the might of the gun. I slowly insert my fingers into the waistband of my pants and pull out the manila envelope, sticky with sweat and smelling of humiliation. The dacoit grabs it from my hand and opens it. He whistles when he sees the crisp new thousand-rupee notes. 'Where the fuck did you get all this money from?' he asks me. 'You must have stolen it from somewhere. Anyway, I don't care.' He drops it in the gunny sack. 'Now none of you move while I meet the other folks in your compartment.'

I just stare dumbly and watch fifty million dreams being snatched away from me, dumped into a brown gunny sack where they jostle with middle-class bangles and wallets.

The dacoit has moved on to the next section of the compartment, but none of us dares to pull the emergency cord. We remain rooted to our seats, like mourners at a funeral. He returns after ten minutes with the sack on his back, its mouth tied, the gun in his right hand. 'Good,' he says, hefting the sack to show us it is full and heavy. He looks at me and grins, like a bully who has just snatched someone's toy. Then he looks at Meenakshi. She has covered her front with her *chunni*, but through the gauzy fabric the white cloth of her bra is visible. He smacks his lips.

The dacoit's partner shouts, 'I am ready. Are you ready?'

'Yes,' calls our dacoit in reply. The train suddenly begins to slow down.

'Hurry!' The other dacoit jumps down from the train.

'I am coming in a second. Here, take the sack.' Our dacoit sends the sack – and fifty million dreams – spinning out of the door. He is about to jump down, but changes his mind at the last second. He comes back to our cabin. 'Quick, give me a goodbye kiss,' he tells Meenakshi, waving the gun at her. Meenakshi is terrified. She cowers in her seat.

'You don't want to give me a kiss? OK, then take off your *chunni*. Let me see your breasts,' he orders. He holds the gun with both hands and snarls at

Meenakshi. 'Last warning. Quick, show me some skin or I'll blow your head off before I leave.' Meenakshi's father closes his eyes. Her mother faints.

Sobbing and weeping, Meenakshi begins to unfurl her *chunni*. Underneath will only be a piece of white fabric. With two straps and two cups.

But I am not seeing this happening. I am seeing a tall woman with flowing hair. The wind is howling behind her, making her jet-black hair fly across her face, obscuring it. She is wearing a white sari whose thin fabric flutters and vibrates like a kite. She holds a baby in her arms. A man with long hair and a thick moustache, wearing black trousers and a white shirt approaches her. He points a gun at her and grins. 'Open your sari,' he barks. The woman begins to cry. Lightning flashes. Dust scatters. Leaves fly. The baby suddenly jumps from the mother's lap and leaps at the man, clawing at his face. The man shrieks and pulls the baby away, but the baby lunges at his face again. The man and the baby roll on the ground while the woman in the sari wails in the background. The man twists his hand and points his gun at the baby's face, but today the baby is blessed with superhuman powers. With tiny fingers he pushes at the barrel of the gun, reversing its direction. Man and baby wrestle again, going left and right, rolling on the ground. They are locked in a death struggle. At times the man gains the upper hand and at times the baby appears to be winning. The man finally manages to free his gun-carrying arm. His fingers curl round the trigger. The baby's chest is directly in front of the barrel. The man is about to press the trigger, but at the last moment the baby manages to twist the gun away from himself and towards the man's own chest. There is a deafening explosion and the man rears back as if hit by a powerful blast. A scarlet stain appears on his white shirt.

'Oh, my God!' I hear Akshay's voice, like an echo in a cave. The dacoit is lying on the floor, inches from the door, and I have a pistol in my hand, from which a thin plume of smoke is drifting upwards. The train is beginning to gather speed.

I have still not quite understood what has happened. When you are woken up suddenly in the middle of a dream, the brain takes some time to respond. But if you have a smoking gun in your hand and a dead man at your feet, there is little room for misunderstanding. The dacoit's shirt is suffused with blood, the stain darkening and expanding all the time. It is not like they show you in the movies, where a bullet produces an instant little red patch and it remains like that till they cart away the body in an ambulance. No. The blood doesn't even come out at first. It begins to seep out very gradually. First there is a tiny red dot, no bigger than a thumbtack, then it becomes a circular patch the size of a coin, then it grows as large as a saucer, then it expands to the size of a dinner plate, and it just keeps growing and growing till the flow becomes a torrent. I begin gasping for breath and the whole compartment is about to drown in a red river when Akshay's father shakes my shoulders violently. 'Snap out of it, I say!' he shouts, and the redness lifts.

I sit on my berth with a crowd of people around me. Virtually the entire compartment has come to see what has happened. Men, women and children crane forward. They see a dead dacoit, whose name nobody knows, lying on the ground with a dark-red patch on his white shirt, a father with a gash on his forehead, a terrified mother from whose breasts every drop of milk has been squeezed by a famished baby, a brother who will never read *Archie* comics on a train again, a sister who will have nightmares for the rest of her life. And a street boy who, for a brief moment, had some money, and who will never have middle-class dreams again.

The yellow light in the cabin seems unusually harsh. I blink repeatedly and hold the gun limply in my hands. It is small and compact with a silver metallic body and a black grip. It says 'Colt' in chiselled letters and has a picture of a jumping horse on either side of the inscription. I flip it over. On the other side of the muzzle it says 'Lightweight', but it feels ridiculously heavy. The pistol has some letters and numbers engraved on it which have become faded. I make out 'Conn USA' and 'DR 24691'.

Meenakshi glances at me furtively. She looks at me like Salim looks at film stars. I know that at this moment she is in love with me. If I propose to her now, she will marry me. Happily have my children. Even without the fifty thousand. But I don't return her glances because everything has changed. I look only at the pistol in my hand and the face of the dead dacoit, whose name I don't know.

He could have died in any number of ways. He could have been shot dead in the middle of a crowded market in a police encounter. He could have been butchered by a rival gang as he sipped tea at a roadside stall. He could have died in hospital from cholera, cancer or AIDS. But no, he did not die from any of these. He died from a bullet fired by me. And I didn't even know his name.

Train journeys are all about possibilities. But a hole in the heart has a certain finality to it. There is no more travelling for a dead body. Perhaps to a funeral pyre, but it will definitely not meet any more hawkers or ticket examiners. I, however, am likely to encounter not just hawkers and ticket examiners, but also the police. How will they treat me? As a hero who protected the modesty of a girl and rid the world of a notorious dacoit, or as a cold-blooded killer who shot dead a man without even knowing his name? I know only one thing: I cannot gamble on finding out. And then Colonel Taylor's words crash into my consciousness like a bolt from the sky. 'CYTLYT, Confuse Your Trail, Lose Your Tail.' I know exactly what I have to do.

Just as the train is about to pull into the next station, where, without doubt, a posse of policemen will be waiting for me, I leap out of the door with the gun still in my hand. I race across the track and jump into another train which is about to steam away from the platform. I don't sit in any compartment; just hang out at the door. As the train passes over a cantilever bridge, I send the gun spinning into the dark river. Then, as the train comes to a stop at the next station, I hop out and find another train going somewhere else. I do this the entire night, moving from station to station, train to train.

Cities go by in a blur. I don't know whether I am travelling north or south, east or west. I don't even know the names of the trains. I just keep changing them. The only thing I know for certain is that I cannot go to Mumbai. Akshay might have told the police about Salim and they could arrest me in Ghatkopar. I also don't want to get off at a dingy, deserted station and attract needless attention. I wait for a station with plenty of light, sound and people.

At nine o'clock in the morning, the train I am travelling in steams on to a bustling, crowded platform. I alight wearing a hundred-per-cent-cotton bush shirt which is torn and has three buttons missing, Levi jeans which are caked with soot and grime, and a fake digital watch. This city seems like a good place to hole up for a while. I see a big yellow board at the edge of the platform bearing its name. It proclaims in bold black letters: 'AGRA. Height above mean sea level 169 metres.'

Smita holds her hand over her mouth. 'Oh, my God,' she says. 'So all these years you have been living with the guilt of having killed a man?'

'Two men. Don't forget how I pushed Shantaram,' I reply.

'But what happened in the train was an accident. And you could even justify it on the grounds of self-defence. Anyway, I'll first find out whether a case was even registered. I don't think the other passengers would have wanted to implicate you. You rescued them, after all. By the way, what happened to that girl, Meenakshi? Did you see her again?'

'No. Never. Now let's return to the show.'

In the studio, the lights have been dimmed again.

Prem Kumar turns to me. 'We now move on to question number seven for two hundred thousand rupees. Are you ready?'

'Ready,' I reply.

'OK. Here is question number seven. Who invented the revolver? Was it a) Samuel Colt, b) Bruce Browning, c) Dan Wesson, or d) James Revolver?'

The music commences. I go into deep thought.

'Have you heard any of these names?' Prem asks me.

'One of them sounds familiar.'

'So do you want to withdraw or would you like to take a chance?'

'I think I will take a chance.'

'Think again. You might lose the one lakh rupees you have won up to now.'

'I have nothing to lose. I am ready to play.'

'OK. So what is your final answer?'

'A. Colt.'

'Are you absolutely, one hundred per cent sure?'

'Yes.'

There is a crescendo of drums. The correct answer flashes.

'Absolutely, one hundred per cent correct! It was indeed Samuel Colt who invented the revolver in 1835. You have just doubled your winnings to two lakh rupees!'

I can't believe it. I have won back my fifty thousand rupees with three times interest. Thanks to a swarthy dacoit, whose name I didn't know.

There are 'oohs' and 'aahs' from the audience. The signature tune is repeated, but the only sound reverberating in my ears is the relentless piston movement of a train travelling from Delhi to Mumbai, via Agra.

Prem Kumar suddenly leaps out of his chair to shake my hand, but finds it limp and unresponsive. If you are taken by surprise in the middle of a game show, the brain takes some time to respond.

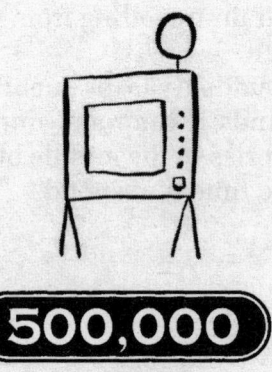

500,000

A Soldier's Tale

Like clockwork, the air-raid warning siren wails at precisely eight-thirty in the evening, leading to frenzied activity in the chawl. Residents follow the instructions which were announced by loudspeaker the whole of last week in anticipation of an outbreak of hostilities. Switch off all the lights, disconnect all gadgets, turn off the gas, close the house, make an orderly file and proceed to the bunker.

The bunker is beneath the school building. It is a large, rectangular hall with subdued lighting. It has a faded and dusty red carpet on the floor, and the only furniture consists of a couple of rickety chairs and an old metal table, on which stands a fourteen-inch television set. The bunker feels hot, suffocating and claustrophobic, but it is for our protection, so we cannot really complain. Though there are rumours that the one in Pali Hill has a thirty-two-inch TV, Dunlopillo cushions and air conditioning.

The residents gather in front of the television set, which is tuned to the news channel. I look around the hall. Almost the entire chawl is here. The Gokhales, the Nenes, the Bapats, Mr Wagle, Mr Kulkarni, Mrs Damle, Mr Shirke, Mrs Barwe ... Only Mr Ramakrishna the administrator is missing. He must be busy counting his rent receipts and fixing fused bulbs, leaking taps, broken railings.

First there are the advertisements. This war is sponsored by Mother India Toothpaste and Jolly Tea. Then we have a broadcast by the Prime Minister. Indian forces are winning the war, he tells us earnestly, and it is only a matter of days before the enemy surrenders completely. This war will be a fight to the finish, he says in a high-pitched voice. There will be an end to terrorism. And hunger. And poverty. Contribute generously to the Soldiers' Benefit Fund, he urges us.

After the Prime Minister's speech, a young actress comes on TV and says the same things, but in filmi style. The women gawk at the actress. How young she looks, they say, and how beautiful. Is her sari silk or chiffon, they ask each other. How does she manage to keep her skin so soft? Which soap does she use? She is so fair. She doesn't need Fair and Lovely cream.

The men are full of anger. Those bastards have caused enough problems for us, they say. Enough is enough. This time we should destroy Pakistan completely.

Mr Wagle is the resident expert on the war. A

lecturer at the University, he is the most educated person in our chawl. Pakistan has missiles and atom bombs, he tells us. That is why we are in this bunker – so that we are protected from radiation. But there is no real protection against the atom bomb. When the bomb falls, he says, the water will become air. The air will become fire. The sun will disappear. A huge mushroom cloud will rise in the sky. And we will all die, he concludes solemnly.

But death is difficult to visualize when you are a twelve-year-old like me and Putul or ten like Salim and Dhyanesh and this is your first war. We are full of enthusiasm and curiosity. We camp before the television set, mesmerized by the images of battle.

We don't know and don't care about radiation. We are interested in more important things. Such as:

How much noise does an atom bomb make?

Can we see jets flying over our houses?

Will it be like Diwali?

Wouldn't it be nice if a missile landed next to our chawl?

It is the third night of the war. Our life in the bunker is falling into a predictable pattern. The women have begun to bring their vegetables and knitting to the hall. They sit in a group, chop tomatoes and potatoes, make sweaters, separate chaff from lentils, extract healthy leaves from spinach and coriander bunches, and exchange the latest gossip. Do you know Mrs Goswami has bought a new twenty-five-inch TV? Heaven knows where her husband gets all his money from! Looks like Mr Bapat and his wife had a big fight the other night.

Practically the entire neighbourhood could hear it! Have you seen the latest *Starburst*? It says Armaan Ali might be gay!

The men listen intently to the news and discuss the latest rumours. Is it true that a state of emergency is about to be declared? They say Pathankot has been completely destroyed by bombing. Many civilians have died. Mehta has reliable information, straight from the Ministry, that petrol is to be rationed. Onions and tomatoes have virtually disappeared from the market. Better start hoarding milk.

We youngsters have our own gang. We run around the large hall shouting and screaming and trip over each other, much to the consternation of the women. We play I Spy till we tire of it. Then Putul invents a new game. It's called, appropriately enough, War and Peace. The game is quite simple. We divide ourselves into two teams, one led by an Indian General and the other by a Pakistani General. The two teams have to tag each other. Whoever is caught first becomes a prisoner of war and can only be released in exchange for another prisoner from the opposite team. Tagging the General counts for two prisoners. The team with the largest number of captured prisoners wins the game. There is only one problem: no one wants to be the Pakistani General. Eventually they get hold of Salim. 'You are Muslim,' they tell him, 'so you become Pakistani.' Salim doesn't agree at first, but is bought off with the promise of two packs of bubblegum. I join Salim's team and we thrash the Indians.

After all our games are played, we gather in a corner, resting from our physical exertion, and discuss the war.

'I love this war,' I say. 'It's so exciting. And my employer Neelima Kumari has given me the week off, because of the curfew.'

'Yes,' says Putul. 'My school has also been closed for a week.'

'I wish we had a war every month,' says Dhyanesh.

'Stop this nonsense, I say!' a man thunders behind our backs.

We turn around in alarm to see an old Sikh on crutches standing behind us. He is thin and tall, with a small, whiskery moustache on a weather-beaten face. He wears an olive-green turban to match his army uniform with lots of pockets and a big belt. He looks at us sternly and raises a finger accusingly. 'How dare you trivialize a war? War is a very serious business. It takes lives.'

Only then do we notice that he has a leg missing.

We learn that he is Lance Naik (retd) Balwant Singh. That he recently moved into our chawl, that he lives alone, and that he lost his leg in combat.

Having disciplined us, Balwant Singh hobbles forward on his crutches and sits down in the chair directly in front of the TV set.

The television is broadcasting live pictures of the war. The screen is cloaked in a hazy green light. We are shown a rocket launcher with a rocket loaded in it. A soldier presses a button and the rocket shoots off in a blaze of fire. After half a minute, we see a flash of greenish-yellow light far away in the distance and the sound of an explosion. 'We have hit the target perfectly,' declares an army officer standing next to the rocket launcher. He grins. His teeth seem unnaturally green. Within ten seconds another rocket is launched. The reporter turns around and says right into the camera, 'This was our live and exclusive coverage of the war in the Rajasthan sector. I am Sunil Vyas of Star News, embedded with 5th Division, returning you back to the studio.' We are not told what the target was, whether it was hit, how many people died in the attack, and how many survived. A famous singer comes on and begins singing old patriotic songs with gusto.

Lance Naik (retd) Balwant Singh gets up from his chair. 'This is not a real war,' he says in disgust. 'It is a joke. They are showing you a soap opera.'

Mr Wagle is not amused. 'Well, what is a real war, then?' he asks.

Balwant looks at Wagle with a soldier's contempt for a civilian. 'A real war is very different from this children's film. A real war has blood and guts. A real war has dead bodies and hands chopped off by enemy bayonets and legs blown off by shrapnel.'

'Which war did you fight in?' asks Mr Wagle.

'I fought in the last real war, the one in 1971,' Balwant Singh says proudly.

'Then why don't you tell us what a real war feels like?' says Mrs Damle.

'Yes, tell us, Uncle,' we clamour.

Balwant Singh sits down. 'You really want to know what a real war feels like? OK, then I will tell you my story. Of those fourteen glorious days when we won our most famous victory over Pakistan.'

We cluster around the old soldier like wide-eyed children before their grandfather.

Balwant Singh begins speaking. His eyes acquire that dreamy, far-off look people get when speaking of things long past. 'I will now take you back to 1971. To the most fateful period in the history of the Indian nation.'

A hush falls over the audience in the bunker. Mr Wagle turns down the volume on the TV set. No one protests. The second-hand live report on TV is no match for the first-hand account of a real soldier.

'The last real war began on the third of December, 1971. I remember the date well because on the very day that war was declared, I received a letter from Pathankot, from my beloved wife, informing me that she had given birth to a baby boy, our first child. My wife wrote in her letter, "You are not with me, but I know you are fighting for your motherland, and this fills my heart with pride and joy. I will pray for your safety and, together with your son, I will wait for your victorious return."

'I cried when I read that letter, but these were tears of happiness. I was not crying because I was far away from my family at such a time. I was happy that I was going into battle with the blessings of my wife and fortified by the arrival of my newborn son.'

'What did she name your son?' asks Mrs Damle.

'Well, we had decided long before the birth that if it was a girl we would call her Durga, and if it was a boy we would name him Sher Singh. So Sher Singh it was.'

'How did the war begin?' asks Mr Shirke.

'On the night of December the third there was a new moon. Under cover of darkness, the cowardly enemy launched pre-emptive air strikes on a number of our airfields along the western sector – Srinagar, Avantipur, Pathankot, Uttarlai, Jodhpur, Ambala, Agra – all were strafed. The air strikes were followed by a massive attack on the strategic Chhamb sector in the north.'

'And where were you posted when war broke out?' asks Mr Wagle.

'Right there in Chhamb, with 13th Infantry Division. I belong to the Sikh Regiment and my battalion – 35 Sikh – was deployed at Chhamb in the middle of a brigade group. Now you must understand why Pakistan attacked us in Chhamb. Chhamb is not just a village on the west bank of the river Munawar Tawi. It is also the lifeline to the districts of Akhnoor and Jaurian. You capture Chhamb and you pose a threat to the entire state.

'So that night Pakistan launched a three-pronged attack against us. They came in with a heavy artillery barrage. Guns and mortar. The firing was so intense that in just a few hours nearly all our bunkers were badly damaged and three of our border patrols had been taken out.

'I was in command of a forward post with three men when the attack started. My post was attacked by the enemy in vastly superior strength. You must remember that we had only three battalions across the Munawar Tawi, which faced a division of Pakistani infantry, the 23rd Infantry Division, with a brigade of armour, about one hundred and fifty tanks, and about nine to ten regiments of artillery. Pakistan had more artillery in Chhamb than in the whole of the Eastern Front.

'The three men under me at that time were Sukhvinder Singh from Patiala, Rajeshwar from Hoshiarpur and Karnail Singh from Ludhiana. Karnail was the best of the lot, a tall, muscular man with a booming voice and an infectious smile. He had no fear of war. He had no fear of death. But there was one fear that nagged him each and every day.'

'And what was that?' asks Mr Kulkarni.

'The fear of being buried. You see, we had heard that these Pakistanis, if they found the dead bodies of any Indian soldiers, would never return them to us. Instead, they would deliberately bury them according to Muslim tradition, even if the Indian soldiers were Hindu. Karnail was a God-fearing and devout man, and he was terrified that if he died in battle, his body would be buried six feet under the ground instead of being cremated. "Promise me, Sir," he said to me a week before the war started, "that you will ensure that I am cremated properly if I die. Otherwise my soul will never find peace and will be forced to roam the depths of the netherworld for another thirty-six thousand years." I tried to reassure him, telling him he was not going to die, but he was adamant. So, simply to stop his nagging, I told him, "OK, Karnail, if you die, I promise I will have you cremated with full Hindu rites."

'So, on the night of December the third, we were in a forward bunker – Karnail, Sukhvinder, Rajeshwar and me – when the firing started . . .'

He is interrupted by Putul. 'Uncle, did your bunker have a TV, like ours?'

The soldier laughs. 'No, my son. Our bunker was not

as luxurious. It didn't have a carpet or a TV. It was small and cramped. Only four people could crawl into it. It was infested with mosquitoes and sometimes even snakes would come to visit us.'

Balwant's tone becomes more serious. 'Now I don't know whether any of you is familiar with the topography of Chhamb. It is a flat area, but is known for its grey stones and the *sarkanda* – elephant grass – so tall and thick it can camouflage a tank. Through this thick grass, the enemy came at us under cover of darkness. Before we knew it, mortars were exploding to our left and right. It was pitch dark and I could not see a thing. A grenade was launched at our bunker, but we were able to scramble out before it exploded. As we ventured out of the bunker, a spray of automatic fire from a light machine gun greeted our every step. Quietly, we began advancing on foot, walking in a straight line, trying to determine the source of the firing. We made good headway and had almost reached the Pakistani bunker from where the firing was being directed, when a mortar bomb exploded just behind me. Before I knew it, Sukhvinder and Rajeshwar were dead and Karnail was bleeding from a shrapnel wound to his stomach. I was the only one to escape with superficial injuries. I quickly informed my company commander of the casualties. I also told him that there was an LMG position which was belching deadly fire from the enemy bunker and that if it was not stopped it would cause heavy damage to the company. My CO told me that he could not spare another sub-unit, and asked me to somehow neutralize the LMG position.

' "I am going towards the enemy bunker," I told Karnail. "You provide covering fire for me."

'But Karnail blocked my way. "This is a suicide mission, Sir," he told me.

' "I know, Karnail," I replied, "But someone has got to do it."

' "Then let me do it, Sir," Karnail said. "I volunteer to neutralize the enemy machine gun." Then he told me, "Saab, you have a wife. You have just been blessed with a son. I have no one in my family. No one behind me. No one in front. I might already be dying from this wound. Let me go and do something in the service of my motherland. But don't forget your promise, Sir." And before I could even utter a word, he snatched the rifle from my hand and rushed forward. *"Bharat Mata ki Jai* – Long Live Mother India," he shouted and charged the enemy bunker, bayoneting three enemy soldiers to death and silencing the LMG. But as he stood with the gun in his hands, he received another fatal burst of rifle fire in his chest, and before my eyes he toppled to the ground, with the gun still in his hand.'

The hall goes very quiet as we try to visualize the violent scene of battle. The sound of gunfire and mortar seems to echo around the room. Balwant continues.

'I stood rooted to the same spot for close to two hours. I was under instruction to return to the company, but the promise that I had made to Karnail kept ringing in my ears. His body was now lying in enemy territory and I had no idea how many Pakistani soldiers were still around. I was the only one left in my section.

'By three am the firing stopped completely and there was a deathly silence. A sudden gust of wind rustled the trees nearby. I inched towards the Pakistani bunker, no more than two hundred feet away. Suddenly, in front of me, I heard the sound of muffled footsteps. I strained to hear over the pounding of my heart as I raised my rifle. I cocked it, ready to fire, but hoping that I wouldn't have to use it. Firing in the darkness produces a bright muzzle flash that would betray my position to the enemy. I tried to suppress even the sound of my own breathing. Something thin and slippery crawled over my back. It felt like a snake. I had a desperate urge to shake it off, but fear of alerting the enemy made me close my eyes and hope that it would not bite me. After what seemed like an eternity, it slithered down my leg and I heaved a sigh of relief. My back was drenched in sweat and my arms were aching. My rifle felt as if it was made of lead. The footsteps started again, coming closer and closer. I peered into the darkness, trying to decipher the outline of the enemy, but could see nothing. I knew that death was lurking close by. I would either kill or be killed. A twig crunched and I could even detect faint breathing. It was an agonizing wait. I debated whether I should fire or wait for the enemy to make the first move. Suddenly, I saw the flare of a match and the back of a head floated into view, like a disembodied ghost, not more than ten feet away. I immediately leapt out of the grass and rushed forward with open bayonet. It was a Pakistani soldier, about to urinate. I had almost knocked him down when he turned around, dropped his rifle and pleaded with me with clasped hands, "Please don't kill me. I beg you."

' "How many of you are still in the area?" I asked him.

' "I don't know. I got detached from my unit. I was just trying to go back. Please, I beg you, don't kill me," he cried.

' "Why shouldn't I kill you?" I demanded. "After all, you are the enemy."

' "But I am also a human being, like you," he said. The colour of my blood is the same as yours. I have a wife who is waiting for me in Mirpur. And a baby girl who was born only ten days ago. I don't want to die without even seeing her face."

'I softened on hearing this. "I also have a wife, and a baby son whose face I have not seen as yet," I told the enemy soldier. Then I asked him, "What would you have done in my position?" He went quiet for a while, then he replied haltingly, "I would have killed you."

' "See," I told him, "we are soldiers. We have to be true to our profession. But I promise you this. I will have your body properly buried," and then, without blinking an eyelid, I pushed my bayonet through his heart.'

'Ugh . . . *chi chi* . . .' Mrs Damle closes her eyes in disgust.

Mr Shirke is also unnerved. 'You really don't have to be so graphic,' he tells Balwant as he tries in vain to cover Putul's ears with his palms. 'All this killing and blood, I worry my son may start having nightmares.'

Balwant snorts. 'Ha! War is not for the squeamish. In fact, it is good for these youngsters to understand what it is all about. They should know that war is a very serious business. It takes lives.'

'What happened afterwards?' asks Mr Wagle.

'Nothing much. I went to the enemy bunker, where the bodies of the three Pakistani soldiers were lying alongside Karnail. I picked him up and trudged back to my company base with his body over my shoulders. The next morning we cremated him.' Balwant's eyes are wet with tears. 'I told the CO about Karnail's supreme act of bravery, and on his recommendation Karnail Singh was awarded a posthumous MVC.'

'What's an MVC?' asks Dhyanesh.

'Maha Vir Chakra. It is one of the highest military honours in our country,' replies Balwant.

'And which is the highest?'

'The PVC or the Param Vir Chakra. It is almost always given posthumously.'

'Which award did you get?' Dhyanesh asks again.

There is a pained expression on Balwant's face. 'I didn't get any for this operation. But this is not the end of my story. I still have to tell you about the famous battle of Mandiala Bridge.'

Mr Wagle looks at his watch. 'Oh, my God, it is past midnight. *Chalo chalo*, I think we have had enough excitement for the day. The curfew is over. We should now return to our houses.'

Reluctantly, we disperse.

The next day, we are in the bunker again. Today Mr Bapat's son Ajay is here too. He must have returned from his grandmother's place. He is a big show-off, always boasting about his toys, his computer, his skates, and his numerous girlfriends. We all hate him, but keep it to ourselves. We don't want to quarrel with a fifteen-year-old who looks seventeen. Today he has got a little diary. He calls it an autograph book. He is showing the other children some scribbles. 'This is Amitabh Bachchan, this is Armaan Ali, that one is Raveena's, this one is the famous batsman Sachin Malvankar's signature.'

'And what about this one?' asks Dhyanesh. He points to a dark squiggle which is completely indecipherable. Ajay thinks about it, and then says sheepishly, 'This is my mother's. She was testing the pen.'

Putul is carrying something with him too, but it is not an autograph book. It is a writing book. His dad has told him that no school does not mean no studies. Now every day he will have to sit in the bunker and write essays. Today's topic is: 'My cow', even though Putul doesn't have a cow.

On the TV, a military spokesman is giving a briefing. 'Pakistani air strikes against Indian air bases in Ambala, Gorakhpur and Gwalior were successfully neutralized. Indian forces have taken Baghla and Rahimyar Khan. Pakistani forward bases at Bhawalpur, Sukkur and Nawabshah have been completely destroyed and the Shakargarh bulge is under our control. In Chhamb sector, our soldiers have repulsed a massive Pakistani attack to take the Mandiala Bridge.'

We cheer wildly. There is a lot of clapping and shaking of hands.

Balwant Singh is sitting, as before, in front of the TV.

'So they have attacked Mandiala again,' he says with a shake of the head. 'These Pakis never learn from their mistakes.'

It seems to me that Balwant is waiting for someone to ask him about the Mandiala Bridge, but no one takes the bait.

The TV programme changes to a studio debate. Some experts are discussing the war. A bearded man with glasses is saying, 'We all know Pakistan has close to forty nuclear warheads. Just one fifteen-kiloton fission bomb explosion over an urban area with a population density of about 25,000 per square kilometre is sufficient to kill about 250,000 people. Now if you extrapolate this data to Mumbai, where –'

Mr Wagle says, 'The water will become air. The air will become fire. A mushroom cloud will burst into the sky. We will all die.'

Mr Kulkarni switches off the TV. 'This is too depressing,' he says. 'Why don't we listen instead to the inspiring story of our war hero. Balwantji, you were mentioning the battle of Mandiala Bridge yesterday. Please tell us about it.'

Balwant perks up, stretches his arms and hitches up the sleeves. He scratches the stump of his leg, swivels his chair around to face the group, and begins.

'There is a very high escarpment across the Munawar Tawi called Mandiala North. This is where the enemy attacked on the nights of the third and fourth of December, and because we had virtually no troops holding that particular feature, our posts were overwhelmed. Then the Pakis began moving forward with both tanks and infantry towards Mandiala

Crossing where I was deployed with 35 Sikh, alongside 19 Para Commando.

'By then we had understood that the key objective of Pakistan's 23rd Division was to capture Mandiala Bridge. Once that happened, we would be forced to abandon Chhamb and all the area west of Tawi. So by midday on the fourth of December we had begun fortifying our position. 31 Cavalry was reinforced by one squadron of the 27th Armoured Regiment, and 37 Kumaon were despatched from Akhnoor to launch a counter-attack to recapture Mandiala North. But tragedy struck when the CO of 37 Kumaon was killed instantly by Pakistani artillery shelling before he could join us. So the battalion was rendered leaderless and reached Tawi only after last light. It was therefore diverted to the east bank, overlooking Mandiala Crossing. And so when night fell only 35 Sikh and the para company of 19 Commando were guarding Mandiala Crossing, together with the tank troops of 31 Cavalry, who were holding Mandiala South.

'Two Pakistan battalions – 6 POK and 13 POK – launched a ferocious attack across Tawi at around 0300 hours on December the fifth. They came in with their American Patton tanks and Chinese T-59s, guns booming. Jets from the Pakistani Air Force screamed overhead, strafing the area, dropping thousand-pound bombs on our positions. I saw vehicles burning everywhere, shells exploding, and tanks moving towards us like giant steel insects in the tall elephant grass. The artillery firing was so heavy that within fifty minutes it had gone through the entire depth of our positions. 13 POK ran into our 29 Jat unit and dispersed it. As they advanced, they captured Point 303 after killing the CO. Defence of this feature was also entrusted to 35 Sikh, but unfortunately some of my compatriots did not respond to the call of duty. They just fled in the face of a sustained barrage by enemy artillery. Having secured Point 303, the Pakistanis ordered their reserves to move forward and consolidate the bridge-head. By first light, they had overrun Mandiala Bridge. It appeared that only a miracle could save us now. Can someone get me a glass of water?'

Balwant Singh is an accomplished storyteller. He emphasizes the right words, pauses at the right places and asks for a glass of water at the perfect time, just when the suspense is getting unbearable.

Someone hastily brings him a Styrofoam cup filled with water. We crane forward. Balwant resumes after taking a gulp of water.

'It was at this point that the Commander of 368 Brigade personally joined us from Akhnoor. When he arrived he saw a scene of utter destruction and con-fusion. Soldiers were running hell for leather from the scene of battle. The ground had become a cratered wasteland, scarred with dead bodies, rubble and the burning wreckage of our tanks. There were fires raging everywhere. The waters of the Tawi had turned scarlet with the blood of soldiers. It was total pandemonium. Not like they show you on TV, where you press a button, you launch a rocket and then sip tea.

'The CO, who knew me, said, "Balwant Singh, what is happening? Where have all our men disappeared to?" And I answered him with a heavy heart, "I am sorry to report, Sir, that many have deserted the scene of battle and fled to safety. They could not withstand the overwhelming force deployed by the enemy." We had lost three tanks and many men.

'The CO said, "If we all start thinking like this, how will we win this war?" Then he sighed. "I think this situation is hopeless. We should retreat."

'I immediately protested. "Sirjee," I said, "the motto of our regiment is *Nischey Kar Apni Jeet Karon* – I Fight For Sure to Win. I will never give up without a fight."

'"That's the spirit, Balwant." The CO thumped me on the back and told me to rally the remaining men. My platoon commander had also deserted, so the CO put me in charge of the platoon. Our battalion was given the task of moving forward immediately to recapture the bridge. The Delta company of Gurkha Rifles was also ready for assault, together with the remaining tanks of 31 Cavalry.

'The morning erupted in cannon and machine-gun fire. Mandiala Crossing became an inferno, a cauldron of fire, concussion and explosion. With sniper bullets whizzing past our heads, machine guns spewing out continuous and deadly fire, enemy aircraft wailing overhead and bombs crashing all around us, we charged from our position with fixed bayonets, shouting the Sikh battle cry, "*Bole So Nihal, Sat Sri Akal.*" We fell upon the advancing enemy and bayoneted many to death in bloody hand-to-hand fighting. This bold action completely demoralized the enemy. The tide began to turn in our favour. We started pushing the enemy back.

'At that point, the enemy decided to bring their

tanks across the Tawi river. So far, they had remained on the other side. The moment they crossed the bridge and came over to our side, we would have been completely exposed. It was essential that we stop them from crossing the bridge. Now our T-55 tanks belonging to 31 Cavalry and the 27th Armoured Regiment came into action. At first our tanks withstood the enemy onslaught well, but when the Pakistani Patton tanks began rolling across the bridge, two of our chaps abandoned their tanks and ran away.

'I don't know what came over me. I just ran towards one of the abandoned tanks, opened the hatch and slipped inside. I knew about tanks, but I had never driven one before. Still, it took me only a couple of minutes to figure out the controls and very soon I had put the T55 into motion. As my tank started up, it came under heavy fire from the enemy concealed in bunkers. So I moved my tank towards the enemy trench. They thought I would give up in the face of their sustained firing, but I kept moving relentlessly towards the bunker, till they jumped out and fled. One of them tried to clamber on to my tank. I immediately put the turret on power traverse, swung the 100 mm rifled gun around and knocked him away like a fly from milk. Meanwhile, our other tanks had begun targeting the enemy, and within twenty minutes only one enemy Patton tank was left. I chased it as it tried to get away. My tank received a direct hit from it and went up in flames. But my gun was still functioning. I kept chasing the Patton and shot at it, barely fifty yards from my position. The enemy tank stopped suddenly and reeled backwards, its turret spinning around like a drunken man. Finally it stopped turning and the tank burst into a ball of flame. I got on to the Bravo-I set to my CO and said, "Eight enemy tanks destroyed, Sir. Situation under control."

'Mandiala Bridge was now almost within our grasp. The enemy had scattered. Its tanks were destroyed, but there were still isolated pockets of resistance. The enemy had sited some machine guns and rocket launchers around the bridge which were still active. And, most important of all, the Pakistani flag was still flying atop the bridge. I had to tear it down. Dazed by concussion and ripped and bloodied from shards of flying metal, I began inching towards the Pakistani bunker. All around me, I saw corpses in the churned and muddy ground. I kept on moving forward and advanced to within ten yards of the enemy bunker, which was ringed by a tangle of barbed wire. I then lobbed a smoke grenade into the bunker and three Pakistani soldiers tumbled out, dead and bleeding. There was only one soldier remaining. As I raised my rifle to shoot him, I realized suddenly that it had jammed. The enemy soldier also saw this. He smiled, raised his gun and pressed the trigger. A hail of bullets hit my left leg, and I fell to the ground. He pointed the gun at my heart and pressed the trigger again. I said my prayers and prepared to die. But instead of a deafening blast, there was just a hollow click. His magazine had finished. *"Narai Takbir – Allah O Akbar!"* he shouted and rushed at me with naked bayonet. I met him shouting, *"Jai Hind"* and neatly side-stepped his charge. I then clubbed him to death with the butt of my rifle. Finally, I leapt at the enemy flag, tore it down and replaced it with the tricolour. When I saw our flag fluttering atop Mandiala Bridge, it was the happiest moment of my life, though I knew I had lost one leg.'

Balwant Singh stops speaking, and we see that his eyes are drenched in tears.

Nobody stirs for almost a minute. Then Putul goes up to Balwant Singh and holds out his exercise book.

The soldier wipes his eyes. '*Arrey*, what is this? I cannot do your maths homework for you.'

'I don't want you to do my homework,' says Putul.

'Then what is this book for?'

'I want your autograph. You are our hero.'

Everyone claps.

Dhyanesh raises the same question again. 'So which award did they give you for this battle?'

Balwant goes silent, as if we have touched a raw nerve. Then he says bitterly, 'Nothing. They gave out two MVCs and two PVCs to 35 Sikh. Three of my colleagues got Sena medals and a memorial was constructed in Jaurian. But they didn't give me anything, not even a mention in despatch. There was no recognition of my valour.'

He lets out a sigh. 'But not to worry. I take satisfaction when I see the flame burning over Amar Jyoti, the memorial to the Unknown Soldier. I feel it burns for people like me.' Turning philosophical, he recites a poem in Urdu: 'Unheralded we came into this world. Unheralded we will go out. But while we are in this world, we do such deeds that even if this generation does not remember, the next generation cannot forget.'

Everyone goes quiet again. Suddenly, Mrs Damle

begins singing, '*Sare jahan se achcha Hindustan hamara . . .*' Pretty soon everyone else joins in singing the patriotic song. I don't know what comes over us youngsters, but we organize a spontaneous march past. We form a single line and file past Balwant Singh, our right fists clenched tightly in a gesture of salute to this brave soldier.

This was our war. He was our hero.

Balwant Singh is so overcome with emotion, he starts crying. '*Jai Hind!*' he shouts, and shuffles out of the room, leaving us alone with the rustle of elephant grass, the sound of exploding bombs, the acrid smell of cordite, and the stench of death.

Mr Wagle comes to the dais and makes an announcement. 'Dear friends, I have the honour of informing you that tomorrow we are being visited by a team from the Soldiers' Benefit Fund, SBF for short. Our beloved Prime Minister has made an appeal to all Indians to contribute generously for the benefit of our soldiers, who sacrifice their lives so that we may live in freedom with honour and dignity. I hope all of you will dig deep into your pockets to help the SBF.'

'But what about the soldier in our own midst? Shouldn't we do something to help him as well?' Mr Shirke shouts.

There are cries of 'Hear! Hear!'

'Yes, you are absolutely right. But I think the biggest service we can do to Balwantji is to get his achievements in the 1971 war recognized. We will give a memorandum to the people from the SBF who come here tomorrow.'

We are all excited. It looks as if finally we are also contributing to the war effort.

There are three of them who come. A tall man, a short man and a fat man. All three are ex-officers; the tall one is from the navy, the short one is from the army and the fat man is from the air force. The short man gives a long speech. He tells us that our soldiers are doing a great job. Our country is great. Our Prime Minister is great. We are great. And our donations should also be great. They pass around a basket. People put money in it. Some put five rupees, some ten, some one hundred. One of the ladies puts in her gold bangles. Salim doesn't have any money. He puts in two packets of bubblegum. Balwant Singh is not present. He has sent word that he has a touch of flu.

Then the inquisition starts. 'Did you fight in any war yourself?' Kulkarni asks the army man, a retired Colonel.

'Yes, of course. I saw action in two great wars, '65 and '71.'

'And where did you serve during the 1971 war?'

'In Chhamb, which perhaps saw the greatest battles.'

'And which was your regiment?'

'I am from Infantry. The great Sikh Regiment.'

'Did you get any medals during the 1971 war?'

'Well, as a matter of fact, I got a Vir Chakra. It was a great honour.'

'What did you get this great honour for?'

'For the great battle of Mandiala Crossing, in which 35 Sikh did a great job.'

'What kind of person are you? You take medals yourself and deny others, without whose support you would never have regained that bridge.'

'I am sorry, I don't understand. Who are you referring to?'

'We are talking about our own soldier, who was a hero during the 1971 war at Chhamb, who lost a limb. Who should have got a Param Vir Chakra, but only got tears. Look, Colonel Sahib, we are civilians. We don't know about your army rules and regulations, but a grave injustice has been done here. Can you see whether something can be done even now? It is never too late to honour brave soldiers.'

'Where is this great soul?'

'He is right here in our chawl.'

'Really? That's great. I would love to pay my respects to him.'

So we escort him to Balwant Singh's room. We point out his door and watch as the Colonel goes in. We loiter around, unable to resist prying.

We hear loud voices, like an argument. Then a banging sound. After ten minutes or so, the Colonel comes rushing out, seething with anger. 'Is this the man you were complaining didn't get a PVC? He is the greatest scoundrel I have ever seen. I wish I could wring the swine's neck here and now.'

'How dare you talk about our war hero like this!' admonishes Mrs Damle.

'He, a war hero? That's the greatest joke in the world. He is a bloody deserter. Ran away at the first sight of trouble in the Chhamb sector. I tell you, he is a bloody blot on Sikh Regiment. He should have had

218

fourteen years' Rigorous Imprisonment. Unfortunately, desertion cases are closed after five years, otherwise I would have reported him even now.'

We are astounded. 'What are you saying, Colonel? He recounted to us in great detail his exploits at Chhamb. He even lost a leg in combat.'

'That's a complete lie. Let me tell you his true story, which is actually quite pathetic.' The Colonel adjusts his belt. 'Balwant Singh was not in a good frame of mind when war broke out, because his wife had just given birth to his first child in Pathankot. He was desperate to be with his family. So great was his longing that at the first sign of trouble in Jaurian, when Pakistan attacked with artillery in full strength, he deserted his post and ran away. He managed to reach Pathankot and hid in his ancestral house. He must have thought he had left the war far behind, but the war did not leave him. Two days after his arrival, the Pakistani Air Force strafed Pathankot air base. They didn't hit any of our planes, but two thousand-pound bombs fell on a house close to the airfield. Turned out that the house was Balwant's. His wife and infant son perished instantly in the attack and he lost a leg to shrapnel.'

'But . . . how could he re-create the scene of battle in such great detail?'

The Colonel grimaces. 'I don't know what stories he told you, but twenty-six years is a long time to read up on great battles. The bastard crawled out of the woodwork after all these years just to fool you people and earn some cheap thrills through his fake tales of valour. Meeting him has spoiled my mood completely. It has not been a great day. Goodbye.'

The Colonel shakes his head and walks away from the chawl, flanked by the tall man and the fat man. We return to the bunker. It has not been a great day for us, either. We wonder what Balwant Singh is doing. He does not come out that evening.

They find him the next morning, in his one-room lodging in the chawl. A can of milk and a newspaper lie untouched on his doorstep. His crutches are stacked neatly against the wall. The wooden bed has been pushed into a corner. There is an empty cup on the nightstand containing a residue of brown tea leaves. The only chair in the room lies upturned in the centre. He hangs from the ceiling fan with a pink piece of cloth tied to his neck, wearing the same olive-green uniform, his head bowed over his chest. As his limp body swings gently from side to side, the ceiling fan makes a faint creaking noise.

A police jeep arrives, its red light flashing. Constables rummage through his belongings. They chatter and gesticulate and question the neighbours rudely. A photographer takes pictures with a flash-gun. A doctor in a white coat arrives with an ambulance. A big crowd gathers in front of Balwant's room.

They wheel out his body on a stretcher, covered in a crisp white sheet. The residents of the chawl stand in hushed silence. Putul and Dhyanesh and Salim and I peer diffidently from behind their backs. We stare opaquely at the dead man's body and nod, in fear and sorrow and guilt, as a liquid understanding spreads slowly through our numbed minds. Those of us for whom this was our first war, we knew then. That war was a very serious business. It took lives.

Smita is looking grim and serious.

'Where were you during the war?' I ask.

'Right here, in Mumbai,' she replies and hurriedly changes the topic. 'Let's see the next question.'

Prem Kumar swivels on his chair and addresses me. 'Mr Thomas, you have answered seven questions correctly to win two lakh rupees. Now let us see whether you can answer the eighth question, for five hundred thousand rupees. Are you ready?'

'Ready,' I reply.

'OK. Question number eight. Which is the highest award for gallantry given to the Indian armed forces? I repeat, which is the highest award for gallantry given to the Indian armed forces? Is it a) Maha Vir Chakra, b) Param Vir Chakra, c) Shaurya Chakra or d) Ashok Chakra?'

The suspenseful music commences. The time bomb starts ticking louder.

There is a buzz in the audience. They look at me with sympathy, preparing to bid goodbye to the friendly neighbourhood waiter.

'B. Param Vir Chakra,' I reply.

Prem Kumar raises his eyebrows. 'Do you know the answer, or are you just guessing?'

'I know the answer.'

'Are you absolutely, one hundred per cent sure?'

'Yes.'

The drumming reaches a crescendo. The correct answer flashes.

'Absolutely, one hundred per cent correct!' shouts Prem Kumar. The audience is exultant. There is sustained clapping and cries of 'Bravo!'

I smile. Prem Kumar doesn't.

Smita nods her head in understanding.

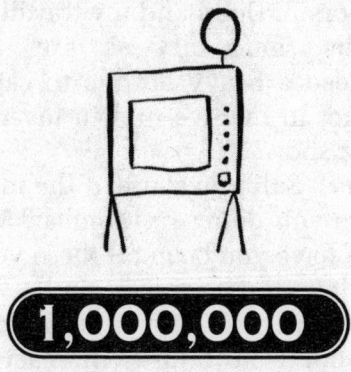

1,000,000

LICENCE TO KILL

There are many hazards of walking in an absent-minded manner on the roads of Mumbai. You can inadvertently slip on a banana peel and go skidding. You can find that without warning your foot has sunk into a pile of soft dog shit. You can be rudely jolted by a wayward cow coming from behind and butting into your backside. Or a long-lost friend you had been avoiding meeting can emerge miraculously from the chaotic traffic and suddenly hug you.

That is what happened to me on Saturday 17 June, in front of Mahalaxmi Racecourse, when I bumped into Salim Ilyasi. After five years.

When I first arrived in Mumbai from Agra three months ago, I had resolved not to contact Salim. It was a difficult decision. I had missed him during my years with the Taylors in Delhi and my travails in Agra, and to be in the same city as him and not see him was indeed a heavy burden to carry. But I was determined not to involve him in my plan of getting on to the quiz show.

'Mohammad!' Salim exclaimed the moment he saw me. 'What are you doing in Mumbai? When did you come? Where have you been all these years?'

Meeting a long-lost friend is similar, I suppose, to eating a favourite dish after a long time. You don't know how your taste buds will react after all this while, whether the dish will still taste as good as it used to. I met Salim after five long years with mixed emotions. Would our reunion be as warm as our friendship used to be? Would we still be as honest with each other?

We didn't speak much at first, but sat down on a nearby bench. We didn't listen to the squawking of the seagulls circling overhead. We took no notice of the little boys playing football on the road. We didn't see the throng of devotees going to the Haji Ali *dargah*. We just hugged each other and wept. For the times we had spent together, for the time we had lost. And then we talked about all that had happened in between. Rather, Salim talked and I listened.

Salim has become taller and more handsome. At sixteen, he looks as good as any Bollywood film star. The hard life of the city has not corrupted him like it corrupted me. He still loves Hindi films and worships the stars of Bollywood (with the obvious exception of Armaan Ali). He still goes to the shrine of Haji Ali every Friday to offer prayers. And, most importantly, the prediction of the palmist is finally about to come true. He no longer works as a *dabbawallah*, delivering tiffins to Mumbai's middle class, but has enrolled himself in an expensive acting school where he is learning to become an actor.

'Do you know who is paying for my acting classes?' he asks me.

'No.'

'It is Abbas Rizvi.'

'The famous producer who has made all those blockbusters?'

'Yes, the same. He has offered me the role of a hero in his next film, which will be launched in two years' time, when I have turned eighteen. Till then he is getting me trained.'

'But that's wonderful, Salim. How did all this happen?'

'It is a very long story.'

'No story can be long enough for me, Salim. Quick, now, tell me from the beginning.'

So this is the story narrated by Salim, in his own words.

'After you went away so suddenly, I was left all alone in the chawl. I continued with my life as a *dabbawallah* for four more years, collecting and delivering tiffins, but I also continued to dream of becoming an actor.

'One day, while I was collecting a tiffin from the wife of a customer called Mukesh Rawal, I noticed that the walls of his house were decorated with pictures of himself with famous film stars. I asked Mrs Rawal whether her husband was in the film industry. She said he was just a sales officer in a pharmaceutical company, but worked in films part-time, as a junior artist.

'I was amazed to hear this. I rushed to Mukesh Rawal's office the same afternoon and asked him if I too could become a junior artist like him. Mukesh looked at me and laughed. He said I was too young to become an actor, but that sometimes they had roles for schoolboys and street kids, for which I might be right. He promised to refer me to Pappu Master, the junior-artist supplier for whom he worked, and asked me to provide him with several glossy eight-by-six photographs of myself in a variety of poses. If Pappu liked my photos, he might choose me for a bit role in a film. Mukesh told me that for a junior artist, acting skills were not required, but I had to look smart in a suit, menacing in a ruffian's outfit and charming in a school uniform. He insisted that I get the photos professionally taken at a studio.

'That night I couldn't sleep. I went to a photographer's shop the very next morning and enquired about the cost of the pictures. The photographer quoted me an astronomical sum, almost equal to my full month's earnings. I told him, "*Arrey baba*, I can't afford so much money." So he advised me to buy one of those cheap, disposable cameras and take my own pictures, which he could then blow up. I did as he told me. I bought a camera and requested passers-by to take my picture. I sat on somebody's motorcycle in front of Churchgate and tried to look as cool as

Amitabh Bachchan in the film *Muqaddar ka Sikandar*. I posed sitting on a horse on Chowpatty Beach, just like Akshay Kumar in *Khel*. I stood in front of Sun 'n' Sand hotel, posing like Hrithik Roshan in *Kaho Na Pyar Hai*. I held an empty Johnny Walker bottle in my hands and tried to look as drunk as Shahrukh Khan in *Devdas*. I grinned in front of Flora Fountain like Govinda does in all his films. I got almost twenty pictures taken of myself, but the roll took thirty-six and I had to finish it before I could get the pictures developed. So I decided to take pictures of interesting buildings and people. I took pictures of Victoria Terminus and the Gateway of India, I clicked a beautiful girl in Marine Drive, snapped an old man in Bandra and even took a close-up of a donkey in Colaba. My final picture was of a swarthy, middle-aged man in Mahim sitting on a bench and smoking. His fingers were adorned with different-coloured rings. Only after I had pressed the shutter button did I realize whose picture I had taken, and I froze.'

'What do you mean?' I ask Salim. 'Was he a famous film star? Was it that swine Armaan Ali?'

'No, Mohammad, it was a man you know equally well. It was Mr Babu Pillai, alias Maman. The man who brought us here from Delhi and almost blinded us.'

'Oh, my God!' I cover my mouth. 'Did he recognize you?'

'Yes, he did. "You are Salim, aren't you? You are the boy who ran away from me. But you won't get away from me this time," he cried and lunged at me.

'I didn't even think. I just turned around and ran

towards the main road. A bus was pulling away and I jumped on it just in time, leaving Maman panting behind me on the road.

'I was sitting on the bus, thinking what a lucky escape I'd had, when guess what happened?'

'What?'

'The bus stopped at a traffic light and a group of ruffians wearing head bands and armed with swords, spears and tridents got on.'

'Oh, my God! Don't tell me it was a mob.'

'Yes, it was. I realized then that we had landed in the middle of a communal riot. The wreckage of a smouldering vehicle lay directly in front of us. Shops had been reduced to rubble, splashes of blood could be seen on the pavement, stones, sticks and slippers littered the street. The driver immediately bolted from the bus. My mind went numb with fear. I had thought I would never have to see such a horrifying sight again. I heard sounds which I thought I had forgotten. My mother's shrieks and my brother's cries echoed in my ears. I began shivering. The ruffians told everyone on the bus that a Muslim mob had set fire to Hindu houses and now they were out for revenge. I learnt later that the whole trouble had started over a simple quibble about a water tap in a slum. But people's minds were so full of hate that within hours buses were being burnt, houses were being torched and people were being butchered.

' "Each one of you say your name. All those who are Hindu are allowed to step down from the bus, all those who are Muslim should keep sitting,' the ruffians announced. One by one the trembling passengers said their names. Arvind. Usha. Jatin. Arun. Vasanti. Jagdish. Narmada. Ganga. Milind. The bus started emptying. The ruffians watched each of the passengers with hawk-like eyes. They checked the vermilion in the partings of the ladies' hair, asked some of the men further questions to establish their religion, and even forced a little boy to open his shorts. I was nauseated by this barbaric display, but was also quivering in my seat. Finally, only two passengers were left on the bus: me and a man sitting two seats behind me.

'You know, Mohammad, in films when such a scene happens, the hero stands up and appeals to the humanity of the mob. He tells them that the blood of both Hindus and Muslims is the same colour. That it doesn't say on our face which religion we belong to. That love is preferable to hate. I knew so many dialogues, any of which I could have recited before those ruffians, but when you actually stand face to face with such savagery, you forget all words. You only think of one thing. Life. I wanted to live, because I had to fulfil my dream of becoming an actor. And now the dream and the dreamer were both going to be set ablaze in a Mumbai bus.

' "What is your name?" the leader asked me.

'I could have said Ram or Krishna, but I became tongue-tied. One of the attackers pointed to the *tabeez* around my neck. "This bastard is definitely a Muslim, let's kill him," he urged.

' "No. Killing him would be too easy. We will burn this motherfucker alive in this bus. Then he and his community will learn never to touch our homes," said the leader, and laughed. Another man opened a can of

229

petrol and started sprinkling it inside the bus. I used to love the smell of petrol, but since that day I associate it with burning flesh.

'The man sitting two rows behind me stood up suddenly. "You have not asked for my name. Let me tell you. It is Ahmed Khan. And I want to see the bastard who will touch this boy," he said.

'There was momentary silence from the ruffians, before their leader spoke. "Oh, so you are a Muslim too. Very well then, you will also be torched along with this boy."

'The man was unperturbed. "Before you torch me, have a look at this," he said, and took out a revolver. He pointed it at the ruffians.

'You should have seen the faces of all those rowdies. Their eyes popped out of their sockets. They left their swords and tridents in the bus and ran helter-skelter for dear life. My life was saved. I had tears of gratitude in my eyes.

'The man saw me crying and asked me, "What is your name?"

' "Salim . . . Salim Ilyasi," I replied, still sobbing.

' "Don't you know how to lie?" he said. "But I value people who speak the truth even when confronted with death."

'He told me he had an import–export business and lived alone in a big house in the Byculla locality. He said he needed someone to do the cooking and cleaning, and generally look after the house whenever he had to travel on business. I did wonder why a businessman like him was carrying a gun on the bus, but he promised me double what I was earning as a tiffin carrier, and I instantly agreed to become his live-in servant.

'Ahmed had a large, spacious flat with three bedrooms, a good-sized kitchen and a drawing room with a thirty-six-inch TV. I did the cooking, cleaning and dusting, but I did not forget my ambition of becoming an actor. In a way, working for Ahmed was good, because he would be away from the house most of the day and sometimes even for a week or two. During that time I would do the rounds of the studios. I developed my roll of film and got excellent eight-by-six blow-ups made. I gave them to Mukesh Rawal, who in turn showed them to Pappu Master, the junior-artist supplier. Believe it or not, after just three months I received my first film offer.'

'Really?' I exclaim. 'Which role did you get and in which film?'

'It was as a college student in the Abbas Rizvi film *Bad Boys* starring Sunil Mehra.'

'Then let's go and see it right away. I would love to watch you on screen and hear your dialogues.'

'Well . . .' Salim hesitates. He looks down at his shoes. 'You see, my role was cut at the last minute. So on screen you see me for just three seconds, sitting at a desk in a classroom with thirty other students. The only dialogues in that scene are between the hero Sunil and the class teacher.'

'What?' I cry in disappointment. 'Just three seconds! What kind of role is that?'

'Junior artists are supposed to do just those kinds of roles. We are not heroes and heroines. We are merely part of the scenery. Remember those big party scenes in films? Junior artists are the extras who stand around sipping their drinks while the hero and heroine waltz on the dance floor. We are the passers-by on the street when the hero chases the villain. We are the chaps who clap in a disco when the hero and heroine win a dance competition. But I didn't mind working as a junior artist. It allowed me to fulfil my dream of seeing behind the scenes. And it enabled me to meet the producer, Abbas Rizvi. He liked my looks and promised to give me a longer role in his next film.

'Over the course of the next six months, I discovered many things about Ahmed. All in all, he was a rather strange man. He had just two interests in life: eating good food and watching television. On TV he watched just two programmes – cricket and *Mumbai Crime Watch*. He was fanatical about cricket. Whenever a match was being played, with or without India, he had to watch it. He would get up at three o'clock in the morning if there was a match in the West Indies and at midnight if it was in Australia. He would even watch matches between novice teams like Kenya and Canada.

'He kept a diary in which he recorded every cricket statistic. He knew by heart the batting average of each and every batsman, the bowling figures of each and every bowler, the number of catches taken by a fielder, the stumpings done by a wicket-keeper. He could tell you the highest and lowest-ever scores in a match, the maximum number of runs scored in an over, the biggest victory margins and the narrowest.

'But he stored all this information for a purpose – to bet on cricket matches. I found this out during the

India–England series. Ahmed was watching the match on TV and trying to call someone on his mobile. So I asked him, "What are you doing, Ahmed *bhai*?"

' "I am about to play satta," he replied.

' "Satta? What's that?"

' "It is another name for illegal betting. Satta is organized by powerful underworld syndicates in Mumbai with a daily turnover of millions of rupees. Millions are bet on every cricket match, thousands on every ball. I am one of the biggest punters. This house that you see, this expensive TV, the microwave in the kitchen, the air conditioner in the bedroom, are all due to my winnings from satta. Three years ago, I made a killing in the India–Australia match. You remember the famous match in Eden Gardens? At a time when India were 232 for 4 and staring at an innings defeat, and the odds were a thousand to one against India, I bet on Laxman and India and cleaned up ten lakh rupees!"

' "Ten lakhs!" My eyes popped out.

' "Yes. Today I am only betting ten thousand on India. I have been trying to ask my bookie for the odds, but his number is continuously engaged." He slapped his mobile a couple of times, looked impatiently at his watch and punched in the number once again. This time he got through. "Hello, Sharad *bhai*? AK here. Code 3563. What's the rate on the match?" I heard the bookie's voice over the phone with a lot of static. I could hear the commentary in the background: "India already has a lead of 175 over England. Once the lead crosses 250, the odds will turn heavily in favour of India. With less than a lead of 250 it is fifty–fifty either way, but crossing the 250 mark will change that to three to one in India's favour."

' "And what are the odds on an England victory?" Ahmed asked him.

' "Are you crazy?" the bookie replied. "There is no way England can win; their best bet is to hold out for a draw. But if you ask for the odds, they are eight to one. Do you want to book now?"

' "Yeah. Put me down for ten thousand on India losing," said Ahmed.

I was astounded when I heard Ahmed place this bet, because India was in the lead. But Ahmed obviously knew more than the bookie, because by the end of play England had won the match, English flags were fluttering all over Lord's cricket ground, and Ahmed was punching his fists in the air and exulting, "Yes! Yes! Yes!" He called up his bookie again. "*Kyun* Sharad *bhai*, wasn't I right? How much have I cleaned up? Eighty thousand? Ha! Not a bad profit for a few hours' work!"

'Ahmed went out and got a bottle full of frothy liquid, and that evening I had my first sip of champagne.

'Ahmed's second interest in life was watching *Mumbai Crime Watch*. Have you ever seen it?'

I shake my head. 'No, it wasn't on the TV in Delhi.'

'Well, it is a very boring programme. It is like a news bulletin, except they don't tell you about floods and riots and war and politics. They tell you only about violent crime. Who has been murdered, who has been raped, which bank has been looted, who has escaped from jail, that kind of thing.

'Ahmed would sit in front of the TV with a plate of seekh kebabs and laugh loudly whenever he heard the bulletin on *Mumbai Crime Watch*. For some reason, he found it very amusing.

'From time to time, Ahmed would receive large yellow envelopes by courier. I had strict instructions not to touch his mail and to leave it on the dining table for him. One afternoon, a large yellow envelope was brought by the delivery boy just when I was having tea. By mistake I spilt tea on the envelope and went into a panic. I knew if Ahmed saw that I had spoilt his packet he would be angry. It might contain valuable commercial documents which could have been damaged. So I sat down and carefully prised open the gummed flap. I inserted my fingers and pulled out the documents . . . and whistled in surprise.'

'Why? What was there?'

'Nothing much. The packet contained just one glossy eight-by-six colour photograph of a man's face and half a sheet of neatly typed details. Even I could read that much. It said:

```
Name:     Vithalbhai Ghorpade.
Age:      56.
Address:  73/4 Marve Road, Malad.
```

That was all.

'I presumed these were the details of some business-man Ahmed had dealings with, and didn't think too much about it. I carefully resealed the flap and put the envelope on the dining table. In the evening, Ahmed came home and opened the envelope. He received a phone call shortly afterwards. "Yes, I have received the packet," is all he said.

'Almost two weeks later, Ahmed was sitting in front of the TV, watching *Mumbai Crime Watch*. I was in the kitchen, chopping vegetables, but I could hear the presenter speaking. ". . . In yet another gruesome incident in Malad, police are looking for clues to the murder of a prominent businessman named Vithalbhai Ghorpade, who was found murdered in his house on Marve Road." The name rang a bell. I glanced at the TV and almost cut my finger, because on screen was the same photograph that had been in the yellow envelope. The presenter continued, "Mr Ghorpade, who was fifty-six, was shot dead at point-blank range while he was alone in the house. He is survived by his wife and son. According to Malad police, robbery appears to have been the main motive as the house was ransacked and many valuables were missing."

'I noticed Ahmed laughing when he heard this. This, too, surprised me. Why should Ahmed laugh over the death of a business associate?

'A month later, there was another yellow envelope. Ahmed was out and I could not resist taking a peek at its contents. This time I steamed it open, so that no marks were left. I opened the flap and pulled out yet another glossy photograph. This one showed the face of a young man with a thick moustache and a long scar running from his left eye to the base of his nose. The typed sheet of paper said:

```
Name:      Jameel Kidwai.
Age:       28.
```

Address: 35 Shilajit
         Apartments, Colaba.

I memorized the name and put the photo back.

'Ahmed came home that evening and looked at the envelope. There was a phone call, as before, and he confirmed receipt of the packet. Exactly a week later, I heard the news on *Crime Watch* that a young lawyer called Jameel Kidwai had been shot dead while getting out of his car near his residence in Shilajit Apartments. The presenter said, "Police suspect a gangland motive in this killing, as Mr Kidwai had represented several mafia dons in court. An investigation has been launched, but there are no clues at present." Ahmed, sitting with a glass of whisky, guffawed when he heard this.

'I was now seriously worried. Why did Ahmed receive pictures of people in the mail and why did those people die soon afterwards? This was still a mystery to me. So when the next yellow envelope was delivered three weeks later, I not only took a peek at the photograph, which was of an elderly man, I also wrote down the address. It was of a house on Premier Road in Kurla. The next day, I followed Ahmed. He took a local train to Kurla and walked to Premier Road. But he didn't enter the house. He just passed it three or four times, as if checking it out. Two weeks later, *Crime Watch* announced that the same elderly man had been found murdered in his house on Premier Road in Kurla.

'I am not a fool. I knew there and then that Ahmed had murdered the man and that I was living with a contract killer. But I didn't know what to do. Ahmed had saved my life once and I couldn't even contemplate betraying him to the police. Meanwhile, Abbas Rizvi called me up and made a firm offer of a supporting role in his next film. When I heard this I ran all the way to the shrine of Haji Ali. I touched my forehead to the cloth covering the tomb and prayed for Rizvi's long life.

'For the next two months I lived an uneasy double life. If Ahmed was a contract killer masquerading as a businessman, I was an actor masquerading as a servant. Ahmed had licence to kill, but I knew that a day would come when he himself would get killed. I simply hoped that I wouldn't get caught in the crossfire. And then everything fell apart.'

'What happened?'

'It was four months ago – the twentieth of February, to be exact. I remember the day very well, because India was playing Australia in the last match of the series and Ahmed had just placed another bet. He used to bet on everything: not only on which team would win, but also the first wicket to fall, the bowler to take the first wicket, who would win the toss, whether there would be rain during the match. Sometimes he would bet on virtually every ball in the match – whether it would be a four, a six or a dot ball. That morning, Ahmed had just spoken to his bookie. "Sharad *bhai*, Code 3563. How do you think the pitch will behave? Yesterday it was flat, but will the ball start turning from today? The weather forecast is good, but do you think it might rain later in the day?" Then he placed his bet. "Book me on Sachin Malvankar making his thirty-seventh century today. What's the rate?" The bookie said, "He is already on seventy-eight and everyone feels a century is a sure shot, so the odds are not very promising. The best I can do is thirteen to ten." "OK," said Ahmed, "then put me down for ten lakhs. This way I will at least make a profit of three lakhs."

That whole afternoon Ahmed sat in front of the TV set and watched Malvankar play, cheering his every run with loud whistles. As Malvankar inched towards his century, Ahmed became more and more excited. By the time Malvankar entered the nineties Ahmed was a nervous wreck, biting his fingernails, praying before every ball, cringing whenever Malvankar was beaten by a delivery. But Malvankar played like the master batsman he is. He moved from ninety-one to ninety-five with a magnificent straight drive for four. Then he took a single to reach ninety-six. Another single. Ninety-seven. Then Gillespie bowled a short ball and Malvankar pulled it majestically to the cover boundary. Hayden was running after it, trying to stop it from crossing the rope. Malvankar and his co-batsman Ajay Mishra were running quickly between the wickets. They took one run. Ninety-eight. Then they raced to complete the second. Ninety-nine. Hayden gathered up the ball inches inside the cover boundary and sent in a looping throw, not to Adam Gilchrist, the wicketkeeper, but to the bowler's end. Malvankar saw the throw coming and shouted "Nooooo!" to Mishra, who was running towards him for the third run. But that idiot Mishra kept on charging down the pitch towards Malvankar. In desperation, Malvankar was forced to set out to complete the third run. He had almost made it to the bowler's end when the ball from Hayden landed directly on the stumps! Malvankar was caught just six inches outside the crease and declared run out by the third umpire. On ninety-nine.

'You can imagine what happened to Ahmed. He had bet ten lakhs on Malvankar's thirty-seventh century and now he had lost it all by one run. He cursed Gillespie, he cursed Hayden, and most of all he cursed Mishra. "I want to kill that bastard," he growled and charged out of the house. He probably went to a bar to drown his sorrows.

'That same afternoon, another yellow envelope came. I was worried that it might contain the picture of a certain Indian batsman, but when I saw what was inside I almost died.'

'Why? What was inside? Tell me quickly.'

'Inside the envelope was a glossy, eight-by-six photograph of Abbas Rizvi, the producer, and a type-written piece of paper containing his address. I knew that he would be Ahmed's next victim, and that with his death, my dream of becoming an actor would also die. I had to warn Rizvi. But if Ahmed found out, he would have no qualms about killing me either. After all, he was a professional hitman with a licence to kill.'

'So what did you do?' I ask breathlessly.

'I did what I had to do. I immediately went to Rizvi and told him about the contract on him. He didn't believe me, so I showed him the picture and the address which had come by courier. Once he saw the photo in my hand, all his doubts vanished. He told me he would run away to Dubai and lie low for a year or so. He was now so indebted to me, he promised that on his return he would make me a hero in his next film and till then he would get me trained. So that is why he is funding my acting course and why I am counting the days till I turn eighteen.'

'My God, what a story, Salim,' I say, letting out a deep breath. 'But by taking that packet to Rizvi, didn't you expose yourself to Ahmed? He would have received a phone call that evening and he would have known about the missing envelope.'

'No, I didn't expose myself, because Ahmed did get a packet on the dining table when he returned that evening.'

'But . . . then Ahmed would have killed Rizvi.'

'No, because the packet contained a new picture and a new address, which I got typed at the nearby typing institute.'

'Brilliant. You mean you gave a fictitious address? But how could you give a fictitious picture?'

'I could not. So I did not. I gave Ahmed a real picture and a real address, and he actually went and carried out the hit. But before he could discover that he had killed the wrong guy, I told him I had to go urgently to Bihar and left his employment. I hid here and there, I didn't enter Byculla, I even stopped going to Haji Ali, which is just opposite. And then last week I saw on *Crime Watch* that the police had shot a dreaded contract killer by the name of Ahmed Khan in a shoot-out near Churchgate Station. So today I came to Haji Ali to offer my thanks to Allah, and behold, who do I see when I come out but you!'

'Yes, it is an amazing coincidence. But I have just one more question. Whose picture and address did you give Ahmed?'

'The only one worth giving. I gave him a glossy eight-by-six photo of Mr Babu Pillai, and Maman's address!!'

Smita claps her hands. 'Marvellous! I know by now that you are a smart cookie, but I didn't know that Salim is also a genius. He got licence to kill by proxy, and he chose the perfect target. So what happened after? Did you tell Salim about your participation in the quiz?'

'No. I didn't reveal why I had come to Mumbai. I simply said that I was in Delhi, working as a servant, and was visiting the city for a couple of days.'

'So Salim has no clue about your appearance on *W3B*?'

'No. I was going to inform him, but before I could do so the police arrested me.'

'I see. Anyway, now let's see how the fortuitous meeting with Salim helped your fortunes on the show.'

In the studio, the lights have been dimmed again.

Prem Kumar addresses the camera. 'We now move on to question number nine, for one million rupees.' He turns to me. 'Are you ready?'

'Ready,' I reply.

'OK. Here is question number nine. This one is from the world of sport. Tell me, Mr Thomas, which sport do you play?'

'None.'

'None? Then how come you are so fit? Look at me, I have gained so much flab despite going to the gym every morning.'

'If you had to work as a waiter and commute thirty kilometres every day, you too would become fit,' I reply.

The audience titters. Prem Kumar scowls.

'OK, here comes question number nine, from the world of cricket. How many Test centuries has India's greatest batsman Sachin Malvankar scored? Your choices are a) 34, b) 35, c) 36 or d) 37?'

The music commences.

'Can I ask a question?'

'Yes, sure.'

'Has India played any other country since the recent series with Australia?'

'No, not to my knowledge.'

'Then I know the answer. It is C. 36.'

'Is that your final answer? Remember, there is a million rupees riding on your reply.'

'Yes, it is C. 36.'

'Are you absolutely, one hundred per cent sure?'

'Yes.'

There is a crescendo of drums. The correct answer flashes.

'Absolutely, one hundred per cent correct! Sachin Malvankar has indeed scored 36 Test centuries. You have just won a million rupees! Ladies and gentlemen, we will now take a short commercial break.'

'Cut!' I say.

$10,000,000$

TRAGEDY QUEEN

A family drama with doses of comedy and action, ending eventually in tragedy. In film parlance, this is how I would describe the time I spent with Neelima Kumari. She was an actress. And I worked for three years in her flat in Juhu Vile Parle.

It all began on that same night that Salim and I escaped from the clutches of Maman and his gang. We took the local train and landed in Juhu. We walked up to Neelima Kumari's flat, pressed the doorbell and waited.

After a lengthy interval the door is opened. 'Yes?' A lady stands before us. Radhey, the lame boy, was right. She is tall and beautiful, just like a heroine, only older. Salim falls at her feet. '*Arrey.*' She hurriedly steps back. 'Who are you two? What are you doing here at this hour of night?'

'We are friends of Radhey,' I reply with folded hands. 'He told us you are in need of a servant. We have come to offer our services. We know you are a very kind lady. We are in desperate need of food and shelter and promise to do anything you ask us.'

'Yes, I do need a servant, but I cannot keep someone so young.'

'Madam, we are young only in looks. We can do the work of four men. I can also speak English. Do try us.'

'But I don't need two servants. I have space only for one.'

Salim and I look at each other. 'Then at least pick one of us,' I say.

'What is your name?' she asks Salim.

'Salim.'

'Oh, you are Muslim, aren't you?'

Salim nods.

'Look, I am sorry, but my aged mother who lives with me cannot eat anything touched by a Muslim. I personally don't believe in all this polluting-contact nonsense, but what am I to do?' She shrugs her shoulders. Salim looks crestfallen.

Then she turns to me. 'And what about you? What is your name?'

'Ram,' I tell her.

So I got the job, and only then did I discover that life with a movie star is not as glamorous as it appears from the outside. When you get to see them without make-up you find that they are exactly like you and me, with the same anxieties and insecurities. The only difference is that we are mainly concerned with money, or lack of it, and they are mainly concerned with fame. Or lack of it.

They live in a fish bowl. First they hate it, then, as adulation grows, they start loving it. And when people no longer shower attention on them, they just shrivel up and die.

Neelima Kumari's flat is spacious and contemporary, tastefully furnished with expensive wall-to-wall carpets and paintings. It has five bedrooms. The large master bedroom with attached bathroom is Neelima's, and her mother has the next-largest. As far as I know, Neelima has no other relatives.

Neelima's bedroom is the best room in the flat. It has a huge bed in the middle with a velvet bedspread. The walls have tiles made of glass so you see your image reflected in a thousand tiny pieces. There is a dresser full of perfumes and bottles. Next to the dresser is a twenty-nine-inch Sony TV, a VCR and the latest VCD player. An expensive chandelier hangs from the ceiling. A soundless air conditioner keeps the room delightfully cool. Glass shelves line the walls, loaded with trophies and awards of all kinds. There is another glass case full of old film magazines. All of them have Neelima Kumari on the cover. Looking at all this, I feel privileged to be working in her house. In her time, she must have been the most famous actress in India.

Neelima's mother is a real pain in the neck. Though she is nearly eighty, she has the energy of a forty-year-old and is always after me. I am the only full-time servant in the house. There is a Maharashtrian brahmin lady who comes to cook in the evening and also does the dishes, and a part-time maid who does the washing. I do everything else. I do the dusting and the cleaning, I iron the clothes and make evening tea, I do errands outside the house, buy the milk and pay all the utility bills. But Neelima's mother is never satisfied, even though I address her very respectfully as 'Maaji'. 'Ram, you have not brought my milk,' she will say. 'Ram, you have not ironed my bed sheet . . . Ram, you have not dusted this room properly . . . Ram you are again wasting time . . . Ram you have not heated my tea.' Sometimes I get so irritated at her constant nitpicking, I want to tape her mouth.

Neelima, though quirky at times, is not so demanding. She wants me to become a live-in servant. There are plenty of empty bedrooms in the flat where I could stay, but her mother refuses to allow a 'male' to live in the house. So I am banished to a chawl in Ghatkopar, from where I commute every day to her flat. She pays rent for the room in the chawl. In a way it suits me, because Salim can also stay with me in the same room.

I am out shopping with Neelima. She doesn't own a car, so we take a taxi. I don't enjoy going out with her. She only buys cosmetics or clothes and I have to carry her heavy bags. She never goes to a McDonald's or a Pizza Hut. And she never, ever, buys me anything.

Today, we are in Cuff Parade, in a very expensive shop which sells saris. She looks at hundreds of them for over two hours, then she buys three for fifty thousand rupees, which is almost equal to my salary for two years. As we are stepping out of the air-conditioned showroom, a group of girls dressed in school uniform approaches her. They look very excited.

'Excuse me, are you Neelima Kumari, the actress?' asks one of them.

'Yes,' says Neelima, looking quite pleased.

'See,' the girl screams to her friends. 'I told you she is Neelima.' Then she turns to us again. 'Neelimaji, we are great fans of yours. Seeing you is like a dream come true. We are not carrying autograph books, but will you please sign our exercise books?'

'Of course, with pleasure,' says Neelima and takes a pen from her handbag. One by one the girls hold out their exercise books, thrilled to bits. Neelima asks each one her name and then records in her sprawling handwriting, 'To Ritu with love, Neelima.' 'To Indu with love, Neelima.' 'To Malti with love, Neelima.' 'To Roshni with love, Neelima.' The girls read their inscriptions and squeal with delight.

Neelima is positively glowing from all this adulation. This is the first time I have seen anyone recognize her and I marvel at the impact it has on her. Suddenly she looks at me with concern, sweating in the heat, holding a heavy shopping bag. 'Ram, you must be feeling quite hungry by now. Come, let's have an ice cream,' she says. I squeal with delight.

From time to time, Neelima teaches me about the art of film-making. She tells me about the various technicians involved in the making of a film. 'People think that a film is made only by the actors and the director. They don't know about the thousands of people behind the scenes, without whose efforts the film

would never be made. It is only after these technicians have done their work that a director can snap his fingers and tell his actors, "Lights, camera, action!" '
She tells me about sets and props and lighting and make-up and stunt men and spot boys.

Then she teaches me about genres. 'I hate the movies they make these days, in which they try to cram everything – tragedy, comedy, action and melodrama. No. A good film has to respect its genre. I always used to choose my films carefully, after fully understanding what the story meant and what it involved for me. You will never catch me singing and dancing in one scene and dying two reels later. No, Ram. A character has to be consistent. Just as a great painter is identified by his unique signature style, an actor is known for his unique niche. A genre of his own. A great artist is not one who merely fits into a genre, but one who defines the genre. Did you see the review of that new film *Relationship of the Heart* in the *Times of India?* The reviewer wrote that Pooja, the actress, made a complete hash of the death scene. "How I wish Neelima Kumari had been in this film to do justice to the character. The young actresses of today should learn their craft from legends like her." It really gladdened my heart to read this. To be held out as an example, as the epitome of a genre, is the ultimate compliment an actor can receive. I am getting the review framed.'

'So what was your unique style?'

She smiles. 'I know you are too young to know that Neelima Kumari is called the Tragedy Queen of India. Come, let me show you something.'

She takes me to her bedroom and opens a metal

almirah. My eyes almost pop out because the *almirah* is crammed with video cassettes. 'Do you know that all these cassettes are of films in which I have actually played a part?'

'Really? So how many cassettes are here?'

'One hundred and fourteen. That is the number of films I worked in over a career spanning twenty years.' She points out the first row. 'These are among my earliest films. Most of them are slapstick comedies. I am sure you know what comedy films are, right?'

I nod my head vigorously. 'Yes. Like the ones Govinda acts in.'

Neelima indicates the next two rows. 'These are films from my middle period. Mostly family dramas. But I also did the famous thriller *Name the Murderer* and the classic horror film *Thirty Years Later.*'

Finally she points out the remaining four rows. 'And all these are tragedies. You see the hundreds of awards and trophies I have received over the years? Almost all of them are for films in this section. My favourite is this one.' She taps a cassette. I read the label. It says *Mumtaz Mahal.* 'This is the film in which I played the role of a lifetime, that of Emperor Shahjahan's wife Mumtaz Mahal. I even received the National Award for my performance. See that trophy in the centre? I received it from the hands of the President of India.'

'So, Madam, was that the greatest role you ever played?'

She sighs. 'It was a good role, no doubt, with a lot of potential for emotion, but I feel that I have yet to play the greatest role of my life.'

* * *

Neelima's mother is no longer keeping well. She coughs and groans a lot. Her carping is becoming unbearable. She is always complaining about her medical condition and doesn't even spare Neelima, reminding her constantly of her obligation towards the person who brought her into this world. I think Neelima is beginning to chafe a little. Apart from my other errands, I now have to spend half a day buying medicines for Maaji and then ensuring that she takes the tablets, capsules and drops on time.

There is excitement in the flat. Doordarshan, the national TV channel, is going to show a film of Neelima's called *The Last Wife* this evening. It is one of her famous tragedies and she wants all of us to watch it with her in the drawing room. Come eight pm, we are all gathered in front of the TV. There is the cook, the maid and me sitting on the carpet and Maaji reclining on the sofa next to Neelima. The film starts. It is not really my cup of tea. It is about a poor middle-class family coping with a whole heap of problems. There is a lot of crying and wailing in it. And a lot of groaning in the background from Maaji. The film shows life too realistically. I think it is ridiculous to make such movies. What is the point of watching a film if you can see the real thing in your neighbour's house just across the street? Neelima, though, looks very young and beautiful in the film and acts really well. It is a strange sensation to watch a film and have its heroine sitting behind you. I wonder what she feels when she watches herself on the TV screen. Does she remember the spot boys and make-up artists, the lighting technicians and sound recordists who worked behind the scenes?

Neelima dies in the film after delivering an emotionally charged speech. The film ends as soon as she dies. We stand up to stretch our legs. Then I notice that Neelima is crying. 'Madam,' I ask with concern, 'what happened? Why are you crying?'

'Nothing, Ram. I just felt a sense of kinship with my character on screen. See, I am smiling now.'

'How can you actors laugh one minute and cry the next?'

'That is the hallmark of a great actor. Do you know why they call me Tragedy Queen?'

'Why, Madam?'

'Because I never used glycerine to weep in any of my films. I could summon tears to my eyes at will.'

'What is so great about that? I also never need glycerine to bring tears to my eyes,' I tell the maid when Neelima is out of earshot.

The more I see of Neelima, the more I begin to understand why she is called the Tragedy Queen. There is a core of melancholy which surrounds her. Even in her smile I detect a hint of sadness. I wonder about her past life, why she never married. She seems to have no real friends. But she goes out of the house from time to time and returns late in the evening. I wonder whom she meets. I doubt that it is a boyfriend or a lover, because she never returns looking radiant. She comes back looking haggard and depressed and goes straight to her bedroom. This is one mystery I would love to get to the bottom of.

I also wonder about her obsession with beauty. Physical beauty. She is good looking, yet she spends hours doing her make-up and preening before the mirror. Her dressing table is full of creams. I try to read the labels one day. There are anti-wrinkle creams, anti-cellulite creams and anti-ageing lotions. There are deep radiance boosters and hydrating age-defence creams, revitalizing night creams and skin-firming gels. Her bathroom is full of strange-smelling soaps and scrubs and face-masks which are supposed to make you look youthful. Her medicine cabinet has as many medicines for her as for Maaji. There are human-growth hormones and breast-firming creams, pharmacy-grade melatonin and antioxidants.

I finally say to her one day, 'Madam, if you don't mind my asking, why do you need all this make-up? You no longer act now.'

She looks me in the eye. 'We people who work in films become very vain. We get so used to seeing our-selves in make-up that we no longer have the courage to look in the mirror and see our real faces. Remember, an actor is an actor for life. Films may end, but the show must go on.'

I wonder whether she said this from her heart, or just recited some lines from a film.

Something truly wonderful has happened today. Maaji has died in her sleep. Aged eighty-one.

Neelima weeps a little, then gets down to the practical business of making funeral arrangements. It seems as though almost the entire film industry comes to her flat to offer condolences. She sits stoically on a sofa in the drawing room, wearing a white sari and light make-up. I recognize many of the people who come. There are actors and actresses and directors and producers and singers and songwriters. The drawing room is overflowing with visitors. I crane my neck to catch a glimpse of the famous stars whose pictures I have seen in *Starburst* and whose films I have seen on screen. I wish Salim could be here with me. But he would be disappointed. Because the visitors don't look like the glamorous stars we see on screen. They are not wearing make-up and flashy clothes. They are all clad spotlessly in white and look grim and sombre. Even those who are famous for comedies.

I don't know how Neelima took her mother's death. But to me Maaji's departure from this world felt like welcome relief after a depressing film.

Within a month of Maaji's demise, Neelima asks me to become a live-in servant. She knows that Salim is staying with me in the chawl, so she continues to pay rent for Salim's room. I shift to her flat. But I am not put in any of the four empty bedrooms. I am given the tiny ironing room.

I notice that after Maaji's death, Neelima begins to go out more frequently, at times not even bothering to return at night. I am convinced she is seeing someone. Perhaps there will soon be a marriage.

I am wakened by a scraping noise coming from the direction of the drawing room. The sound is quite faint, but sufficient to disturb my sleep. I rub my eyes and look at the alarm clock by my side. It says two-thirty am. I wonder what Neelima is doing pottering about the flat at this hour. Suddenly I realize that her lover might have come to visit her and I get all excited. I tiptoe out of my room and move towards the drawing room.

The room is in darkness but there is a man there. He doesn't look like a lover. He wears a black mask over his head with slits only for the eyes. In his left hand he holds a black sack. In his right hand is a flashlight which is pointed at the VCR. He quickly disconnects the cables, picks the VCR up and inserts it in his black sack. I know now that he is no lover. He is a thief. And I scream. It is a piercing scream which shatters the silence of the night like a bullet. It wakes up Neelima Kumari, who comes running to the drawing room. It completely unsettles the thief, who drops the sack and the flashlight and covers both his ears with his hands. And it shatters a glass figurine which was poised delicately on top of the television cabinet.

'What is the matter?' Neelima asks breathlessly. She switches on the drawing-room light. Then she sees the thief and lets out a scream too. The thief has almost gone deaf by now. He falls down on his knees and begins pleading with us. 'Please, Madam, I am not a thief. I have just come to look at your house.'

'Ram, bring me the phone. I will call the police immediately,' Neelima tells me. I bring her the cordless phone with alacrity.

The thief tears off his mask. He is a youngish man with a goatee. 'Please, madam, please don't call the police, I beg you. I am no thief. I am a final-year student at St Xavier's. I am one of your greatest fans. I have come to your house only to see how you live.'

I notice that Neelima softens visibly on hearing the fan part. 'Don't listen to him, Madam,' I warn her. 'This fellow is a thief. If he is a fan, why has he stolen our VCR?'

'I'll tell you why, Neelimaji. I have purchased cassettes of each and every film you have acted in. All 114 of them. I watch at least one of your movies every day. Due to heavy use, my VCR has become defective. I am having it repaired. But I cannot bear to pass a day without watching one of your films. So I thought I would take one of your VCRs. Just the fact that I am watching a movie on your VCR will make the experience so much more memorable. I was going to return your VCR when my own comes back from repairs. Please believe me, Madam. I swear on my dead father I am not lying.'

'This is all a lie, Madam,' I cry. 'You'd better call the police.'

'No, Ram,' says Neelima. 'Let me first test whether this man is indeed telling the truth. If he has seen all 114 of my films then he can answer a few questions. OK, Mister, tell me in which film I played the role of a village girl called Chandni?'

'Oh, how can I forget that, Neelimaji? It is one of my favourite films. It is *Back to the Village*, right?'

'Right. But that one was too easy. Tell me, for which film did I get the Filmfare Award in 1982?'

'That's even easier. For *The Dark Night*, surely.'

'My God, you are right. OK, tell me in which film did I act with Manoj Kumar?'

'It was that patriotic film, *The Nation Calls*.'

'Oh, you even saw that one?'

'I told you, Neelimaji, I am your greatest living fan. Tell me, why did you agree to do that two-bit role in *Everlasting Love*? I always thought the director under-utilized you.'

'It's amazing you ask me about *Everlasting Love*. I too feel that I shouldn't have done that role. All the credit for the film's success went to Sharmila, and I got a raw deal.'

'But you were fantastic in *It's Raining over Bombay*. I think the monologue that you deliver in the temple after your father's death is the most memorable scene in the whole film. You really should have got the Filmfare Award for it, but they gave it to you for *Woman* instead.'

'Yes. If I were to choose between *Woman* and *It's Raining over Bombay*, I would probably also choose the latter. I must say, you know a lot about my films. What is your name?'

'My name is Ranjeet Mistry. I am twenty-four years old. I have always wanted to ask you about *Mumtaz Mahal*, which I consider to be the greatest film ever made. That childbirth scene, when you are dying and Dileep Sahib, who plays the Emperor, is sitting by your bedside, you ask him to make a promise, and then you take off your gold bangle – but you never give it to him. Why did you do that?'

'This is amazing. You have gone into the minute details of that film. I will tell you the answer. But why are you sitting on the ground? Come, sit here on the sofa. And Ram, what are you doing standing with a phone in your hand? Can't you see we have a guest in the house? Go, get two cups of tea and some biscuits. So as I was telling you, when *Mumtaz Mahal* was being conceptualized . . .'

By the time I return with two cups of tea, Neelima and the thief are laughing and sharing jokes like two long-lost friends. I shake my head in disbelief. This man had come to rob her and just because he has seen a few of her films she feeds him biscuits and tea.

What started as a thriller has turned out to be a family drama.

She calls me one evening. 'Ram, I want you to shift to the chawl tomorrow. Just for a day. I need privacy in the house.'

'But why, Madam?'

'Don't ask questions,' she says in an irritated voice. 'Just do as I tell you.'

These instructions are given to me three times in the next three months. I know that when I am away she will entertain her lover in the house, and does not want me to know about it. So the next time she tells me to stay in Ghatkopar and return the next day, I do not follow her instructions fully. I go back to Ghatkopar for the night, but instead of returning at seven am the next morning, I come back at five and hang around outside the flat. Sure enough, at six am the door opens and a man steps out. He is tall, with a decent face, but his bloodshot eyes and scruffy hair spoil the look. He is clad in blue jeans and a white shirt. He holds a sheaf of currency notes and a lighted cigarette in his left hand and twirls some car keys in his fingers. He seems vaguely familiar, but I cannot place him. He doesn't even glance at me before he walks down the stairs to the ground floor. I enter the house only at seven am.

I get my first shock on seeing the condition of the drawing room. There are cigarette butts and traces of ash everywhere. An upturned glass lies on the centre table, together with an empty bottle of whisky. Peanuts are scattered all over the carpet. There is a strong smell of alcohol in the room.

The second shock is on seeing Neelima Kumari. She has bruises all over her face and a black eye. 'Oh my God, Madam, what happened to you?' I cry.

'Nothing, Ram. I slipped from my bed and hurt myself. Nothing to worry about.'

I know she is lying. That man I saw leaving the flat has done this to her. And in return she has given him cigarettes, whisky and also money. I feel pained and angry, and powerless to protect her.

From that day, a subtle change comes over Neelima. She becomes more introverted and withdrawn. I think she starts drinking whisky, because I often smell it on her breath.

One morning I find her again with a black eye, and a cigarette burn on her arm. I can bear it no longer. 'Madam, I feel very sad seeing you in this condition. Who is doing this to you?' I ask her.

She could have said 'It is none of your business,' but she was in a reflective mood that morning. 'You know, Ram, someone has said that it is better to have loved and lost than never to have loved at all. I wonder at times if this is true. I too have loved. I don't know whether I have lost as yet, but I have received a lot of pain. There is a man in my life. Sometimes I think he loves me. Sometimes I think he hates me. He tortures me slowly, bit by bit.'

'Then why don't you leave him?' I cry.

'It is not that simple. There is some pleasure even in pain. A sweet ecstasy. Sometimes I feel if pain can be this sweet, how exquisitely pleasurable death will be. When he tortures me with cigarette butts I don't want to scream. I want to recite those memorable lines from my film *Woman*. The death scene. "O life, how fickle you are. It is death which is my real lover, my constant companion. Come, death, take me in your arms, whisper the sweet sound of silence in my ears, and waft me away to the land of eternal love." '

'But that was just a film, Madam,' I plead with her.

'Hush! Have you forgotten what I told you once, that an actor is an actor for life? Do not forget that I will forever be known as the Tragedy Queen. And I didn't become a tragedy queen just by reciting lines given to me by a scriptwriter. I lived the life of my characters. Ghalib didn't become a great tragic poet just by writing some lines in a book. No. You have to feel pain, experience it, live it in your daily life before you can become a tragedy queen.'

'If this is the criteria, then can I become a tragedy king?' I ask with the wide-eyed innocence of a twelve-year-old.

She does not answer.

Neelima is giving an interview to a journalist from

Starburst in the drawing room. I enter with a tray of *gulab jamuns* and samosas.

'OK, Neelimaji, we have talked about the past, now let's come to the present. Why did you quit films?' I watch closely as the journalist fiddles with a tape recorder. She is quite young and rather striking looking, with fair skin and shoulder-length black hair. She is wearing smart black trousers with a printed *kurti* and high-heeled black pumps.

'Because they no longer make films like they used to. The passion, the commitment, is gone. Today's actors are nothing but assembly-line products, each exactly like the other, mouthing their lines like parrots. There is no depth. We did one film at a time. Now I find actors rushing to three different sets in a day. It's ridiculous.' Neelima gestures with her hands.

'Well, pardon my saying so, but I heard that part of the reason you quit was because you were not being offered any roles.'

Anger flares up on her face. 'Who told you that? It is a complete lie. I was offered several roles, but I turned them down. They were not powerful enough. And the films weren't heroine-oriented.'

'What you mean is that you were not offered heroine roles any longer, but those of elder sister or aunt.'

'How dare you disparage me and my work? I must say even the journalists of today have lost their manners. Can't you see the awards and trophies lining the shelves? Do you think I got these by not acting? Do you think I earned the sobriquet of Tragedy Queen by singing around trees like today's two-bit heroines, looking like a glorified extra?'

'But . . . but we are not talking about your past caree—'

'I know exactly what you are talking about. Please leave this instant. Ram, show this lady out and do not open the door to her ever again.' She stands up and walks out of the room in a huff. I escort the bewildered journalist to the door.

I am unable to figure out whether this was a comedy, a drama, or a tragedy.

There are many framed pictures in Neelima's flat. But all of them show only her. Neelima receiving some award, Neelima cutting a ribbon, Neelima watching a performance, Neelima giving an award. There are no pictures of any other movie stars, except for two framed pictures in her bedroom. They are of two beautiful women, one white, the other Indian.

'Who are these women?' I ask her one day.

'The one on the left is Marilyn Monroe and the one on the right is Madhubala.'

'Who are they?'

'They were both very famous actresses who died young.'

'So why do you keep their pictures?'

'Because I also want to die young. I don't want to die looking old and haggard. Have you seen the picture of Shakeela in this week's *Film Digest*? She was a famous film star in the fifties and must be ninety now. See how old and desiccated she looks. And this is exactly how people will remember her after her death. As old and wrinkly and haggard. But people always remember Marilyn Monroe and Madhubala as young because they died young. The lasting image people have of you is how you looked at the time of your death. Like Madhubala, I want to leave behind an image of unspoilt youth and beauty, of everlasting grace and charm. I don't want to die when I am ninety. How I wish at times I could stop all the clocks of this world, shatter every mirror, and freeze my youthful face in time.'

A strange sadness spreads through me when I hear this. In a way, Neelima is an orphan, like me. But unlike me, she has a larger family — her fans, producers and directors. And she is willing to make the ultimate sacrifice for their sake. So that they can remember her forever as a young woman.

For the first time, I feel lucky that I am not a film star.

A famous producer is coming to the house. Neelima is very excited. She believes he will offer her a role and she will get to face the camera once again. She spends the entire day applying make-up and trying on various outfits.

The producer comes in the evening. He is short and bald, with a bulging tummy. I am told to bring in *gulab jamuns* and samosas and sherbet.

'. . . is a great role for you, Neelimaji,' the producer is saying. 'I have always been one of your greatest fans. I saw *Woman* fifteen times. That death scene. O, my God, I could die seeing it. That is why I've resolved to drag you out of your retirement. This film, for which I have already roped in a top-level director, is a woman-centric film. I am offering you a fantastic role.'

'Who is this director you have contracted?'

'It is Chimpu Dhawan.'

'But isn't he a comedy film director?'

'So what? Anyway, there will be some comedy in this film. For the lead roles I have already signed up Shahrukh Khan and Tabu.'

'I don't understand. You have already signed a heroine. So will you have two heroines?'

'No, not at all.'

'Then what will Tabu do?'

'She is the heroine.'

'So what role are you offering me?'

'Oh, didn't you understand? I am offering you the role of Shahrukh Khan's mother.'

She kicks him out of the house then and there.

The producer leaves, frothing at the mouth. 'Spoilt bitch, what does she think? She still fancies herself as a heroine. Has she seen herself in the mirror? She is lucky I didn't cast her as the grandmother. Huh!'

I thought this was a good comedy scene.

Her lover has visited her again. But this time things are more serious. She is in bed with a deep cut above her left eyebrow and her cheek is swollen. She has difficulty speaking.

'We must call the police, Madam, have that swine arrested,' I urge her as I apply antiseptic ointment to her bruises.

'No, Ram. I will be all right.'

'At least tell me his name.'

She laughs hoarsely. 'What good will that do? Don't worry, that man is never going to come here again. I finally broke off with him. That is why he did this to me. If he ever comes back, I will spit on him.'

'And how long will you suffer in silence? Look at what he has done to your face.'

'It is the destiny of a woman to suffer in silence. And what he has done to my face is nothing compared to what he has done to the rest of my body. Do you really want to see? Then look.' She unfastens the buttons on her blouse and snaps open her bra. I see a woman's naked breasts for the first time in my life. They are large and pendulous and hang down like udders on a cow. I recoil in shock when I see the cigarette burn marks all over her chest, looking like little black craters on the smooth white flesh. I begin to cry.

She is crying too. 'I do not want to live with a mask any more. I have had enough facelifts, taken enough beauty aids. I want to be a real woman for once in my life. Come to me, my child,' she says and draws my face into her chest.

I do not know what Neelima Kumari was thinking when she drew me to her bosom. Whether she saw me as a son or as a lover, whether she did it to forget her pain or simply to gain a cheap thrill. But as I nuzzled my face between her breasts, all consciousness of the outer world ceased in my brain and for the first time I felt as though I was not an orphan any more. That I had a real mother, one whose face I could see, one whose flesh I could touch. And the salty taste of my tears merged with the sweat and scent of her body in the most moving experience of my thirteen-year-old life. All the pain and suffering, all the insults and humiliation I had endured over the years melted away in that moment. I wanted to stop all the clocks of the world and freeze that moment for ever. For though it was all too brief, even in that short span of time it produced a sensation so genuine, no amount of acting can ever aspire to replicate it.

That is why I will not attempt to define this episode as a drama or a thriller or a tragedy. It was beyond any and all genres.

Neelima and I never speak again about that morning. And what happened then never happens again. But both of us live with the knowledge that our lives have been altered irrevocably.

She wants to remove her mask, but does not have the mental strength to do so. And she refuses to take my help. The inevitable destiny of a tragedy queen tugs at her with renewed urgency. She becomes more depressed. Her drinking increases to such an extent that she is hardly conscious of the world around her. She dismisses her maid and cook. I am the only one left in the flat. And then she prepares for the greatest role of her life.

Neelima Kumari asks me to stack all the film magazines with her pictures in neatly in a pile. She arranges all her trophies and awards personally, putting the platinum jubilee ones in front, followed by the golden jubilees and the silver jubilees. She wears her most expensive sari and puts on her finest jewellery. She spends three hours in front of the mirror making her face look the best it has ever looked. Afterwards, she flushes all her cosmetic creams down the toilet. She goes to the medicine cabinet and throws away all her beauty aids. Then she opens a jar containing painkillers prescribed for her mother. I don't know how many of these tablets she gulps down.

Finally, she enters her bedroom and inserts into the VCR the cassette of her film *Mumtaz Mahal*. She sits down on the bed and presses the 'Play' button on the remote. The film begins on the TV screen. She orders me to get vegetables from the market and settles down to wait.

I find her the same evening on my return from the market, looking like a beautiful new bride sleeping on the bed. But I don't have to touch her cold skin to know that she is dead. In her hand she holds a trophy. It says, 'National Award for Best Actress. Awarded to Ms Neelima Kumari for her role in *Mumtaz Mahal*, 1985.'

What I see before me can only be described as the height of drama.

I gaze at Neelima Kumari's dead body and I do not know what to do. The only thing I am certain of is that I will not go to the police. They are quite capable of pinning the blame on me and arresting me for murder. So I do the only logical thing. I run away to the chawl in Ghatkopar.

'Why have you come here?' Salim asks me.

'I have also been dismissed by Madam, just like she dismissed the maid and the cook.'

'What will we do now? How will we pay rent for this chawl?'

'Don't worry, she has already paid advance rent for the next two months. By then I am sure I will get a new job.'

* * *

Every day that I stay in the chawl I fear that a jeep with a flashing red light will come to take me away, but nothing happens. There is also no news in the papers about Neelima Kumari's death. Meanwhile, I get a job in a foundry.

They discover her body after a month, and only then because one of the neighbours complains about the smell. So they break open the door and enter. They find nothing in the drawing room or the first four bed-rooms. Then they discover a rotting corpse in the master bedroom. The sari looks new, the jewellery sparkles, but the face and body have decomposed beyond recognition. They cart away the body with white masks on their faces and dump the trophy in the dustbin. They confirm her identity only from her dental records. And when they discover who she was, they publish the picture of her rotting body on the front page of all the newspapers. 'Neelima Kumari, famous Tragedy Queen of yesteryear, has committed suicide. She was forty-four. Her badly decomposed body was discovered in her flat only after a month.'

Now this I call a real tragedy.

Smita lets out a long breath. 'No wonder film stars are neurotic! You know, I have seen *Mumtaz Mahal* and I too have always wanted to know the mystery behind that gold bangle. I wonder what Neelima Kumari told that thief.'

'Unfortunately, that will remain a mystery. Now are we just going to talk about Neelima Kumari, or shall I tell you what happened next on the quiz show?'

With a reluctant expression, Smita presses 'Play'.

There is a flurry of activity inside the studio. We are in the middle of a long break. The producer of the show, a tall man with long hair like a woman – or a rock star – is busy conferring with Prem Kumar in a corner. After he leaves, Prem Kumar gestures me to join him.

'Look, Mr Thomas,' Prem Kumar tells me, 'you have done fantastically well on the show. You are sitting pretty with a million rupees in your kitty. Tell me, what do you intend to do now?'

'What do you mean?'

'I mean are you going to just walk away or will you play for the billion-rupee prize? Remember it is Play or Pay now.'

'Well then, I'm going to walk away. I have been lucky up till now, but my luck might just be running out.'

'Now that would be a real pity, Mr Thomas. We think that if you go on to win this quiz you can become the biggest role model for the youth of our country. So we in *W3B* have decided to make it easier for you to win. You remember how I helped you on the second question? If I had not changed the question for you then, you would have been out with not even a rupee in your pocket. I want to do the same for you on the next three questions. I promise you, if you agree to go into Play or Pay we will help you win, because we want you to win. It will be the best thing that ever happened to our show.'

'What kind of questions did you have in mind?'

'It doesn't really matter, because we will secretly tell

you the answers beforehand. If you could trust me on question number two, I am sure you can trust me on questions ten, eleven and twelve. So do we have a deal?'

'Well, if you are guaranteeing my victory, I can hardly say no. So tell me, what is the next question?'

'Excellent.' Prem Kumar claps his hands. 'Billy,' he tells the producer, 'Mr Thomas has agreed to go into the Play or Pay rounds.' He turns back to me and whispers, 'OK, let me tell you about the next question. I am going to ask you, "What is the length of the Palk Strait between India and Sri Lanka? The choices are going to be a) 64 km, b) 94 km, c) 137 km, and d) 209 km. The correct answer will be c) 137 km. Have you understood?'

'Yes. But how can I be certain that it is the correct answer?'

'Oh, don't you trust us, Mr Thomas? Well, I don't blame you. After all, we are talking about a billion rupees here. So I will prove it to you. Here, look in this book. I am sure you can read numbers.' He pulls out a diary which has page upon page of questions and answers, like a quiz book. He jabs at a question. It is the same question that he has asked me. And it has the same answer: 137 km.

'Are you satisfied now that I am not going to pull a fast one over you?'

I nod my head.

'OK. You'd better return to your seat, and I will join you in a second.'

The signature tune comes on and the studio sign says

'Applause'. Prem Kumar addresses the audience. 'Ladies and gentlemen, we are at a historic crossroads in our show. We have with us a contestant who has reached the magic figure of one million rupees. Now he has to decide whether he goes on to compete for the top prize or retires from the game. The moment of truth has arrived, Mr Thomas. What is your decision? Will you play to win or will you run? Do remember, though, that if you play, you risk losing all that you have won till now. So what do you say?' He smiles at me reassuringly.

'I will play,' I say softly.

'Excuse me?' says Prem Kumar. 'Could you say that a bit louder, please?'

'I will play,' I say loudly and confidently.

There are gasps from the audience. Someone says, 'Oh, my God!' Another says, 'What an idiot!'

'Is this your final, irrevocable decision?' says Prem Kumar. He smiles at me again.

'Yes,' I say.

'Then we have made history, ladies and gentlemen,' Prem Kumar exults. 'We have with us a contestant who is prepared to risk it all. We had one other contestant before who risked it all – and lost. We will see today whether Mr Thomas can create history by becoming the winner of the biggest prize in history. OK, so we are ready for the final three questions in Play or Pay. Please give him a big round of applause.'

There is a crescendo of drums. 'Play or Pay' flashes on the screen. The audience stand up in their seats and clap enthusiastically.

After the music dies down, Prem Kumar turns to me.

'OK, Mr Thomas, you have won one million rupees and you are in the sudden-death round which we call Play or Pay. You will either win a billion or you will lose everything you have earned till now. So question number ten for ten million, yes, ten million rupees is coming up. Here it is. Neelima Kumari, the Tragedy Queen, won the National Award—?"

'But this is not the ques—'

'Please, Mr Thomas, don't interrupt me in the middle of the question. Let me complete,' he says sternly. 'So as I was saying, the question is, Neelima Kumari, the Tragedy Queen, won the National Award in which year? Was it a) 1984, b) 1988, c) 1986 or d) 1985?'

I glare at Prem Kumar. He smirks. I understand him now. What he told me in the break was a trick to lure me into this round. But he has not reckoned with my luck. It is still holding.

'I know the answer. It is d) 1985.'

'What?' Prem Kumar is thunderstruck. He is so surprised that he even forgets to ask me whether I am a hundred per cent sure. He presses his button mechanically and the correct answer flashes. It is D.

Prem Kumar looks as though he has seen a ghost. 'Mr . . . Mr Thomas . . . has . . . just won t-ten million rupees,' he stammers, completely flustered.

The audience goes wild. Everyone stands up and cheers. Some people start dancing in the aisles.

Prem Kumar wipes the sweat from his forehead and takes a big swig of lemonade.

What should have been a tragedy has become a farce.

100,000,000

X Gkrz Opknu
(or A Love Story)

Food. That is all I can see, hear, think and smell on the crowded and noisy railway station where I have been standing in my cotton shirt and Levi jeans for the past two hours. If you don't eat for a while, the hunger just shrivels up and dies. But if you don't eat for a long time – and I have not had a meal since yesterday afternoon – your brain does funny things. All around me I can only see people eating and drinking. And my nose follows the trail of food like a dog sniffing out a bone. The aroma of freshly made *jalebis*, *puris* and *kachoris* makes me dizzy. Even something as basic as a boiled egg, which I have never liked, makes me salivate. But when I finger my pocket I discover only a one-rupee coin, and after last night's loss of my fifty thousand rupees, it doesn't seem lucky any longer. So I lick my parched lips and wonder how to kill my hunger.

I am about to trade in my Kasio digital watch for a plate of *chhole bhature* when my eyes fall on a hoarding next to the railway canteen. It says simply, 'M – Just one kilometre away.' I know instantly where I can get food. For free.

I leave Agra railway station and set about searching for the big red M sign. I take one or two wrong turns, ask a couple of shopkeepers, and find it eventually in the heart of a posh market. The smartly attired waiters at McDonald's look at me suspiciously but don't shoo me away. They can't turn back a customer in Levi jeans, however scruffy he might be. I position myself close to the wooden bin, the one with the swinging flap. When no one is looking I quickly push my hand inside and take out as many of those nice brown paper bags as are within arm's reach. I exit after using the clean toilet to wash off some of the dirt and grime from my face.

My first attempt at scavenging is quite successful. I sit on a green wooden bench outside and feed contentedly on a half-eaten vegetable burger, some chicken nuggets, two almost full packets of French fries and half a cup of 7 Up. Scavenging is part of the survival gear of a street kid. I knew some boys who used to live off the leftovers found in the air-conditioned compartment of the Rajdhani Express. There were others who were addicted to the pepperoni pizza from Pizza Hut, managing to extract at least seven or eight perfect slices every evening from the bin inside the outlet. But they all agreed that the easiest way to eat a free dinner was to join a marriage procession. Salim used to be an expert at this. The only requirement is to wear neat clothes and proper shoes. You mingle with the guests and then line up at the buffet dinner. The bride's side thinks you are from the groom's family and the groom's side thinks you are from the bride's family. You get to drink ten or fifteen bottles of soft drinks, eat a lavish spread and enjoy a wide range of desserts. You can even make off with some nice stainless-steel cutlery. Salim had acquired almost a full dinner set. But he gave up the habit after an episode in Nariman Point, when he gate-crashed a marriage where the families of the bride and groom had a massive fight which degenerated into fisticuffs. Salim got beaten up by both parties.

My hunger sated, I decide to explore this unknown town. I walk through its crowded lanes, full of rickshaws, pedestrians and cows. I admire the intricate latticework on old-fashioned *havelis*, savour the smell of food drifting from road-side kebab shops and pure vegetarian *dhabas*, and wrinkle my nose at the stench coming from open drains and tanneries. I read the giant posters stuck on every empty space, urging people to see new films or vote for old politicians. I see old and wizened craftsmen sitting in derelict shops, making exquisite designs in marble, and brash young salesmen selling cellphones in air-conditioned showrooms. I discover that the rich of Agra are no different from the rich of Delhi and Mumbai, living in their marble and Plexiglas houses with guards and alarms. And that the slums of Agra are no different either. They consist of the same cluster of corrugated-iron sheets masquerading as roofs; the same naked children with pot bellies frolic in the mud with pigs, while their mothers wash utensils in sewer water.

I walk along a winding dusty road, and suddenly I see a river. It is yellowish green and muddy. Its receding water level is a pointer to the fact that the monsoons have still not arrived. Pieces of driftwood and plastic debris float on its eddying currents. In another place I would have traced its meandering route with my eyes, bent down to see its high-water mark on the bank, craned to catch a glimpse of a dead body floating on its surface. But not here, not now. Because my eyes are transfixed by something I have seen on the opposite bank. It is a gleaming white structure which rises up from a square base like a swelling dome, with pointed arches and recessed bays. It is flanked on all four sides by spear-like minarets. It glitters in the sunlight against the turquoise sky like an ivory moon. Its beauty overpowers me.

After an eternity, I turn to the first passer-by I see, a middle-aged man carrying a tiffin box. 'Excuse me, can you tell me what that building is on the other side of the river?'

He looks at me as if I am a lunatic. '*Arrey*, if you don't know that, what are you doing in Agra? That is the Taj Mahal, idiot.'

The Taj Mahal. The Eighth Wonder of the World. I had heard about it, but never seen its picture. I stand mesmerized by the monument as the clouds drifting in the sky cast shadows on its dome, the change of light turning the smooth marble from pale cream to ochre to alabaster. The loss of my fifty thousand rupees, the worries about where I will eat next, sleep next, the fear of being caught by the police, pale into insignificance against the purity of its perfection. I decide then and there that I must see the Taj Mahal today. From up close.

Thirty minutes of brisk walking along the embankment brings me to an enormous red-sandstone entrance gate. A large white board says: TAJ MAHAL ENTRY FEES: INDIANS RS.20 FOREIGNERS $20. MONDAYS CLOSED, FRIDAYS FREE. I look at my Kasio day-date wristwatch. It says Friday, 12 June. Looks like today is my lucky day.

I pass through the metal detector, cross the red-sandstone forecourt with its arched gateway and there, in front of me, the Taj Mahal rises in all its beauty and splendour, shimmering in the afternoon haze. I take in the landscaped garden with fountains and wide paths, the reflecting pool with a glassy image of the Taj dancing in its water, and only then do I notice the overflowing crowds. The Taj is swarming with tourists, young and old, rich and poor, Indian and foreign. There are flashbulbs popping everywhere, a babble of voices rises in the courtyard, while stern-faced, baton-wielding policemen try to restore order.

After half an hour of aimless exploration, I notice a group of prosperous Western tourists armed with camcorders and binoculars, listening intently to an elderly guide at the base of the dome. I join them discreetly. The guide is pointing towards the marble dome and speaking in a rasping voice. 'I have explained to you the architectural features of the red-sandstone forecourt, the Chowk-i Jilo Khana, which we have just passed. Now I will tell you a little bit about the history of the Taj Mahal.

'One day in the year 1607, Prince Khurram of the royal Mughal household was strolling down Delhi's Meena Bazaar when he caught a glimpse of a girl selling silk and glass beads in a small booth. He was so entranced by her beauty that he fell in love with her then and there. But it took five years before he was finally able to marry this girl. Her real name was Arjuman Banu, but he gave her the new name of Mumtaz Mahal. She was nineteen at the time and he was twenty. Mumtaz Begum was the niece of Noorjahan or Mehrunnisa, the wife of Jahangir, who in turn was a niece of Akbar's Persian queen, Bilgis Begum. Mumtaz and Khurram were married in the year 1612, and over the next eighteen years had fourteen children together. Mumtaz was her husband's inseparable companion on all his journeys and military expeditions. She was his comrade, his counsellor, and inspired him to acts of charity and benevolence towards the weak and the needy. She died in childbirth on the seventh of June 1630 in Burhanpur, only three years after Khurram ascended the Mughal throne as Emperor Shahjahan. It was when Mumtaz Mahal lay dying that she extracted four promises from the Emperor: first, that he erect a monument to match her beauty; second, that he should not marry again; third, that he be kind to their children; and fourth, that he visit the tomb on the anniversary of her death. Mumtaz's death left the Emperor so heartbroken that his hair is said to have turned grey overnight. But so great was the Emperor's love for his wife that he ordered the building of the most beautiful mausoleum on earth for her. Work started in 1631. It took twenty-two years and the combined effort of over twenty thousand artisans and master craftsmen from Persia, the Ottoman Empire, and even Europe, and the result is what you see before you, the Taj Mahal, described by Rabindranath Tagore as "a teardrop on the cheek of time".'

A young girl in hot pants raises her hand. 'Excuse me, who is Tagore?'

'Oh, he was a very famous Indian poet who won the Nobel Prize. He can be compared to, let's say, William Wordsworth,' the guide answers.

'William who?'

'Never mind. Now, as I was saying, the architectural complex of the Taj Mahal is comprised of five main elements: the *Darwaza* or main gateway, the *Bageecha* or garden, the *Masjid* or mosque, the *Naqqar Khana* or rest house, and the *Rauza* or the main mausoleum. The actual tomb is situated inside the Taj, which we will see in a minute. There I will show you the ninety-nine names of Allah on Mumtaz's tomb, and the pen box set into Shah Jahan's tomb, which is the distinguishing feature of a male ruler. These cenotaphs, in accordance with Mughul tradition, are only representations of the real coffins, which lie in the same positions in an unadorned and humid underground crypt. The mausoleum is 57 metres square in plan. The central inner dome is 24.5 metres high and 17.7 metres in diameter, and it is surmounted by an outer shell nearly 61 metres in height. The minarets on all four sides are 40 metres high. You will see how sophisticated the artwork of the time was, because even a

3-centimetre decorative element contains more than 50 inlaid gemstones. Also notice that the lettering of the Quranic verses around the archways appears to be uniform, regardless of their height.

'As a monument to enduring love, the Taj reveals its subtleties to those who know how to appreciate beauty. You will notice that the rectangular base of the Taj is in itself symbolic of the different sides from which to view a beautiful woman. The main gate is like a veil over a woman's face, which should be lifted very gently and slowly on the wedding night. Like a jewel, the Taj sparkles in the moonlight when the semi-precious stones inlaid into the white marble on the main mausoleum catch the glow of the moon. The Taj is pinkish in the morning, milky white in the evening and golden when the moon shines. These changes, it is said, depict the different moods of a woman. I will now take you inside the mausoleum. Please take off your shoes and deposit them here.'

The tourists take off their shoes and enter the main mausoleum. I remain outside, trying to match the changing colours on the dome with what I had seen of the changing moods of Neelima Kumari.

Someone taps me lightly on the shoulder. I whirl around to see a bespectacled foreigner with a wife and two kids staring at me. He is bedecked with gizmos of all kinds, from digital camcorder to mini disc player. 'Excuse me, you speak English?' he asks me.

'Yes,' I reply.

'Please, can you tell little bit about Taj Mahal. We are tourists. From Japan. We new to your city. We come just today.'

I feel like telling him that I am also new to this city, that I also came just today, but his curious face appeals to me. Mimicking the serious tone of the guide, I begin to tell him what I remember. 'The Taj Mahal was built by Emperor Khurram for his wife Noorjahan, also known as Mumtaz Begum, in 1531. He met her while she was selling bangles in a garden and fell in love with her, but married her only after nineteen years. She then fought with him in all his battles and gave him eighteen kids in fourteen years.'

The Japanese interrupts me. 'Eighteen kids in only fourteen years? You sure?' he asks diffidently.

'Of course,' I rebuke him. 'Some must have been twins, you see. Anyway, when the nineteenth child was being born, Mumtaz died in Sultanpur on the sixteenth of June. But before she died she asked the king for four favours. One to build the Taj Mahal, two not to beat their children, three to make his hair grey, and the fourth . . . I don't remember, but it's not important. Now, as you can see, the Taj Mahal consists of a gateway, a garden, a guest house and a tomb.'

The Japanese nods enthusiastically. 'Yes. Yes. We have seen gateway and garden. Now we see tomb. But where guest house?'

I scowl at him. 'Haven't I told you that the real tombs are underground? Therefore all the area above the ground must have been the guest house. Now inside the mausoleum you will see the tombs of Mumtaz and the Emperor. Don't forget to see the pen with ninety-nine gemstones on it, and every three centimetres you will see fifty names of God engraved on the walls. The verses on the walls all mean the same, regardless of the different lettering. Isn't that wonderful? Remember that the dome is 160 metres high and the minarets are seventeen metres tall. Also, if you view the Taj Mahal from different angles you will see different veils of a woman on her wedding night. Go and try it. Before I forget, I must also tell you that Tagore, our famous poet, won the Nobel prize for his poetry on the Taj Mahal, called "The Slap on the Cheek of William Wordsworth."'

'Really? Wow! So interesting! Guide book no mention all this.' He turns to his wife and speaks to her in rapid-fire Japanese. Then he translates for my benefit. 'I tell my wife it is good we no take expensive official guide. You tell us everything so nicely.' He beams at me. 'We thank you very much. Arigato.' He bows to me and slips something into my hand. I bow back. As he moves on I open my fist to see a neatly folded, crisp new fifty-rupee note. For just five minutes' work!

I know two things now: I want to stay in the city of the Taj Mahal, and I wouldn't mind becoming a tourist guide.

Dusk is beginning to fall by the time I finally tear myself away from the marble monument, now cloaked in a reddish hue. I have to find a place to stay. I accost a young boy in the street. He is around my age, and wears a white T-shirt, grey pants and blue Hawaii slippers. He is standing still, watching an altercation in the street. I tap him gently on the shoulder. 'Excuse me,' I say. He whirls around and looks at me with the kindest eyes I have ever seen. I sense friendship and curiosity and warmth and welcome in those expressive brown eyes. 'Excuse me,' I repeat, 'I am new to this city. Can you show me a place where I can stay?'

The boy nods his head and says, 'Uzo Q Fiks X Ckka Lgxyz.'

'Excuse me?' I say.

'Ykhz Sqpd Hz. Q Fiks X Ckka Lgxyz,' he repeats, flapping his hands.

'Excuse me, I do not understand this language. I am sorry to have troubled you. I will ask someone else.'

'Ejop Bkggks Hz,' he insists and takes my arm. He begins pulling me in the direction of the market. I think of breaking free, but his face is so friendly that I allow myself to be led. He walks in a peculiar fashion, almost on tiptoe. He takes me through narrow labyrinthine by-lanes and twisted alleys, and after fifteen minutes we emerge in front of a large mansion. 'Swapna Palace' says the brass nameplate next to a huge iron door. He opens the door and we step inside. The mansion has a curved driveway, a massive lawn with a painted Gujarati swing and a fountain in it. I see two gardeners toiling on the grass. An old Contessa car stands in the driveway, being polished by a uniformed chauffeur. My friend is obviously known to the occupants of the mansion, because no one tries to stop him as he takes me up the driveway to the ornate wooden entrance of the house and presses the door-bell. A dark, young, good-looking maid opens the door. She looks at my friend and says, 'Oh, it is you, Shankar. Why do you come here again and again?

You know Madam does not like it when you come this side.'

Shankar points at me. 'Dz Izzao X Nkkh.'

The maid looks me up and down. 'Oh, so Shankar has brought you here as a new tenant? I don't think there are any rooms left in the outhouse, but I will call Madam.' She disappears into the house.

Presently a middle-aged woman appears at the entrance. She is wearing an expensive silk sari and tons of gold jewellery. Her face is covered in make-up. She might have been beautiful in her youth, but, unlike Neelima Kumari, her face has lost its glow. Plus she has pinched lips which make her look rather severe. I take an instinctive dislike to her.

Shankar gets extremely excited on seeing the woman. 'Q Gkrz Ukj Hjhhu,' he says with a wide grin, but the woman doesn't even register his presence. 'Who are you?' she asks me, looking closely at my clothes. 'And why have you come with Shankar?'

I begin to wilt under her scrutiny.

'My name is Raju Sharma,' I say. There is no way I am going to use any of my real names in this city. Not after killing an unknown man in a train.

'Oh, so you are a Brahmin?' she asks, her eyes turning even more suspicious. I should have realized that a dark-skinned Brahmin would be something of a novelty.

'Yes. I am new to Agra. I have come to ask if there is anywhere I can stay.'

'We have an outhouse where we keep tenants.' I notice she uses the royal 'we'. 'Right now no room is available, but if you can wait a week, we can arrange for a room. It will cost you four hundred rupees per month, with the rent to be paid in advance in full at the beginning of the month. If this is acceptable, Lajwanti can show you the outhouse. But you will have to manage somewhere else for a week.'

'Thank you, Madam,' I reply in English. 'I will take the room and I will pay you four hundred rupees next week.'

The lady looks at me sharply as soon as I speak in English. Her severe features soften somewhat. 'Perhaps you can stay with Shankar for a week. Lajwanti, show him the outhouse.'

That is the end of the interview, conducted at the door.

Lajwanti escorts me to the outhouse, which is immediately behind the mansion and which I discover to be the North Indian equivalent of the chawl. It has a huge cobbled courtyard, with interconnected rooms constructed all round the periphery. There must have been at least thirty rooms in the tenement. Shankar's room is almost in the middle of the eastern corridor. He unlocks the door and we step inside. There is just one bed and a built-in *almirah* in the room, and, attached to it, a tiny kitchen, just like in our Ghatkopar chawl. The toilets are communal and located at the end of the western corridor. Bathing can only be done in the centre of the courtyard, under a municipal tap, in full view of the residents of the tenement. Lajwanti points out her own room. It is eight rooms before Shankar's. And the room I will get in a week's time is four rooms after Shankar's.

Before Lajwanti returns to the mansion, I ask her a

quick question. 'Excuse me, but who is this boy Shankar? I've just met him in front of the Taj Mahal.'

She sighs. 'He is an orphan boy who lives here. We are all very fond of him. The poor fellow has some problem in his brain and cannot talk sense, just utters nonsense words. He roams around the city aimlessly all day. It is Madam's kindness that she has allotted him a room free of charge and also gives him some money to buy food. Otherwise the mental-asylum people would have picked him up a long time ago.'

I am shocked. Shankar appeared to me to be an intelligent boy, with only a speech defect. Perhaps my assessment of Madam is also off the mark. Given her benefaction to Shankar, she cannot be as stern as she looks. 'And Madam. Tell me more about her,' I ask Lajwanti.

Like a court historian recounting the genealogy of an empress, Lajwanti explains the impressive lineage of her employer. 'Her real name is Queen Swapna Devi. But we all call her Madam or Rani Sahiba. Her father was the King of the Princely State of Jamgarh, Raja Shivnath Singh, of the Rathore dynasty. On the maternal side, her grandfather was the King of Dharela, near Agra, Raja Ravi Pratap Singh, who is the original owner of this *haveli*. When she was just twenty, Swapna Devi was married to the son of the King of Bhadohi, Kunwar Pratap Singh, belonging to the Gautam dynasty, and shifted to Benares, where the family had a mansion. Unfortunately, her husband, the young prince, died within just two years of the marriage, but she did not remarry. She continued to

live in Benares for another twelve years. In the mean-
time, her grandfather Raja Ravi Pratap Singh died,
bequeathing this *haveli* to her. So she moved to Agra
and has lived here for the last ten years.'

'What about children?' I ask her.

Lajwanti shakes her head. 'No. She does not have
any offspring, so she keeps herself busy with
charitable activities and social occasions. She is probably the richest woman in Agra and very well
connected. The police commissioner and the district
magistrate eat at her house every week, so you'd better
not entertain any ideas about staying here and not paying the rent. If you don't pay her rent on the first, you
are out on the second. Better get this straight.'

That evening, Shankar cooks food for me and insists
that I sleep in his bed. He sleeps on the hard stone
floor. This kindness brings tears to my eyes. The fact
that he is also an orphan like me gives rise to a deep
bond between us. A bond beyond friendship. Beyond
companionship. Beyond words.

That night it rains in Agra.

I had to pay four hundred rupees to Madam within
seven days so I wasted no time in acquiring the
knowledge relevant to my chosen vocation. The fifty
rupees I had with me got me admission to the Taj for
two days, and Shankar lent me ten rupees for a third
day as well. I would hang around groups of Western
tourists, listening to English-speaking guides and trying to memorize as many of the facts and figures
mentioned as possible. It was not very difficult, partly
because I took to the Taj Mahal like a pickpocket to a

crowded bus. Perhaps it was in my blood. Mumtaz Mahal could have been one of my mother's ancestors. Or my father might have been of Mughal descent. Anyway, by the fourth day I had picked up enough knowledge about the Taj Mahal to aspire to join the ranks of the hundreds of unlicensed guides in Agra. I hung around the red-sandstone entrance and offered my services to the foreign tourists who came to see the Taj even in the stifling June heat. My first 'clients' were a bunch of young college girls from England with freckles, sun tan, travellers' cheques and very few clothes. They listened attentively to me, didn't ask any difficult questions, took a lot of photographs, and gave me a ten-pound note as a tip. It was only when I converted the note at the forex bureau that I realized I had got seven hundred and fifty rupees, even after deducting the three per cent commission the shop charged me. Almost enough to pay rent for the next two months!

I shifted to my own room in the outhouse after a week, but in the seven days I spent in Shankar's room I learnt many things about him. I discovered that his language was not just meaningless gibberish. Although the words sounded nonsensical to us, for him they held a peculiar internal coherence. I also learnt that Shankar's favourite food was chapattis and lentils. That he hated aubergine and cabbage. That he had no interest in toys. That he had superb artistic skills and could draw a person down to the tiniest detail, simply from memory. And that, like me, he dreamt of his mother. On two nights I heard him cry out, 'Mummy, Mummy' in his sleep. And I knew that deep within him he did possess the ability to speak more than non-sense syllables.

Living with him must have had a psychological impact on me, because I recall dreaming about a tall young woman clad in a white sari with a baby in her arms. The wind howls behind her, making her jet-black hair fly across her face, obscuring it. The baby looks into her eyes and gurgles sweetly, 'Mama . . . Mama.' The mother opens her mouth to reply to the baby, but the only sound that comes out of her lips is 'Q Gkrz Ukj Hu Wxwu.' The baby shrieks and tumbles from her lap. I wake up, and check whether I still have a tongue.

During the next year in Agra, I acquired a wealth of information about the Taj Mahal. I learnt intimate details about the life of Mumtaz Mahal, such as the fact that her fourteenth child, during whose birth she died, was called Gauharar. I memorized detailed accounts of the construction of the Taj, such as that the State Treasury supplied 466.55 kilograms of pure gold, valued at six lakh rupees in 1631, and the total cost of construction came to 41,848,826 rupees, 7 annas and 6 pies. I delved into the controversy of who really built the Taj and the spurious claim of Geronimo Veroneo, an Italian goldsmith. I found out about the legend of a second Taj and the mystery of the basement chambers and a probable third grave. I could hold forth on the art of *pietra dura,* used in the floral patterns on the walls of the Taj, and the gardens modelled on the Persian Char Bagh style. The fact that I spoke fluent English immediately gave me a headstart. Foreign tourists flocked to me and pretty soon the fame of Raju Guide had spread far and wide. But this did not mean that I became an authority on the Taj Mahal. I had information, but no knowledge. Raju Guide was no better than a parrot who faithfully recited what he heard, without really understanding a word.

Over time, I learnt to say 'Konichiwa' to Japanese tourists and 'Dasvedanya' to Russians, 'Muchas gracias' to Hispanic tippers and 'Howdy' to American rednecks. But, to my everlasting regret, I never had an Australian client whom I could slap on the back and say, 'G'day mate, I'm gonna give you the good oil about this rip-snorter of a tomb!'

I also started earning good money from the tourists. Not a fortune, but certainly enough to pay my rent, eat in McDonald's or Pizza Hut once in a while, and still manage to save up for a rainy day. Except that a rainy day ceases to have meaning for a person who has lived in the open under a monsoon cloud most of his life. I had experienced too many misfortunes, and with the constant fear at the back of my mind that a jeep with a flashing red light could come any day to arrest me for the murder of a nameless dacoit or Shantaram or even Neelima Kumari, it felt pointless to make long-term plans for the future. I treated money, therefore, like I treated my life – as an expendable commodity. Easy come, easy go. Not surprisingly, very soon I became famous in the outhouse as a soft touch.

The residents of the outhouse were a motley collection: poor college students from far-off villages, government clerks who were illegally renting out their official accommodation at exorbitant rates, train drivers, laundry workers, gardeners, cooks, cleaners, plumbers, carpenters, and even a poet with the mandatory beard. Many of them became my friends. Living in their midst, I came to realize that Emperor Shahjahan and Mumtaz Mahal's story was not the only one in this sleepy little town.

Lajwanti was the official 'news supplier' of the outhouse. She had an ear to the ground and knew exactly what was going on in the neighbourhood. She knew the wife-beaters and the adulterers, the drunkards and the misers, the rent-evaders and the bribe-takers. Despite her obvious loyalty to her employer, she was also not averse to sharing some titbits about the palace. It was from her that I heard the gossip about Swapna Devi's colourful past. It was rumoured that she had had a torrid affair with her late husband's brother, Kunwar Mahendra Singh, but eventually fell out with him and poisoned him to death. It was also said that her liaison had resulted in an illegitimate daughter in Benares. What happened to the daughter nobody knew, and nobody seemed to care.

Shakil, one of the poor students living in the outhouse, approaches me one evening.

'Raju *bhai*, if you don't mind, can I ask you a favour?' he asks diffidently.

'Yes, Shakil, what is it?' I reply, sensing the purpose of his visit.

'Actually, my father has been unable to send me the money order this month because of the drought in the village, and unless I pay the university fees by Monday I will be rusticated. Can you please lend me one hundred and fifty rupees? I promise to repay you as soon as I receive the money order next month.'

'Of course, Shakil. I have already lent fifty to our great poet Najmi and a hundred to Gopal, and I had been keeping a hundred to buy a new shirt. But your requirement is greater than mine, so take it all.'

Shankar and I have been invited by Lajwanti to her room for dinner. She is unmarried and lives alone in the outhouse, but has a younger sister who lives in a village approximately thirty kilometres from Agra. The first thing I notice about Lajwanti's room is its obsessive tidiness. It is the cleanest room I have ever seen. The stone floor has been polished to a sparkle. There is not a speck of dust. The bed is very neatly made, with not even a crease on the cotton bedspread. There are little decorative objects displayed on a mantel with geometric precision. Everything is painfully neat. Even the kitchen looks so sanitized that I can almost imagine the soot from her *chulha* being white rather than black. Shankar and I sit on chairs; Lajwanti sits on the bed, wearing a pink sari. She seems very excited and tells us that she has started searching for a suitable bridegroom for her sister, Lakshmi, who is now nineteen years old.

'But what about you?' I ask her. 'Shouldn't the elder sister get married first?'

'Yes, she should,' she replies. 'But I am not just a sister to Lakshmi, I have been her father and mother ever since our parents died five years ago. That is why

I cannot act selfishly and think only about myself. Once I have married off my sister, my responsibilities will be over and I can then look for my own prince.'

'So how are you going about searching for suitable grooms?'

'I placed an ad in *Dainik Ujala*, the Hindi newspaper, two months ago, and due to the blessings of Goddess Durga the response has been very good. See how many letters have come.' She holds out a bundle of letters and envelopes. From these she extracts six photographs and shows them to us. 'Tell me, which one of these boys will be suitable for Lakshmi?'

Shankar and I examine the prospective grooms. We find fault with almost all of them. This one looks too old. This one has a wicked smile. This one is ugly. This one has a scar. This one picture looks like a prisoner's mugshot. That leaves only one photo. It shows the face of a handsome young man with stylish hair and a thick moustache. 'Yes, this boy looks to be the best of the lot,' I tell Lajwanti. Shankar also nods his head in fervent approval. 'Q Gqfz Pdz Wku,' he says.

Lajwanti is delighted with our selection. 'He is my choice too. Apart from being the best looking, he is also the most qualified and comes from a very respectable family. Do you know that he is a very high-ranking government officer?'

'Really? What does he do?'

'He is the Assistant Sugarcane Officer in the District. Lakshmi will live like a queen with him. So should I commence negotiations with his family? Take

Goddess Durga's blessings to move the process forward?'

'Of course, without any delay.'

Lajwanti serves us an excellent meal that evening, of *puris*, *kachoris*, potatoes, lentils and *muttar paneer*, on steel plates so clean they could double up as mirrors. I feel almost guilty eating off her spotless crockery, worried that it might get scratched. I cannot resist asking her, 'Lajwanti, how come your house is so neat and clean? Do you keep a maid?'

She appreciates my noticing. 'Don't joke with me. How can a maid employ a maid? I am the one who keeps this house in tip-top order. This has been my habit since childhood. I cannot live in an unclean house. My fingers start itching the moment I see a speck of dirt on the floor, a piece of food sticking to the dining table or a crease on the bed cover. My mother used to say, "Lajwanti cannot tolerate even a leaf sticking out wrongly from a tree." That is why Rani Sahiba is so happy with me. I overheard her telling Commissioner Sahib's wife the other day that Lajwanti is the best maid she has ever had and she will never let me go.' She beams with pride.

'Yes, I agree, you must be the most efficient maid in the whole world. But you'd better not visit my room, otherwise you will get sick.'

Shankar also agrees that Lajwanti is the greatest. 'Q Gkrz Gxesxipq,' he says with a wide happy grin.

My last patrons today are a group of four rich college students from Delhi. They are a young, boisterous lot in designer jeans and imported sunglasses who make flippant remarks about the Taj Mahal, rib each other incessantly and crack vulgar jokes. At the end of the guided tour they not only give me my fee but a fat tip as well. They then invite me to join them on a night out in their chauffeur-driven minivan. 'Raju Guide, come with us, we will give you the time of your life,' they implore. I decline at first, but they are insistent and I am so beholden to them for their generous *baksheesh* that I cannot say no. I hop into the vehicle.

First we go to the Palace Hotel. This is my first-ever visit to a five-star hotel. I sit in its air-conditioned restaurant and take in the gleaming, softly lit chandeliers, the liveried waiters, the light instrumental music and the well-dressed clientele exuding wealth and influence. The men speak in confidential low tones, the women are like delicate dolls. The food is mouth-watering. One of the boys passes me the menu. 'Here, Raju. Order whatever you fancy.' I take a look at the menu and almost choke on seeing the prices. A plate of butter chicken costs six hundred rupees! At the roadside stall near the outhouse I can buy the same thing for a mere fifty-five rupees. But I realize that here you do not pay simply for the food, you pay for the ambience as well. The boys order practically everything on the menu and two bottles of Scotch whisky.

The sight of all this opulence makes me uneasy. In Mumbai, Salim and I would gatecrash the weddings of the rich for free food, but we never grudged them their wealth. But seeing these rich college boys spending money like paper, I am gripped by a totally new sense of inadequacy. The contrast with my own imperfect life pinches me with the force of a physical hurt. Not surprisingly, my hunger just shrivels up and dies, despite the mounds of tempting dishes lying on my table. I realize then that I have changed. And I wonder what it feels like to have no desires left because you have satisfied them all, smothered them with money even before they are born. Is an existence without desire very desirable? And is the poverty of desire better than rank poverty itself? I think about these questions, but do not arrive at any satisfactory answers.

After they have eaten enough food and drunk enough whisky, the boys ask me to hop in the minivan once again.

'Where are we going now?' I ask.

'You'll see,' they say and laugh.

The driver takes us through narrow streets and teeming bazaars towards the outskirts of Agra. He finally enters a strange-looking settlement close to the National Highway called Basai Mohalla. There is a billboard at its entry which says: 'Enter the Red Light Area at your own risk. Always remember to use a condom. Prevent AIDS, Save Lives.' I do not understand the reference to red light on the billboard. There are no red lights on any of the houses, as far as I can see. There are at least a dozen trucks parked along the road. Some barefoot children loiter in the streets – there is no sign of their mothers. The faint sound of music and dancers' ankle bells floats into the night air. In the distance, I can see the dome and minarets of the Taj Mahal shimmering under the golden moonlight. The halo of the moon and the sight of the marble monument imbue even this dusty and dirty enclave of single- and double-storey shacks with a bit of gold dust.

The college students alight from their vehicle and move towards a cluster of small buildings. I hesitate, but they pull me along. I now see that the area is bustling with people. Vile-looking men in *kurta* pyjamas loaf in front of the houses, chewing betel leaf. I see girls of various ages sitting on the steps wearing just petticoats and blouses, with heavy make-up and jewellery. Some of them give us come-hither looks and make obscene and suggestive gestures with their fingers. I now understand what a red-light area is. It is a place where prostitutes work. I had heard about the existence of Falkland Road in Mumbai and G B Road in Delhi, but had never actually visited a red-light area. And I didn't even know there was one in Agra. This was indeed turning out to be a night of new experiences for me.

The boys step inside a large, two-storey house, which looks less seedy than the others, making sure that I am with them. We enter a foyer, from which narrow corridors lead off to sets of small rooms.

A man meets us. He is young, with a scarred face and shifty eyes. 'Welcome, gentlemen, you have come to the right place. We have the youngest and best girls in Agra,' he says.

The boys go into a huddle with him, negotiating the price. A sheaf of notes exchanges hands. 'We are paying for you as well, Raju. Go, enjoy at our expense,' they say, before each one of them disappears into a room with a girl. I am left alone in the foyer. Presently an old woman chewing *paan* comes along and takes me with her. I follow her up a flight of stairs. She stops in front of a green wooden door and tells me to enter. Then, with tired steps, she troops back down the stairs.

I cannot decide whether to enter the room or go back to the minivan. One part of my brain tells me to leave immediately. But the other impels me to stay, driven by an almost manic curiosity. In the Hindi films I have seen, the prostitute heroine is inevitably a good-hearted girl who has been forced into the profession against her will. At the end of the film the prostitute almost always commits suicide by consuming poison. I wonder whether I have been brought to this whorehouse with a purpose. Whether there is a heroine waiting for me behind this door. Whether I am her hero, who is supposed to rescue her. And whether I can change the ending and prevent her death.

I push open the door and enter the chamber.

It is a small room, with a bed in the centre. Somehow the surroundings do not register on me at all. My eyes are drawn only to the girl sitting on the bed in a shocking-pink sari. She is dark and beautiful, with lovely kohl-lined eyes, luscious painted lips and long black hair plaited with fragrant white flowers. She wears excessive make-up and her arms and neck are bedecked with jewellery.

'Hello,' she says. 'Come and sit here with me on the bed.' The words come out of her mouth like musical notes from a piano.

I approach her reluctantly. She senses my hesitation and smiles. 'Don't worry. I won't bite you.'

I sit down near her on the bed. I notice that the bed sheet is rather dirty, with strange splotches and stains on it.

'You are new,' she says. 'What is your name?'

'Ram Mohammad Thom – no, no . . . Raju Sharma,' I reply, catching myself just in time.

'Looks like you forgot your name for a second.'

'No – not at all. What is your name?'

'Nita.'

'Nita what?'

'Meaning?'

'I meant what is your full name? Don't you have a surname?'

She chuckles. 'You have come to a brothel, Sahib, not a marriage bureau. Prostitutes don't have surnames. Like pet cats and dogs, we are called only by our first names. Nita, Rita, Asha, Champa, Meena, Leena, take your pick.' She says this in a matter-of-fact tone, without any rancour or regret.

'Oh, so you are a prostitute?'

She laughs again. 'You are a strange one. *Arrey baba*, when you come to Basai Mohalla you only meet prostitutes. You will definitely not meet your mother and sisters in this part of Agra!'

'How old are you?'

'Now that is a more relevant question. I am seventeen. Don't tell me that you wanted someone even younger. You yourself don't look a tad over sixteen to me.'

'I am also seventeen. Tell me, how long have you been doing this work for?'

'What difference does it make? All you need to know is whether I'm a virgin or not. Well, I'm not. You would have had to pay four times what you paid for me if you wanted a virgin. But try me, I am even better than a virgin. You won't be disappointed.'

'Aren't you worried that you might catch some disease? There is even a billboard at the entrance warning against AIDS.'

She laughs again, a hollow, empty laugh. 'Look, this is a profession for me, not a hobby. It gives me enough to feed me and my entire family. If I was not doing this, my family would have died from hunger long ago. We prostitutes know about AIDS. But it is better to die of disease tomorrow than hunger today, don't you agree? Now are you just going to ask questions or are you going to do something? Don't blame me later if your time runs out and Shyam sends in the next customer. I am much in demand.'

'Who is Shyam?'

'He is my pimp. You gave money to him. Now come, I am taking off my sari.'

'No. Wait. I want to ask you some more questions.'

'*Arrey*, have you come here to fuck or to talk? You are like that *firang* reporter who came here with his tape recorder and camera. Said he was not interested in me and was only doing some research. But the moment I opened my *choli* he forgot all about his research. The only sounds on his tape recorder will be his own moaning and groaning. Let me see now whether you're the same.'

She snaps opens her blouse in one motion. She isn't wearing a bra. Two pert breasts pop out like domes of a brown Taj Mahal. They are perfectly round and smooth and the nipples stand out like exquisite pinnacles. My mouth goes dry. My breathing becomes shallow. My heart starts hammering against my ribs. Her hand slithers down my chest and finds my hardness. She laughs. 'You men are all the same. One look at a woman's tits and all your morals go out of the window. Come.' She pulls me into her and I experience a moment of pure, unadulterated rapture. An electric current darts through my body which thrills rather than shocks. I shiver with pleasure.

Afterwards, when we are lying side by side under the rickety ceiling fan and I have also contributed a stain to the dirty bed sheet, I inhale the fragrance of the flowers in her jet-black hair and kiss her clumsily.

'Why didn't you tell me it was your first time?' she says. 'I would have been more gentle. But go now, your time is over.' She gets up from the bed abruptly and begins gathering her clothes.

Her sudden brusqueness upsets me. Five minutes ago I was her lover, but now I am just a customer whose time has expired. I realize then that the moment has indeed passed. The magic has gone, and now that I am no longer blinded by my desire, I see the room in its true colours. I see an antiquated cassette player on a side table, connected to the mains by an ugly black cord. I see the mouldy walls with peeling paint. I see the torn and faded red curtain at the window. I see the stains on the sheet and the tears on the mattress. I feel a slight itching sensation, probably from the mites infesting the bed. I sniff the decaying, musty smell of the room. Everything now seems sordid and sleazy. Lying in the soiled bed, I feel polluted and unclean. I, too, get up and hastily gather my clothes.

'What about my tip?' she asks, pulling her blouse back on.

I take out a fifty-rupee note from my wallet and hand it to her. She tucks it gratefully inside her blouse.

'Did you enjoy that? Will you come again?' she asks.

I don't reply and leave hastily.

Later, sitting in the minivan going back to the city, I reflect on her questions. Did I enjoy that? Yes. Will I come again? Yes. A strange new sensation tugs at my heart and makes me giddy. Is it love? I ask myself. I don't know the answer, but I know this – I entered the red-light district at my own risk. I met a hooker, had sex for the first time. And now I was hooked.

There is a rabies scare in the city. Many children have died after being bitten by infected dogs. The health department is advising citizens to be extra vigilant and take preventive steps. I warn Shankar, 'Be careful when you go outside. Don't go near any dogs. Understood?'

Shankar nods his head.

It's the turn of Bihari the cobbler today. He is the only one who has not asked me for any money till now. 'Raju, my child Nanhey is very sick and has been admitted to Dr Aggarwal's private clinic. The doctor says I have to buy medicines urgently, which cost a lot of money. I have managed to scrape together four hundred so far. Can you please lend me something? I beg you.'

I give two hundred rupees to Bihari, knowing that I will never get them back. But he is still unable to buy all the medicines. Two days later, six-year-old Nanhey dies in the clinic.

That evening, Bihari comes back to the outhouse with the body of his son covered in a white shroud. He is obviously drunk and walks with unsteady steps. He places his son's dead body in the middle of the cobbled courtyard, near the municipal tap, and calls everyone out of their rooms. Then he launches into a monologue full of slurred invective. He abuses no one in particular and yet everyone. He abuses the rich, who live in their palatial homes and do not care for the poor who serve them. He abuses the fat-cat doctors who fleece their patients. He abuses the government which makes promises only on paper. He abuses all of us for being mute spectators. He abuses his children for being born. He abuses himself for still being alive. He abuses God for creating an unjust world. He abuses the world, the Taj Mahal, Emperor Shahjahan. Not even the electric bulb hanging outside his house, that once gave a shock to Nanhey, or the municipal tap escape his ire. 'You rotten piece of junk, when we need it, you don't give us two drops of water, but when it came to my son, you allowed him to frolic for two hours and gave him pneumonia. May you soon be uprooted, may you rust in hell,' he curses and kicks the tap. Then, after half an hour of non-stop ranting and raving, he collapses on the ground and begins to sob. He holds his dead son in his arms and wails till his tears run dry, till his voice fails.

In my own room, I lie on the bed and think about the iniquities of life. Images of little Nanhey frolicking in the outhouse flit through my mind. I want to cry, but tears refuse to flow from my eyes. I have seen too many dead bodies. So I pull the crisp white sheet up over my head and go off to sleep. And dream of a Taj Mahal in a special shade of brown. With two exquisitely shaped domes.

I visit Nita again after a week. This time I have to pay the full fee to Shyam, her pimp. Three hundred rupees. I lie in her soiled bed, make love to her and listen to her dirty talk.

'So do you like being a prostitute?' I ask her after our lovemaking.

'Why? What's wrong with it? It is a profession, like any other.'

'But do you like it?'

'Yes. I love sleeping with strangers. Like you, for instance. It gives me enough money to provide for my family. And I get to see a brand-new film at the theatre every Friday. What more could a girl possibly want?'

I look into her doe-like eyes and I know she is lying. She is an actress playing a role. Except she wouldn't win any awards, like Neelima Kumari.

The more Nita seems a mystery, the more desperate I become to know her. She arouses a hunger in me unlike anything I have ever experienced before. I may have entered her body, but now I want to enter her mind. So I begin visiting her on Mondays, when the

Taj Mahal is closed. After four or five visits I finally succeed in breaking down her defences.

She tells me that she is a Bedia tribal girl from the Bhind district in Madhya Pradesh. Both her parents are still alive and she has a brother, and a sister who is happily married. In her community, it is the tradition for one girl from each family to serve as a communal prostitute, called the *Bedni*. This girl earns money for her family, while the males spend their time drinking alcohol and playing cards. 'That is why the birth of a girl is an occasion to celebrate in our community, not a cause for gloom. A boy is, in fact, a liability. You can find *Bednis* from my village in brothels, truck stops, hotels and roadside restaurants, all selling their bodies for money.'

'But why did your mother choose you? She could have chosen your sister.'

Nita gives a hollow laugh. 'Because my beauty became a bane. My mother had the right to decide which of her two daughters would marry and which one would become a prostitute. She chose me to become the *Bedni*. Perhaps if I had been plain looking, like my sister, I would not have been sent here. I might have gone to school, married and had children. Now I am in this brothel. This is the price I have to pay for beauty. So don't call me beautiful.'

'And how long have you been doing this?'

'Ever since puberty. Once the *nathni utherna* ceremony for the removal of the nose ring and the *sar dhakwana* ritual for covering the head are over, you are deemed to have become a woman. So at the age of twelve, my virginity was auctioned to the highest bidder and I was put on sale inside this brothel.'

'But surely if you want to you can quit this profession and get married, can't you?'

She spreads her hands. 'Who will marry a prostitute? We are supposed to work till our bodies start to sag or till we die of disease, whichever is sooner.'

'I know you will find your prince one day,' I declare, with tears in my eyes.

She doesn't accept any tip from me that day.

I reflect later on my conversation with Nita and wonder why I had lied to her. I didn't really want her to find any other prince. Without even realizing it, I had fallen in love with her.

Till now, my conception of love has been based entirely on what I have seen in Hindi films, where the hero and the heroine make eye contact and whoosh, some strange chemistry sets their hearts beating and their vocal chords tingling, and the next you see of them they are off singing songs in Swiss villages and American shopping malls. I thought I had experienced that blinding flash of love when I met the girl in the blue salwar kameez in that train compartment. But real love visited me only that winter in Agra. And I realized again that real life is very different from reel life. Love doesn't happen in an instant. It creeps up on you and then it turns your life upside-down. It colours your waking moments and fills your dreams. You begin to walk on air and see life in brilliant new shades. But it also brings with it a sweet agony, a delicious torture. My life was reduced to feverish meetings with Nita and pining for her in between. She visited me in the oddest places and at the oddest moments. I visualized her beautiful face even when lecturing a haggard, eighty-year-old day-tripper. I smelt the fragrance of her hair even when sitting on my toilet seat. I got goose bumps thinking of our love-making even when buying potatoes and tomatoes from the vegetable market. And I knew in my heart of hearts that she was my princess. The burning ambition of my life was to marry her one day. The consuming worry of my life was whether she would agree.

A jeep with a flashing red light has come to the out-house. An inspector and two constables alight from it. My heart lurches. A cold knot of fear forms in the pit of my stomach. My crimes have finally caught up with me. This is the pattern of my life. Just when I begin to feel on top of things, fate yanks the rug from under my feet. So it is to be expected that just when I have dis-covered true love, I should be taken away to a jail where, like Emperor Shahjahan, I will sit in solitary confine-ment and pine for Nita, my own Mumtaz Mahal.

The Inspector takes out a megaphone from the jeep to make an announcement. I expect him to say, 'Will Ram Mohammad Thomas, alias Raju Sharma, come out with his hands in the air?' But he says instead, 'Will all the residents of the outhouse come out? There has been a robbery in the Bank of Agra and we have reason to believe that the thief is here. I have to con-duct a search of the premises.' When I hear this, I feel a heavy weight lift from my heart. I am so happy, I want to go out and hug the Inspector.

The constables enter each room in turn and conduct a thorough search. They come to my room and ask me for my name, my age, my occupation, whether I have seen any suspicious characters lurking about in the area. I don't tell them that I am an unauthorized guide. I say I am a student at the University and am new to the outhouse. This satisfies them. They look under my bed. They peer into the kitchen, tap the pots and pans, overturn the mattress and then move on to the next room. The Inspector joins the constables.

They are now in Shankar's room.

'Yes, what is your name?' the Inspector asks Shankar gruffly.

'Hu Ixhz Qo Odxifxn,' Shankar replies, slightly confused.

'What? Can you repeat that?'

'Odxifxn.'

'Bloody bastard, you are making fun of me?' the Inspector says angrily, and raises his baton to hit Shankar.

I quickly intervene. 'Inspector Sahib, Shankar has a mental problem. He cannot speak.'

'Then why didn't you say so before?' He turns to his constables. 'Let's go to the next room. We won't get anything out of a lunatic.'

They search all thirty rooms during the next three hours, and eventually unearth a cache of currency in the room belonging to Najmi, the bearded poet, who claimed to be a Bollywood songwriter. We are all astonished to discover that our young poet is a part-time bank robber as well. Just goes to show that appearances can be deceptive. Well, I can hardly complain. The outhouse *wallahs* would be just as scandalized if they found out about my own chequered past!

Lajwanti has come to my room to offer some crumbly fresh *laddoos* from the nearby Durga Temple. She is very excited.

'*Arrey*, Lajwanti, what are the sweets in aid of? Have you got a raise?' I ask her.

'This is the happiest day of my life. With Goddess Durga's blessings, the Sugarcane Officer has finally agreed to marry Lakshmi. My sister will now live like a queen. I am preparing for a wedding to beat all weddings.'

'But what about dowry? Hasn't the groom's family made any demands?'

'No, not at all. They are a very decent family. They do not want any cash. They have only requested some very small things.'

'Like what?'

'Like a Bajaj scooter, a Sumeet Mixer, five Raymond suits and some gold jewellery. I was, in any case, going to give all this to Lakshmi.'

I am scandalized. 'But Lajwanti, this will cost you a packet – at least a lakh rupees. Where will you get this money from?'

'I have been saving up for Lakshmi's wedding. I have accumulated nearly fifty thousand rupees. And I will borrow another fifty thousand from Rani Sahiba.'

'Are you sure she will give you such a large sum of money?'

'Of course. I am the best maid she has ever had.'
'Well, good luck then.'

I continue to meet Nita, but the atmosphere inside the
brothel stifles me. And I hate dealing with that shifty-
eyed pimp Shyam. So on Nita's suggestion we start
meeting outside. She goes alone to see films every
Friday. I join her. She loves popcorn. I buy her a big
packet and we sit in the back row of the dark and
dingy Akash Talkies. She eats popcorn and giggles
when I slip my hand through her thin muslin dress to
feel her soft breasts. At the end of the film, I come out
of the hall hot and flushed, not knowing whether I've
seen a family drama, a comedy or a thriller. Because I
have eyes only for Nita, and I hope that our own story
will turn slowly but surely into an epic romance.

Shankar enters my room crying.
    'What's the matter?' I ask.
    He points to his knee. It is cut and bruised. I im-
mediately become concerned. 'How did you get hurt,
Shankar? Did you fall down?'
    Shankar shakes his head. 'X Akc Wqp Hz,' he says.
    For once, I wish he could speak sense. 'I am sorry, I
don't understand. Why don't you come outside and
show me how you got hurt?'
    Shankar takes me out and points to where the cobbled
courtyard joins the main road. There is a little parapet in
the corner, from which the kids in the outhouse are
always jumping up and down.
    'Yxi Ukj Ozz Pdxp Akc? Dq Wqp Hz Dznz,' Shankar
says and indicates his knee.

I trace the direction of his finger and nod in understanding. I reckon that he must have jumped down from the parapet and grazed himself. 'Come, Lajwanti has a medical kit in her room. I will get her to put a dressing on your wound.'

I fail to see the mangy little street dog with black spots huffing on the cobbled pavement just below the parapet, spit dribbling from its sharp white teeth.

A new year has dawned, bringing with it new hopes and new dreams. Nita and I have both turned eighteen – the legal age for marriage. For the first time, I begin to think about the future and to believe I might even have one. With Nita by my side. I stop lending money to people in the outhouse. I need every penny now.

Today is a Friday, and also a night of the full moon, a very rare combination indeed. I persuade Nita not to go to the movies, but instead to come with me to the Taj Mahal. We sit on the marble pedestal late in the evening and wait for the moon to appear beyond the jets of fountains and the rows of dark-green cypresses. First comes a glimmer of silver through the tall trees on our right, as the moon struggles to break free of the cluster of low buildings and foliage, and then, suddenly, it rises majestically in the sky. The curtain of the night is pushed aside and the Taj Mahal stands revealed in all its glory. Nita and I are awestruck. The Taj appears like a vision of paradise, a silvery apparition risen from the Yamuna river. We clasp hands, oblivious to the hordes of foreign tourists who have paid fifty dollars each for the privilege of seeing the Taj by the light of the full moon.

311

I gaze at the Taj and then I gaze at Nita. The sterile perfection of the Taj begins to pale in comparison with the flawless beauty of her face. And tears start falling from my eyes as all the love I have bottled up in my heart for eighteen long years comes out in a tumultuous rush. I sense an emotional release like the bursting of a dam, and experience for the first time what Emperor Shahjahan must have felt for Mumtaz Mahal.

This is the moment I have been waiting for all my life and I have practised for it well. Najmi, the bearded poet, left a book of Urdu poetry for me before going to jail, and I have memorized several romantic verses. In a burst of inspiration, Najmi had even composed an original ghazal in praise of Nita, for my use. It went something like this:

> *Your beauty is an elixir,*
> *Which has given an orphan life,*
> *Lovesick I will die, from the grave I will cry,*
> *Should you decline to become my wife.*

I also recall many immortal dialogues from famous celluloid love stories. But sitting with Nita under the moonlit Taj Mahal, I forsake the world of poetry and films. I look into her eyes and ask her simply, 'Do you love me?' And she replies with just one word, 'Yes.' That one word holds more meaning for me than all the books on poetry and all the guidebooks on Agra. And when I hear it, my heart takes a joyous leap. My mighty love breaks free of the earth, takes wing and soars into the sky, like a kite. And then, for the first time, the Taj Mahal feels like a living house instead of an impersonal tomb; the full moon over our heads becomes a personal satellite, shining a private light, and we feel blessed to be bathed in its celestial glow, in our own exclusive heaven.

Shankar comes running to my room. 'Ykhz Mjqyfgu. Gxesqipq qo ynuqic,' he announces and directs me to Lajwanti's room.

Lajwanti is crying on the bed. The drops falling from her eyes like little pearls and darkening the fabric of her creaseless bed cover seem out of place in the spartan neatness of her room. 'What's wrong, Lajwanti? Why are you weeping?' I ask her.

'Because of that bitch Swapna Devi. She has refused to give me a loan. Now how will I pay for my sister's wedding?' she says and wails again.

'Look, nobody in the outhouse has that kind of money. Can't you get a loan from a bank?'

'Huh, which bank will lend to a poor maid like me? No, now I have only one alternative.'

'What? To cancel your sister's wedding?'

Anger flashes in her eyes. 'No. I will never do that. Perhaps I will have to do what our poet Najmi did. Steal the money.'

I jump up from my chair. 'Are you out of your mind, Lajwanti? Don't even think about it. Didn't you see how the police took Najmi away?'

'That is because Najmi was a fool. I have a foolproof plan, which I am going to share with you because you are like my younger brother. Don't mention this to any-one, not even to Shankar. You see, I have seen the location of the safe where Swapna stashes all her precious things. In her bedroom there is a huge framed painting on the left wall. Behind the painting is a hole where a steel safe is embedded. She keeps the keys to the safe underneath her mattress, in the left-hand corner. I secretly observed her opening the safe once. It is full of money and jewellery. I am not going to steal money, because that will be detected immediately, but I am thinking of making off with a necklace. She has so many in that safe, she wouldn't even notice. What do you think?'

'Lajwanti, Lajwanti, listen to me. If you consider me to be your brother, then follow my advice. Don't even think about this idea. Trust me, I have had many brushes with the law and I know your crime will eventually catch up with you. And then, instead of participating in your sister's wedding, you will be grinding a mill in some jail.'

'Oh, you men are all sissies,' she says in disgust. 'I don't care what you say. I will do what I have to do.'

In desperation, I turn to my trusted old coin. 'Look, Lajwanti, if you don't believe me, that's fine. But believe in the power of this magic coin. It never sends you the wrong way. So let us see what it says. I am going to toss it. Heads, you don't carry out your plan, tails, you do what you want. OK?'

'OK.'

I flip the coin. It is heads. Lajwanti sighs. 'It looks like even luck is against me. OK, I will go to my village and try to raise funds from the headman, who knows me. Forget that we spoke.'

Three days later, Lajwanti locks up her room, takes a week's leave and departs for her village.

'I want you to stop working as a prostitute,' I tell Nita.

Nita agrees. 'I don't want to die before I am twenty like Radha. Take me away from here, Raju.'

'I will. Should I have a chat with Shyam about this?'

'Yes, we must get his agreement.'

I speak to the pimp the same evening. 'Look, Shyam, I am in love with Nita and I want to marry her. She will no longer work in the brothel.'

Shyam looks me up and down as if I am an insect. 'I see, so you have been giving her all these stupid ideas. Listen, you bastard, nobody tells Nita to stop working. Only I can tell her that. And I don't want her to stop working. She is the goose which lays the golden eggs. And I want those eggs to keep coming for a long, long time.'

'That means you will never allow her to marry?'

'I can allow her to marry, but only on one condition. That the man who marries her agrees to compensate me for my loss of earnings.'

'And how much is your estimated loss of earnings?'

'Let's say . . . four lakh rupees. Can you get me that sum of money?' He laughs and dismisses me.

I check my savings that night. I have a total of 480 rupees. Leaving a shortfall of only Rs. 399,520.

I feel so angry I want to strangle the pimp. 'Shyam will never agree to you marrying me,' I tell Nita the next day. 'The only option for us is to run away.'

'No,' Nita says fearfully. 'The brothel people are bound to find us. Champa tried to run away last year

315

with a man. They found her, broke the man's legs and starved her for ten days.'

'In that case I will just have to kill Shyam,' I say with a malevolent glint in my eyes.

'No,' Nita says vehemently. 'Promise me you will never do that.'

I am taken by surprise. 'But why?'

'Because Shyam is my brother.'

A jeep with a flashing red light has come to the out-house. Constables pour out. This time there is a new Inspector. We are all called out again. 'Listen, all you good-for-nothings, something very serious has happened. Someone has stolen a very precious emerald necklace from Swapna Devi's house. I have a strong suspicion that the thief is one of you bastards. So I am giving you an opportunity to make a clean breast of it, otherwise when I catch the thief I am going to give him a hiding.'

I am immediately concerned about Lajwanti, but when I see the lock on her room and remember that she is in her village, I heave a sigh of relief. It is good she dropped that ridiculous idea of stealing a necklace. She thought Swapna Devi wouldn't notice the loss, and now the police are on to it in a flash.

One by one all of us are questioned. When Shankar's turn comes, the same scene is re-enacted.

'Name?' asks the Inspector.

'Odxifxn,' replies Shankar.

'What did you say?'

'Q Oxqa Hu Ixhz Qo Odxifxn.'

'Bastard, trying to act smart with me . . .' the

Inspector says through gritted teeth. I explain again and the Inspector relents. He waves Shankar away.

This time the policemen go away empty handed. Without any necklace and without any suspect.

The same evening a mangy little street dog with black spots dies near the Taj Mahal. No one takes any notice of this fact.

Lajwanti returns from her village the next day and is immediately arrested. A sweaty constable drags her from her room to the jeep with the flashing red light. She wails inconsolably.

Helplessly I watch the spectacle unfold. I am with Abdul, who works as a gardener in Swapna Palace.

'Abdul, why are the police taking Lajwanti away? Why doesn't Rani Sahiba do something? After all, Lajwanti is the best maid she has ever had.'

Abdul grins. 'Madam has herself called the police to arrest Lajwanti.'

'But why?'

'Because Lajwanti stole the necklace from her safe. The police searched her house in the village and found it today.'

'But how did Swapna Devi know it was Lajwanti who stole the necklace? She wasn't even here when the robbery took place.'

'Because she left behind a tell-tale sign. You see, she did not go to her village straight away. She stayed in Agra and waited for an opportunity to break into the house unnoticed. When she finally entered the bedroom to steal the necklace, Madam was at a party. But just before leaving for the party, Madam had combed her hair on the bed and there were a few of her pins and clips lying on the satin bedspread. When Madam returned late at night, she discovered all her pins and clips neatly arranged on her dressing table. This immediately alerted her. She checked her safe and found a necklace was missing. So she knew instantly that it could have been none other than Lajwanti.'

I thump my forehead. Lajwanti couldn't resist being the perfect maid, even when on a mission to steal!

I try to intercede with Swapna Devi on Lajwanti's behalf, but she rebuffs me with icy disdain. 'I run a household, not a charity. Why did she have to arrange such a lavish wedding for her sister? You people who are poor should never try to overreach yourselves. Stay within your limits and you will not get into trouble.'

I feel genuine hatred towards her that day. But perhaps she is right. Lajwanti made the cardinal mistake of trying to cross the dividing line which separates the existence of the rich from that of the poor. She made the fatal error of dreaming beyond her means. The bigger the dream, the bigger the disappointment. That is why I have small, manageable dreams. Like marrying a prostitute after paying off her crooked pimp brother the minor sum of four hundred thousand rupees. Only.

I have barely recovered from Lajwanti's arrest when another tragedy strikes me.

Shankar comes coughing to my room and flops down on the bed. He looks tired and complains of pain in his arms and knees. 'Q Xh Oqyf,' he says, flapping his hands.

I check his forehead and find he has a slight fever. 'You have caught a chill, Shankar,' I tell him. 'Go to your room and rest. I will come round soon to give you some medicine.' He gets up from the bed and tiptoes to his room. He seems restless and irritable.

Later that night, I give Shankar some painkillers, but his condition continues to deteriorate. By the second day, he is becoming violent. He is unable to move his arm and shrieks when the light is switched on. With great difficulty I manage to take his temperature and am shocked to discover that it has shot up to 103 degrees. I immediately go out to call a doctor. The physician working in the government dispensary flatly refuses to come with me, so I am forced to go to a private doctor. He charges me eighty rupees to come to the outhouse. He examines Shankar and asks me whether I have noticed any recent cuts or bruises on him. I tell him about the grazed knee. The doctor nods his head and pronounces his diagnosis. Shankar has got rabies – probably from a mad dog. He should have had a series of injections of human diploid cell vaccine and human rabies immune globulin as soon as he was infected, but now it is too late. His condition is very serious. He will soon develop an aversion to water. He might show signs of agitation and confusion and even have hallucinations. He could have muscle spasms and seizures. And he may stop speaking completely as the vocal cords become paralysed. Finally, he will slip into a coma and stop breathing. In simple language, he will die. And all within forty-eight hours.

The doctor explains this catalogue of horrors in his normal bedside manner. I am utterly devastated. Even thinking about Shankar's death brings tears to my eyes. 'Doctor, is there absolutely nothing that can be done to save Shankar?' I implore him.

'Well,' the doctor hesitates. 'There was nothing till a month ago, but I am told a brand-new experimental vaccine from America has just been imported to India. It is called RabCure and is only available at the Gupta Pharmacy.'

'The one in Rakab Ganj?'

'Yes. But I don't think you can afford it.'

'How much does it cost?' I ask with a sinking heart.

'Approximately four lakh rupees.'

I reflect on the irony of the situation. Shankar's treatment requires four lakh rupees and Nita's pimp has also demanded exactly this amount. And I have the princely sum of four hundred rupees in my pocket.

I do not know where I will get money from for Shankar's treatment, but I know that he cannot be left alone, so I decide to take him to my room. I pick him up in my arms. Even though he is almost my age, his body seems weightless. His hands and legs droop limply by his side, and it feels as if I am not carrying a living person but a sack of potatoes. I deposit Shankar on my bed and lie down on the ground, in an exact reversal of what he did for me almost two years ago, although it now seems like twenty.

Shankar tosses and turns and sleeps fitfully. I too have a difficult night, my sleep interspersed with nightmares about mad dogs and babies who speak only in nonsense syllables. And then, suddenly, in the middle of the night, I seem to hear the words 'Mummy, Mummy' shouted loudly. I wake up, and find Shankar sleeping peacefully. I rub my eyes and wonder whether Shankar's dream had unexpectedly inter-sected with mine.

The whole of the next day, Shankar stays in bed, getting weaker and weaker. I know that he is under sentence of death, but I pretend he has got nothing more than a mild case of flu. It breaks my heart to see his gentle face and to imagine that I will never see it again. Even his nonsense syllables today seem like profound statements which should be memorized.

Night comes and Shankar begins having spasms in his arms. He has difficulty taking in fluid and eats just one chapatti with lentils, his favourite dish. His fore-head burns. I take his temperature and find it has shot up to 105 degrees. 'Q Akip Sxip Pk Aqe, Nxej,' he says and begins crying. I try to comfort him as best I can, but it is difficult to give strength to another when you yourself feel completely hollow inside.

I sleep fitfully again, tormented by the demons of my past. Late that night, when it is almost two o'clock, I hear a sound coming from Shankar's bed, like some-one moaning. I get up slowly, still quite disoriented. I look at Shankar's face. His eyes are closed, but his lips are moving. I strain to hear what he is mumbling and almost jump out of my skin. Because I swear Shankar says, 'Please don't beat me, Mummy.'

'Shankar! Shankar!' I scramble to his bed. 'You just said something, didn't you?'

But Shankar is completely oblivious to me, lost in his own private world. His eyes are lolling upwards and he is clearly delirious. His chest convulses as if in a spasm and phlegm drips from his mouth. 'Why did you throw me out, Mummy?' he mumbles. 'I am sorry, I should have knocked. How could I know Uncle was inside with you? I love you, Mummy. I draw pictures of you. My blue diary is full of pictures. Your pictures. I love you, Mummy. I love you very much. Don't hit me, Mummy. I promise I won't tell anyone, Mummy, Mummy, Mummy . . .'

Shankar speaks in the voice of a six-year-old. He has regressed to a long-lost time. To a time when he had a mother. To a time when his life, and his words, had a meaning. I do not know how he can suddenly speak so sensibly and lucidly when the doctor said he would stop speaking completely. But I have no desire to find out the reason. One doesn't question a miracle.

That is all I hear from Shankar that night, and when he wakes up the next morning, he becomes the same sixteen-year-old who speaks in nonsense syllables. But I remember his reference to a blue diary. I search his room and find it hidden underneath his bed.

It contains loose sheets of drawing paper, all with beautiful pencil drawings of a woman. The drawings are very accurate, down to the last detail. But I stand transfixed not by the excellence of the drawings, but by the identity of their subject. Because the woman in the pictures is Swapna Devi.

'I know what you have been hiding from me all this while, Shankar. I know that Swapna Devi is your mother,' I tell Shankar, holding aloft the blue diary.

His eyes dilate with fear and he tries to grab the diary from my hands. 'Cqrz Hz Wxyf Hu Aqynu,' he shrieks.

'I know it is true, Shankar. I think you discovered her dirty secret and that is why she threw you out of the house. And that is when you lost the ability to speak like a normal boy. I think your mother has lived with this guilt all her life. Perhaps for this reason she pays your rent and gives you money. But I am going to your mummy right now, to ask her to pay for your treatment.'

'Ik, Ik, Ik, Lgzxoz Akip Ck Pk Hu Hjhhu,' he cries. But I have already set off for Swapna Palace for a heart-to-heart chat with Rani Sahiba.

Rani Sahiba refuses to meet me at first, claiming that she meets people only by appointment. I camp on her doorstep for two hours, until finally she relents.

'Yes, why have you come to bother me?' she asks insolently.

'I know your secret, Swapna Devi,' I tell her to her face. 'I have discovered that Shankar is your son.'

Her regal mask slips for an instant and her face turns pale, but she regains her composure equally swiftly and her haughty manner returns to freeze me with contempt. 'You worthless boy, how dare you make such a scurrilous allegation? I have no relationship with Shankar. Just because I showed a little bit of sympathy for that boy, you made him my son? Get out of here right now, or I will have you thrown out.'

'I will go,' I tell her. 'But only after collecting four lakh rupees from you. I need the money for Shankar's treatment. He has contracted rabies.'

'Are you out of your mind? You think I will give you four lakhs?' she shrills.

'But if I don't get the money, Shankar will die of hydrophobia within twenty-four hours.'

'I don't care what you do, but don't bother me.' And then she says the most spiteful thing I have ever heard a mother say. 'Perhaps it is for the best that he dies. The poor boy will be put out of his misery. And don't you dare repeat that lie to anyone about him being my son.' She closes the door.

I stand on her doorstep with tears in my eyes. I was at least lucky enough to have been discarded by my mother at birth, but poor Shankar was cast off by his mother midway through life, and now she was refusing to lift a finger even to prevent his imminent death.

I return to Shankar's room with a heavy heart. Swapna Devi's words resonate in my ears with the force of a hammer blow. She wants Shankar to die like a rabid dog. At no other time has my poverty riled me as much as it does now. I wish I could explain to the dog that bit Shankar that before biting he should have checked whether the person he was attacking could afford the antidote.

The next day, I do something which I have not done for a decade. I pray. I go to the Durga temple and offer flowers for Shankar's recovery. I go to the Church of St John and light a candle for Shankar. I go to the Kali Masjid and bow my head before Allah, asking him to have mercy upon Shankar. But even the power of prayer proves to be insufficient. All day Shankar remains in agony, with pain in virtually all parts of his body. His breathing becomes more irregular.

Night falls. It is moonless, but it does not appear so in the outhouse because of the reflected glow of the thousand lights which have lit up Swapna Palace like a giant candle. There is a party in the palace. The Police Commissioner has come, as well as the District Magistrate, and a whole host of businessmen, socialites, journalists and writers. The sound of soft music and laughter drifts down to the outhouse. We hear the clink of wine glasses, the buzz of conversation, the jingle of money. In my room there is an eerie silence, broken only by Shankar's laboured breathing. Every half-hour or so his body is racked by convulsions. But he is most bothered by the constriction in his throat, where a viscous, stringy spittle has formed, causing him great discomfort. Now he goes into a spasm even at the sight of a glass of water. The slightest gust of air produces the same result.

Of the many ailments a person can die from, perhaps the cruellest is hydrophobia, where water, which is supposed to give life, becomes the cause of death. Even a cancer patient is able to entertain some hope, but a rabies patient has none.

Watching Shankar's slow death, I can only imagine how utterly heartless Swapna Devi must be, to allow her son to die in this horrible fashion while she was having a party in her house. It is lucky that I threw that Colt revolver into the river, otherwise I would definitely be committing another murder tonight.

As the night progresses, Shankar's spasms become more frequent, he shrieks in agony and begins foaming at the mouth. I know that the end is near.

Shankar finally dies at twelve forty-seven am. Just

before dying, he has another lucid moment. He holds my hand and utters a single word, 'Raju.' Then he clutches his blue notebook and cries, 'Mummy, Mummy,' and then he closes his eyes for ever.

Agra has become the city of death. I have a dead body in my room and a blue notebook in my hands. I flip through the pages aimlessly, staring at pencil sketches of a woman who was a heartless mother. No, I will not call her 'mother', because to say that would be an insult to all mothers.

I do not know how to react to Shankar's death. I could scream and shout like Bihari. I could abuse all the gods in heaven and all the powers on earth. I could batter down a door, throw some furniture, kick a lamppost. And then I would break down and cry. But today, the tears refuse to come. A slow, molten rage builds up in my guts. I tear the pages from the notebook and shred them into tiny little pieces. Then, all of a sudden, I pick up Shankar in my arms and proceed towards the lighted palace.

The uniformed guards bar my way, but as soon as they see the dead body in my hands they hastily open the gate. I pass along the curved driveway, where the expensive imported cars of the guests are lined up one after the other. I reach the ornate entrance and find it open in welcome. I pass through the marbled foyer into the dining room, where the guests are about to be served dessert. All conversation ceases the moment they see me.

I climb on to the table, and place Shankar's body gently in the middle, in between a creamy vanilla cake and a bowl of *rasagullas*. The waiters stand as still as statues. The smartly attired businessmen cough and shift uncomfortably in their seats. The ladies take hold of their necklaces. The District Magistrate and the Police Commissioner watch me with worried eyes. Swapna Devi, sitting at the head of the table, clad in a heavy silk sari and loaded with jewellery, looks as if she is going to choke. She tries to open her mouth, but finds her vocal chords paralysed. I look directly at her with as much contempt as I can muster and speak.

'Mrs Swapna Devi, if this is your palace, and you are its queen, then acknowledge the prince. I have come to deliver the dead body of your son Kunwar Shankar Singh Gautam to you. He died half an hour ago, in the outhouse where you have kept him hidden all these years. You did not pay for his treatment. You did not fulfil the duty of a mother. Now honour your obligation as a landlady. Please pay for the funeral of your penniless tenant.'

I say my piece, nod at the guests who watch in frozen silence, and walk out of the stuffy palace into the cool night. I am told that no one had dessert.

Shankar's death affects me deeply. I sleep, cry and sleep again. I stop going to the Taj Mahal. I stop meeting Nita. I stop seeing films. I press the 'Pause' button on my life. For a fortnight or so after Shankar's death, I roam around Agra like a crazed animal. Shakil, the university student, finds me standing outside Shankar's room one evening, staring at the lock on the door like a drunkard looks at a bottle of whisky. Bihari, the cobbler, discovers me sitting next to the municipal tap, with water dripping from my eyes instead of from the tap. Abdul, the gardener at Swapna Palace, catches me tiptoeing around the outhouse like Shankar used to. In the peak of winter, the city becomes a hot and lonely desert for me. I try to lose myself in its anarchic existence. I try to become a nonsense syllable in its ceaseless chatter, and I almost succeed in sending myself into a stupor.

By the time I wake up, it is too late. There is a phone call at the local public call office and Shakil comes running to tell me. 'Raju, Raju, someone called Nita phoned. She wants you in the Emergency Ward of Singhania Hospital right now.'

My heart leaps to my mouth when I hear this and I run the entire three miles to Singhania Hospital. I narrowly avoid crashing into a doctor, almost overturn a trolley and charge into the Emergency Ward like an Inspector bursting in on an armed robbery.

'Where is Nita?' I demand of a bewildered nurse.

'I am here, Raju.' Nita's voice sounds weak. She is behind a curtained partition, lying on a trolley. One look at her and I almost faint from shock. She has livid bruises all over her face and her lips are peculiarly twisted, as if her jaw has been dislocated. There is blood on two of her teeth, and her left eye is blackened.

'Who . . . who has done this to you?' I ask, barely recognizing my own voice.

She has difficulty speaking. 'It was a man from Mumbai. Shyam sent me to his room at the Palace Hotel. He tied me up and did all this to me. What you see on my face is nothing. See what he did to my body.'

Nita turns on her side and I see deep red welt marks on her slim back, as if someone has used a horsewhip. Then she pushes up her blouse and I almost die. There are cigarette burn marks all over her chest, looking like ugly pockmarks on the smooth brown flesh of her breasts. I have seen this before.

My blood begins to boil. 'I know who has done this to you. Did he say his name? I will kill him.'

'I don't know his name, but he was tall and—'

Shyam enters the room at this point, clutching a packet of medicine. He takes one look at me, and goes berserk. 'You bastard,' he yells and catches me by the collar. 'How dare you come here? It is only because of you this has happened to Nita.'

'Are you out of your mind, Shyam?' I cry.

'No, it is you who is mad. You think Nita is your personal property, and you have been telling her to quit the profession and not oblige customers any longer. Do you know how much this party from Mumbai paid for her? Five thousand rupees. But my sister believed you; she must have resisted him and look what happened. Now let me tell you something. If you want to see Nita again, then come to me with four lakh rupees. If you cannot produce this sum, then forget about Nita. If I see you even lurking about the hospital, I will have you killed, understand? Now get out.'

I could have killed Shyam that very instant, throttled him and choked the breath out of his lungs, or gouged out his eyes with my fingernails. But I remembered the promise I had made to Nita and some-how kept my simmering anger in check. I could not bear to see Nita's face any longer, and left the Emergency Ward. I knew only one thing. Somehow I had to get hold of four lakh rupees. But from where?

I make my plans and wait for an occasion when Swapna Devi is not at home. Two nights later, I see Rani Sahiba being driven away in her Contessa car to yet another party in town, and I break into the grounds of Swapna Palace through a hole in the boundary wall. Lajwanti had explained to me the detailed topography of the house and I have no difficulty in locating the window which opens into Swapna Devi's bedroom. I jimmy open the window and step inside her lavish bedroom. I have no time to admire her massive carved walnut bed or the teak dressing table. I look only for a large framed painting and discover it on the left wall. It is a brightly coloured picture of horses and is signed by someone called Husain. I hastily remove the painting from its hook and discover a square hole in the wall where a steel safe is embedded. I look underneath the left-hand corner of the mattress and find that there is no key there. I am momentarily put off balance, but relieved to discover the key in the right-hand corner. The key fits perfectly into the lock and the heavy door swings opens slowly. I look inside the safe and get another shock. It is practically empty. There are no emerald necklaces and gold bangles. There are just four thin stacks of currency, some legal documents and a black and white photo of a toddler. I don't have to look very closely to know that it is Shankar's picture. I feel no qualms about stealing from the safe. I stuff the four bundles into my pockets, close the safe, return the painting and the key to their original locations and exit the way I came.

I rush to my room in the outhouse, lock the door behind me and sit down to count the loot. The four bundles total 399,844 rupees. I rummage through all my pockets and find 156 rupees. Together they make exactly four lakh rupees. Looks like even Goddess Durga has given me her blessings.

I put the money in a brown paper bag, hold it tightly in my right hand and rush to the hospital. As I am entering the Emergency Ward, a bespectacled, middle-aged man with an unshaven face and unkempt hair barges into me. I fall down on the tiled floor and the brown packet slips from my grasp. The currency notes tumble out of the bag. The man sees the notes and a maniacal glint enters his eyes. He starts picking up the notes like an excited little child. For a second I freeze, wondering whether I am seeing a repeat of the train robbery. But after collecting all the notes, the man returns them to me and folds his hands. 'This money is yours, but I beg you, brother, please lend it to me. Save the life of my son. He is only sixteen. I cannot bear to see him die,' he implores like a beggar.

I hastily stuff the notes back into the brown paper bag and try to get rid of him.

'What is the matter with your son?'

'He was bitten by a mad dog. Now he has got hydrophobia. The doctor says he will die tonight unless I can buy a vaccine called RabCure which is only available at the Gupta Pharmacy. But it costs four lakh rupees and there is no way a schoolteacher like me can raise such a huge sum of money. I know you have that money, brother. I beg you, save my only son's life and I will become your slave for life,' he says and starts crying like a baby.

'This money is required for the treatment of someone very dear to me. I am sorry I cannot help you,' I say and enter through the glass door.

The man runs after me and catches hold of my feet. 'Please wait a minute, brother. Just see this picture. This is my son. Tell me how can I live if he dies tonight?' He holds out a colour photo of a young, good-looking boy. He has expressive black eyes and a warm smile on his lips. He reminds me of Shankar, and I hastily look away. 'I told you, I am sorry. Please don't trouble me,' I say and extricate my legs from his arms.

I don't look back to see whether he is still following me, but hurry over to Nita's bed. Shyam and another man from the brothel are sitting on chairs like guards in front of Nita. They are eating samosas from a soggy newspaper. Nita appears to be sleeping. Her face is heavily bandaged.

'Yes?' says Shyam, chomping on a samosa. 'Why have you come, bastard?'

'I have got the money you asked for. Exactly four lakh rupees. Look.' I show him the bundles of notes.

Shyam whistles. 'Where did you steal all this money from?'

'That is none of your business. I have come to take Nita away with me.'

'Nita is not going anywhere. The doctors say it will take her four months to recover. And since you are responsible for her injuries, you'd better pay for her treatment as well. She requires plastic surgery. It's bloody expensive, costing me nearly two lakhs. So if you really want Nita, come back with six lakhs, or my friend here will take care of you.'

The man sitting alongside Shyam takes out a switchblade from his pocket and twirls it in his fingers like a barber about to shave a customer's beard. He grins evilly, showing *paan*-stained teeth.

I know then that Nita will never be mine. That Shyam will never let her go. That even if I somehow bring six lakhs, Shyam will increase the demand to ten lakhs. My mind seems to go numb and I see blackness all around me. A wave of nausea assails me. When I recover, I see a soggy newspaper lying on the floor. It has an advertisement showing the face of a man who is grinning and holding several thousand-rupee notes in his fingers. Underneath the picture is a caption that says, 'Welcome to the greatest show on television. Welcome to *W3B – Who Will Win A Billion?* Phone lines are open. Call now or write to us to see if you will be the lucky winner of the biggest jackpot on earth!' I look at the address given in the advertisement. It says, 'Prem Studios, Khar, Mumbai.' I know in that moment that I am going to Mumbai.

I step out of the Emergency Ward as if in a trance. The antiseptic smell of the hospital doesn't irritate my senses any longer. The bespectacled man is still in the corridor. He looks at me with hopeful eyes, but doesn't try to accost me this time. Perhaps he has reconciled himself to his son's death. I still have the brown paper bag in my hand. I gesture to him. He comes shuffling to me, like a dog expecting a bone. 'Here, take this.' I hand over the bag. 'It has four lakh rupees inside. Go and save your son's life.'

The man takes the packet, falls down at my feet and begins crying. 'You are not a man, you are a god,' he says.

I laugh. 'If I were God, we wouldn't need hospitals. No, I was just a small tourist guide with big dreams,' I say and try to move forward, but he bars my way again. He takes out a worn leather wallet from his pocket and extracts a card. 'The money you have given me is a debt I owe you. This is my card. I will repay it as soon as I can, but from this moment I am your servant.'

'I don't think I will need you. In fact, I don't think I will need anyone in Agra. I am going to Mumbai,' I tell him in an absent-minded way and slip his card into my shirt pocket. The man looks at me again with tearful eyes, then rushes out of the hospital, running towards Rakab Ganj and the all-night Gupta Pharmacy.

I am just about to step outside the hospital when a jeep with a flashing red light comes screeching to a halt. An Inspector and two constables jump out. Two more men emerge from the back seat whom I recognize. One is a guard at Swapna Palace and the other is Abdul, the gardener. The guard points at me. 'Inspector Sahib, this is that boy Raju. He is the one who has stolen Rani Sahiba's money.' The Inspector instructs his constables. 'Since we found nothing in his room, the cash must be on him. Check the bastard's pockets.' The constables grope through my shirt and trousers. They find a small packet of bubble gum, some corn kernels and a one-rupee coin, which doesn't seem lucky any longer.

'He is clean, Sahib. He doesn't have any money,' one of the constables replies.

'Really? Still, let's take him in for questioning. We'll find out where he was this evening,' the Inspector says brusquely.

'Ztyjoz Hz?' I reply, my lips twisting in a deformed way.

'What did you just say? I didn't get it,' says the Inspector, a little baffled.

'Q Oxqa Ukj Xnz Xi Qaqkp.'

'What is this nonsense?' the Inspector says angrily. 'Are you trying to make fun of me, bastard? I'll teach you a lesson.' He raises his baton to strike me, but Abdul intervenes. 'Please don't hit him, Inspector Sahib. Raju has become mentally unbalanced since his friend Shankar's death. Shankar also used to speak like this.'

'Oh, is that the case? Then why did you even think of him as a suspect? We won't get anything out of a lunatic. Come, let's go,' he gestures to his constables. Then he looks at me. 'Sorry to have bothered you, you can go home now.'

'Pdxif Ukj,' I say. 'Pdxif Ukj Rznu Hjyd.'

I am sitting on Smita's bed with tears falling from my eyes. Smita takes my hand in hers and gently squeezes it. I notice that her eyes too are misting with tears. 'Poor Shankar,' she says. 'From what you've told me, he seems to have been an autistic child. What a horrible death he endured. You have really gone through hell, Thomas. You didn't deserve all that pain.'

'But my hell is still preferable to Nita's. Just imagine what she has had to undergo since the age of twelve.'

Smita nods her head. 'Yes, I can imagine. Is she still in Agra?'

'She should be, but I can't know for sure. I have had no news of her for the last four months. I don't know whether I will ever see her again.'

'I am sure you will. Now let's see the penultimate question.'

The studio sign says 'Silence' but the audience refuses to heed it. They point at me and chatter excitedly among themselves. I am the idiot waiter who has staked a hundred million rupees on one question.

Prem Kumar addresses the camera. 'We now move on to question number eleven for ten crores. Believe me, I am getting goosebumps just thinking about it. So, Mr Thomas, are you nervous?'

'No.'

'That's amazing. Here you are, gambling with the ten million rupees you have already won and you don't feel even a trace of anxiety. Remember, if you give the wrong answer, you lose everything. But if you give the correct answer, a hundred million rupees are yours. No one has ever won such a large amount, not even in a lottery. So let us see whether history is about to be made, right here, right now. OK, here comes question number eleven, and it is from the world of . . .' Prem Kumar pauses for dramatic effect, then completes the sentence . . . 'English Literature!' The studio sign changes to 'Applause'.

'Tell me, Mr Thomas, do you have some knowledge of English literature? Have you read English books, plays, poems?'

'Well, I can recite "Baa, Baa, Black Sheep", if that is what you mean by English poetry.'

The audience laugh loudly.

'I must confess, I had something slightly more complex in mind, but never mind. You must have heard of Shakespeare?'

'Sheikh who?'

'You know, the Bard of Avon, the greatest playwright in the English language? Oh, how I wish I could return to my college days, when I spent all my time acting in Shakespeare's plays. Do any of you remember your Hamlet? "To be, or not to be, that is the question. Whether 'tis nobler in the mind to suffer the slings and arrows of outrageous fortune, Or to take arms against a sea of troubles, And by opposing end them?" But enough of me. It is Mr Thomas who has to answer the next question – and here it comes, for the astronomical sum of a hundred million rupees. In which play by Shakespeare do we find the character Costard? Is it a) *King Lear*, b) *The Merchant of Venice*, c) *Love's Labour's Lost* or d) *Othello*?'

The music commences. I stare blankly at Prem Kumar.

'Tell me, Mr Thomas, do you have any clue at all as to what we are talking about here?'

'No.'

'No? Then what do you propose to do? You must give an answer, even if it is based on the toss of a coin. Who knows, if your luck continues to hold, you just might hit on the correct reply and win a hundred million rupees. So what's your decision?'

My mind goes blank. I know I have been cornered at last. I think for thirty seconds, and then make up my mind. 'I will use a Lifeboat.'

Prem Kumar looks at me quizzically. It seems he has forgotten that this game has something called Lifeboats. He snaps awake at last. 'A Lifeboat? Yes, of course, you have both of your Lifeboats available. Tell me, which one do you want to use? You can either ask me for Half and Half or go for A Friendly Tip.'

I am confused again. Who can I turn to for an answer to this question? Salim will be as clueless as me. The owner of Jimmy's Bar would have as much awareness of Shakespeare as a drunk has of direction. And literature is as far from the minds of the residents of Dharavi as honesty is from the police. Only Father Timothy could have helped me out on this question, and he is dead. Should I ask for Half and Half? I insert my fingers into my shirt pocket to take out my trusted old coin and am surprised to brush against the edge of a card. I pull it out. It is a visiting card which says, 'Utpal Chatterjee, English Teacher, St John's School, Agra' and then it gives a phone number. I don't understand at first. I have no recollection of anyone by this name or even how this card got into my shirt pocket. And then, all of a sudden, I remember the scene at the hospital: the bespectacled, unkempt man with a sixteen-year-old son who was dying of hydrophobia. An involuntary cry escapes my lips.

Prem Kumar hears it and looks at me sharply, 'Excuse me, what did you say?'

'I said can you please call this gentleman?' I hand over the card to Prem Kumar. 'I am using my Friendly Tip Lifeboat.'

Prem Kumar turns over the card in his fingers. 'I see. So you do know someone who can help you with this question.' He has a worried look on his face. He makes eye contact with the producer. The producer spreads his hands. The word 'Lifeboat' flashes on the screen. We see the animation of a boat chugging along on the sea, a swimmer shouting for help and being thrown a red lifebuoy.

Prem Kumar picks up a cordless phone from underneath his desk and passes it to me. 'Here you are. Ask whatever you want, from whoever you want. But you only have two minutes, and your time starts,' he looks at his watch, '. . . now!'

I take the phone and dial the number on the card. The call goes through and the phone starts ringing at the other end in Agra. But it simply rings and rings and rings and rings and nobody picks it up. Half a minute passes. The suspense in the studio could be cut with a knife. The audience is watching me with bated breath. To them, I am no different from a trapeze artist in a circus doing a high-wire act without any safety net below. One false move and the trapeze artist will plunge to his death. Ninety more seconds and I will lose a hundred million rupees.

Just when I am about to hang up, someone picks up the phone. I have just over a minute left now. 'Hello?'

'Hello. Can I speak to Mr Utpal Chatterjee?' I say hurriedly.

'Speaking.'

'Mr Chatterjee, I am Ram Mohammad Thomas.'

'Ram Mohammad . . . what?'

'Thomas. You may not know my name, but I helped you out in Singhania Hospital, where your son was hospitalized. Do you remember?'

'Oh, my God.' Suddenly the tone changes completely. 'I have been desperately seeking you for the last four months. Thank God you have called. You saved my son's life, you have no idea how much I have tried to—'

I cut him short. 'Mr Chatterjee, I do not have much time. I am a participant in a quiz show and I need you quickly to answer a question for me.'

'A question? Yes, of course, I am ready to do whatever you want.'

Less than thirty seconds are left now. All eyes are on the wall clock, busily ticking away the seconds.

'Tell me, very quickly, in which one of Shakespeare's plays is there a character called Costard? Is it a) *King Lear*, b) *The Merchant of Venice*, c) *Love's Labour's Lost* or d) *Othello*?'

The seconds tick away and there is silence from Chatterjee.

'Mr Chatterjee, can you tell me the answer?'

Only fifteen seconds are left by the time Chatterjee replies, 'I don't know.'

I am dumbfounded. 'What?'

'I am sorry, I don't know the answer. Rather, I'm not sure. I don't remember this character in *The Merchant of Venice* or *Othello*. It is either from *King Lear* or *Love's Labour's Lost* – I am not sure which.'

'But I can only give one answer.'

'Then go for *Love's Labour's Lost*. But as I said, I am not very sure. Sorry, I cannot be more helpf—'

Prem Kumar cuts him off. 'Sorry, Mr Thomas. Your two minutes are up. I need your reply now.'

The music in the background doesn't sound suspenseful any longer. It is positively chilling. I go into a deep thought.

'Mr Thomas, how well do you know this Mr Chatterjee?' Prem Kumar asks me.

'I have met him just once.'

'And how good an English teacher is he?'

'I have no idea.'

'So can you trust his reply, or would you rather go by your own instinct?'

I make up my mind. 'I will go by my instinct, and my instinct tells me to trust the answer given by Mr Chatterjee. It is C. *Love's Labour's Lost*.'

'Think again. Remember, you give me the wrong answer and you not only don't win the hundred million rupees, you also lose the ten million rupees you have won till now.'

'My final answer is still C.'

'Are you absolutely, one hundred per cent sure?'

'Yes.'

'I am asking you again. Are you absolutely, absolutely, one hundred per cent sure?'

'Yes.'

There is a crescendo of drums. The correct answer flashes on the screen.

'Oh, my God, it is C. You are absolutely, one hundred per cent correct!' Prem Kumar stands up. 'Ram Mohammad Thomas, you are the first person on

this show to have won a hundred million rupees.
Ladies and gentlemen, history has been made! And
now we simply have to take a break!'

The audience goes wild. Everyone stands up and
claps for more than a minute.

Prem Kumar's face is flushed. He is perspiring
profusely.

'So how do you feel?' he asks me.

'Q Bzzg Cnzxp!' I say.

Prem Kumar looks baffled. 'Excuse me, what did
you just say?'

'I said I feel great,' I reply and look up. I see Shankar
smiling at me from above. And it seems that Goddess
Durga is really looking out for me tonight.

1,000,000,000

THE THIRTEENTH QUESTION

We are still in the commercial break. Prem Kumar is in a corner, conferring with the long-haired producer. I look around the studio, at the nice panelling, the spotlights, the multiple cameras, the high-tech sound system. Many members of the audience are watching me, wondering perhaps what is going through my mind.

Prem Kumar ends his consultation and walks up to me. He has a sinister grin on his face. 'Thomas, we don't know how you have managed to answer eleven questions so far, but there is no way you will be able to answer the final question.'

'We'll see.'

'No, I'll see. Prepare yourself to lose all,' says Prem Kumar and sits down on his seat.

The studio sign changes to 'Applause'. The

signature tune comes on. The audience claps loudly.

Prem Kumar looks at the camera. 'Ladies and gentlemen, we are standing at the brink of a historic moment, not just for this show but perhaps for posterity. Ram Mohammad Thomas, an eighteen-year-old waiter from Mumbai, has gone further than any other contestant on this show. He is now about to create another milestone. If he answers this last question correctly, he will win the biggest jackpot in history – one billion rupees. If he fails to give me the correct answer, he will lose the single largest sum of money ever to be lost by an individual in sixty seconds – one hundred million rupees. Either way, history will be made. So please clear your minds, fill your hearts and join me in saluting once again our contestant tonight, Mr Ram Mohammad Thomas!'

The studio sign changes to 'Applause'. Everyone, even Prem Kumar, stands up and there is sustained clapping.

I must admire the tactics of *W3B*. I am being fêted before being sent off the show without a penny. Like a lamb, they are fattening me with adulation before slaughtering me on the next question. The moment I have been waiting for, and dreading, has finally arrived. I take a deep breath and prepare to face my destiny.

'Ladies and gentlemen, I am about to reveal question number twelve, the final question, for one billion rupees, the biggest prize ever offered in the history of the planet. And remember, we are still in Play or Pay mode, so it is win all or lose all. OK, without any further ado, here is the last question for you, Mr Thomas, and this is from . . . the pages of history! We all know that Mumtaz Mahal was the wife of Emperor Shahjahan and that he built the world-famous Taj Mahal in her memory, but what was the name of Mumtaz Mahal's father? This is the billion-rupee question. Your choices, Mr Thomas, are a) Mirza Ali Kuli Beg, b) Sirajuddaulah, c) Asaf Jah, or d) Abdur Rahim Khan Khanan.

'Think about the answer carefully, Mr Thomas. Remember, you are at a historic crossroads. I know you need time to reflect on your answer, and to allow you just that, we will now take another quick commercial break. Ladies and gentlemen, please don't even think of going anywhere.'

The studio sign changes to 'Applause'. The signature tune plays again.

Prem Kumar grins widely at me. 'Got you, didn't I? Unless you have an MA in Medieval History, there is no way you will be able to answer this. So bid good-bye to the hundred million you have just won and prepare to resume your career as a waiter. Who knows, perhaps I may come by Jimmy's Bar tomorrow. What will you serve me? Butter chicken and lamb vindaloo?' He laughs.

I laugh back. 'Ha! I've got no MA in history, but I do know the answer to this question.'

'What? You must be joking, surely?'

'I am not joking. The answer is Asaf Jah.'

Prem Kumar looks aghast. 'How . . . how do you know this?'

'I know it because I worked as a guide for two years at the Taj Mahal.'

Prem Kumar's face turns ashen. For the first time he

looks at me with a trace of fear. 'You . . . you are casting some kind of magic, I am sure,' he says and runs to the producer. They whisper amongst themselves. Prem Kumar gesticulates several times in my direction. Then someone brings in a fat book and they pore over it. Ten minutes pass. The audience begins to get restless. Eventually, Prem Kumar comes back to his seat. His expression is neutral, but I am sure he is squirming inside.

The studio sign changes to 'Applause' and the signature music commences.

'Ladies and gentlemen, before we went into the break I asked the question, what was the name of the father of Mumtaz Mahal? I am sure all of you thought that that was the final question, but it was not.'

The audience is astounded. I am stunned. Are they introducing another question? The air becomes thick with tension.

Prem Kumar continues. 'Not only was that not the last question, it was not a question at all. We were simply recording a commercial for Mumtaz Tea, which is one of the sponsors on this show. For this reason, we had to introduce a dummy question.'

The audience members start whispering among themselves. There is suppressed laughter. Someone shouts, 'You really fooled us, Mr Kumar!' The tension dissipates. The studio sign changes to 'Applause' again.

I am the only one not smiling. I know now that this is really a show run by crooks.

The studio sign changes to 'Silence' and the

signature music commences. Prem Kumar speaks into the camera. 'Ladies and gentlemen, I am now about to reveal question number twelve, the final question, for one billion rupees, the biggest prize ever offered in the history of the planet. And remember, we are still in Play or Pay mode, so it is win all or lose all. OK, without any further ado, here is the last question for you, Mr Thomas, and this is from the world of . . . Western classical music! Beethoven's Piano Sonata No. 29, Opus 106, also known as the 'Hammerklavier Sonata', is in which key? Is it in a) B flat major, b) G minor, c) E flat major, or d) C minor?

'Think about the answer carefully, Mr Thomas. Remember, you are at a historic crossroads. This is the most momentous decision of your life. I know you need time to reflect on your answer, and to allow you just that, we will now take another quick commercial break. Ladies and gentlemen, please don't even think of going anywhere.'

The studio sign changes to 'Applause'. Prem Kumar looks at me with a sly grin. The audience start chattering amongst themselves.

Prem Kumar stands up. 'I am just going round the corner. I will be right back.'

I stand up as well. 'I need to go to the toilet.'

'Then you'd better come with me,' he says. 'The rules stipulate the contestant must be accompanied everywhere.'

I am in the fluorescent-lit washroom of the studio. It is extremely clean. The tiles are gleaming white. There are huge mirrors. And no graffiti on the walls.

Prem Kumar and I are the only people in the wash-room. He whistles as he urinates. Then he notices me looking at him. 'How come you are simply standing? Don't tell me that the last question is so tough that you have even forgotten how to empty your bladder.' He throws his head back and laughs. 'Too bad it had to end this way. But without my help you would have been out a long time ago, on the second question itself. Which means you would have gone home with just one thousand rupees. So how about we make a deal? Tomorrow, when I come to your restaurant, I promise to give you a thousand-rupee tip. And, believe me, this is a promise I will keep.' He smiles patronizingly at me.

'You didn't do me any favour by telling me the answer to question number two, you did yourself a favour,' I say.

Prem Kumar looks at me sharply. 'What do you mean?'

'What I mean, Mr Prem Kumar, is that I did not come on your show to win money. No, far from it.' I shake my head exaggeratedly. 'No, I came on your quiz show to take revenge.'

Prem Kumar's peeing is cut short midstream. He zips up his trousers hastily and looks at me sidelong. 'Revenge? What do you mean? Revenge on whom?'

'On you,' I say defiantly. I step backwards and pull a gun from the waistband of my trousers. It is a small, snub-nosed revolver, very compact, no bigger than my fist. I grip it tightly in my hand and point it at him.

The blood drains from Prem Kumar's face. 'You . . . you have made a mistake, Mr Thomas. We have never met before,' he says, his voice barely a whisper.

'No, *you* have made a mistake. We did meet once, outside Neelima Kumari's flat. It was early in the morning. You swaggered out in blue jeans and a white shirt, with bloodshot eyes and unwashed hair. You were carrying a sheaf of currency notes which you had forced Neelima to part with, and you were twirling a car key in your fingers. You ruined her. But that was not enough for you. You did the same to my beloved Nita.'

'Nita?' Prem Kumar raises his eyebrows. 'That name means nothing to me.'

'She is the girl who almost died in Agra thanks to you, and now,' I grip the gun tighter, 'it is your turn.'

Prem Kumar looks anxiously at my hand. He stalls for time. 'Did you say Agra? But I haven't been to Agra for months.'

'Let me refresh your memory. Four months ago you stayed at the Palace Hotel. You called a girl to your room. You tied her up. And then you brutally beat her and burned her with a lighted cigarette, just as you did to Neelima.'

I see his lip begins to quiver. Then it begins to curl.

'She was a prostitute, for God's sake. I paid her pimp five thousand rupees. I didn't even know her name.'

'Her name is Nita.' I raise my gun.

Prem holds his palms towards me. 'No . . . No . . .' he cries and steps back. His right foot plunges into the open drain behind him. 'Don't shoot – drop that thing now, please.' He pauses to step out of the drain.

I point the gun directly at his heart. I can see he is trembling. 'I swore I would avenge the person responsible for hurting Nita. But I didn't know how to find you. And then I saw an advertisement in a newspaper in Agra. It showed your face, grinning like a monkey, inviting people to participate in a quiz show in Mumbai. That is why I am here. I would have shot you at the first question I couldn't answer, but miraculously I have been able to answer every single one. So when you helped me on question number two you didn't do me a favour at all, you merely prolonged your life a little bit longer. But now there is no escape.'

'Listen to me,' pleads Prem Kumar. He is cracking now. 'I did treat Neelima badly and I did get rough with that prostitute in Agra. But what will you gain by shooting me? You will not get your money. Drop that gun now, and I promise you I will allow you to win the top prize. Just think, you will have wealth beyond the wildest dreams of a waiter like you.'

I laugh bitterly. 'What would I do with all that wealth? Eventually a man needs just six feet of cloth for his shroud.'

He is turning paler and holding out his hand defensively. 'Please, don't pull the trigger. Look, the moment you kill me you will be arrested. And then you will be hanged. You will die, too.'

'So what? The only thing I live for is revenge.'

'Please reconsider the situation, Thomas. I swear to you, spare my life and I will tell you the answer to the last question. You will be our biggest winner.'

'I am not returning to the quiz show, and neither are you,' I say and remove the safety catch.

Prem Kumar's bravado is shattering. I see him for the coward that he is. He grips the wall behind him and closes his eyes tightly. The moment I have been waiting for for the last four months has finally arrived. I have Prem Kumar before me and a loaded gun in my hand. The gun is really good. I have fired a test bullet and found the recoil minimal. In any case, at point-blank range I can hardly miss.

I increase the pressure on the trigger, but the more I try to squeeze it the more resistance I encounter. It is almost as if my finger is turning to stone.

In films they show you that killing a man is as easy as popping a balloon. Bam, bam, bam . . . people in films fire guns as though bullets are going out of circulation. They kill people like we squish ants. Even a novice hero, who has never even seen a gun in his life, is able to shoot and kill ten baddies in the villain's den from five hundred feet away. But real life is very different. It is easy to pick up a loaded gun and point it in someone's face. But when you know that a real bullet will strike a real heart and that the scarlet liquid will be blood and not tomato ketchup, you are forced to think twice. It is not easy to kill a man. You need to first switch off from your brain. Drinking can do that. And so can anger.

So I try to summon up as much anger as I can. I call to mind all that has brought me to this pass in life. Images of Neelima Kumari and Nita float through my mind. I see the black cigarette-burn marks on Neelima's body, the red welts on Nita's back, the bruises all over her face, her blackened eye, her dislocated jaw. But instead of a rising anger, I feel a spreading sadness, and instead of a bullet coming out of my gun, I find tears coming out of my eyes.

I try to drum up support from other quarters. I think

of all the indignities I have suffered, all the hurt and humiliation I have endured. I see the bloody corpse of Father Timothy, the kindest man I have known, and the limp body of Shankar, the gentlest boy I have met. I recall all the merchants of suffering who have passed through my life. Images of Swapna Devi, Shantaram and Maman buzz through my brain, and I try to compress all these emotions into that split-second in which the bullet will be fired. Despite my effort, I find I cannot pin the blame for all my misfortunes on the man in front of me. I do not have enough anger in me to justify his death.

And I realize then that, try as I might, I cannot kill in cold blood, not even a vermin like Prem Kumar.

I lower the gun.

All this happens within a space of half a minute. Prem Kumar endures it with eyes tightly closed. When he hears no sound of gunshot, he opens one eye. He is sweating like a dog. He stares blankly at me, a gun in my hand and indecision writ large on my face.

Finally, he opens both his eyes. 'Thank you for sparing my life, Thomas,' he says with his chest heaving. 'In return for your mercy, I will tell you the answer to the last question. You have already won fair and square. The question on Mumtaz Mahal was indeed the last question, and you knew the answer. So now I will tell you the answer to the new question.'

'And how do I know that you won't change it again at the last minute?'

'Hold on to your gun. But believe me, you won't have to use it, because now I sincerely want you to win the top prize. A billion rupees is a billion rupees. And you will get it all in cash.'

For the first time, I am tempted by the prospect of all this money. With a billion I can achieve many things. I can buy Nita's freedom. I can fulfil Salim's dream of becoming a star. I can light up the lives of thousands of fellow orphans and street kids like me. I can get my hands on a beautiful red Ferrari. I make up my mind. It is 'yes' to a billion and 'no' to murder.

'OK, so what's the answer?' I ask.

'I will tell you,' says Prem Kumar. He looks down at his feet and pauses.

'What's the problem?' I ask.

'I have realized that if I tell you the answer, I will be in violation of my contract and also the rules of the show. Your prize could be invalidated.' He shakes his head slowly. 'No, I will not tell you the answer.'

I am confused.

A hint of a smile begins to cross Prem's face. 'I said I can't tell you the answer, but there's nothing in my contract which prevents me from dropping a hint. Now listen carefully. I am going to the railway station immediately after this show and I am going to board a train. I have been invited to visit four friends in Allahabad, Baroda, Cochin and Delhi, but I can only visit one of them. So I have decided to go to Allahabad, to wash off all my sins by taking a dip in the Sangam. OK?'

'OK,' I nod.

We leave the washroom and return to our seats. Prem Kumar gives me an anxious look. I wonder if he will keep his word. Everyone claps when I sit down.

My gun is sitting uncomfortably in my side pocket. I lay my hand over it.

The studio sign changes to 'Silence'.

Prem Kumar turns to me. 'Mr Ram Mohammad Thomas, before we took our last break I asked you the final question, question number twelve, for one billion rupees. I will repeat that question again. Beethoven's Piano Sonata No. 29, Opus 106, also known as the 'Hammerklavier Sonata', is in which key? Is it in a) B flat major, b) G minor, c) E flat major, or d) C Minor? Are you ready with a reply?'

'No.'

'No?'

'I mean I do not know the answer to this question.'

The camera zooms in on my face. There are audible gasps from the audience.

'Well, Mr Thomas, as I told you, you are standing at a historic crossroads. One path leads to unimaginable wealth and fortune, but the other three simply take you back to your starting point. So even if you take a wild guess, guess carefully. You can win all or lose all. This is the most important decision of your life.'

'I would like to use a Lifeboat.'

'OK, you still have one Lifeboat left, and that is Half and Half. So we will take away two incorrect answers, leaving one correct answer and one wrong answer. You then have a fifty–fifty chance of getting the right answer.'

The word 'Lifeboat' flashes on the screen. We see an animated boat chugging along on the sea, a swimmer shouting for help and being tossed a red lifebuoy. The screen changes to display the full question once again.

Then two answers disappear and only choices A and C flash on the screen.

'There you have it,' says Prem Kumar. 'It is either A or C. Give me the right answer and you will become the first man in history to win a billion rupees. Give me the wrong answer and you will become the first man in history to lose a hundred million in less than a minute. What is your decision?'

I take out my lucky one-rupee coin. 'Heads my answer will be A, tails my answer will be C. OK?'

The audience gasps at my audacity. Prem Kumar nods his head. The glint in his eye has returned.

I toss the coin.

All eyes are riveted as it goes up, almost in slow motion. This must be the only one-rupee coin in history on which a billion is riding. It comes down on my desk, and spins for a while before becoming still. Prem Kumar bends to look at it and announces, 'It is heads!'

'In that case my answer is A.'

'Are you absolutely sure, Mr Thomas? You can still choose C if you want.'

'The toss of the coin has decided my answer. It is A.'

'Are you absolutely, one hundred per cent sure?'

'Yes. I am absolutely, one hundred per cent sure.'

There is a crescendo of drums. The correct answer flashes on the screen for the last time.

'It is A! Absolutely, one hundred per cent correct! Mr Ram Mohammad Thomas, you have made history by winning the world's biggest jackpot. One billion rupees, yes, one billion rupees are yours, and will be paid to you very shortly. Ladies and gentlemen, please give a very warm round of applause to the greatest winner of all time!'

Confetti starts to fall from the ceiling. Red, green, blue and yellow spotlights bathe the entire stage. For almost two minutes, everyone stands up and claps. There are whistles and catcalls. Prem Kumar bows like a magician. Then he winks at me slyly. I don't wink back.

Suddenly the producer comes up to the dais and takes Prem Kumar away with him. They exchange heated words.

Houston, I think we have a problem.

Smita looks at her watch and gets up from the bed. 'Phew! What a show, what a story, what a night! So now I know how you won a billion rupees. The coin toss at the end was just for show, wasn't it? You already knew that the answer was A.'

'Yes. But you decide whether I deserve the top prize or not. I have not kept anything from you. I have told you all my secrets.'

'And I think it is only fair that you should know mine. You must be wondering who I am and why I suddenly appeared in the police station.'

'Well, yes, but I decided not to question a miracle.'

'I am Gudiya. I am the girl you helped in the chawl. And don't feel remorse that you pushed my father to his death. He merely broke a leg, and that one act set his brain right. He did not bother me after that. I owe everything to you. For years I tried to find you, but you had disappeared. Then yesterday I saw your name in the newspaper. It said a boy named Ram

Mohammad Thomas had been arrested by the police. I knew that there could only be one Ram Mohammad Thomas and came running to the police station. So just think of this as a very small repayment of the debt I owe you.'

I am overcome with emotion. I grasp Smita's hand, feel its flesh and bone, and my tears start falling. I hug her. 'I am so glad you found me. I have got a lawyer, a friend and a sister in one go.'

'All your troubles are now mine, Ram Mohammad Thomas,' Smita says, with fierce determination in her eyes. 'I will fight for you, just as you fought for me.'

EPILOGUE

Six months have passed since the longest night of my life.

Smita remained true to her word. She fought for me like a mother fights for her children. First she dealt with the police. She proved to them that they had no basis on which to arrest me. She also found out that nobody had even heard about the dead dacoit on the train and there was no pending investigation. So the nameless dacoit remained nameless, even in death.

Then she dealt with the quiz company. They threatened me with allegations of cheating and fraud, but Smita proved that the DVD footage clearly established me as a legitimate winner on the show. After four months of dilly-dallying, the company was forced to concede that they had no grounds on which to withhold payment of the top prize to me.

I did not get a full billion rupees. I got a little less. The government took some. They called it 'gameshow tax'. The company producing *W3B* folded after the massive payout. So I became the first and last winner on the show.

Prem Kumar died two months ago. According to the police, he committed suicide by gassing himself to death in his car. But there are press reports of foul play. My own hunch is that the thugs financing the show probably took their revenge on him.

I realized a long time ago that dreams have power only over your own mind; but with money you can have power over the minds of others. What I discovered after receiving the payout was that with money I had power even over the police. So, accompanied by a sizeable police contingent, I paid a visit to Goregaon last month, to a large decrepit building set in a court-yard with a small garden and two palm trees. The police arrested five people and freed thirty-five crippled children. They are all now in the care of a well-known international child-welfare agency.

Lajwanti's release from jail was also secured last month and she is now staying with me in Mumbai. In fact, she returned just last week from her sister Lakshmi's wedding in Delhi to a top-level officer in the Indian Administrative Service. The groom's family made no demand for dowry, but Lajwanti still gave her sister a Toyota Corolla car, a thirty-two-inch Sony TV, twenty Raymond suits and one kilo of gold jewellery.

Salim has landed the role of a seventeen-year-old college hero in a comedy film directed by Chimpu Dhawan, and these days is busy shooting in Mehboob Studios. He thinks the producer is a man named Mohammad Bhatt, but it is actually me.

The love of my life has joined me in Mumbai. She is now my lawfully wedded wife, with a proper surname. Nita Mohammad Thomas.

Smita and I are walking along Marine Drive. A pleasant wind is blowing, occasionally sending a misty spray from the ocean where giant waves crash and roll against the rocks. The uniformed driver is following us at a snail's pace in a Mercedes Benz, maintaining a respectful distance. The rear bumper of the Benz carries a sticker. It says 'My other car is a Ferrari'.

'I have been wanting to ask you something,' I tell Smita.

'Shoot.'

'That evening, when you saved me from the police station, why didn't you tell me straight away that you were Gudiya?'

'Because I wanted to hear your stories and find out the truth. Only when you narrated my own story, without realizing that I was in front of you, did I know for sure that you were telling me the truth, the whole truth and nothing but the truth. That is why I told you at the very beginning that I didn't need you to swear on any book. I was your witness, just as you were mine.'

I nod my head in understanding.

'Can I also ask you a question?' Smita asks me.

'Sure.'

'That same evening, when I first brought you home, before you told me your stories, you flipped a coin. Why?'

'I was not sure whether to trust you. The coin toss was my decision-making mechanism. Heads I would have told you everything. Tails it would have been goodbye. As it turned out, it was heads.'

'So if it had turned up tails instead of heads, you wouldn't have told me your story?'

'It wouldn't have come up tails.'

'You believe in luck so much?'

'What's luck got to do with it? Here, take a look at the coin.' I take out the one-rupee coin from my jacket and hand it to her.

She looks at it, and flips it over. Then flips it again. 'It . . . it's heads on both sides!'

'Exactly. It's my lucky coin. But as I said, luck has got nothing to do with it.'

I take the coin from her and toss it high into the air. It goes up, up and up, glints briefly against the turquoise sky, and then drops swiftly into the ocean and sinks into its cavernous depths.

'Why did you throw away your lucky coin?'

'I don't need it any more. Because luck comes from within.'

THE END

ACKNOWLEDGEMENTS

This book would not have been possible without the support of Peter Buckman. I owe him a debt of gratitude for being friend, guide and agent, in that order. Thanks are also due to Rosemarie and Jessica Buckman, who put so much effort into making this debut a truly international one.

I must record my appreciation for Transworld, both for accepting this novel so enthusiastically and for giving me the best editor a writer could hope for. It was a treat working with Jane Lawson, who, over the course of some really long long-distance phone calls, made editing such a collaborative and enjoyable task.

Brigadier S. C. Sharma provided valuable input for 'A Soldier's Tale'. I would also like to thank Navdeep Suri, Humphrey Hawksley, Patrick French, Tejinder Sharma, Maureen Travis, the British public-library system and Google for helping out in various ways.

Above all, this book owes its existence to my wife Aparna and my sons Aditya and Varun, who gave me the space to begin this project and the strength to complete it.

Q & A

VIKAS SWARUP

A READING GROUP GUIDE

About the Author
Profile of Vikas Swarup
Interview with Vikas Swarup

About the Book
Facts behind the Fiction
Questions for Discussion

Read On
Further reading and website information

SECTION 1: ABOUT THE AUTHOR
Profile of Vikas Swarup

Born in Allahabad, India, into a family of lawyers and solicitors, author Vikas Swarup grew up amidst conversations about judges and court cases at the dinner table. 'One advantage of growing up in this environment was that I was probably the only seven-year-old in Allahabad who could spell "jurisprudence" and "habeas corpus"!' says the Indian diplomat who has served in Turkey, the United States, Ethiopia and Great Britain. As a child, Swarup dreamt of becoming a pilot or an astronaut when he grew up since the family profession had been ruled out as a possible career by his mother in the form of a curt ultimatum: 'If any of my [three] sons becomes a lawyer, I will throw him out of the house.' A career in science was similarly ditched because of discouraging experiences with frog dissections in the biology lab and such thousand-page tomes as 'The Principles of Theoretical Physics'. The idea of becoming a civil servant gradually took hold and Vikas graduated university with majors in Modern History, Psychology and Philosophy, ultimately joining the Indian Foreign Service.

By self admission, Vikas Swarup has always been a creative thinker although *Q & A* is his first published work of fiction. His hyperactive imagination initially manifested itself in an essay on bad luck assigned by his sixth-grade teacher. While other children wrote about such run-of-the-mill occurrences as a black cat crossing their path, Vikas chose to recount the trials of a trio of Japanese thieves that manages to get trapped in an earthquake after pulling off a flawless bank heist.

Vikas tried his hand at another story titled *The Autobiography of a Donkey* in school before finally embarking on the globally successful project, *Q & A*.

Interview with Vikas Swarup

Vikas, even though you are not in the hot seat here and there's no jackpot at the end of it, here's your slice of the 15-questions pie:

1. Is *Q & A* your first work of fiction?

I have been telling stories since childhood but, sadly, didn't write anything beyond my school days. It was only during my diplomatic posting in London that I had the urge to write. I tried my hand at a full-length novel about a contract killer, but didn't really show it around to publishers. I used it as a learning experience to work on *Q & A*, which I finished in two months flat. And that's the truth, the whole truth and nothing but the truth!

2. Was there a particular 'aha' moment that gave you the inspiration for this book?

It was a series of 'aha' moments. I wanted to write something off-beat. I did not want to write a generational family saga or a magical realist fable with talking monkeys. And then it struck me: Why not tap into the global phenomenon of the syndicated televised quiz show? After all *Who Wants to be a Millionaire?* was a top rated show in a number of countries the world, including India. The issue was:

Who would be my contestant? It was around this time that a scandal involving an army major broke out in England. The man had apparently won a million pounds on the show but was accused of cheating. I thought to myself, if someone as well educated as an officer of the British Army can be accused of cheating, why could I not have a contestant who would *definitely* be accused of cheating? Incidentally, I had also come across a news report of how street children in an Indian slum had begun using a free mobile internet facility entirely on their own. So I decided to juxtapose these two themes – of a game show and of a contestant who has had no formal education, who has 'street' knowledge as opposed to 'book' knowledge. That is how *Q & A* was born.

3. The structure of the novel seems to be one of its strengths; how did that evolve? Were these chapters always meant to be individual episodes strung together to form a coherent whole?

The novel essentially move on two planes. There is the life story of the quiz show contestant Ram Mohammad Thomas, and there are the goings on in the quiz show itself. To my mind, the pace of the novel stems from the fact that there is this dualism, this contradiction, this tension between these two strands of the novel. What links these two strands is 'memory'. Having been an avid quizzer myself, I was interested in the ideational and psychological processes that are at work in a contestant's mind. As one of my characters in the book says, 'A quiz is not so much a test of knowledge as a test of memory.' And our memories are produced by various things: by our experiences, our dreams and desires, not just what we are taught in school. *Q & A* is built around a series of stories that the protagonist tells his lawyer, which eventually link up to the questions on the quiz show. Some are his personal stories, some he has heard. My aim was to make each story complete in itself, to make it stand on its own, even without the larger context of the novel. The difficulty was doing this while following the conventions of a quiz show where the questions follow a certain progression: easier questions come first, difficult questions come later and the topics have to keep changing. Since Ram Mohammad Thomas' life could not follow the order of the questions in a strictly chronological sequence, the additional difficulty was to ensure that the reader does not lose the thread when my protagonist goes back and forth in time. Above all, I wanted to ensure an organic connection between the stories and the questions – they needed to appear natural rather than gimmicky and forced.

4. Have you ever visited Dharavi or come in prolonged contact with a resident to be able to paint such a vivid picture of the (in)famous slum, its inhabitants and their lifestyle?

I have never lived in Mumbai for any sustained period of time, and I have never visited Dharavi. But then India is a country where no one leads the life of an island. The lives of the rich and the poor, the high and the low, intersect every day. And if one observes, and learns, then one can also project. One may not have seen Dharavi but one has seen slums. You just have to magnify the slums you have seen ten times, or maybe a hundred times, to visualize the scenario in Dharavi.

5. How much effect, if any, do you think your own exposure to Mumbai's film industry has had in directly or indirectly shaping the overall theme and pace of this novel?

I admit there is an undercurrent of Bollywood running through the novel. That is because Hindi films are an inescapable part of popular Indian culture. You cannot conceptualize an Indian matrix without bringing in Bollywood. The potboiler Hindi films have traditionally been considered escapist entertainment, perhaps highlighting their appeal to the masses. They almost become an alternate reality for the poor. So, throughout the novel, you have my protagonist contrasting 'reel' life with 'real' life. But the real treat for me, personally, is that *Q & A* itself is likely to become a plot for a Bollywood film! Though Film Four have optioned the film rights, several top Indian directors have approached me for the Hindi remake.

6. For viewers of *KBC*, or for the general Indian audience for that matter, most of the characters of the novel might seem thinly disguised. Did the possibility of celebrity recognition ever become an issue while writing *Q & A*?

A few reviewers have commented that they found some of my characters – the action film hero, the famous cricketer, and even Neelima, the tragedy queen – to be tongue-in-cheek caricatures of real people. All

I can say is that the characters I have drawn are entirely fictional but I wouldn't be surprised if some people find familiar echoes in them.

7. What were some of the research methods you used while writing the book?

The book required considerable research. The maximum investigation was undoubtedly needed for 'A Soldier's Tale' in which I had to document the India-Pakistan War of 1971. I read a number of books on the famous battles of that war, delved into actual soldier accounts of the course of the war in Chhamb and received some excellent feedback from my colleague, the Military Attaché in the High Commission in London. I undertook similar painstaking research to get fully acquainted with life in juvenile homes, betting on cricket matches, the practice of selling tribal girls into prostitution, the modus operandi of contract killers, voodoo, the Taj Mahal, and even Australianisms. My neighbourhood library in Golders Green gave me access to a number of useful books and the Internet also proved to be a mine of information.

8. Throughout the novel one of the major themes that arises repeatedly is the rampant apathy in India – the slum dwellers, the game show authorities, the cinema industry, for example. Do you think this feeling somehow characterizes modern India itself?

There is a quote in the book. When Ram Mohammad Thomas approaches the administrator of his chawl, asking him to intervene before Shantaram does something terrible to his wife and daughter, he is told: '*We Indians have this sublime ability to see the pain and misery around around us, and yet remain unaffected by it. So, like a proper Mumbaikar, close your eyes, close your ears, close your mouth, and you will be happy like me.*' So apathy does exist in the nation of a billion people, but one also sees evidence of tremendous compassion and solidarity, such as during the recent tsunami disaster.

9. You have tackled difficult issues – incest, rape, torture – in almost every chapter of the novel. What was your experience writing these passages?

The novel opens somewhat bleakly and then continues in the same vein for the first few chapters. This bothered me a bit when I had finished the novel, but the structure of the novel was such that if I changed even one story or altered the timeline, the whole edifice would have collapsed. In the end I just trusted the reader to find light at the end of the tunnel. By the same token, I had to find my own illumination in writing some of the darker chapters. The writing of 'A Brother's Promise' and the section in the Agra chapter relating to the death of Shankar were the toughest. Even finding the right words to describe those emotions was gut wrenching. But the fact that I myself had tears in my eyes when I re-read the Shankar episode convinced me that it had been written with heart and soul.

10. Any interesting anecdotes behind writing/ researching *Q & A* that you'd like to share?

I wrote *Q & A* in complete secrecy. No one, not even my closest friends, knew that I was working on a novel! For two years I kept my professional world as a diplomat and my private world as an author completely apart. But now everyone knows.

11. We know that you were born in Allahabad and were a champion debater and an avid quizzer at school. Tell us some more about your formative years and your family's influence on your literary aspirations.

I come from a family of lawyers. My grandfather had a magnificent library full of leather bound, gold embossed volumes of legal books. But he was a man of eclectic tastes and his interests embraced history, philosophy and art as well. Thus a first edition of Hitler's *Mein Kampf* would be nestling next to Tolstoy's *War and Peace*. I learnt a lot from him, most importantly, a love of books. Since I grew up in an era without cable TV and the Internet, my favourite pastime was to read, and I devoured everything, from *Aesops Fables* to Albert Camus, from Enid Blyton to Irving Wallace. And, I believe, a good writer is first and foremost a good reader.

12. What are some of your favourite books (fiction or non-fiction) of all time?

Till I joined the Indian Foreign Service, I used to be a very big reader. I have read many authors and many books over the years. I have been a big fan of the thriller genre, but I have enjoyed contemporary

374

literary works as well such as Coetzee's *Disgrace*, Alan Hollinghurst's *A Line of Beauty*, David Mitchell's *Cloud Atlas* and the novels of Haruki Murakami. Some of my all-time favourite works are:

Of Mice and Men by John Steinbeck
The Old Man and the Sea by Ernest Hemingway
The Trial by Franz Kafka
Animal Farm by George Orwell
Dracula by Bram Stoker
The Story of Philosophy by Will Durrant

13. Which faction of creative thinkers might you belong to: One that thinks that good writing is one that pleases the reader? Or another for which writing is a personal process unhindered by audience pressure?

As they say, 'Any fool can write a book; it takes a genius to sell it'. So readers remain critical to the writing process. Writing is, indeed, a personal process, but I feel that what a writer writes must, in the final analysis, be accessible to the reader. If the writer cracks a joke which the reader doesn't get, then what's the point? The key to a good novel is to ensure a degree of congruence between the subjective vision of the writer and the objective reaction of the reader.

14. How has your experience been with the world-wide publishing industry?

When I set out to write this book I had no idea it would appeal to readers in Brazil and Barcelona, in Seattle and Sydney. The book is now being translated into 25 languages so it has enabled me to interact with publishers and readers in five continents. The experience has been uniformly positive. The reason for the novel's global appeal, I imagine, is that though it is set in India, the themes and the emotions evoked are universal and the underlying message is one which applies to every community and culture – of creating your own luck, of the underdog beating the odds and winning!

15. Is there a follow-up novel to *Q & A* in the works? If not, might there be one in the future?

I have a number of ideas, so, yes, there will be another book. Perhaps in a year or two.

SECTION 2: ABOUT THE BOOK
Facts behind the Fiction

In September 2000, when Harshvardhan Vinayak Nawathe answered the 15th question correctly on *Kaun Banega Crorepati* (the Indian version of *Millionaire*), little did he realize that he had changed history – not only television history but also his own. An unknown youth hailing from a middle class family residing in one of Mumbai's middle class neighbourhoods, he suddenly became a media sensation. Overnight, a person for whom traveling incognito in public buses was no big deal had to temporarily change residences for fear of being hounded by paparazzi. Harsh Nawathe, the new face of the teeming Mumbai millions, had arrived.

24 September 2000. *Kaun Banega Crorepati* Episode number 64. More than 50 million eyes stare unblinkingly at their TV screens. Hot seat contestant Harshvardhan Nawathe is on the precipice of the million-rupee question. The random question flashes, he doesn't know the answer. He phones a friend who doesn't know it either. Without an alternative, Nawathe makes a painstakingly wild guess. And wins.

As 300 people from the audience descended on the disorientated winner, and his building residents back home lit up the evening sky with fireworks, the boy next door became an instant celebrity and one of India's most eligible bachelors. Nawathe, who, before the competition, was preparing for his entrance exams for the Indian Civil Services, is now studying business management in London, England. His family still lives in their modest apartment in Mumbai.

Nawathe's 15 jackpot-winning questions:

1. Which is the largest key on a computer keyboard?
a) Enter   b) Back space   c) Number lock   d) Space bar
Correct answer was d

2. If you visit the Tirupati temple which state would you be in?
a) Karnataka   b) Andhra Pradesh   c) Tamil Nadu
d) Kerala
Correct answer was b

3. Who composed the bhajan 'Pag ghungroo bandh Meera naachi re'?
a) Tukaram   b) Surdas   c) Meerabai   d) Chaitanya
Correct answer was c

4. Which angle is formed by the hour and minute hands of a clock when it's exactly 3 o'clock?
a) 45°   b) 90°   c) 360°   d) 180°
Correct answer was b

5. What name is given to the zodiac sign usually represented by a lion?
a) Cancer   b) Taurus   c) Leo   d) Pisces
Correct answer was c

6. Which Asian Games gold medallist played Bheema in the TV serial 'Mahabharatha'?
a) Bhim Singh   b) Praveen Kumar   c) Dara Singh
d) Pangal Singh
Correct answer was b

7. What was the first name of the wife of the last Viceroy of India?
a) Diana   b) Sara   c) Elizabeth   d) Edwina
Correct answer was d

8. Which of these do not reproduce by laying eggs?
a) Whales   b) Hens   c) Crocodiles   d) Snakes
Correct answer was a

9. The rivers Brahmaputra and Sutlej originate near which source in the upper Himalayas?
a) Gangothri   b) Siachen   c) Manasasarovar
d) Yamunanatri
Correct answer was c

10. Who is the President of Pakistan?
a) Musharraf   b) Ghulam Ishaq Khan   c) Rafiq Tarar
d) Farooq Ahmed Leghari
Correct answer was a

HERE HE USED HIS FIRST LIFELINE 'AUDIENCE POLL'. BUT HE GOES AGAINST THE AUDIENCE POLL.

11. In one-day cricket how many fielders can stay outside the 15 yard circle for the first 15 overs?
a) 3   b) 4   c) 5   d) 2
Correct answer was d

12. Who was the world's first woman Prime Minister?
a) Indira Gandhi   b) Golda Meir
c) Srimavo Bandarnaike   d) Margaret Thatcher
Correct answer was c

13. In the Mahabharatha, who was Draupadi's twin brother?
a) Parikshit   b) Drupada   c) Dhristadyumna
d) Ikshvaku
Correct answer was c

14. Which Indian state has the highest percentage of Hindus?
a) Uttar Pradesh   b) Madhya Pradesh
c) Himachal Pradesh   d) Orissa
Correct answer was c

HERE HE USED HIS SECOND LIFELINE '50:50'

HE ALSO USED HIS THIRD LIFELINE 'PHONE A FRIEND' – BUT THE FRIEND DIDN'T KNOW IT EITHER

15. Who among these does the Indian Constitution permit to take part in the proceedings of Parliament?
a) Solicitor General   b) Attorney General
c) Cabinet Secretary   d) Chief Justice
Correct answer was b

Questions for Discussion

1. Ram has been described as an 'Everyman Underdog'. Is he someone you might like to meet? What would you talk about?

2. *Q & A* shows a side of India we don't often see or read about. Do you think this is true? What makes the book so atmospheric?

3. Were you able to guess any of the questions before the end of the chapter? What other question might you have asked, if you were writing it?

4. Ram is infinitely resourceful and versatile. How does he show it? What does this say about the rigid social and religious structures in India?

5. Why is the Bollywood actress so tragic? How far does she reflect the darker side of celebrity lifestyle? What is Ram's attitude to celebrity culture?

6. Ram has also been described as a Forrest Gump figure. Do you agree?

7. What do you think the author's underlying message is? Is it a very radical one?

8. How sweet is this story? And how sour?

9. Who is your favourite character? Which is your favourite episode?

10. Do you think this story could be set in any deprived area of the world – in London? New York? Mexico? What makes it especially Indian, and what makes it universal?

SECTION 3: READ ON

Other works set in Mumbai's underprivileged backgrounds:

Fiction:

Love and Longing in Bombay: Stories, by Vikram Chandra (Faber, 1998)

Baumgartner's Bombay, by Anita Desai (Heinemann, 1988)

Bombay Ice, by Leslie Forbes (Weidenfeld, 1998)

A Fine Balance, by Rohinton Mistry (Faber, 1997)

Bombay, Meri Jaan: Writings on Mumbai, Edited by Jerry Pinto, Naresh Fernandes (Penguin Books India, 2003)

The Death of Vishnu, by Manil Suri (Bloomsbury, 2001)

Show Business, by Shashi Tharoor (Picador, 1994)

Bombay Time, by Thrity Umrigar (Picador USA, 2001)

Non-fiction:

Maximum City, by Suketu Mehta (Review, 2005)

Rediscovering Dharavi: Stories from Asia's Largest Slum, by Kalpana Sharma (Penguin Books India, 2000)

Web Detective

http://en.wikipedia.org/wiki/Bombay
A comprehensive history of Mumbai (formerly Bombay), including descriptions of the city's geography, demographic, culture and media

http://www.himalmag.com/may2001/review.html
An insightful review providing background on some of the issues tackled in *Rediscovering Dharavi: Stories from Asia's Largest Slum* by author Kalpana Sharma

http://www.searchindia.com/search/bombay-pictures/dharavi.html
A photo depicting the squalid living conditions in Asia's largest slum located within rock-throw distance of the metropolis' downtown

http://icmr.icfai.org/casestudies/catalogue/Leadership%20and%20Entrepreneurship/LDEN028.htm
A feature on the Mumbai Tiffin Carrier service, or 'dabbawalas' in Hindi, which was noted by *Forbes* magazine as one of the world's foremost entrepreneurial successes – in the same league as multinationals Motorola and GE

http://kbc2.indya.com/index.html
The official website of *Kaun Banega Crorepati* (literally, 'Who Will Become a Millionaire'), the Indian version of *Who Wants to be a Millionaire?*

http://kbc2.indya.com/kbc1/kbc1_crorepati.html
A link to the mini-biography of the only jackpot winner in the Indian *Millionaire* history

http://abc.go.com/primetime/millionaire/
showhighlights/players.html
A list of the jackpot winners on ABC's original *Millionaire*

http://www.imdb.com/name/nm0000821/bio
http://www.imdb.com/name/nm0451321/bio
Biographies of Bollywood superstars Amitabh Bachchan and Shahrukh Khan, cited in the pages of *Q & A*

http://www.indialawinfo.com/bareacts/ipc.html#_Toc 496765206
Link to Indian Penal Code sections 330 & 331 cited by Ram Mohammad Thomas' lawyer upon demanding his release from the police station

Six Suspects

By Vikas Swarup

There's a caste system, even in murder.

Seven years ago, prominent playboy Vivek Rai murdered Ruby Gill simply because she refused to serve him a drink. Now 'Vicky' Rai is dead, killed at a party he had thrown to celebrate his acquittal. Six guests are discovered with guns in their possession. Who are these six suspects? And what were they doing at the party that night? Vicky Rai had enemies, and many had wanted him dead – but only one had the nerve to pull the trigger...

Audaciously and astutely plotted, with a panoramic imaginative sweep, *Six Suspects* is the work of a master storyteller, from the acclaimed author of *Q & A*.

'Unusual, witty, quirkily, cleverly plotted, intelligent...a rollicking good read'
Mercel Berlins, *The Times*

9780552772518